KENDRELL
PUBLISHING

RED BLUE

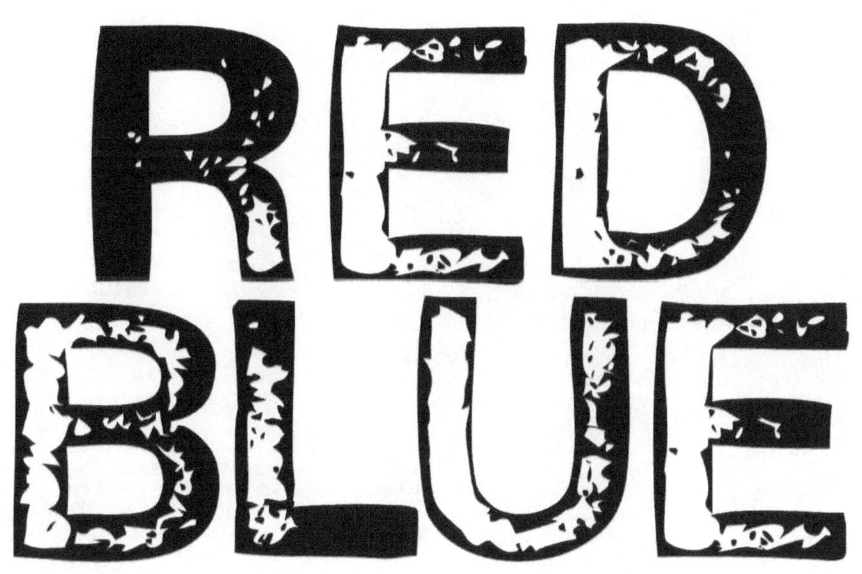

Micah House

Red Blue

First published 2025

Copyright © 2025 by Micah House

All rights reserved.

Published by Kendrell Publishing, Birmingham, Alabama

Edited by Crystal Castle

Cover design by Paul Palmer-Edwards

ISBN: 979-8-9922157-6-2

Library of Congress Control Number: 2025918232

Also by Micah House

The Blanchard Witches of Daihmler County

Prodigal Daughters

Stitches in Time

The House of Duquesne

Half Sick of Shadows

Becoming Olympia

My Soul To Keep

CONTENTS

CHAPTER 1

THE UNRAVELING

How it began was anybody's guess. Not that it mattered anymore. It happened, and however it happened, all that mattered was survival. The world plunged into chaos as if someone had flipped reality inside out overnight. There wasn't time to wait for explanations from the mouths of those in authority. Whatever this was, it spread fast and violently. There was no stopping it. There was no containing it.

Some called it an infection, while others whispered darker causes—government experiments gone wrong, an alien infestation, a devastating virus escaped from some covert lab, or God's little game He forced his children to play. Each explanation was as good as the next in a world that no longer needed them. Nothing mattered anymore except surviving the apocalypse. The infected seemed to shed their humanity like a husk pulled from an ear of corn. They became something primal. They hunted. They killed. And they didn't stop.

Two months was all it took to unravel civilization. Families slaughtered each other, lovers turned on one another, and neighbors became the executioners of those they once waved to while watering a lawn. Perhaps the lucky ones died quickly, escaping the torture of having to watch the world end.

Farrah and Penn Fletcher were newlyweds, beginning their new life together in the seclusion of Farrah's family's cabin in Mentone, Alabama. She had always felt at peace on the majestic mountain, in the picturesque log cabin her grandfather had built. As a child, she spent some of her most treasured memories there, nestled among the trees, trails, and running brooks. There was no other place where she wanted to begin her new life as a wife.

Their leisurely spent mornings in bed were a far cry from the digital screech of workday wake-up times. Penn and Farrah could linger beneath the sheets for as long as they liked, wrapped in each other's arms. The most alluring thing calling them from the bed was their empty stomachs. Answering that call, they'd cook breakfast together over the cabin's stove, feeding each other fresh fruit while the eggs and bacon sizzled in the pan, and sipping on whatever remained from the previous night's champagne. Afternoons found them walking the wooded trails to watch the mid-spring sunset settle between the mountain peaks. Neither of them had a very reliable cell signal at the cabin, but it being their honeymoon, they didn't much care. It was only on the fourth day when it mattered.

Penn and Farrah ventured down the mountain to buy a few things they'd need before their peaceful week of solitude was over. Capshaw Marketplace was a familiar sight. Its rustic log structure seemed like a snapshot of the past, when time moved slower. The gravel parking lot crunched beneath the tires as they pulled in. Neither paid any attention to the sloping downhill village below. Farrah heard a raised voice trickling uphill towards them but didn't turn to look as she and Penn proceeded into the market.

As the bell above the glass door jingled, Mrs. Capshaw was not wearing her usual smile of welcome behind the counter. In fact, she seemed aggressive and frightened. "What do you want?" she snapped.

The rudeness took Farrah aback, it being so unlike the cordial old soul she'd known all her life. Forcing a smile to her lips, she offered a friendly wave towards the apprehensive woman. "It's me, Mrs. Capshaw, Farrah Carter—uh, sorry. Farrah Fletcher now." She held up her ring finger as a reminder, although the woman shouldn't have needed one. She'd fawned over Farrah's ring and marriage for ten minutes only a few days ago when they arrived for their honeymoon.

"Farrah, sweetie!" the old woman said, placing her shaky hands against her temples. "I'm sorry, but I don't know what's gotten into people. Everyone is losing their minds!"

Penn stepped closer. "How do you mean?"

Mrs. Capshaw, still flustered, flailed her hands as her breath came in short spurts. "The Douglas folks just swept in here a little while ago and screamed at me, saying they don't want *my kind* on *their* mountain no more!"

"What?" Farrah gasped. She'd known the Douglas's a long time. They were friends of her parents. Mr. Douglas used to fish with her father, and Farrah used to play with Shelly Douglas on their weekends in Mentone. "They don't own this mountain! And why would they be upset with you?"

"Beats me!" the frazzled woman cried. "But then Jasper Dole, from the post office, came storming up here right after with an axe in his hand." Mrs. Capshaw scurried down the counter to show them a section of busted glass. "Look what he did! He smashed into the ammunition cabinet and stole all the boxes of shells! Then he hightailed it out of here!"

Farrah exhaled sharply, just as shocked by the account as Mrs. Capshaw. "That is insane! Mr. Dole is usually a perfectly nice man. Did you call the police?"

"I tried calling, but nobody answered."

A prickle of unease crawled up Farrah's spine. She was on the verge of offering to drive further down the mountain to the station for the old woman when a sudden explosion of glass blew across them. Penn pulled his bride to the ground, shielded behind a shelf, as shell casings clattered against the wooden floor.

Mrs. Capshaw, still behind the counter, began screaming at the gunman. "Please, Jasper! Why are you doing this?"

The man stalked forward, bits of glass crunching under his boots. "You aren't a'going to ruin our land, you damned gremlin!" he bellowed as he cocked open the barrel of his rifle, reloading shells into the chamber. Shells undoubtedly stolen from her a little while ago.

Penn pulled Farrah towards the back of the store where an EXIT sign showed the way out. He pushed it open for them to get away from the madman, but as they slipped out, Farrah heard Mrs. Capshaw offer a final plea as Jasper took aim at her chest. "I don't understand! What are you saying? Why are you upset?"

The old man raised the barrel and fired.

Mrs. Capshaw collapsed as Farrah barely swallowed her scream.

Penn grabbed her wrist, tugging her through the back door, where they sprinted around the building to their car. Penn slipped on the uneven gravel, grabbing the hood of the car to break his fall. The sound drew Jasper's attention from the broken store window. The moment Penn thrust the car in reverse and backed out, Jasper was there, his rifle aimed directly at Penn's head through the windshield.

Farrah acted on instinct, throwing her hands up in surrender. "Mr. Dole!" she cried from the passenger window. "It's me! It's Farrah Carter!"

"Farrah! Don't!" Penn hissed.

She could see the old man's expression register her name, familiarity breaking through his madness. "He knows me, Penn," she stammered. "God, I hope he does." She looked back at Jasper. "Mr. Dole, it's Farrah Carter!"

"Farrah?" he muttered, his gun beginning to lower to his side. He stepped closer to her window, scratching his head with his free hand. "Haven't seen you in a coon's age. Heard you got married."

"Yes, sir," she said nervously.

At her window now, Jasper leaned down, resting his forearm on the door. "This here your husband?"

"Yes, Mr. Dole, this is Penn Fletcher, my husband." Her eyes kept edging downward to the rifle leaning against his hip. There was no way to get it away from him at her angle.

"Nice to meet you, young feller," Jasper raised up and nodded towards the store. "Hope I didn't scare y'all none. But we gotta get this mess under control right quick."

"What mess?" Penn asked, a knot started to tie in his throat. "What did that old woman do?"

Jasper's expression darkened, a slow and sinister grin curling at his lips. "That there was no woman, young man. That was one a' those things what's sprouting up all over. Tryin' to wreck our country. Maybe the world."

"Things?" Penn asked.

"Yep," Jasper said, spitting on the gravel as his hands gripped his rifle again. Penn in turn gripped the wheel, ready to slam his foot on the gas pedal, but Jasper didn't point his gun at them. Instead, he casually laid it upright against his shoulder, readying himself to leave. But he had one more word of warning for the newlyweds. "They look like us at first, but they ain't one of us. You'll see for yourself soon enough."

"They aren't one of us?" Farrah repeated, placating his madness. She had known him most of her life, but the eyes looking back at her were not those of the man she remembered fondly.

"Naw, and if you ain't got your wits about you," Jasper explained. "They'll kill you soon as look at you. So, we gotta get them first."

Farrah tried to tread lightly by saying, "I've known Mrs. Capshaw for years. It seemed like it was her."

"Naw, it weren't," Jasper asserted. "Didn't you hear her gibberish? Those things—those demons, or whatever you wanna call it. They can't speak our language. That's how you know. You two youngens be careful out there."

He patted the top of Penn's car, as if giving him permission to drive away. Then the old man started on foot down to the village. Slowly and wordlessly, Penn drove the car out of the gravel lot. Farrah watched Jasper descend the hill, taking aim and shooting two other people when they came into his view. Farrah shuddered but did not scream. She understood he mustn't think she and Penn weren't on his side.

Old Jasper wasn't alone in his rampage. As Penn turned onto the road leading up the mountain, a woman ran frantically from her house wielding a kitchen knife. At first, they weren't sure of her plan. But then the hum of a lawn mower rounded her house, where a teenage boy was cutting her grass. Penn reached out his hand, turning Farrah's head away, then his own as the boy's cries competed with the roar of the mower. Penn stepped on the gas and took them back up the mountain. They watched the road ahead and nothing else. If more chaos was happening in the few homes they passed, they didn't look at it. Penn's only goal was to drive them uphill to safety until they could decide what to do.

Farrah's family cabin, a retreat which an hour ago stood as a symbol of solace and solemnity, now faced her with an eerie stillness. Somehow the landscape seemed tarnished, as if an ominous cloud was settling over the mountain, casting an otherworldly shadow.

"We can't just sit here!" Farrah argued, after they'd locked themselves inside.

Penn paced the open living room, kitchen, and dining space. "Maybe it's just those two crazies we saw. That knife woman and Mr. Dole."

"But he said *everyone*," Farrah reminded him. "Has something happened we don't know about."

Penn looked at his cell phone. No signal, still. He remembered how much they liked that when they had first arrived. Now, it sucked. Farrah's was on the dining table. He walked over to check it too, even though he knew there was no use. They were on the same account, which meant same carrier, same nonexistent signal.

Suddenly, Farrah released a forced laugh. "We are so stupid! TV's *do* pick up news channels."

Penn grabbed the remote off the coffee table and clicked on the television. It took him a minute to figure out what he was doing. "Jesus! How do you get channels on this thing?"

He fumbled around, figuring out how to switch from streaming channels to the more archaic live TV. He felt like a caveman trying to conjure fire, but he got there. When they finally found a news station broadcasting from nearby Birmingham, they discovered what awaited them in the outer world. The first report was already half over when they found it. Video footage captured by shoppers in Birmingham's Galleria mall showed what looked like a civil war battle waging through the colonnade. People, bloodied and screaming, ran for their lives as attackers pursued them with makeshift weapons and blunt objects.

Penn perched on the end of the coffee table while Farrah curled her legs against her chest with her arms cradled around them, as report after report came in on the horror unfolding across the nation. Each incident was more gruesome than the last, as the world descended into a nightmarish version of its former self.

"Is this real?" Farrah whispered as clips played, each capturing random murders of unsuspecting people. Some footage depicted victims screaming into their cameras that monsters were after them. Some tried to film the frenzy until phones fell to the ground, presumably caught by their pursuer. Other reels showed people fighting back against their aggressors, armed with guns and knives, hell bent on surviving.

Unable to form words for what he was seeing, Penn simply reached his hand over to touch his wife's leg. Between scenes from national news reporters, other clips showed from viral social media uploads, all showing the same bedlam. People killing other people, claiming they were monsters. The images were often blurry, often jerky-as panicked men and women ran for their lives. But occasionally, the look on an attacker's face might easily be construed as monstrous.

An Instagram reel showed a man recording his actions as he walked towards three people on a city sidewalk. His phone camera locked onto his victims as his other hand waved a pistol at them. "Look at those twisted faces," he told his viewers. "This is what they turn into after a few days. And listen to the sounds they make. It's like an alien language!"

The grainy footage paused on the man's gun the moment it fired, but the sounds still playing were horrible. The echoing blast of *crack*, *crack*, *crack* caused Farrah to recoil in her own chest, as if she'd been the one shot. The news anchor's voice, chillingly shaken, cut through the animalistic screams of the man's prey until the footage cut off. The ashen, stunned face of the news anchor revealed her own horror and fear. The station may have blacked out of images for the viewers, but it clearly didn't censor what the anchor had seen.

The broadcast switched to a jarring, bright-lit TikTok stream. A girl, no older than seventeen, with eyes enlarged with the same mania sweeping the country, was laying out her handgun and bullets on a white laminate table. Against an almost distasteful backdrop of upbeat pop music, she was energetically telling her subscribers about her plan. "Guys, it's real easy to spot one," she said. "They've got these messed up faces and their skin is kinda blue. Not Smurf blue, but definitely not like us. You know, like how a dead person looks. That's what these freaks are, I think. *Dead*. I'm telling ya, we got us a zombie epidemic going on."

Penn exchanged glances of disbelief with his wife. Both seemed to say the same thing with their eyes. The apocalypse had arrived, and soon their fight for survival would begin.

"So, get out there people!" the girl instructed. "When you see one, kill 'em! That's how we take our world back!" Her high energy and enthusiastic spirit may have been meant to convey strength and courage, but to Farrah and Penn it carried a casual brutality.

Penn clicked the television off as the broadcast turned back to more footage of murder. "I didn't see anything strange," he said, barely above a whisper. "Did you?"

"What do you mean?" Farrah asked, only half listening because her mind was in shock.

Penn shrugged, running a hand through his curly brown locks. "I don't know. It was jumping around too fast. Forget it."

A shrill ringing of bells exploded in the background, causing them both to jump. Their heads turned frantically, following the sound. Farrah, as if reuniting with a long forgotten friend, leaped to her feet. "The landline!"

Tucked unassumingly away on a corner end table next to a comfy, quilt-draped chair, was the telephone, which Farrah had only seen used once or twice in her lifetime when her grandparents owned the cabin.

"Hello?" she cried desperately into the receiver.

Penn watched her face twitch through several intense emotions as the person on the other end said something he couldn't hear. Farrah pulled the receiver away from her face, allowing Penn to hear her mother's muffled voice sounding out its panicked warning. He only heard broken sentences as his mother-in-law cried out in panic.

"...don't know...nobody does...stay up there!"

Farrah laid the receiver back onto the phone cradle after the line went silent. She looked at her husband in terror. "What do we do?"

"We stay here, for now." Penn advised. "Getting out into this could be dangerous, honey."

Penn moved quickly to the windows. "Nobody is out there yet. Maybe we are safe up here." Looking back at Farrah, he asked, "Does your dad keep tools here? Hammer, nails? Any wood? We need to board up these windows."

Snapping out of her panic, Farrah crossed the room to one of the front windows. "It's okay," she said, showing him. She unlocked and lifted the windowpane, then reached out to the thick wooden shutters mounted outside. She swung them closed from the inside, showing Penn how they locked shut from within by a sliding latch.

"Perfect!" he cried. "Do they all do that?"

He ran through the house, securing all the windows below while she did the same upstairs. The doors were the only concern now, but they seemed solid enough to hold. "I guess we just wait now?" Farrah asked.

He placed his arm around her shoulder and walked her back to the couch, where they remained in virtual silence for a long time. Though he wanted to say something comforting to her, Penn could find nothing convincing to say. Perhaps they were safe for the moment, but he couldn't shake the feeling he and Farrah were mere spectators to the end of the world. And the cozy cabin where they'd spent the first days of their marriage in blissful content now felt like a trap—a refuge which could just as easily become their tomb.

WHERE THERE'S SMOKE...

The food inside the cabin was running out. Penn had known this moment would come. On the first night of boarding the windows, he and Farrah lay in bed, staring at the beams across the ceiling. Very little sleep came to either of them, the image of Mr. Dole killing Mrs. Capshaw clinging to their minds. Her mind continuously raced through the shocking event, while Penn couldn't stop reminding himself that they'd gone to Capshaw's for more food and left with nothing but fear on their backs.

They waited out the next couple of days and nights, making do with the very last of their provisions, hoping the madness would calm. Farrah had flinched at every noise—and there had been noises. Penn dismissed them all as the natural sounds one hears in nature, but he wasn't sure she'd believed him anymore than he had believed himself. What he'd explained as the groan of wind through the eaves, did sound a little like faraway screams echoing from the surrounding hills. And those sharp cracks he'd explained as tree branches shifting in the wind or acorns falling onto the roof, did sound a lot like distant gunfire.

Whatever carnage may have been happening below them in the village had not crept upward towards their cabin, but distance hadn't masked the reality. Even from their perch on the mountain, the haunting sounds below could be heard if the wind carried them right. And then the sounds appeared to be gone.

Penn and Farrah remained safe, it seemed, but with the food nearly diminished he knew he'd have to venture down the mountain. Farrah was against the idea but also knew they couldn't last long without something to eat.

"We could go home," she offered. "I am worried about my family, and you are worried about yours. Let's just get out of here."

Penn shook his head. "I think right now, where we are is the safest place to be. No one has tried to come up here and bother us. Until this dies down a little more or we know more..."

"How will we find anything out?" she asked. "Local news stopped broadcasting last night. It's only station identification letters now."

"I'll go down and see what's up in town." Penn told his wife. "Maybe I can get something on the car radio."

"Not without me," she snapped.

"Baby, I'll be fine. I want you here where it's safe."

Farrah waved her hands expressively, the way she always did when she had no intention of backing down. "No way. Then you end up dead, and I'm up here all alone wondering. We are a team. We go together."

He didn't argue with her. And truthfully, he didn't want to go alone. They took what they had as weapons, the gun, a tire iron, a hunting knife from a drawer in the desk. Penn locked the cabin door behind them, hoping when they returned, they would not be empty-handed.

"If everything looks okay," Farrah said hesitantly. "Then we just keep rolling right through town and go home."

"There's no telling what home might be like," Penn pointed out. "We live in the city. Birmingham has a million people. I think we have better odds here."

She didn't like his answer, despite knowing he was probably right. "What about our families, Penn? Are they okay? And all our friends? We can't just hide here forever. I want to go home."

He took her in his arms, not knowing what to say. He shared her fear about their loved ones but overriding that concern was her personal safety. "Right now, this is where we need to be, Farrah. If the people we care about were in danger, that already happened. There's no way we can change their fate even if we return home."

"Maybe we can find out more if we go down the mountain to find more food." Her voice was hopeful, if not convincing.

They drove down the winding mountain road where all seemed relatively as it should be for a few minutes. There weren't many homes along the stretch, but the first couple they passed appeared undisturbed. However, a little further down, Penn had to maneuver the car around an abandoned truck. Someone smashed the driver's side window, and streaks of dried blood were visible on the side of the door. Neither said anything as Penn steered around it.

Further down the mountain, they encountered a lone figure —a woman, staggering along the roadside. Her clothes were torn and bloodied. She turned towards the car as she heard the engine approaching. Waving her arms frantically, her mouth open in a silent scream. Penn slowed the car, but Farrah shook her head. "We can't help her," she said with much remorse in her voice. "She's infected." The woman lunged at the car as it drove past, her eyes wild with anger, but Penn kept driving. Nearing the bottom of the mountain, Penn noticed a light fog dwindling between the trees.

Even though Capshaw's Marketplace was the first official start of the village when coming down the mountain, the downward slope of the hill offered a condensed view of the other streets and businesses. It all seemed eerily quiet. However, the fog was a little thicker now, drifting slowly up the rise. The color was off though, and the composition. It looked like smoke, although there were no signs of fire within eyesight.

They pulled into the market's gravel lot again. There did not appear to be anyone in sight. The birds in the trees chirped as if nothing at all had changed. It was a sweet song. But just underneath it, wind hissing through the broken glass shards in the market window played a disturbing dirge.

They walked slowly into the store. The smell was putrid, hitting them like a slap. Penn had not even thought about Mrs. Capshaw. Her decaying body behind the counter was bloated now and crawling with flies. Farrah began to wretch from the odor. Penn didn't speak; afraid another mad killer would overhear them. But he gestured to her to cover her mouth and nose with her shirt collar. It helped only minimally, but they didn't intend to be there long.

Taking a few cloth shopping bags from the counter, they moved along the three aisles quickly, gathering what they could carry. They slipped back out to the car, careful to scan their surroundings as they laid their items in the back seat. Penn held up a finger and rotated it, silently signaling he thought it was safe to go back in for more things.

A second raid of Capshaw's seemed risky to Farrah, but it made sense. While it appeared safe, they should take all they could rather than risk coming back later for another raid. She grabbed more meat, eggs, butter, and cooking oil while Penn made a few trips back and forth to the car loading packs of bottled water, soda, juice, and various liquids to drink. With the car loaded, Farrah glanced back at the shattered store window and felt a twist of guilt.

Starting back up the mountain, Farrah tapped Penn's shoulder. "Our phones! Let's see if they'll work down here!"

Penn stopped the car. No one was in sight behind or ahead of them. He looked at his screen and dropped his mouth open. "I have 34 missed calls."

"28 on mine," Farrah said.

They each began dialing members of their families, but no one answered. With apprehension in his eyes, Penn played his voicemails. Farrah did the same. Staring into each other's teary eyes, they heard terrified messages from their loved ones. One after another, someone they knew had tried to reach them. Each caller conveyed the same panic and confusion in their voices.

"Mom and Dad were shouting about people killing people in the street," Penn said, his hand on his forehead in shock.

"My folks too," Farrah stammered. "Then Jessica…Jessica said her parents…and her brother and sister-in-law…"

"Are dead?" Penn asked. "Jessica's family got killed?"

Farrah shook her head, barely comprehending what she'd heard about people she'd known her whole life. "They were trying to kill *her*."

"What!" Penn cried, reaching over the car and clasping Farrah's hands. "Her parents and brother!"

"She was so scared!" Farrah began to sob and shake. "Her voice, Penn. She was screaming at me in her message that they were outside her house. They were breaking through her windows trying to come in." Farrah paused a second, imagining the terror.

"What about Jim? Where was her husband?"

"They killed him in the yard." Farrah revealed. "I could hear him yelling in the background. Jessica was screaming, *'They're killing him! They're tearing him apart with their bare hands.'*"

Penn gripped his wife in his arms, unable to believe any of what they'd heard. Part of him still did not believe any of it. Surely, this was some elaborate prank all their friends managed to pull together on them. Even as he tried to rationalize how they might have pulled off such a ruse, he knew that was a ridiculous wish. No one would do anything so cruel, and none of their friends had the time or fortitude to go to such outrageous lengths. Then, as if a guiding hand placed it before them, a flap of paper being carried in the wind slapped against the side of the car. It was a newspaper, Birmingham News, dated five days ago. In big black letters…MONSTERS ARE REAL!!! IS THIS

TRULY HAPPENING???

"What do we do, Penn?"

He sat silently gripping the steering wheel for a moment, then said, "We go back to the cabin. We have food. We know it is safe there. Let the world settle down before we rejoin it."

"But our family?" Farrah reminded him. "What if they need us?"

Gently, he placed his hand onto her soft cheek, his grim expression on the verge of tears. "Baby, I think you and me are all the family we've got."

CHAPTER 3

SHORT TERM FRIENDS

Time passed like an hourglass choked by wet sand—slow, uneven, almost unwilling to move. Yet somehow the seasons still changed. Life for Farrah and Penn had become more a resistance to defeat than a yearning for survival. They had watched their world die before their eyes through news broadcasts and viral posts until the electricity stopped working on the mountain. Gasoline was too scarce to waste running the car to charge a phone and had to be conserved strictly for driving down the mountain whenever food ran low. And it wasn't as if keeping track mattered anyway; after a while, nothing new was left to report or learn. The last seen broadcast had been as full of unanswered questions as the day it all began. Something happened. A virus? Biochemical warfare? Little green men from outer space? Only in this case, big green, blue, red, purple, gray, monsters no one seemed to describe reliably.

New meaning came to the term "the honeymoon is over" as Penn and Farrah learned to operate as teammates and not merely lovers.

He became proficient at chopping wood to keep the fireplace going for light in the dark hours, as well as warmth when cold set in. Farrah learned how to make bread from a recipe book using a few supplies found at Capshaw's, and one or two other nearby markets they had been forced to pillage. She was rather proud of her yeast dough, which she nurtured and kept alive for future baking. It was like pioneer times, only unromanticized—probably how actual pioneers had lived. Scraping by and terrified of what lay beyond their barred door at night. With Farrah's replenishing supply of bread, along with a supply of jellies, jams, and peanut butter, they never starved while they stretched out the rest of their food stores.

Though it was a lonely existence, the young couple did have friends. Tom and Nancy Parker were an older couple living a few doors down from the second-closest market. Having run into each other while scavenging for food, Penn and Farrah did their best to remain in touch whenever they came down the mountain. It had become a habit for Penn to tap his horn whenever nearing the Parker's small house on the little country lane. Without fail, Tom and Nancy would unbar their door and venture out to the porch to greet their new...and now only friends. It was Tom who first shared the frightening news about the monsters.

"Don't know exactly where they come from," he warned one afternoon, leaning over his porch rail. "But me and Nancy saw three or four of them stalking around a house about a mile up the highway."

"What were they like?" Farrah asked.

"Tall and twitchy, like shadows that got too heavy."

"Looked like some kind of lizard if you ask me," Nancy chimed in. "Like those old dinosaur movies where something extinct comes back to life. It was dark though, hard to see. But Tom's headlights lit them up for a couple of seconds. Scariest things I've ever seen."

"What do you think they are?" Penn asked.

"Before the radio conked out," Tom informed them. "I heard 'em telling about some weird lights glowing off in woods near Choctaw County. Sounds like some sort of thing from another world to me."

"Aliens?" Farrah gasped. "But that doesn't explain why people were killing each other at the beginning."

"Right?" Tom gave a humorless chuckle. "We get rid of one thing then get sent another! First, people go killing crazy. Now we got these things skulking around in the dark."

Nancy folded her arms across her chest as if she were about to impart something invaluable. "That alien nonsense is a bunch of hooey. We got poisoned is what happened! Russia or China or somebody put something in our water or gassed up our atmosphere."

It wasn't a mystery any of them would be solving anytime soon, but before Penn and Farrah continued on their way, Nancy called Farrah inside where she gave her a foil-covered pan of salted meat.

"Tom killed one of the pigs the other day, and I set aside some meat for you two kids."

Farrah was almost speechless by the kind woman's generosity. "No, ma'am, we can't accept that. Food is too hard to come by now. You and Tom need this—"

"Without a working refrigerator we ain't got no way of storing meat," Nancy countered with a smile. Her weathered, caring face was about the only beautiful thing Farrah had seen in some time. "You kids have got to eat too and be strong enough to fight these things if they come up the mountain at you."

When the women came back outside, Penn was beside himself with gratitude. He hadn't had meat in weeks, and with the power out, any the market had was rancid now. "I don't know how to thank you," Penn said to them, shaking Tom's hand.

"No thanks needed, son." Tom said. "We all gotta look out for each other now."

* * *

And they did look out for each other...for a while. When winter came, the visits grew less frequent. Rain turned to ice on the frosty nights, making it impossible for Penn and Farrah to get down the mountain until daytime temperatures grew high enough to make the roads passable. But dense trees and indirect sun sometimes took days to melt even the thinnest sheet of ice.

It had been nearly three weeks since the last time they'd seen Tom and Nancy, when Penn honked the horn as he and Farrah neared the house.

"Don't get out," he warned Farrah as he brought the car to a stop before the porch.

Her eyes saw the same thing as his. The door torn from the hinges, raccoons stirring in and out of the open doorway where windblown leaves stretched inside the house from the porch. Penn got out of the car.

"Penn, don't go in!" Farrah begged. "Something might still be in there. Just look through the side windows.

It was an excellent suggestion, one he followed. When she saw her husband turn quickly from the windowpane to wretch into the gray dead grass, she knew. And when he got back into the car, she didn't ask. They had been a genteel and generous couple, and she'd rather not have to know the details.

CHAPTER 4

VERNON

Winter in the mountains painted a dismal landscape of the diminished world for Penn and Farrah. Brittle branches, crisp brown fallen leaves, and remnants of a once picturesque community gave an impression of a civilization left in ruins. But as spring arrived, leaves budded. Wildflowers bloomed. And green grass sprung up around the rotted husks of animal-picked bodies across the lawns of fractured houses. As the early hours of summer dawned, it felt hopeful somehow, as if life might renew.

Whenever Penn used to watch zombie movies or binge any post-apocalyptic series—back when things were normal—the *end of days* always seemed a good deal more apocalyptic than they did now driving down the interstate. Of course, it was still early. It had been less than a year since he and Farrah had left on their honeymoon to Mentone. If the "end of the world" was still an event in progress, maybe there was still time remaining until the closing act.

While nature remained seemingly undisturbed by Armageddon,

man-made nature looked very different. The interstate was eerily uncongested, although not exactly empty. Other vehicles passed them from time to time—some heading toward the city and some disappearing into the safety of rural distance. No one tried to run them off the road. They did not display blatant animosity or antagonism. In fact, a few drivers even honked and waved in some kind of cosmic solidarity. Still, overall, it seemed wrong in its quietness.

"I was second-guessing leaving the mountain," Penn remarked after tossing up a friendly hand to acknowledge the man who had just passed him. "But doesn't it seem a little friendly for the Apocalypse?"

"It does," Farrah replied beside him. "Is it possible it's all over?"

"God, I hope so," he said under his breath.

Then the realization hit her like a slap. She grabbed his arm, panic in her face. "Penn, it has been months. Months! What if all that ended a long time ago? Have we been hiding in the mountains for no reason at all?"

Penn glanced at her sweet, hopeful face. He understood why she might think that. The same thought had crossed his own mind a few miles back, but he knew better now. "No, honey, I don't think so."

"Look around, though!" she cried. "Nothing seems all that bad."

She hadn't been paying attention to the signs. Penn understood that now. He found it interesting how two people looking out onto the same environment could perceive it in such different ways. Farrah noticed the sunlight, the wildflowers blooming in the medians and across the meadows. Her eyes hadn't taken in the rest. The signs. The literal signs.

"How many times did we drive down the mountain to hit up a store or abandoned café for some food over the last few months?"

"A lot," she admitted.

"We never saw a soul but us," he reminded his wife.

Farrah sighed. "Yeah, Penn, but we were way out in the country, secluded."

Penn patted her leg, replying, "Exactly my point, Farrah. We are not secluded now, and very few vehicles have passed us on the road. And then there are the signs you clearly aren't noticing."

"What signs?" she asked. "Like, intuition?"

He laughed, "No, honey! Like actual written signs!" Penn's finger shot across her chest to her window. "See! There's one right now."

Farrah twisted in the seat to glimpse the small scrap of torn cardboard staked into the ground off the road's shoulder, but they passed too quickly. "I missed it," she moaned. "What did it say?"

Staring straight ahead, hands tight on the wheel to keep from shaking with his growing anxiety, he answered. "It said...We're fucked!"

They continued along the highway into Birmingham, growing more apprehensive with every mile as to what they might encounter in the city. Sadly, they'd each come to terms with the fact that their families were most likely dead months ago. The last messages they'd heard before the cell phone service disappeared gave every indication they were under attack. The likelihood of survival was dismal. Their phones, when charged, could still take pictures, operate as a flashlight, and work as a calculator—but they were no longer tools for communication. Farrah disregarded hers, but Penn still liked to keep his on him. Looking back at the pictures of his family at their wedding made reality a little less painful.

Penn glanced at the fuel gauge. "We need gas."

It hadn't occurred to them until that moment how involved the task of getting gas might be. Would stations even have gas? Were any open? Was it safe to stop anywhere? The panic of running out of gas with no way to acquire any, and no ability to call for help, put a knot in their gut.

Looming ahead stood a towering gas station sign, the kind intended to drive traffic in. It was perfect timing as Penn wasn't sure how many miles he had left on an empty tank. He turned off the exit ramp with butterflies in his stomach, not knowing what they might find. Farrah noticed his fingers tightening around the steering wheel. Relief washed over them to find another car parked at a pump, but their relief was short-lived. Farrah and Penn exchanged wary glances as they looked out at the sight of five fuel pumps completely enclosed by a makeshift cage of welded bars, blocking access on all sides and over the top. Only one pump was assessable, the door to its caged housing open. Next to it, a young man in a black cap was filling his pickup truck's tank.

Penn eased his car up behind it, unsure what the protocol was for this changed world. "I'll be done in a sec," the young man shouted to Penn.

"Stay here," Penn told Farrah as he got out of the car, approaching the other man cautiously. "Don't worry!" Penn called out to him. "I'm not one of the deranged people. I won't hurt you. Just want to talk."

The younger man didn't appear worried as he returned the gas nozzle back to the pump. He lifted the brim of his cap a little, allowing easier eye contact with Penn. "I'm not worried," he replied with an easy-going smile. "Those deranged people, as you call 'em, don't come out much in the day. And believe me, I'd have known if you were one of them well before you pulled in."

"What do you mean they don't come out in the day?" Penn asked. "We saw people out killing in broad daylight. Saw it on the news too."

"When was this?" the younger man asked with a curious look on his face.

Penn shrugged, "I don't know. Months ago, late last fall. Back when we could get a signal."

The other guy nodded as if Penn's earlier claim now made sense. "Yeah, in the beginning the light wasn't an issue. But when they started turning into what they really are, I guess the light hurts them."

A shiver ran down Penn's spine. "What do you mean...*what they really are?*"

The young man studied Penn a moment. "You're sorta out of the loop, aren't ya?"

Penn exhaled with an awkward grin. "Guess so. We were up in the mountains. No cell reception. And the power went out after a while. My wife and I have been alone for a long time. Then food ran out, so we decided to come home."

The man nodded again, understanding. "They got service in the bigger cities. Ain't got anybody to tend the downed lines, I guess. Too many dead. Too many turned. Guess we're all on our own now."

Penn rubbed his hand through his hair, pushing his bangs away—he was overdue for a haircut...if barber shops were even a thing now? "What do you mean when you say *turned?*"

The guy propped his hand on the fuel pump as he leaned against it. "I dunno exactly," he said. "They just...changed. Like those zombie movies, ya know?"

"Zombies?"

The man shrugged from a lack of answers. "My dad says it's toxic waste. Big business dumping into rivers and oceans. Whatever caused it, turned people into the sickest looking things you ever saw." He looked out across the afternoon sky, then remarked, "Heard a preacher say on the radio, when it all started, that it is demons, if you can believe that! And I read something somebody wrote online—before the internet crashed—it is all these hormones we used to get in our food. Changes some of us."

"How?" Penn scoffed, finding that theory the most ridiculous, which in itself sounded ridiculous considering the implausibility of the other explanations.

The young man chuckled. "That science stuff is over my paygrade. But the article mentioned some new medicine that come out a couple years ago. Said something about those medicines, reacting to hormones, then maybe a new strand of virus...Man, I really don't know anything for sure. Nobody does." His amused smirk faded, and he added with a twinge of hopelessness in his tone, "I think the house just caught on fire. And when the house is burning down, does it make a shit who lit it?"

As the man wished him luck and was about to leave, Penn motioned towards the gas pump. "How does this work now? Can we still use our credit card to turn it on?"

The guy grinned and shook his head. "I'm afraid those days are over. Whoever worked here must have died or left before shutting the pumps off. Few of us welded these cages together to conserve what gas there is. Don't know when or if anything is coming to refill the tanks underground."

"Oh," Penn replied. "Can I pay you for some?"

"Naw, man," he chuckled. "Go ahead and fill up, just do me a favor... Make sure you lock it all back up when you're done."

"Absolutely," Penn said. "I appreciate your letting me fill up."

The young man tugged at his cap. "Our side's gotta look out for each other, Mister." He slid into his truck to go. "The more of us there is alive, the more chance we got to kill those creatures."

Penn watched the truck drive off, the younger man's words still replaying in his mind. It sounded like a very different world now and Penn could only hope he and Farrah could survive within it.

* * *

They drove further in the direction of town as the sun dipped lower in the afternoon sky. The closer they came to the city, the more man-made signs Penn saw. Farrah was on the lookout for them now. Whenever they passed under a bridge crossing the interstate, their eyes were drawn to the messages spray painted onto the sides or the signs draped over them written on sheets.

They can look like us. Trust nobody!

Martin Ford. House got attacked. Mom's dead. Me and Dad at Shirley's barn.

The Devil has opened Hell. Repent and Pray!

No food left at this exit

Each sign further filled them with dread as they pushed along the almost empty highway. The late-day sky caused the trees along the roadside to cast inward shadows, making it seem as if a black tide was rolling in on both sides with no way to escape. Neither Farrah nor Penn said it aloud, but the sight of the setting sun aroused a dread in each of them after what the man at the gas station had said. Had they known the "creatures" came out at night, they would not have started from the cabin so late.

The original plan was to drive to Penn's parents' house in Mountain Brook. It was doubtful they would still be alive, but it was worth finding out. Even if they weren't, their house had a wall around the backyard, and it was large enough that he and Farrah could board themselves up in the pool house. It was all too risky now. Not enough time to get there. Instead, they would go to their apartment. It was on the third floor, easier to protect.

Penn pulled into the parking lot, deserted except for a single abandoned truck, stripped of its tires and engine.

"Let's do this fast," he told Farrah. "We can come down tomorrow for our stuff."

They had barely stepped out of the car when they heard the silent air shatter with the sounds of shouting. Penn turned sharply to see two men, guns drawn, charging between the two buildings towards them. Their shouts, competing with each other, were unintelligible from so far away. Farrah ran around to Penn's side of the car, taking his hand in fear. His eyes darted ahead to the stairs leading up to the third floor. Did they have time? He couldn't be sure. A dozen thoughts raced through his mind in a few quick seconds as the men grew closer to the end of the building. There was a chance to run for it, taking the steps two at a time, and maybe—just maybe—Penn could unlock their apartment door and get Farrah inside before the men shot them.

Another sound rang through the air, turning Penn's attention away from the apartment building. A van came to a screeching, sliding halt several feet from them. The driver, a rugged-looking man, locked eyes with them through the window. Then came the gunfire. A bullet slammed into the van's metal siding. They heard a woman's shriek from inside, then watched as the van's side door slid open.

A woman's voice shouted out to them. "Get in! NOW!"

Penn hesitated, looking back at the gunmen. There was no way to reach their apartment now.

The first shot had been distant, but when the second came it was much closer, barely missing the passenger side window. The deafening blast made Farrah gasp, digging her fingers into Penn's arm as the woman in the van screamed. For some reason he didn't understand, Penn trusted these people. He pushed Farrah into the van and slammed the door shut after him. The man driving roared off through the parking lot, jumping the median to meet the road leading away from the chaos. Birmingham blurred past them through the windows as the man navigated around abandoned cars and debris-strewn streets, weaving between what was left of a city Penn and Farrah once knew well but could now only barely recognize.

"What are we doing?" Farrah whispered to her husband.

"Escaping with the people not shooting at us." Penn answered with his gaze locked straight ahead toward the battered streets.

The woman in the passenger seat turned to face them. She was blonde, with shoulder-length curly—almost frizzy—hair. "What were you guys doing?" She asked Penn and Farrah. "Trying to get killed? If we hadn't been on a supply run...or was that what you were doing too?"

"Supply run?" Farrah repeated.

Penn glanced around the van. Now that he wasn't dodging gunfire, he could notice the stacks of bottled water, crates of canned goods, and crates of meat packages lifted from a grocery store. There were also sodas, beer, rice, and crates of potatoes and fruits rolling around in plastic bins. These people weren't just rescuers, they were scavengers. Survivors.

Running a trembling hand through his dark curls, "What is going on around here?"

The driver glanced back from the rear-view mirror. His hair was hidden under an Alabama Football hat, but the bits sticking out from under were the same blonde as the woman's. "Where have you two been?" he asked Penn. "Do you not know the world ended?"

Farrah and Penn exchanged glances, then Farrah attempted a joke. Recalling the wind-swept headline, she said in a cracking voice, "Did zombies take over while we were on our honeymoon?"

The grim face of the woman confirmed Farrah's little joke was not remotely funny. "Yeah, that's basically it."

Farrah squeezed closer to Penn as the words hung in the air under the hum of the tires against the pavement. The blonde man looked back at them again, his face sympathetic. "It's a lot. We get it. But accept it. We've seen too many people stuck in disbelief and they weren't ready when the bad shit hits." He exhaled through his mouth as if releasing some of the haunting images he'd witnessed, then added. "And they're all dead now."

His warning shook their new companions, and he saw it in their reflected faces from the rear-view mirror. He lightened his tone and introduced himself and the woman beside him. "I'm Rylan, and this is my sister Allie."

Allie emitted a little chuckle. "Our granddad used to call us Rye and Ale. Sorta stuck. You can call us that too if you want."

Farrah tried to smile in return. "I'm Farrah and this is Penn. If we didn't say it earlier, thank you for picking us up before those men shot us."

Allie winked. "Anytime, but those weren't men." She turned back towards the windshield, commenting to her brother, "Sun's setting. They are going to be freaked out at Vernon."

The van twisted through the streets of town. It was a heart-chilling ride for Farrah and Penn, to see things so desolate. It wasn't the way it was in movies, where nature had crept back in to take the urban places back over. Everything looked just as it should be, only no people. It was the lack of people that made it all seem so unrecognizable. In a city once so full of noise and motion, the silence was the most unnatural thing of all. Traffic lights flashed their reds, yellows, and greens to the one moving vehicle which paid no attention to them. It might have been Christmas morning, or one of those rare holidays when people are usually already where they intended to be. But even then, the streets had movement. Occasionally, as the van passed a building, something would flash behind a window, or a random face would look from a doorway. Farrah could feel the unseen eyes watching them.

"There are communities," Rylan informed them. "People living together, or alone, in some buildings or houses. It's best to be in a group. Easier to protect each other."

"Do you guys live in a group?" Penn asked.

"A good one too," Allie said with a hint or pride. "We've got a sweet setup. We're luckier than some."

Farrah regretted asking the moment the words left her lips, but she had to know. "Our families are from Mountain Brook. Do you know—"

Allie shook her head solemnly. "I'm sorry. Rye and I have been all through Birmingham. A great many areas have been..."

She didn't finish, perhaps not knowing tactfully how. It was only a confirmation of what they'd already assumed. Farrah and Penn continued looking from the van window. The noise of the vehicle drew attention, not only from behind boarded windows but from around corners where a few people, like the men with guns, swarmed like locusts towards the escaping van. Thankfully, the vehicle was too far ahead of them to be in any real danger. Farrah looked through the windows, trying to see for herself the bluish tint to their skin and distorted appearance that the clips on the news back at the cabin warned about, but the fading sun and the distance from them made it difficult to distinguish.

"Take the long road, Rye." Allie said.

He did as directed, and though neither he nor his sister explained why, Penn and Farrah knew it was to ensure if any of the monsters were watching, they wouldn't know the exact location the van was moving towards. Soon the winding back road twisted onto a side street running beside a high school. The sign said *Vernon High*. The road passed beside an overgrown football field enclosed by a tall fence woven with razor wire. Vines covered the goal posts on each end of the field and stretched diagonally to the ground below. Though it was growing too dark to see for sure, the vines had to be held that way by stretched cables.

"Is that a garden?" Farrah asked.

Allie smiled. "It was one of the first things our founders did when they took the school over. They knew growing food would be vital for survival. This summer should yield a good harvest."

Rylan steered the van into the opening of an asphalt driveway behind the school, where two men with rifles slung over their shoulders stood behind a tall gate. Rylan gave the high sign through the van window, and one of the men rolled back the iron-barred gate. As they pulled in, the gate quickly rolled shut behind them as Penn and Farrah scanned the camp. What probably once operated as school bus lanes, the road behind the school held many parked vehicles. Trucks, vans, cars, buses, and even a U-Haul sat ready for use when needed.

"We're good on transportation," Rylan called back to them from the steering wheel. "And thankfully, this school has its own diesel fuel tank for the buses. But we try not to use them unless necessary, to conserve fuel."

A covered walkway ran against the back of the school with several doors standing open to the night air. An elderly woman with a broom lifted her hand to them as she paused from sweeping the walk. "Hi, Mrs. Yardley!" Rylan shouted to her, waving back. "We found more Ensure for you! The old woman blew a polite kiss as they drove past and resumed her sweeping.

"Mrs. Yardley is our oldest resident," Allie told Penn and Farrah. "She used to be a teacher here before she retired. She lives in her old classroom; I guess because it makes her feel centered. But those exterior rooms are really too far from everything for someone her age."

"We've tried to get her to move to the main hall," Rylan added. "But she likes where she is."

The van drove around the building to the official front of the school. He parked the van in front of the auditorium and told the new arrivals they could get out now. Allie opened the back doors of the van as two men and a woman came outside to unload. They eyed Penn and Farrah with a welcoming suspicion while offering a polite nod as they went about their work.

"Come on," Rylan said, gesturing for Penn and Farrah to follow. "We'll get you checked in."

He made it seem like a hotel concierge welcoming weary travelers, but once they walked into the auditorium, Penn and Farrah saw for themselves it wasn't a bad analogy. The school was a thriving center of survival. Just inside the auditorium entry stood three long tables where those unloading the van placed the new inventory. Behind the tables two middle-aged women stood sorting the finds into individual clusters.

One of the women looked up from her work with a welcoming smile to Penn and Farrah. "I see Rye and Ale found more than rations today! Welcome to Vernon. I'm Marian."

Marian bore the signs of the new world thrust upon her. Once heavyset, she'd lost weight at a rapid pace, most likely from limited indulgences. Her formerly plump arms now sagged underneath when she lifted them to move something, and her face and neck seemed more jowly than it probably once had.

"Hi," Farrah said meekly.

The men unloading the van continued bringing in more supplies, which Marian and her co-worker quickly organized into departments. These were people with a system, a process. And it appeared to be a successful one.

"Marian and Emma," Allie informed the new arrivals, "Make sure everything brought in gets dispersed to the proper storage room." As a crate was placed on the table, Allie instantly removed a 12-pack of vanilla flavored supplemental milk. "But this," she said to Marian. "Goes to—"

"Mrs. Yardley," Emma answered for her, swiping them across the table to a separate area. "You were so sweet to find these for her. Are there more than these 12?"

Allie nodded. "I'm not sure how many, but we took all we found."

The hands of the sorters moved with precision skill, almost like a grocery store clerk swiping groceries across the scanner. Marian and Emma knew what they were doing and where everything would need to go, pushing things into piles or creating new ones. And as a crate became empty, they immediately refilled it with items being transferred to the same storage area.

Emma pushed a crate of frozen meat and vegetables to the end of her table, shouting, "Billy! Cold storage!"

Farrah turned to watch for a few seconds as the boy, Billy, quickly loaded the frozen crates onto a wagon where he dashed off through a door in the auditorium's center wall.

"Billy's got to get that to the freezer before things thaw!" Allie grinned, ushering Farrah along.

Rylan turned to Allie. "Can you settle them in?" He looked almost embarrassed.

"Yeah," his sister replied. "You go take the wrath you're in for."

As Allie led Penn and Farrah through the door where Billy had disappeared, she turned back to confide in them. "Rye's husband Dillon gets really worried whenever we are on supply runs. And we are not supposed to be out past dark. My brother is in for it."

Allie led them out of the auditorium into the school's main corridor. It felt like being in high school again. Just outside the auditorium stretched a wide staircase, turning at the landing to reach upward to the floor above.

"That narrow little hall between the auditorium and stairs goes to the old art room and music room," Allie explained. "There is a piano and an organ, but no one knows how to tune the piano, and it is really off-key."

Her eyes scanned the newcomers, but when Farrah and Penn shook their heads, she knew that problem wasn't any closer to being solved.

"People do use the art room," she continued. "Kids mostly. And Lauryll. She was an artist in the old life and still paints now that she's here."

Allie explained that the little hall ended in a small switchback staircase leading to the outside walkway where they'd seen Mrs. Yardley earlier. "Do many people live on that stretch?" Penn asked.

"Not many. Mrs. Yardley...and Patrice Wilson lives next door with her little daughter Lakeisha."

Continuing down the main hall, lockers still lined the walls between the closed classroom doors. Overhead, fluorescent lights buzzed softly with an all too familiar hum. "Electricity is...dependable, but not guaranteed to work all the time," Allie warned. "You'll want to keep some candles in your room at night, but enough sun gets in during the day to see your way around."

Between the doors of the Boy's and Girl's bathrooms was a bulletin board, still decorated with the sentiment expressed by whatever teacher had last laid hands on it. *Show who* you are *by showing who you* want to be.

Penn looked back at the bathroom and asked, "Do you have running water?"

"We do," Allie answered. "We have no idea why the electricity, gas, and water still function, but thank God they do. Although you can always rely on them to operate better on some days than others, we try to conserve."

"How is it that the utilities are all still operational?" Penn asked.

Allie chuckled, "Hey, don't look a gift horse—you know? Maybe the monsters haven't found a way to disable them, or maybe computers run the grid. If it's people, we owe somebody a great deal of thanks."

Farrah trailed a little behind as Allie and Penn moved on. Her eyes were fixed on a girl no older than seventeen hurrying down the hall balancing a crate stacked with folded towels and shampoo bottles. She stopped at a classroom, fumbling for the key to the lock. Farrah proceeded to help, taking the crate from her arms.

"Thanks!" the girl smiled, unlocking the door.

As the door swung open, Farrah could see many tables spread around the room. One was neatly piled with towels. Another had soaps. Another toilet paper. There was even a table of battered hair dryers and curling irons, and one for hairbrushes and combs. The girl took back the crate and placed it on an empty table to unload and sort.

"That's Maddie," Allie explained from the doorway. "This is her storeroom. She knows where everything goes." Then, lowering her voice to Penn, she whispered. "Check out those towels and bath cloths. Maddie is a bit compulsive. You'll never see anything in her domain not perfectly aligned and in order."

Farrah started back towards the door, but Maddie called out for her to wait. Dashing off to a few tables, the girl returned with a cardboard box of items. "Towels, toothbrushes, cloths, and bed linen."

"Thank you," Farrah said, taking the box.

"No, thank you," Maddie grinned. "You just saved me from having to find your room and deliver it all. If you need anything else hygiene-wise, just tell Dolores and I'll get it to you."

Allie led them back into the hall. Penn turned to her and commented, "So that's how you keep it all together. Shopping in the post-end-of-the-world era."

"It works—when everyone does their part." Allie said, moving along.

"Who is Dolores?" Farrah asked.

But her question went unanswered as they passed another open classroom where a woman was sorting clothes onto shelves. As she saw them pass, she rushed to the door and called out, "Something going on out there today, Ale?"

Allie paused. "What do you mean, Beth?"

"Just wondered if there was trouble outside," Beth remarked. "You and Rye got back so late and...Dasha and Shane still aren't back."

Allie looked concerned. "They still haven't come back?"

Beth shook her head.

"We had a flat tire," Allie said, explaining her and her brother's tardiness. "Then we had to find a tire to change it with." Allie turned back to Penn and Farrah. "After we got the tire on, we saw these two across the street about to be attacked. Sun was setting, and the ghoulies were already coming out. Nearly got them."

Beth gave them a wave, then returned to her work as Allie moved the new additions along. It was obvious to Farrah that Allie was troubled. "Do you think your friends are okay?"

Allie frowned. "I hope so. It's never good to be out after dark." They walked along a few more feet before Allie said anything else about it, and when she did, it seemed more to her benefit than theirs. "But Shane and Dasha are pros in a tight spot. If they can't get back, they know how to hide until morning."

Continuing through the school, Penn was curious. "Do you ever run into those monsters out there?"

"Used to, before the sun started messing with their chemistry. Rye and I killed them anytime we ran across one. But now they roam at night. And the more they degrade into whatever they really are, the more brutal they become."

"Are we safe here?" Farrah worried.

"As safe as can be."

It was one of those sentences left up for interpretation. "As safe as you can be" meant something far different from "As safe as you can be." Farrah didn't ask which she meant. She wasn't sure she really wanted to know. Allie brought them to the center of the building, where the high school office was still the hub of this community's government.

"Just a heads-up," she said in a low voice before going in. "Dolores is...enthusiastic."

Penn raised an eyebrow. "Enthusiastic like a *cheerleader*, or *cult recruiter*?"

"Yes."

Before Farrah could laugh, Allie opened the door, where a thin, pale woman stood. She looked to be in her forties, with large glasses and a pinched, severe face. The impression she gave was that of a mousy librarian who'd be quick to shush the slightest noise in her proximity. However, when she spoke, it was a rather high-pitched, shrill tone accompanied by far too much excitement.

"I heard we had newbies!" she exclaimed. "Welcome to Vernon! I am Dolores. I suppose you two need accommodations!"

Penn exchanged glances with Farrah before replying, "Yes. Please, I guess." He took the box Maddie had given them and placed in a chair.

A door at the back of the office swung open, and a young man came out. He had short, choppy cut light brown hair and a scruffy face that hadn't been shaved lately. Allie's immediate attention moved to him, leaving the newcomers on their own with bubbly Dolores.

"Decker?" Allie exclaimed. "Is everything okay?"

The man came toward the counter with a salty swagger and a mischievous grin. He placed his hands on the counter and jumped across it, sweeping Allie into his arms. "Now it is! I was pleading with Gusty for permission to take a car out looking for you!"

Flirtatiously, she smirked back at him before they kissed. "My knight in shining armor. But I know my way around out there better than you. You'd have only gotten yourself killed."

A woman came out of the door behind Decker. She was older, maybe 60, African American, and dressed in a purple wrap dress, which seemed far too fashionable for the end of the world.

"I told him the two of you would be fine, Allie," she said. She smiled, taking notice of the new arrivals. "Welcome to Vernon High. My name is Augusta, but everyone calls me Gusty. I am the principal, I suppose you would say. At least I was before everything went bonkers."

Dolores turned giddily to Augusta, chirping, "Gusty, I was just about to decide where we should put Penn and Farrah." She turned back to the newcomers. "Now, I assume you're married? I see rings. That makes it easier to know where to place you."

"Place us?" Penn repeated.

"Yes, Penn, if I may?" Augusta replied. "We have limited accommodations here for the long run. Although for the moment, new arrivals are lucky in that they get to have choices."

"Choices?"

"Yes," Augusta explained. "Your quarters, your jobs. Everyone at Vernon contributes. And we try, while we can, to provide our residents with adequate quarters—although not everyone can have their own space, we try to be fair."

Dolores took it from there. "Since you are married, you probably do not want to be divided up in one of the male/female dorms."

Penn blushed. "No. I had enough guy roommates in college."

Dolores released an exaggerated giggle, which everyone took uncomfortably, even Augusta. "We have an opening in the Duplexes. One has just been freshly painted a lovely light yellow." This tidbit excited her even more than the thought of Penn having once lived with other guys. "We have two available annex rooms if you wish to be private, and two portables."

Augusta filled them in. "Annex rooms are rather small, but private. They open to the outdoors, which can be a hardship during cold months or stormy weather, but other than that it is perfectly private. The portable buildings are larger, but again, they are outside and, unlike the annex rooms, they do not have a covered walkway. Duplexes are one large classroom, divided into fourths. We've built walls so they are private but shared with three other residents. Though small, they are indoors and close to all the common areas."

The new arrivals opted for an annex room, which they learned was right next door to the older lady Rylan and Allie had been waving to when they drove in. Allie told Dolores she would show it to them later. "I don't think these two have had a bite to eat all day."

Leaving the office, Allie escorted them further down to the end of the main hall where it branched right into an adjacent corridor. They didn't tour that wing; instead, they entered the large cafeteria. The dining facility was alive with chatter and the smell of food. As they came inside, heads turned to look at Penn and Farrah as if they were two movie stars coming down the red carpet.

Allie laughed, shouting over the room, "You will all meet them later! His name is Penn. Her name is Farrah. Go back to your own conversations."

A light chuckle moved across the room as Allie led the newcomers to the back of the cafeteria, where a modest buffet awaited. The young man behind the glass put his hands on his hips and scolded, "I don't know if I am willing to feed you at all tonight, Allie!" He presented a nicer smile to Penn and Farrah, expressing that his irritation was not with them. "But I set you both aside plates already. They're in the warming drawer."

He disappeared to the back of the kitchen, returning with three plates on a tray, proving he was not going to punish Allie after all.

"Farrah, Penn," Allie introduced with a smile. "This is my brother-in-law, Dillon."

He handed Penn a tray with two plates, each filled with potatoes, green beans, and a braised hamburger patty topped with gravy and onions. He handed the third plate to Allie without a tray. "I hope it burns your hands. You had me scared to death."

She laughed, offering Dillon a playful wink. "We ran over a nail and got a flat."

"Was Rylan driving?"

Grimacing, Allie answered. "Yes."

"He drives like a fool. You should be the one driving!"

"Then please drive that point home to your husband," she quipped. "He never listens to me."

Penn couldn't tell whether Dillon was truly upset or if Rye needed a defender. "Your husband and Allie saved our lives."

Without missing a beat, Dillon leaned over the counter and said, "Please do not repeat that to people. Rylan is quite cocky enough already."

Allie high-fived Dillon over the remark, then led her new friends to a table.

CHAPTER 5

THE DEDICATED PRINCIPAL

It surprised her how many thoughts could run through a mind during a ten-second tailspin in a car you can't control. Regret hit first. She suspected she'd punctured that tire but decided to keep moving unless it lost air. Next came recrimination. Why hadn't she considered that the weeds overgrowing the bridge might conceal nails, spikes, or shrapnel? Then, lastly it was irony she thought about, as the old adage about taking the road less traveled mocked her because she'd been told not to deviate from the known route. The car spun, tires screaming, until the guardrail crumpled under the impact. Then every prior thought—every existing memory—emptied from her mind as she plunged over the bridge.

Dasha slammed the brakes of the pickup truck when she saw the car tumbling downhill directly in her path. "Reverse!" Shane shouted while rock pelted the hood like hail and debris from the disintegrating car sprang downhill in their path. Dasha threw the gear into reverse, racing backward, leaving her own trail of black rubber on the road in front of her. The neatly arranged crates in the bed of the truck shifted violently towards the cab, feathers flying out of the wire tops and sides. Dasha turned back to look quickly at their haul. The chickens weren't happy about the sudden jolt, but none of them appeared injured.

The toppling car landed ahead onto the spot they had just been. A swirl of dirt, smoke, glass, and twisted metal clouding the view. A human hand flopped out from the shattered side window, clawing at the pavement and the side of the door.

"Shit!" Shane yelled. "They're alive!"

He bolted from the truck with Dasha directly behind him. The woman inside the car was choking, gasping for air. Initially, it seemed she had internal injuries and might be coughing up blood, but after they unbuckled the seatbelt and slid her through the window, they saw the blood on her chin came from the wound on her head.

"What's your name?" Dasha asked. "Can you speak?"

The woman coughed again, gasping for breath. "Give her a sec," Shane suggested. "I think she's had the wind knocked out of her. And maybe a concussion."

"Let's take her back," Dasha said, glancing up at the rapidly darkening horizon. "Doc can treat her at Vernon." *If she makes it that far.*

Shane hesitated, his eyes locking onto his partner. "Do you think we should take her with us?" he asked. "We don't know her. What if she's trouble?"

Dasha frowned at him. "She's not trouble. She's *in trouble.* Clearly, she's not one of the monsters."

"Doesn't mean she's one of the good guys," Shane barked back. "And it doesn't mean she hasn't turned yet."

With a quick nod, Dasha acknowledged the point but still argued. "Yeah, but we can't leave her here alone. It'll be dark in a few minutes, and those things will rip her to pieces."

He knew she was right. Risky or not, the injured woman was clearly human—for now at least. The creatures would crawl out of their lair at any moment. They hefted her into the back of the truck next to the cages of chickens they'd collected from the outskirts of town. Shane took the wheel while Dasha stayed in the truck bed with their rescue.

The headlights of the truck swept the streets, cutting through the growing dark as they tore through town headed home, only the streets were no longer empty. The monsters were awake now. As the truck roared past buildings and abandoned houses, doors flung open, revealing the twisted, gruesome beings coming out to kill. Their narrow-slit eyes crowning their malformed heads turned to catch sight of the humans trying to escape. Twice, a few charged towards the road, but Shane kept his speed too high for anyone to make an ambush. In the truck bed, Dasha watched the bluish-skinned creatures scurrying outside as she clutched the woman's still unconscious body close to her. The chickens weren't at ease either, squawking and rustling within their crates.

In the distance, Dasha saw a pair of headlights flashing through patches of trees and brush. Someone else was out there driving. They weren't close enough to see the truck yet, and she wondered if the other driver weaving through the trees might be one of their own teams caught out past dark, trying to get to Vernon. Or it could just as easily be another vehicle of people from another settlement or living on their own, desperate to get themselves to safety before any of the diseased creatures overtook them.

Shane pulled the truck through the gates of Vernon High School, the gatekeepers pushing it quickly closed behind them. He readied himself for a scolding because cutting it this close after dark put the entire community at risk. He made his way quickly around to the auditorium entrance. Dasha leaped from the back of the truck as the helpers came out to unload.

"Who is she?" Billy asked as he saw the woman.

"We don't know," Dasha told him. "Just tend to the chickens. We'll take care of her."

* * *

Most of Vernon had gone to bed, except for the night guards patrolling the campus. Normally, Augusta would have long since retired to sleep, but she stayed up waiting for the last two supply runners' safe return. And now, with an unconscious stranger in their midst tonight, Augusta worried about the safety and wellbeing of her people.

Usually, when someone new joined Vernon, there was no question about their status. When Penn and Farrah were brought in earlier that day, their ability to speak audibly proved they were uninfected. The monsters were not so easily recognizable in the beginning. Back when the plague began, they looked like anybody else. It could be days before the external metamorphosis fully transformed them into the bluish-purple things with such exaggerated extremities. Until then, the only indicator of a human being infected was their inability to utter any sounds other than gurgling gibberish, clicks, and growls.

This mystery woman Dasha and Shane rescued, remained unconscious. No one would know if she was infected until she woke up. If she could speak, she was still human. If she couldn't, she would have to be killed before risking everyone else.

Augusta walked to the nurse's office; her purple pumps echoed through the empty hallway. She opened the door, finding the lights off. She flipped the switch, washing the space with fluorescent light. No one was there, and all three of the cots were empty. Someone parked the stainless-steel rolling cart against the wall, but something was amiss on the supply shelves above it. Augusta took her responsibilities seriously. She knew the lives of dozens of people depended upon her rational and educated judgement. Few things went unnoticed by her at Vernon, and she made it a point to ensure that the medical unit remained stocked with essentials. She also knew that Corinne, affectionately referred to by most as "Doc", had a propensity to prefer things in even numbers. Perhaps it was a tick, or maybe a superstition. Whatever the reason, when Augusta's eyes saw three rolls of bandages instead of four, five rolls of adhesive tape, and three bottles of antiseptic, she knew Corinne had taken an extra precaution. She probably deviated to Vernon's former protocol, quarantine in the armory.

Augusta made her way to the east end of the hall and rounded the corner by the staircase. Walking past the art room, she saw a light on under the door. She hesitated a moment. There was no actual need to look, she knew...but Augusta poked her head inside, anyway. It was as she expected. Lauryll was at the canvas, brush gripped tightly in her fingers, adding thin streaks of color to the work she'd been painting for a week. She hadn't heard the door open, unaware the principal was watching. The artist's hand swept across the canvas, carefully adding minutiae to details she'd already captured. Her lips moved softly as if whispering something only the painting could hear.

Augusta quietly pulled the door closed again. She made a mental note to check in on Lauryll tomorrow. This was becoming something of an obsession, this latest painting. But grief did strange things to people. This was what it had done to Lauryll.

The principal made her way down the twisting stairs to the tiny vestibule where a lone classroom stood opposite the exit door. For a moment, her mind wandered into the past, when she'd been the official school principal here. No teacher ever wanted that isolated classroom. That's why when she smelled cigarettes on Mrs. Rice's breath, she struck a deal. Move her Spanish classroom down there, and she'd be able to have easy access sneaking out between classes to grab a smoke behind the parked buses in the bus lane. Augusta now wondered what had happened to Mrs. Rice? Did the monsters get her...or the cigarettes?

Exiting the main building, Augusta followed the walkway between the gymnasium and the outer bank of classrooms. She could see a light on in the small square window at the top of Mrs. Yardley's door. It seemed curious for the most senior resident in Vernon to still be up.

Augusta nuzzled the door open. "Just checking on you, Imogene. It's a little late for you to be up, don't you think?"

The elderly woman was in her bed, tucked in with her Bible folded open on her lap. "One might say the same about you, Augusta."

"Yes. It is way past my bedtime. I was just going to look in on Dasha and the injured lady before I retire. But when I saw your light...did you forget to take your nighttime medicine?"

Mrs. Yardley flushed with embarrassment. "That may be why I can't fall asleep."

Augusta went inside and inspected Mrs. Yardley's pill dispenser. The two evening pills were still in their compartment. She removed them and a small bottle of water from the shelf. Closing the pills into Mrs. Yardley's frail, weathered hand, Augusta told her, "Here you go. Take them now. If you sleep past breakfast, I'll make sure Dillon brings you down a plate."

She watched while the old woman swallowed her pills with a few sips of water. The plastic bottle made a crackly sound as it flexed against her fingers—the nuisance of having to refill bottles for repetitive use. Eventually, the durability wears out. Augusta made a mental note to make sure someone gave Mrs. Yardley a fresh bottle in the morning.

Dasha rose from the desk when she felt a hand on her shoulder. Pushing her swath of black bangs from her eye behind her ear, she got her bearings within a few seconds. "Shit, Gusty," she whispered. "I fell asleep. Sorry."

"I understand," the principal replied. "You have had quite a long day. Making a run out to one of the remote farms, then finding and rescuing this woman. But I must caution you until we know..."

"You're right," Dasha answered. "I can't be caught off guard. But Doc and I did tie her hands to the cot frame."

"Where is Corinne?" Augusta asked.

"Oh, I sent Doc to bed. No reason for her to stay in here and risk herself."

Augusta walked over to the unconscious woman, examining her injuries. Corinne had stitched up the patient's head and bandaged the scrapes and cuts on her arms. Her flesh seemed normal. The texture and color, quite human. Of course, that didn't prove anything until she woke up.

"I'd say she's in her mid-to-late twenties."

"How can you tell?" Dasha asked.

The principal chuckled. "Dingy blonde hair at the ends, brown midway to the scalp, but no gray roots mixed in. She colored her hair up until civilization fell." Augusta lifted the hands, turning each over to inspect. "No dirt under her nails. No blisters or calluses. Wherever she's been living, she didn't have much manual labor assigned to her."

Dasha stepped closer. "I can't see any injuries except head trauma. Hopefully, she'll wake up tomorrow."

Augusta looked into Dasha's eyes, making a serious pronouncement. "If she cannot speak. Or if she speaks in a manner you cannot understand..." Augusta removed a knife from her dress pocket, unsheathing the blade. "End her and alert the Janitors."

"Yes, ma'am."

Augusta moved towards the door to leave, but stopped short, turning back to offer another warning. "Dasha, I want you and Shane to be extra careful in the future. This woman's car blew a tire. Rye and Ale also lost a tire on the road. It is possible the monsters are laying traps now to disable our vehicles. Drive with awareness and never leave Vernon without two spares on you."

CHAPTER 6

MEET JANE DOE

A soft groan escaped her lips as she opened her weak eyes to confront the light shining into them. Wincing from the light or from her throbbing headache, she turned her face into the coarse pillow. It felt rough against her cheek and had the faint smell of antiseptic.

"It's alright," she heard a reassuring feminine voice say. "Stay still and don't be alarmed. We are friends."

The patient jerked at her hands, tied to the sides of the cot, then sent the strange woman a questioning look.

"Well…" Corinne blushed. "We are cautious friends."

The speaker turned her head gently back, shining the penlight into her pupils again. She tried to sit up, but the restraints made it impossible. All she could do was stare up blankly at the woman with the light. It was then she saw a second woman, younger, with black hair cut at an angle on the left side of her head and buzzed short on the right.

"Do you remember anything?" the younger woman asked. "Can you speak?"

"What happened?"

The woman with the penlight and the younger woman exchanged communicative glances, conveying a message with their eyes but saying nothing. They seemed relieved.

"What is it?" the woman exclaimed, beginning to panic. "What's wrong?"

"Nothing...now," the younger woman with the odd haircut grinned, slicing a knife through the zip ties holding the patient's arms down.

With her hands freed, she sat up on the cot, clutching her head from pain or dizziness. It occurred to her as she thanked the lady for cutting her ties that hearing her own voice felt foreign to her.

The older woman patted her leg gently. "Don't get excited. You are perfectly fine. I am a doctor. My name is Corinne Chambers, but most people around here just call me Doc." She gestured to the younger woman. "This is Dasha. She and her partner Shane pulled you from the wreckage."

"Wreckage?"

"Do you remember your accident?" Doc questioned the patient.

The woman appeared rather confused, stunned perhaps. Her brows pushed together as if she were straining to remember. "No, I don't remember anything."

"Let's start simple," Doc advised. "What is your name?"

The woman swung her legs over the cot as if about to stand. Her eyes looked erratic, and her hands trembled. "I have to get out of here."

Dasha stepped forward, placing a firm but unthreatening hold on her shoulders. "You can't do that just yet," she said. "We need information so we may help you. Doc asked your name."

The woman dug her fingers into her scalp in frustration but flinched from the pain. "What is wrong with my head?"

"You have a concussion," Doc explained. "You were pulled from a car that crashed and rolled downhill. Do you recall that happening?"

The woman glanced into Corinne's eyes; she seemed to be genuinely afraid. "I don't. I don't remember a thing!"

"It is all right," Corinne said soothingly. "It will come back to you later. Let's begin with your name."

"That's just it!" the woman shouted as she pressed her fists into the cot's fabric. "I don't know!"

Doc eased her back down on the cot, looking again into her eyes, but this time she didn't use the light, only her fingertips to widen the pupil. "It might be the concussion. What is the very last thing you can remember?"

The answer was nothing. Nothing came to her. No images. No names. No faces. No history at all. It was all just a void.

* * *

Augusta was in her office when Corinne knocked at the door. "Well, Gusty," she said, taking a seat across from her desk. "The accident victim is not infected. But she also has no idea who she is."

The principal's eyes widened. "Amnesia?"

"Appears so," Corinne replied. "I don't believe she has bad intentions. And she is definitely not one of *them*."

Augusta leaned back in her chair, exhaling a sigh of relief. "So, what do we do with her? We can't allow her to leave. In her condition, she shouldn't be left to fend for herself. We should invite her to join Vernon."

"I agree," the doctor said. "We even asked her if she'd like to remain here, and she isn't opposed to the idea."

Augusta nodded. "Can she be assigned a room yet, or do you want to keep her under medical observation?"

"Another day or two should do it," Doc replied. "Besides the concussion and her memory loss, there isn't anything really wrong physically.

Dolores can assign her a room once she can walk without dizziness."

Augusta chuckled to herself. "She'll need a name."

"Dasha already gave her one," Corinne laughed. "Doe. As in Jane."

* * *

Days passed, and Doe's recovery progressed. Physically, she was not seriously harmed in her accident. Her dizziness and headaches subsided, but memory did not return. Once Corinne released her from the infirmary, Dasha took it upon herself to introduce Doe to the rest of the community. Other than stepping outside to visit the restroom, Doe had seen nothing of the complex. Now, as they walked the west wing of the repurposed school, Doe took in the new world she had unknowingly entered.

"That over there," she pointed out, showing Doe a building set apart from the school on the west lawn. "That is the old vocational building—it houses the shop, garage, and some classrooms we use now for tool storage."

Doe noticed another building much lower where the land sloped. The building was set against the hill under the vocational wing. "Is that also part of it? That fenced off section?"

Dasha shook her head. "No, that is the armory where the school's former ROTC classes were. Now we use it for weapon storage due to the built-in fortifications." Dasha forced down an amused grin. "It's also where we kept you on your first night. But you probably don't remember."

Swiping a bit of her chin-length cold blonde hair from her eyes, Doe smirked as if amused. "Who would have guessed high school, the place everyone can't wait to escape, would be the sanctuary people run back to?"

Dasha laughed, "Ironic, isn't it?" She paused for a second, asking, "Can you remember high school?"

"Not at all," Doe answered. "But some knowledge is universal, I guess." As they continued moving towards the main building, Doe must have thought more about the paradox of her situation. "How can I not know my own name, but know I probably hated high school? For that matter, how do I know what ROTC is? Or how to speak English?"

Dasha grinned. "How do you know how to use a fork? Some things are just ingrained, I guess."

Upon entering the school, Dasha explained that each resident receives two lockers to store their personal belongings, in addition to what they keep in their sleeping quarters. "Many are empty because this school has four hundred of them," she added. "And the cooks use the ones closest to the cafeteria for additional can and dry good storage." She let out a hearty laugh before confiding, "They turned the storage room off the kitchen into a smokehouse for meat."

"Meat?" Doe repeated.

"Surprises you?" Dasha asked. "One of the territories Shane and I scope is rural. When the world went crazy, it left a lot of farm animals without care. We keep them tended and bring a few at a time back here to Vernon."

"To kill?"

Dasha frowned and shrugged. "Cows we keep for milk. Occasionally we bring a pig or two home to smoke. But a couple of the guys go deer and turkey hunting sometimes. Actually, we were bringing back chickens when we saw your crash."

They continued the tour, following the end of the corridor, where the scent of seasoned meat and baked bread filled the air. When Dasha opened the cafeteria doors, heads turned to check out the amnesiac they'd heard about. Feeling the eyes on her, Doe felt anxious in her skin, but presented a few nods to those who appeared to be greeting her, and those who were merely staring, she ignored. Dasha escorted her back to the long three-rod buffet rail against the plexiglass window.

"Hi Chef!" Dasha waved to the brunette-haired man by the stoves.

He was stirring a large pot with tendrils of steam swirling around his face.

"Tonight is meatloaf!" he shouted back to her. "And thanks to your chicken run I have more than enough eggs to spare for the mixture! And I'm making a few cakes!"

Dasha whispered to Doe, "That's Dillon." They started down the line, a bright-smiling Hispanic woman began filling two lunch trays with creamed corn, peas, and a square slice of pizza. "And this is Trisha!" Doe exchanged nods with Trisha and accepted the lunch tray given to her over the counter.

The women settled at a nearby rectangular table already occupied by two men. "Doe," Dasha introduced. "This is Shane. He helped rescue you. In fact, technically, he pulled you free."

"Then, thank you, Shane." Doe nodded with a polite smile.

He gestured back with a thumbs up as he spread grape jelly over a piece of cornbread. "Glad you are on your feet."

"And this is Billy," Dasha said, pointing to the second guy.

"Hi."

Conversation flowed between the three, but Doe stayed quiet, listening and taking everyone in. Not only those she was dining with, but occasionally sneaking glimpses around the cafeteria. A few tables over, a middle-aged woman was helping an elderly man cut his food into smaller bites. Another woman sat alone at a table, staring off into nothing as she mechanically chewed her food. Doe noticed she had splotches of dried paint on her arms. But then Dasha's next statement drew her back into the conversation.

"We need more hands to raid a farm," Dasha insisted. "If Shane drives the U-Haul, I can get a bus, remove the seats, and load up some cows."

Shane rubbed his chin with a hearty laugh. "Dasha, do you know how heavy a bus full of cows would be?"

"We need meat, Shane!"

Billy scarfed down the last of his pizza and, after a subtle hiccup, argued, "What you guys need to bring back here is a bull. Get the bull from that farm, and we'll make our own cows."

"I am not getting gored by a bull!" Shane gasped. "No, sir. Besides, Doc needs some medical supplies from our next run."

It was now that Doe entered the conversation. "Sounds like you need more supply runners. One team out searching farms and one out getting the other things this place needs."

Shane glanced her way. "That would be great, but it can be a dangerous job. You've not only got those monsters out there to avoid, but not all the people out there are docile. The end of the world tends to change man's willingness to share. We don't get too many folks here willing to go back outside once they come here."

Dasha picked up from there. "Most of the folks here at Vernon barely escaped the outside world with their lives. Supply Runner is not a job most people are willing to take."

"I'll do it," Doe announced.

Shane narrowed his eyes and replied sarcastically, "Uh...Doe, I've witnessed firsthand how you handle a car. Maybe you should go to work in the stockrooms."

His remark didn't offend her, strangely. There was no malice in his tone; in fact, it was rather familiar. It made Doe feel less left out and more as if she were already one of them. She liked the feeling.

"I have no memories of the outside to make me afraid," she said, addressing the pros of her idea. "I am also new, so if I get killed it isn't a big loss anyone will suffer."

Dasha lightly slapped her hand. "Don't say that."

Doe addressed Shane now directly, realizing that he seemed to be the one in charge of the Supply Run force. "You said no one volunteers. I'm volunteering. Train me."

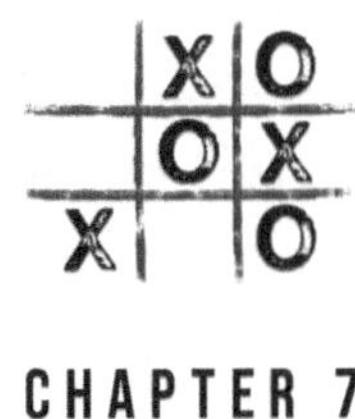

CHAPTER 7

WHAT SHE MISSED

Doe was going a little stir crazy in her small quarter-section of one of the female dormitory rooms. She didn't mind her new sleeping space, but an apartment, it wasn't. With merely a single bed and nightstand, it wasn't a space she planned to spend too much waking time in. She ventured out into the corridor, strolling across the worn tiled floor. The interior hall had no windows; with the only light being the overhead fluorescence, she wasn't sure if it was still daylight outside. Regardless, it seemed too early to sleep, so she strolled through the hall looking for the library she'd passed before but couldn't recall its direction.

It didn't take long to find, and Doe went inside hoping to find a book, magazine, or something to pass the empty time. Immediately, the scent of aged paper and dusty bindings filled the air. It didn't bother her; however, her brain now had considered the idea she might see or read something which might evoke a memory of who she used to be.

She wasn't alone in the library. Another woman was there, seated at a table, perusing a few books. Her bright auburn hair shone under the light and she glanced up with a friendly wave when she saw Doe come in.

"Hi! You're...Doe, right? Or is it Jane, and Doe is the last name you picked? I'm sorry, I only briefly heard about the girl with amnesia." She seemed embarrassed by her clumsy introduction, quickly adding, "My name is Farrah. I'm new here too, if that helps explain me."

Doe strolled to the table to make her acquaintance, greeting her with a forgiving smile. "It's just Doe. For now. Until I remember my real name, I guess."

Farrah gestured to a chair at the table, inviting Doe to join her. " I'm very sorry about your memory," she offered with a frown. "As if we aren't all experiencing enough uncertainty, you lose your memory on top of everything else." She seemed sympathetic. Doe liked her right away.

"It is definitely strange," Doe replied. "But maybe I'm lucky. I don't have an old life to miss like the rest of you do."

"Now that is a positive way to view things!" exclaimed Farrah. "I do miss my life, and my family. But my husband, Penn, and I are like you in a way. We missed most of the worst that everybody else faced. We were in the mountains when it all started and stayed there until we couldn't find food anymore. These stories some others tell about what they went through is mind-blowing."

"Did you two go through quarantine too?" Doe asked.

Farrah's smile fell slightly, explaining, "I think they worried you might be infected until you woke up. They say the first thing affected is speech. I think they just needed to hear you talk."

Doe shook her head. "They might wish I couldn't once they know me better." She folded her hands on the table and admitted, "I don't know anything that happened, except what Dasha told me. And all she said was that some people woke up one day and began killing other people for no reason. Then they transformed into some kind of monster."

"Basically, that sums it up," agreed Farrah.

Doe gave her a peculiar fisheye look and asked, "Doesn't that sound outlandish though? Granted, I have no memories, but even I can't help but feel it all sounds impossible."

"I would have said the same," Farrah answered, closing the book she'd been reading and running her finger across the title. The Viral Storm: The Dawn of a New Pandemic Age *by Nathan Wolfe.* "I have been reading up on all the scientific books and journals this library has since I came to Vernon. Trying to understand."

"Had any luck?"

"Not really," Farrah admitted. "But I have learned some pretty fascinating things about how viruses mutate. Of course, I've found nothing to explain how people turned into reptiles."

"Reptiles?" Doe exclaimed. "Like a snake?"

"Well..." Farrah sighed. "Maybe 'reptile' is strong. But some people here who've seen them say they look like purple lizards or something. Maybe it's some weird thing from the other side of the universe. Bacteria trapped in a meteor that crashed—like in that old *Blob* movie! Nobody really knows."

Doe glazed over the covers of Farrah's assorted books with mild interest. "Contagions, toxic chemicals, DNA structures...you're covering wide territory."

Farrah giggled. "What else is there to do?" She took a pause and then added, "Well, I did take a job working in the gardens. Have you chosen a job yet?"

"I volunteered for Supply Run, but Shane and the others have to talk it over."

"That would scare me to death!" Farrah admitted. "Penn hasn't chosen a job yet, but if he tried to pick that, I'd have a big problem with it."

Doe opened one of the books Farrah had been reading. Gruesome images of radiation burns, physical malformations, and historical epidemics filled each page. "Fun stuff," she commented. "I came in here hoping to find a book to lull me to sleep. This isn't it, though."

Farrah grinned. "It isn't a fun read, that's for sure. And I still can't find anything that would remotely link any virus or bacteria to something strong enough to change human DNA into a blue-skinned lizard thing."

The doors to the library swung open, and a man swept in with an excited look on his face. "There you are, honey!" he rushed over to the table and placed his hands on Farrah's shoulders. "I figured out what job I want!"

Farrah clasped his hand and introduced him to her new friend. "Penn, this is Doe. Doe, my husband Penn."

Penn shook Doe's hand and offered his sympathy for what she'd been through. Then he returned his attention to his good news. "I've been talking with that Decker guy. He runs the security patrol. He says I can shadow him tonight if I want—see if I like it."

"Patrol guard?" Farrah repeated. "That could be dangerous, Penn."

"But it's doing something," he replied. "Something useful and significant. It's just a tagalong tonight. Nothing's been decided yet."

Doe released a soft moan. "Maybe I'll pick something like that too if they don't approve me for Supply Runner."

"You should work in the gardens with me," Farrah smiled, running her hand across her forehead to push her bangs away. "We would have a great time working together out in the open air!"

With a bit of a smirk on her lip, Doe remarked. "Someone with your fair skin and hair probably isn't suited for daily outdoor sun exposure."

Farrah laughed. "I know! But I have always loved the outdoors. I think it's why I have so many freckles."

Penn asked his wife if she was ready to go to bed and started helping pick up the books she'd been studying, to re-shelve. "Farrah, why are you reading all this? This shit will give you nightmares."

"We are already in a nightmare," she exclaimed. "I want to know why it happened."

* * *

Doe went to the locker she was assigned and removed some comfy clothes before going to the gym. For nighttime, it bustled with more activity than she'd expected. A group of men and two women were playing basketball. Doe sent a wave to Dasha and Shane, who were on opposite teams, interestingly enough.

Doe went into the girl's locker room to shower. Another woman was bathing in one stall already, and Doe gave her a nod hello as she stepped into the stall beside her. Doe pressed the spout on the repurposed milk jug, and it spit out a very watered down homemade bath soap.

"It isn't going to foam, no matter how much you use," the woman said under the other shower head.

"Yeah, I am discovering that." Doe replied.

"The ladies in the bath supply room do their best with what they get," the woman explained. "It took my little girl a long time to stop whining about not having bubbles when she washed her hair."

Doe nodded, turning to rinse, then looked back over at the woman, realizing she should be polite and ask. "How old is your daughter?"

"Eight, almost nine. I'm Patrice."

"Doe," she answered, shaking over the half wall. "How long have you two been here at the school?"

Patrice stared at the rafters, trying to remember. "I guess...about ten or eleven months. It was right near the start of this place. Keisha and I were down to our last two cans of beans when we heard Rylan and Allie's truck going by our little house. We'd been hiding under the floorboards at night when those creatures would come out. It was no place for a little girl." Patrice's face lifted a little as she recalled that eventful day. "We ran out the second we heard that truck coming down the road."

"And they stopped for you." Doe replied.

"They did more than that," Patrice grinned. "They practically adopted us into their family. Rye and Dillon fell in love with my little girl from the start. They help me out a lot when I work patrol."

"I haven't met them yet," Doe admitted. "Except for the chef, Dillon, for a brief second."

As Patrice rolled her head under the shower, she continued talking to Doe. "They've been so great for Keisha. Our world turned scary, especially for a child. We lost my son. Rye and Dillon and Allie became family to us when we needed one."

"I'm sorry," Doe muttered, not quite knowing how to respond. "Was it...those things?"

Patrice dried her face with the towel slung over the wall. "Don't know. Dre just never came home to find us. His phone didn't work anymore. He's just gone..." she dabbed her eyes once more, but this time Doe suspected it was from tears. "...or he's one of those things now."

Dasha's stroll into the locker room interrupted the heavy moment. She was covered in sweat as she peeled off her clothes. "Everybody prepare for a trickle," she warned stepping into the stall on Patrice's left. "These pipes aren't known for quantity,"

"Who won the game?" Doe asked. "Your team or Shane's?"

Patrice sighed, shutting off her own shower now. "Dasha is kind of unbeatable," she groused. "Which is why I don't play anymore. They always split up the women, but if Dasha plays, nobody else stands a chance."

Dasha pumped a few handfuls of the watered-down soap and exclaimed, "Oh, I forgot to tell you, Doe. Augusta approved you to train as a runner on the next supply day!"

CHAPTER 8

SUPPLY RUN

Rylan sneaked into the empty cafeteria like a seasoned thief, keeping to the wall to avoid being seen from the kitchen's limited vantage point. He tossed up a hand to Trisha, signaling her to keep silent and not reveal his presence as he crept behind the buffet warmer and plexiglass sneezeguard. She was busy slicing potatoes, but when she caught sight of him, she gave him a wink and a conspiratorial nod. Trish knew this game. She'd seen it before.

He continued past her, creeping around the long aluminum counter, staying low to be unseen. He saw Dillon's back turned to him inside the storeroom closet. Rylan tiptoed nearer, seeing his husband oblivious to the approach as Dillon clutched a clipboard to his chest while absently tapping the eraser end of a pencil to his chin. Scanning the stores of ingredients and dry mixes, he was too occupied to hear Rylan sneaking up on him.

With a mischievous grin playing at his lips, Rylan jabbed his fingers under the chef's arms, tickling him as he blurted, "Got enough sugar!"

Dillon yelped! Dropping the clipboard and pencil, he whirled around with blazing eyes to scold his husband. "Why do you *do* that!?"

"Because it's funny." Rylan chuckled, drawing Dillon in for a kiss.

Dillon melted into the kiss and held it for several moments before pulling away and folding his arms with an exasperated huff. "No."

Rylan blinked. "What?"

"No!" Dillon repeated, shaking a finger at him. "I said it, and it stands. No. You *are not* going back out again today."

"How did you—"

"Because that was your *'remember I love you if anything happens'* *kiss*." Dillon deduced. "I was scared out of my mind when you were late the other night. Let another team go out today."

"I don't get to decide those things." Rylan smiled, trying to pull him close again, but Dillon ducked it.

"Well, I do!" Dillon shot back, stomping past Rylan as if marching to war. "If Augusta and the rest of the school board don't dismiss you from duty for a week, they can do their own damn cooking around here for a while!"

Trisha shot Rylan one of her sympathetic looks. If there was anyone else at Vernon who frequently found themselves on the receiving end of Dillon Daily's rants, it was his assistant cook. As Rylan rushed after his fuming husband, she leaned in and whispered a single word into his ear.

"Paprika."

Catching up to Dillon before he made it out of the cafeteria, Rylan stepped in front of him, pressing a firm hand to his chest. "Ease up, cowboy. No need to go shooting both barrels at the principal."

Dillon refused to disarm. "Why, Rye? What is so damned urgent that you must go out thrice in a week?"

"Thrice? Really?" Rylan tried not to laugh. Sighing in frustration and understanding, he wrapped his arms around Dillon's neck. Dillon stubbornly avoided any eye contact, turning his head side to side to dodge Rylan's gaze. But Rylan outsmarted him, turning right when

Dillon thought he was turning left, and locked him in with that Rylan Daily signature lop-sided grin. There was no escape. Not for Dillon anyway. It got him every time.

Dillon groaned in defeat. "Stop."

"Stop what?" teased Rylan.

"That stupid smile on your stupid face," Dillon grinned, pressing his hand across his husband's mouth and pushing him back.

They kissed again, Dillon softening now, but barely. "Please let somebody else go."

"It is a simple run," Rylan promised. "Doc is low on bandages and peroxide. And…" Rylan glanced around as if checking for eavesdroppers, but no one else was anywhere near them. "The feminine hygiene shelves are low, and the baby formula is almost gone."

Dillon's indignation sprouted once more. "There are *two babies* at Vernon! You can get bandages next week. Nobody's injured. And I hardly think a tampon run is worth your life!"

Rylan started laughing.

"It isn't funny!" Dillon snapped.

"It really *kind of* is, honey," Rylan replied. "Obviously, there is going to be more to the list. Somebody said the janitors need new shovels. They're already borrowing from the gardens. I have to go."

Dillon stood silently, pouting. Then Rylan heard a throat clear in the distance. Trisha, reminding him.

"What if I promise to find you some paprika?"

Dillon squirmed a little on his feet, his resistance beginning to waver. He knew Rylan would go no matter what, but this dance was necessary to maintain balance in their marriage. In reluctant defeat, Dillon gave a nod, but demanded, "I want lots of paprika! And mustard seed. And cinnamon. A bunch of cinnamon!"

"Deal."

"Then get out of my face before I slap yours," Dillon snorted. "You always get your way."

Rylan leaned in, nuzzling his stubbly cheek against Dillon's ear. "When I get home, you can have *your* way...with *me*."

"You're a jerk," Dillon laughed, kissing him again. "Please be careful. I swear if you die, I will marry someone a thousand times hotter than you."

"No one is hotter than me," Rylan smirked, slapping his husband on the rear before slipping out of the cafeteria.

In the hallway, his sister Allie was waiting. "Pissed?"

Rylan sighed, "Oh yeah."

"Told ya so." Allie smirked as they stepped through the outer doors by the cafeteria. "Oh, we have a trainee today."

Rylan spotted Doe waiting in the van when he climbed into the driver's seat. She appeared ready, but he worried about her going out so soon after her accident. "You sure about this?"

Doe met his eyes in the rearview mirror. "Physically, I'm fine," she replied. Then with a look of determination, she added, "To tell the truth, I'm hoping driving around the city may jog my memory."

"You never can tell," Allie said. "You had to come from somewhere. Maybe one of the other communities or the stragglers living alone. If anything looks familiar, just speak up and we can check it out."

As the van rumbled through the empty city streets, Rylan watched the traffic lights blinking yellow—a haunting ghost of the order they once provided. The Lakeview District loomed ahead. It was a name he never understood, having never seen a lake near it in all the years he'd lived in Birmingham. Doe watched from the back seat as well, scanning every building and house hoping for something that might seem familiar, but nothing did.

Soon Rylan pulled into the lot of a dialysis center, one of many that had sprung up through the city over recent years. He used to wonder what was up with the kidneys in Alabama, that so many renal clinics were needed? But it didn't matter now. The three scavengers left the van, each holding an empty crate, and went into the facility through a side door Rylan had broken through months ago. The sunlight streaming through the windows illuminated the building enough to see without artificial light.

Allie nudged Doe in the back with her crate, explaining, "You and I will clear out bandages, adhesive tape, and plastic tubing. Rye can grab antiseptics and heavier things."

"I am surprised all this is still here," Doe remarked as she filled her crate with rolls of tubing.

"Other communities raided the hospitals first," Allie explained, tossing in several boxes of needles. "Nobody ever thinks of these places." The needles weren't on the list, but she knew Doc wouldn't complain about having extra inventory.

After loading the van, Rylan crossed over a few streets and parked in the restaurant district. "I'll be back in a few," he told the girls. "You two check out the pharmacy over there."

"In the doghouse, Rye?" Allie smirked, understanding he hoped to bribe his way back into Dillon's good graces.

"Ale," he said, shaking his head. "More like the dog pound."

He set off with another empty crate, squeezing through a large broken pane of glass of what was once a Thai themed restaurant. Allie and Doe took crates across the street to a corner pharmacy. Someone had previously looted it, but what they needed might still be in stock.

"Is everything alright with Rye and Dillon?" Doe asked Allie as they entered the store.

"Dillon does not like that we are Supply Runners. Coming back so late the other night got to him."

"But that was because you saved Farrah and Penn," Doe replied. "He can't be upset over that."

"Not about rescuing them," Allie explained. "But this is a dangerous job, away from the protection of Vernon. Any run has risks. Rye, Dillon, and I are all the family we have left. It scares the hell out of him every time we leave."

While she neatly packed her crate with feminine products, Doe asked more questions. "You lost the rest of your family?" Allie was about to answer, but Doe quickly grabbed her arm, signaling trouble. Outside, two figures approached the front of the store. Doe squinted to see from the other end of the pharmacy. Were they people? "Ale," she whispered. "Look."

Two beings slithered through the broken doors at the front of the drugstore. The women stood still, not yet seen by the intruders. Allie and Doe, crouched behind a shelf, watched the figures intently, studying their movements. Each step taken seemed disjointed and unnatural, as if entities who had only now learned to walk. Their appearance was unlike any animal known to humankind. With only the natural light from outside illuminating the space, their body covering appeared too textured for skin. In the light, it shone iridescently in varying shades of grays, blues, and greens much the way sequins might...or scales. Their heads were inhumanly oblong, and their eyes appeared to be nothing more than dark slits. In their exaggeratedly large hands, they held long empty sacks. But unlike Allie and Doe, who were out for supplies, these entities were stuffing their bags with *everything*.

It was methodical. The two creatures positioned themselves between the two lengths of shelving on the nearest aisle, then starting at the top shelf and working down, they removed every item, placing it in their bags.

"They aren't even looking at what they're taking," Allie whispered to Doe.

The scene became more disturbing when, behind the figures, more beings infiltrated the store. In assembly-line precision, the invaders formed distinct lines behind the original two, working in unison to remove everything in sight. After they filled a bag, their taloned fingers passed it down until it left the store, while a fresh, empty bag moved forward. Like ants, they were devouring the inventory, inch by inch, leaving nothing on the shelves except the dust.

"Can they really need all that?" Doe whispered.

The look on Allie's face told the frightening reality facing them. "This is a tactile strike. Take it before humans can."

Communication between the creatures was hard to decipher other than a few throaty grunts repeating down the line. If they weren't using telepathy, their language was rudimentary. Regardless, the choreography of their raid proved a formidable hive mentality.

Allie realized that she and Doe had to get out before being seen. She tapped Doe's shoulder, her eyes wide with fear, gesturing to the exit door twenty yards behind them. The two women prepared for a sprint they hoped would be faster than the monsters could move.

"Go!" Allie shouted, bolting towards the exit with Doe at her side. One creature let out a high-pitched shriek, alerting its comrades to the escaping humans. Abandoning their strip mining of the drugstore, the hostiles lurched forward towards the exit door like a swarm of locusts.

Allie and Doe fled the pharmacy, their feet pounding asphalt as they rounded the building to reach the van. Neither dared look behind them, afraid that doing so might slow them down or cause a stumble, but they could hear their pursuers on their heels.

Rylan was in the van already, watching them cross the street. He reached back to open the sliding door just in time for Allie and Doe to jump in as he slammed into gear and sped off. A few of the monsters diverted to the road, attempting to form a barrier, but Rylan didn't blink, mowing them down in his path. The strange blue-skinned lifeforms screeched and writhed under the wheel; their haunches crushed from the impact.

The van hurtled down the avenue while the remaining creatures gave chase, but Rylan was too clever, and the van was too fast to keep pace with. He steered down a hidden alley, gliding block by block unseen between buildings until he was well away from that section of the city.

"What the hell are those things!" Doe exclaimed once they were safe.

Rylan whipped the van onto a proper road and shouted, "Some scary-ass motherfuckers is all I know!"

CHAPTER 9

SCHOOL BOARD MEETING

Perhaps it was because their community lived in a former high school. Or it could have been the fact Augusta Davis had actually been the principal of Vernon High School when the epidemic broke out. Either way, the need for structure had driven the residents of Vernon to model their little government much like a school.

Over breakfast, Allie did her best to explain the system to newcomers Farrah and Penn, who were still adjusting to life at Vernon. "Gusty, as you know, is the equivalent of mayor to our little society," she said, propping her elbows on the cafeteria table. "But whenever something big happens, we have what we call *school board meetings*."

Farrah, mid-sip of her coffee, perked up. "*That's* what all those signs in the halls are about! Penn and I wondered what *School Board Meeting Tonight* meant."

Allie gave a nod and continued. "We have one every month unless something urgent pops up everyone should know about."

"Does Augusta make all the decisions?" Penn asked.

"On basic things around here, but with big stuff she lets all residents have a say." Allie explained. "It is also a great time to bring any issues up or make suggestions. Vernon's government works a lot better than our Congress ever did!"

Swelling in the background, raised voices began spilling out from the kitchen, causing more than a few heads to turn in that direction.

Allie rolled her eyes in frustration. "Here we go again."

Penn looked across the table at her. "Isn't that your brother-in-law Dillon's voice?"

Looking embarrassed, Allie glanced around the dining room, then waved to a little girl seated a few tables back with her mother. The mother smiled Allie's way, then gave her permission to her little girl. The bright-eyed child left her chair, skipping to them. Allie slid her arm around the girl's shoulders, introducing her. "Farrah, Penn, this is Lakeisha."

"What a pretty girl you are," Farrah said. "I love your pink dress."

"Ale got it for me!" Lakeisha grinned, exposing her two missing front teeth.

"You hear that mess in the kitchen?" Allie asked the child.

"Sure do!" Lakeisha giggled. "This one sounds like a doozie!!"

Allie placed a hand on the child's shoulder, giving her a very serious look. "What did I tell you *your job* was at Vernon?"

Lakeisha laughed. "Keeping the peace!"

Allie winked at Penn and Farrah, then looked back at Lakeisha. "Well then, I'd say you have some work to do."

Lakeisha grinned and then sprinted off, disappearing into the kitchen. As Farrah and Penn shared confused faces, Allie explained. "Neither of those guys can resist Keisha. She has them both wrapped around her finger."

Sure enough, within a few minutes the arguing from the kitchen fell silent. Lakeisha returned, leading a very subdued Rylan by the hand. The child glowed with self-satisfaction, having quelled the latest argument between husbands.

Allie shot Penn and Farrah a look. "Told you." She glanced at her brother and asked, "What was this one about?"

"What do you think?" Rylan shook his head. "He's mad about the close call we had yesterday when he hadn't wanted me to go in the first place. I'm never going to hear the end of this."

* * *

The auditorium was filling up fast when Penn came in with Farrah. Although they'd met many other residents since arriving, there were still quite a few they hadn't. Of course, only one of them fit both categories. A balding, older man with sun-spotted skin rushed toward them with an outstretched hand, grasping Penn's for an enthusiastic handshake.

"I think we are all on different meal schedules," the older man said gregariously. "My name is Andy Sims. I head up the garden squad, and *boy*, we sure could use more hands! I hear you two ain't picked a job yet, and I'm hoping you'll join up with us."

Before Penn could answer, a middle-aged woman with short gray hair moved quickly to take Andy gently by the arm. She looked apologetic at the Fletchers. "Now, Mr. Andy, you have already met Farrah, remember? Farrah started working with us several days ago."

"She did?" Andy exclaimed, placing his hand absently on the side of his head. "Well, I am sure sorry. Can't believe I'd forget meeting a pretty little thing like her."

Farrah smiled, unfazed by his dementia. Someone had warned her on her first day in the gardens. "Mr. Andy, you and I haven't talked much. I don't blame you for forgetting. I've been mostly working with Miss Ashley on the peas and bean vines." She turned to her husband and introduced the gray-haired woman to Penn. "This is Miss Ashley, Penn. I've told you about her."

Penn shook the lady's hand and watched her escort the elderly gentleman back to their seats. "He's the one with Alzheimer's?"

Farrah nodded, pulling Penn to a couple of empty chairs. "Yes, unfortunately. What's astounding is that he is a living catalogue of fruits, vegetables, seeds, soil nutrition and growing regions. Mr. Andy used to teach horticulture at University of Georgia. It's just everything else he forgets."

"Thank goodness he has that Miss Ashley looking after him," Penn remarked. "Are they related?"

"She is his daughter-in-law." Farrah's eyes lowered sadly. "Her husband—his son—got killed by a couple of those monsters while he was erecting fencing around the gardens."

Doe entered the auditorium from the main hall, catching Farrah's eye. She waved her over. "We saved you a seat."

Within a few minutes, the auditorium filled with residents. Doe, Penn, and Farrah, being so new to Vernon, were happy to see how many people in the community they already knew. Corinne and Dolores both waved friendly hellos their direction. A few seconds later, Allie and Decker tapped their shoulders to say hi as they took seats directly behind them.

"Thank you all for coming tonight," Augusta began, standing to call the meeting to order at the front of the auditorium. "I know this isn't our usual monthly meeting, but I received some concerning reports yesterday which I feel should be known by everyone in our community." Murmurs rippled through the large room, as Augusta continued. "I will let the head of our supply team fill you in."

Eyes watched as Shane stepped to the front of the assembly. He recounted the experience Rylan and Allie had with Doe in the drugstore. "The predators are no longer night-bound," Shane informed the crowd, who all looked around at their neighbors with grim, frightened expressions. "Whatever sensitivity they once had to sunlight, has been overcome."

A hand raised from the crowd. "Yes, Lauryll?" Augusta said, acknowledging the woman as she stood. Fortyish in age, Lauryll had a thin, stick-like figure, with graying hair pulled into a tight ponytail.

"Are you saying they can attack us in the daytime now too?" she asked anxiously. "It was frightening enough at night, but at least we could breathe easy when the sun came up."

Dolores, seated next to Lauryll, arose to wrap a calming arm around the anxious woman. "It is going to be alright, Lauryll. We are perfectly safe here."

"But what if we're not?" Lauryll stammered. "I can't go through it all again, Dolores."

"You won't have to," Dolores calmed, stroking Lauryll's arm gently as she settled her back into her seat.

A rather tall, stout man stood next. His wooden chair made a creaking sound as he did, giving the impression it was relieved he'd risen. "Ms. Lauryll, they *won't* get in Vernon."

Allie leaned forward, whispering to the newcomers. "That's Terry Hoagland. He's in charge of keeping our fences strong."

Terry continued reassuring Lauryll and the others that Vernon was sound. "None of those slimy beasts have managed to get through our fences at night. Seems to me daytime makes them even easier to spot. We got us an electrified fence they can't climb without getting fried. We got spiked battering rams for any that try. Our patrol monitors are alert and capable. You don't need to worry."

More than just Lauryll appeared relieved by the man's assessment. Augusta took over again. "We have a very protected perimeter around Vernon, thanks to Mr. Hogland and his fortification team. However, we will need more patrol monitors to cover the new daytime rotations." She searched the crowd for the head of security. "Decker, I will need you to recruit for day shifts."

"I'll get on it, Gusty!" Decker shouted from the back. "Anybody interested in becoming a Patrol Monitor, just come see me."

Farrah cringed when Penn stood up. "Augusta?" he called from the middle row. "I've been talking with some monitors. I think I'd like to join the Patrol."

"See how good I am at my job, Gusty!" Decker quipped, slapping Penn on the back. "One down! Thanks Penn. We'll take a shift tonight, and I'll get you all trained."

Penn gave him the thumbs up, sitting back down beside Farrah, who did not appear exactly thrilled with her husband's decision. Shane took the floor once more, compelled to share even more disturbing news relayed by Rylan and Allie.

"Yesterday while Rye and Ale were out with their trainee, Doe, they witnessed something even more upsetting than the creatures' adaptation to daylight. The monsters are emptying stores now themselves. Not for consumption, but to starve us out. To remove food, medicine, and anything else we need from our reach."

A grim hush fell over the auditorium as each resident understood how vital to survival outside food sources were. "How does the board plan to combat that?" a man asked. "If we run out of food or medicine…"

"We are fully aware of the repercussions of the creatures' new tactical measures," Shane said. "However, we have always known the day would come when outside resources would be scarce, whether used up by us or taken by other settlements. Vernon has planned for this from its inception."

"How?" a middle-aged woman asked from somewhere in the middle of the auditorium.

"We need more replenishing food sources," Shane answered. "Supply Runners will now make it a priority to locate more livestock. With the baseball field grass knee-high, we have both the space and nourishment to house more animals."

Augusta addressed the issue as well. "Miss Ashley and Mr. Andy have done such a marvelous job on the creation of the football field garden and the proper way to rotate crops to keep the soil nutrient rich, we are harvesting stores of fresh vegetables every season now."

Shane nodded in agreement. "Gusty is right. Between the gardens and our chicken eggs, along with the staples Supply Runners always manage to find, we are not in any immediate danger of starving. With that said, we do need more livestock, and we must increase supply run days to ensure we get to the things before the monsters do."

Dillon jerked forward to stand in protest, but before he could, Rylan popped his arm across his chest like a mother slamming on the brakes, forcing him back down in his seat. In perfect sync with Rylan, Dasha pitched forward from the row behind and clamped her hands across Dillon's mouth.

"Stop. Shut up. Don't say a word," Rylan whispered into his husband's ear. "I have to. It's my job. It's for the whole of Vernon. Otherwise, we all die from starvation, infection, or sickness."

Dasha's fingers continued pressing across Dillon's mouth, but he had had enough. She jerked them away with a loud "Ouch!" as he bit them. Surprising everyone who knew him, Dillon remained uncharacteristically quiet throughout the remainder of the meeting. He did not voice any opinions. Of course he didn't have to; the way his chest was heaving up and down as he clenched his fists said everything Rylan needed to hear about the firestorm he would encounter once they got back to their private quarters.

As the meeting was called to an end and the community began drifting out of the auditorium to their own rooms, Rylan quickly found Patrice Wilson on her way out, stopping her with a beseeching look on his face. "Can Keisha stay with us tonight? Please."

Patrice laughed. She lifted her hand to his stubbled cheek and shook her head. "Oh, baby, I am afraid you can't avoid Dillon's wrath this time. Might as well get it over with."

Rylan's eyes were wild, as if genuinely afraid, and made a final plea. "But he's relentless when he's pissed at me, Patrice."

Patrice's eyes grew larger right before Rylan's eyes, and she was no longer looking at him, but just over his shoulder. As she cleared her throat in warning, Rylan winced. "Shit. He's right behind me, isn't he?"

Patrice placed her hand on her daughter's shoulder, guiding Lakeisha and herself aside out of the way of battle. Allie and Decker were approaching as Rylan's back still faced his husband. Dillon stood still and silent. He knew eventually Rylan would have to turn around and face him. Then, unexpectedly, Lakeisha's sassy commentary rang out as she yelled at Allie and Decker. "Hey Ale! He's gonna get read for filth tonight!"

Slowly, cautiously, Rylan turned around to face Dillon, who was smiling pleasantly, making him all the more terrifying. "I am not angry," Dillon said.

"You aren't?" Rylan sighed, instantly relieved.

"No," Dillon offered. "I understand the community must come first."

Rylan took him into his arms for a thankful embrace. "You are the best, baby!"

Lakeisha glanced up at her mom. "Rye ain't stupid enough to think that's the end of it, is he?"

Patrice smirked down at her child, waiting for the shoe to drop just like Keisha was.

"I understand you have no choice but to go back out again," Dillon continued. "That's why I am going with you."

"There it is!" Lakeisha quipped. Patrice escorted her away, leaving the husbands to fight it out audience-free.

"No," Rylan replied.

With an icy glare, just daring him to argue, Dillon said, "It wasn't a question."

Dillon turned, following behind Patrice and Lakeisha, leaving Rylan standing in the auditorium, unsure of what to do now. Out of the corner of his eye, he saw Decker and Allie watching him from several feet away.

"What the fuck are you two looking at?!" he huffed, stomping off.

The couple shared a snigger and left the auditorium behind Penn and Farrah. Decker tapped Penn's shoulder and asked, "Ready for an orientation?"

He glanced at Farrah, who begrudgingly agreed with a nod. Penn gave her a peck on the cheek, promising, "I'm sure it'll be safe. Safer than we were in the mountains, at least."

Decker shot Farrah a playful wink. "Almost nothing ever happens. He'll be fine. I'll just show him around the armory tonight. He can start officially tomorrow night."

* * *

The two men left the building and walked down to the armory. The outbuilding on the edge of the school property was well protected with a high razor-wire fence, steel gate over the doors, and barred windows—where there were windows. Decker flipped on the lights and showed Penn around the main room. He was surprised to see a jail cell, although its emptiness and dirtiness proved it hadn't been used for anything other than storage in a long time.

"Once in a while, in the early days," Decker explained. "We'd lock up a trespasser trying to steal from us. After a couple of days, we'd let him go and didn't have any further trouble. But once Terry got our fences all the way around the property and we took some other precautions around the adjoining roads, we haven't had to use it."

Across from the cell were three tall, caged cabinets with chained metal doors. Decker unlocked all three to reveal the display of weapons on hand at Vernon. He could see by Penn's expression; it was a larger supply than he'd expected.

"Most of the rifles in this first section were here already. Students used them, I think."

"Sounds like a lawsuit waiting to happen," Penn joked.

"Yeah, it does, doesn't it?" Decker agreed. "Mr. Andy swears this place used to be a headquarters for the National Guard when he was young...but you've met Andy. Not the most reliable source." Decker continued the tour. "We've added shotguns, long-range rifles, and three assault rifles."

Penn asked if he could hold one, and Decker gave him permission. Penn seemed more interested in the ordinary military rifles and the shotgun than the assault weapons. "These I know how to handle," he admitted.

"That's good," Decker remarked. "Assault rifles spend way too many bullets too quickly for patrol. Those are here just in case...which we pray never happens."

The second cabinet held revolvers, pistols, Glocks, and other handheld guns. The third cabinet was more of the same, although it also housed an array of knives, daggers, one sword and even a scythe. Penn was a traditionalist and opted to make his regular weapon a simple rifle like the one his grandfather taught him to shoot as a boy.

"Great!" Decker exclaimed. "So, every shift, this will be your gun, and the corresponding shells are in the drawer beneath the rack."

Penn pulled open one of the deep metal drawers in the wall cabinet and saw the various boxes of shells. Pulling the bottom drawer open, assuming there would be more of the same, Penn's mouth hung open as his eyes caught sight of what lay dusty in the drawer.

"Is this what I think it is, man!"

Decker peered down and looked at the dusty contraption. "Some old intercom, I guess. I've seen it in there before, but we've never fussed with it."

Penn looked at him with amazement sparkling in his eyes. "Decker, this is a HAM!"

"A what?"

"A radio! The kind you call other shortwave radios on. We could talk to other settlements!"

Decker didn't seem impressed. "Who'd have a relic like that? What is it from World War II?"

"You'd be surprised how many guys may have one of these things." Penn moved to lift it out but paused. "Is it okay if I try to set this bad boy up?"

"You know how to use one?"

"My uncle had one of these. He and I used to call people all over with it." Penn inspected the one in the drawer. "It's pretty old and beat up, but worth a try."

Decker scratched at his beard. "What do you think using that thing will do?"

Penn shrugged. "Give us answers, maybe. Or help us keep in contact with other places and see what they know."

"What else do we need to know?" Decker scoffed. "The fucking world ended."

Penn lifted the radio out of the drawer and placed it on a nearby table, his eyes admiring the find. "We talk about the world ending," he told Decker. "We say everybody in the world started killing each other. Or monsters have taken over the world. But do we *know that*, know that?"

"I don't follow, Penn," Decker said.

"Where did the monsters come from? Was it a virus that started it all? Is this just happening here or everywhere in the world? What if some place, like Europe, has found a cure?"

Decker groaned in hopelessness. "Penn, I don't even know what's happening right next door in Georgia! And without risking my life to drive there, I don't see any way to find anything out."

"If this thing is still operational, we don't have to drive to Georgia, or anyplace else to see what's going on."

"Go ahead," Decker permitted. "Give it a try and see."

Penn frowned. "Well, tomorrow. This looks like it'll take a lot of work to fix up. Wires are pulled out and frayed. And there's got to be an antenna somewhere I'll have to mount on the roof before I can string the wires up. Then I need a car battery to power it."

"We have electricity," Decker reminded Penn. "Not reliable, but we have it."

"Won't work on anything but batteries. That's how they used to use these out in battle."

Penn could barely wait until morning to see if he could get the radio working. Decker told him he could set it up in the back, in the former sergeant's office, but with one caveat. "You are a Patrol monitor first. This little radio project comes second."

CHAPTER 10

WATCHING OUT FOR MONSTERS

Penn spent several hours that morning mounting the antenna he found in an old closet to the top of the armory roof and connecting the wires and battery to the newly found long-range radio. He had only a couple of hours to play around with it before he was due to start his first night of official patrol duty. Terry Hogland stood over him with piqued interest while Penn tested the knobs and switches.

"Man, I've heard of these things," Terry commented, leaning over Penn's shoulder at the desk in the old armory sergeant's office. "Old war movies, disaster flicks and such, but I have never seen one in real life before. Think it'll really work?"

"No reason it shouldn't." Penn tinkered with the knobs, wishing Terry wasn't so close over him, but understanding his interest and the possibilities this device brought if successful. Penn gave Terry a quick tutorial, recalling how patient his uncle used to be with him over a very similar model years ago. "This is the tuning knob to scroll frequencies," he explained, touching the largest knob on the far-right side. "On the left are the volume and squelch controls."

As he flipped the power switch, a green backlit screen ignited, garnering a gasp of excitement from over his shoulder. "It works!" Terry exclaimed, slapping Penn on the back.

"It has power," Penn clarified. "Doesn't mean it works yet. That coaxial cable was in ratty shape. I had to cut it and splice a second cord to it I found in the closet. I hope it holds a connection up to the pole on the roof."

Penn started turning the large knob, which emitted a series of faint clicking noises. The thin red needle in the meter window jumped with each turn, then settled back to zero, reporting little to no signal strength from the bands Penn searched.

"Terry..." Penn muttered; his eyes affixed to the red pendulum flopping around on the tiny screen. "There's a little leather book on the cabinet. It has call signs written in it. Will you hand it to me?"

Such a simple task filled Terry with even more excitement, making him feel like he was part of the experiment. Flipping a few pages, Terry found the listings and put the book on the desk in front of Penn, pointing to one. "Wanna try Washington first?"

"Worth a shot!" Penn answered.

The former owner had written the radio's call signal on the first page, and Penn was glad he had. He would sound much more impressive to whoever he reached instead of simply shouting, *Help!*

He dialed the knob to 14MHz, remembering his uncle telling him it was a good long-distance band for daytime. As his fingers turned across the different bands watching for the meter needle to pitch higher, static sounds intermixed with warbles drifted from the small speaker. He glanced up at Terry, who was grinning with anticipation.

"Sorta like dialing on the old AM FM car radios!" Terry remarked.

"Let's give it a try," Penn smiled anxiously as he leaned into the small microphone. "Hello? This is..." he scanned the notation of his call sign and read it aloud. "K4RGT...that's me, I guess."

Terry tapped his shoulder, pointing to the notebook before he turned back a few pages to something he'd seen scribbled down earlier. "Says you say CQ three times. For emergency. I don't know why, but he wrote it down."

Penn nodded and started again, edging the dial slowly across the broadbands. "CQ CQ CQ. This is K4RGT in Birmingham, Alabama. Can anybody hear me? Over."

Breathlessly they waited, hearing only the faint sound of hissing as if someone had trapped some of an ocean tide in a tin can. Penn continued turning the dial, trying again. Crackles jumped between long bursts of nothing like teasing whispers out of reach. Penn's fingers rolled across the different frequencies with resolved patience but found nothing. His shoulders slumped in defeat after a quarter hour passed.

"Don't get discouraged," Terry cheered him on. "Screw Washington! What about something closer? Atlanta or Nashville, maybe? How do we dial them?"

Nodding, Penn checked the book and found the Georgia region number was also 4. Then the realization slapped him in the face like an insulted woman. "Dammit Terry! We are calling out over all frequencies, not one specifically. That last try went out to anybody with a radio, not just Washington."

"Shit," Terry moaned. "So, we were basically trying Atlanta, Nashville, Memphis, New York...every fucking where!"

"It's okay," Penn said, trying to convince himself as well. "It was a good first attempt. We'll try again tomorrow. I've got to start my patrol shift soon. Better grab a bite first though."

Terry said he would stay and keep trying a while longer, and Penn trusted the radio in his hands. Terry now knew how it operated, so maybe he'd have better luck. As he ducked out of the office, he could hear Terry giving it his best across the empty bandwidth. Terry stayed with it another hour but found it was like listening to snowfall in the woods, only a few crackles and hissing wind sounds in a wilderness of dead air.

* * *

Penn's first night of training began with a walk around the perimeter with Decker. As they walked away from the armory to begin Penn's training session, it became clear how much he, and most likely others at Vernon, took for granted the colony's security measures. Things were far more advanced than he'd given Vernon credit for. As Decker showed him around the outer perimeter of the school, he emphasized the importance of teamwork.

"Everyone here at Vernon," Decker began explaining as they walked along the outer fence line. "Relies on the contributions of every resident. Your wife, Farrah, for example. Now that she's in the gardens, she helps keep us fed. Not only fed, but garden workers also keep us from becoming sick."

Decker stopped walking, pausing just under a tall hackberry tree at the edge of the school's property. "A garden worker doesn't merely raise, fertilize, water, and pick the tomato. They inspect each tomato for worms, rot, or disease. If a spoiled piece of fruit or vegetable somehow made it into Dillon's soup, it could cause sickness throughout Vernon. Sickness depletes a person's ability to do a job. If a Patrol Monitor isn't on patrol, something bad may find a way in. And not just the monsters..." Decker's tone sent a chill up Penn's spine. "...sometimes people are just as deadly."

"You mean you've had to fight back ordinary people too?"

Decker smirked, with his hand on the back of his neck. "Well, we usually take in anyone who comes here for help. It's the ones who want to take what we have that I'm referring to." He looked Penn directly in the eye with cold seriousness. "Penn, killing monsters is one thing. Killing people is another. If someone comes here intending to tear through our defenses and attack Vernon, are you willing to take their life to defend us?"

It was a thought he hadn't considered before. Having spent the months of anarchy and violence tucked away in a mountain cabin, it wasn't a situation Penn ever had to face. But he sighed deeply and answered. "Yes. I think I could. I think if I saw a guy out doing harm to what you've all built here, I would stop him. Whatever it takes."

"Glad to hear it," Decker said. "And you just said exactly what I'm trying to show you here. We have built something—all of us, together. Everyone at Vernon plays a role, and no one role is more important than the next."

"I understand."

Decker looked pleased. "A Patrol Monitor's role consists of multiple gears and switches. Meaning, like a gardener can't simply grow and pick food without the possibility of sickness breaking out, a Patrolman can't just circle this property with a flashlight and assume we are safe simply because you don't find a killer at the fence."

Not quite following his meaning, Penn asked, "Tell me about the gears and switches I need to know about."

Decker raised his hands toward the tree. "Exactly why I stopped here. You tell me. We are walking along this fence, and we see no danger. Do you mark us safe? Or do you see a rotten part on the tomato?"

Penn almost answered too quickly but stopped himself. He knew his first observation was too simple to be the only one. It was a test. Not a test to disqualify him but to educate him on seeing more than the eye perceives. He nosed around the hackberry tree a bit. He spent a moment squatting down, looking at the root system, then he flashed his light through the fence a few feet away as if searching for something.

"Just right off," Penn began, piquing his boss' attention. "There is an upper limb that looks a bit iffy up there. But it's on the lawn side, not fence side, so if it falls, I doubt it would land on the fence."

"Correct," Decker said with folded arms and a nod. "But looking up is key. I'm glad you figured that out. If a storm or simple rot weakens a limb that's over the fence, our perimeter will be breached."

"Also," Penn went on. "There is a very slight hump in the bottom line of the fence across the ground right over here." He pointed his flashlight beam at where he meant. "There's a root from this tree pressing up under the fence. In a year or two, it might weaken where this section latches to the poles."

Decker beamed proudly! "You are the only one to catch that Penn! Since I've been in charge of patrol at least."

He could tell Penn felt proud for figuring it out, and he eagerly addressed the third thing. "This one limb here," he observed, flashing his light across the underside of a long, outstretched branch. "It is just about over the top of the fence."

Decker stepped back to see for himself and discovered Penn was right.

"If a monster can get high enough to reach that limb from the other side, it could crawl through the branches and bypass the electric fence altogether."

Decker covered his mouth with his hand. "And now you have shown me something even I have not noticed before. I think you fully comprehend my little lesson."

They continued moving ahead, Decker pointing out how every ten yards a large overhead motion-sensitive floodlight triggered on. Any creature or invader of any kind approaching the fence would set off the motion and draw attention from patrol during the dark of night.

"Two patrol monitors stand lookout on the roof day and night. They'll see any floodlight flash on and walkie-talkie you there."

Penn rested his foot on a bit of chain stretching between two parking posts where the old lot used to be. "Are the blue slimy things the only danger we look out for? What about other people? We have a good setup here."

Decker grinned once again. "You, my man, are made for this job!" He slapped Penn on the shoulder, and they started off again, crossing the parking lot.

He pointed to the stretch of road running perpendicular to the parking lot. "This used to be the main road into the school. We do not use it now. All access in or out goes through those tall iron gates in back. We tarred nails and spikes over this road after a few bands of aggressive humans tried getting in a couple of times."

"You'd think with the world in ruins, mankind would join together in unity instead of trying to take each other down too." Penn sighed.

Decker shook his head. "When people are scared and desperate, they'll do just about anything."

Once they'd covered the outer perimeter, Decker showed Penn the spiked battering rams on every lawn. Welded onto the old blocking sleds the football coach once used when Vernon was a school with a varsity team, the sleds had been repurposed to rush at the fences if something managed to be undeterred by the electricity. The sleds, when rushed forward at the fence, would push their sharp metal spikes through the holes in the fence, impaling multiple wounds on their target.

"We have men called Janitors," Decker snickered. "Yes, they do what you think they'd do. But they also clean up the mess if we ever have to kill one of those things. So, if you see danger at the fence, stab it through and keep walking your route. Radio the lookout, and they'll call in the janitorial staff. Patrice usually works night shift lookout. Have you met her yet?"

"I did," Penn answered. "She and her little girl live right next to me and Farrah."

"She's the best. Nothing gets by her." Decker remarked. "She prefers nights so that she can have her days with Keisha."

"Is the little girl alone in their room at night?" Penn asked with concern. "I never knew that. We could check in on her—"

Decker laughed. "No need. Lakeisha can take care of herself if she has to, but she never has to. Rye and Dillon keep her when Patrice works the after-midnight shift."

* * *

When Penn's shift was over, he hurried excitedly back to the room, eager to share his first night on the job with Farrah. Coincidentally, he ran into Patrice coming in his direction on the outside walkway to their rooms.

"I know you just got off your shift too, because I heard you on the walkie-talkies," Penn chuckled. "But you are going the wrong way if you're headed to bed."

Patrice smiled. "Not quite yet. I need to get Keisha. She stays with Rylan and Dillon when I work nights."

Penn nodded. "Yeah, Decker told me. But you know, now that we're neighbors, anytime you need Lakeisha to come over to our room until you get off, she is welcome."

Smiling in gratitude at the offer, Patrice explained. "That is really sweet, thank you. But you may have to fight Dillon and Rye over her. They think she hung the moon."

Penn disappeared into his room while Patrice followed the walkway to the thin switchback staircase leading to the main level. Passing the music room, she couldn't help but see the patch of light coming under the art room door. *She's at it again*, she thought to herself.

Tired as she was, Patrice would feel guilty if she didn't check on Lauryll. The artist often fell into melancholy, and whenever she did, the only thing that soothed her was painting long into the night. Patrice knocked lightly, just to let Lauryll know she was there before going in. Lauryll glanced up from the canvas and did her best to smile politely, but it wasn't convincing.

Patrice strolled by the display wall, long cleared of former high school students' work, now housing paintings and charcoal sketches made by Vernon residents. It was the colony's own private little art museum. Of course, most of the canvases on the lower row belonged to Lauryll, and the subject never changed. She'd drawn the same thing since she'd arrived at Vernon.

Lingering a few moments longer on the previous renditions of the subject matter, Patrice always preferred these three portraits best. The further out the paintings stretched, the more disturbing the image became.

"That one is your favorite," Lauryll noted from her artist stand across the room. "You spend more time on the second painting than any other."

Patrice nodded in agreement, turning around to reply. "Probably because she is the same age in this picture as Keisha."

"Heather was a beautiful child at that age," Lauryll recalled with a sweet sad smile.

The first painting on the wall had been of the girl as a baby. Big cheeked, plump arms, and her wiry brown hair only beginning to fill out over her round head. The second painting, Patrice's preferred one, was of the same girl at age 7 or 8. Longer hair, brighter smile, thinner face and body, and angelic. Lauryll had captured the memory of her daughter in a way perhaps only the old masters might have done. That one painting had an allure about it none of the others had. It was sublime.

Patrice moved along, glimpsing Lauryll's daughter's growth, until she became stuck on the portrait of Heather at 20. It wasn't the painting keeping her there; it was Patrice's own melancholy.

"Your son?"

Patrice nodded tearfully as Lauryll left the easel to comfort her friend. "Dre is about her age here. Or was. I wish I knew whether I should speak past tense or present."

"Which gives you the most peace inside?" Lauryll asked.

It was an odd question, and one no one had ever asked. Until now, Patrice hadn't even considered it herself. "Past means he's dead," Patrice began. "So obviously not that."

"Yet present means he's lost," Lauryll pointed out. "Possibly even in danger. It is okay to mourn the loss if it gives you comfort. If it only makes the wound deeper, then keep imagining him alive out there."

Patrice stepped to the next painting. Lauryll's daughter was different, a few years older. Something cold crept in around the eyes and mouth. "It began there, I believe," Lauryll offered. "Marriage and motherhood changed her."

"How?" Patrice asked. "Didn't you like her husband?"

Lauryll returned to her easel and resumed her work. "I liked him very much," she answered as her hand busily swiped across the canvas. "It was Heather, I found difficult to like."

Patrice's eyes fell to the next canvas. There was darkness captured within the brushstrokes and color choices. It was in the eyes, dimming from their early-life blue into something too morose to assign any color to. The only spark of light on the canvas came from a small golden cross held by a thin gold chain, prominently centered under Heather's tight high-collared neck.

"We stopped getting along after she involved herself in church," Lauryll admitted. "Maybe it was my fault for never introducing her to religion when she was growing up. I wanted her to be responsible for her decisions. To understand whatever happened in life stemmed from her own choices. That nothing was predestined."

Patrice nodded, understanding a little more now. "And then she dove headfirst into faith?"

"She practically drowned in it," Lauryll sighed. "We didn't talk together as we once had. We couldn't laugh anymore. She was much too serious, and I seemed far too laid back for a world so filled with sin. Heather became a severe mother, and her girls shrank inside themselves."

Patrice knew the story. It wasn't even that unique. She'd known a few Heathers herself in the old life. Women who grabbed a mantle of faith after marriage and motherhood. Often it was just a show, conforming to what they perceived they were supposed to be. But it was the truly devoted who became unrecognizable.

"That had to be hard," Patrice said softly. "What was your relationship like with your daughter after that?"

The regret on Lauryll's face was answer enough, even before she responded. "I took a step back. Didn't visit as often. Didn't call anymore, only texts. It was harder to get into an argument with a short text. I felt uncomfortable in her home, so I avoided it. But that meant I also rarely saw my grandchildren." Lauryll's eyes shifted to the last painting on the wall. "And this is what it cost me."

Lauryll beckoned Patrice to the easel, allowing her to see the current painting she had almost completed. It was the end of Heather's story, and her family. Lauryll was painting what she had encountered the last time she had seen them. Two small bodies, both drenched in blood, laying halfway from escape with their cherub faces sunk into the grass. In the doorway, something shimmered with a flush of blues, greens, purples, and grays. It was the monster who'd slaughtered Heather's family.

"Because I didn't understand my daughter's choices, I missed so much time." Lauryll confessed. "The day the world went mad, I arrived too late to save them. I should have been there all along. And I live with that every single day."

CHAPTER 11

NOT ALONE

With ant-hive precision, the creatures had stripped places around town of provisions, causing an urgency for Vernon's Supply Runners to get to shelves first. Shane let Doe take his place as Dasha's partner for the next supply run so that they, and Rylan and Allie, could salvage as much inventory from the remaining warehouses as possible. While the two teams pillaged for necessities around town, Shane and a few other Vernon men could go out searching for livestock to bring back.

Dasha and Doe decided it might be a good idea to venture further than normal as well, hoping the payoff would be worth it. It was a gamble, for sure, straying that far from Vernon, but now that the enemy had learned to maneuver in daylight, Augusta ordered each team to pull guns from the school armory before heading out. They wouldn't be defenseless.

They found a reasonably sized chain grocery store on the outskirts of town, which looked to be in far better condition than anything Dasha had seen before. She kept the van idling outside in the empty parking lot and told Doe to slide over to the wheel. "I'm going to check it out, see that it's safe. If it is, I'll signal you."

Doe waited in the van, her eyes glued to the glass door, as Dasha aimed her gun to shoot out the glass. Before she fired a shot, the electronic doors surprisingly parted, startling them both. The store still had power. This was a good sign in Dasha's estimation. She and Shane, as well as Rylan and Allie, made a point of shutting off the electricity at the breaker box of the stores after they'd taken everything worth taking. This not only helped keep track of where either team may have already looted, but it also reduced some of the drain on the fragile power grid, which still miraculously worked somehow. Of course, other survivors pilfered shops as well, but she hoped they too had the forethought to reduce the electricity for the greater good.

Doe waited with bated breath for several minutes after Dasha disappeared into the market. It was only when she felt an ache in her hands that she realized she'd been gripping the wheel tight enough to cut off her circulation. Dasha soon came back out, giving Doe the all-clear salute. Letting out a breath she hadn't realized she'd been holding, Doe shut off the engine and joined Dasha inside.

"This place is completely untouched," Dasha whispered. "I don't think anyone has looted it at all."

Doe grabbed a cart. "Where do we start?"

Dasha thought for a second. "Dry goods first. Flour, sugar, cornmeal, tea, coffee. Load up everything you can get in the van, and if the freezer section still works, we'll grab all the meat they have last."

"Where are you going?" Doe asked curiously.

"To the back. If the storeroom is full, we can drive around back and load up even faster."

Dasha disappeared down a side aisle, leaving Doe alone to shop in the eerily untouched supermarket. Working quickly, Doe grabbed what she could with her nerves misfiring through her body. Something in her gut told her she wasn't alone, but she dismissed the fear. The shrieking wheels of the shopping cart were enough to send any monster within a mile straight at her. However, as she moved down the freezer aisle, she heard the unmistakable hiss of the sliding doors up front. She stopped immediately, hiding behind the tall freezers. The same paralyzing fear she'd felt in the drugstore with Allie came over her.

She braced herself, waiting to hear the inhuman sounds of communication between the creatures. Soon she should hear the noise of swift pillaging again as they stripped the shelves with their tidy rows of helpers. But that wasn't what she heard.

"Whose van is that out there?"

It was a man's voice.

Human. But was he dangerous?

Another voice rang out. Like the first speaker, it had a Southern accent. "Think those fiends killed whoever it belongs to?"

"I don't smell rotting corpses in here," replied the Southern one. "Maybe whoever owns the van is still in here."

Then, a third voice spoke out. His voice was cautious, and thick with an accent she could not place. But underneath it was the sound of a cocking rifle. "Somebody in here?" he shouted.

Doe froze, unsure what might happen if she made her presence known. How many men were there? And where on earth was Dasha through all this? Doe remembered the pistol tucked in the back of her jeans and drew it out. *Do I even know how to shoot a gun?* It was a little too much for her nerves. Monsters, she understood. People were different. Her mind suddenly raced with questions her amnesia couldn't answer. *Are other people friendly or hostile?*

She hadn't answered the man yet, though his footsteps sounded to be a few rows over from her. Then Dasha, emerging from the stockroom, shouted out unwittingly from the back. "Doe! There's a ton of stuff in back!"

Doe flinched. "Dasha, stay back! We aren't alone."

Tension seized the air. The men had zeroed in on Doe's location and started advancing. Dasha, halfway back in the center aisle, stopped and drew her gun.

The man with the rifle spoke once more, his accent thick. "You sound human." His slow footsteps echoed in the silence as he went down the aisle. "We are human too."

The original voice called out now. "My name is Rex Brewster. I have two friends with me. We are in Row 5. We aren't here to hurt you. You are human, right?"

"We're human." Dasha yelled across the market. "I'm armed as well," she warned. "I'll meet you on 5, with my gun drawn. But if you don't fire on me, I won't fire on you."

"That sounds real good to me, ma'am." Rex answered.

Dasha and Doe moved cautiously toward the end of their rows, meeting each other in the back of the supermarket by a refrigerated section of sour-smelling meat. Together they approached Aisle 5 with trepidation. Dasha rounded the corner first, her gun firmly in her grip as she saw the man with the rifle. Behind him, also moving with caution, were his two friends, including the one with the gun.

"Okay, we're all human." Dasha noted. "Now let's establish if we are friendly. It's a big store, plenty to go around."

"We are all for sharing, ma'am," Rex nodded, adjusting his green baseball cap. It had a purple dragon on the side breathing fire. Dasha recognized it immediately. His friends wore the same cap.

"I am 32," Dasha remarked. "*Ma'am* me again, and I will shoot your ass."

Rex laughed, blushing. "Sorry, ma'—lady. I'm 18, and my grandma taught me to 'sir and ma'am' everybody."

"Southern gentleman," Dasha smiled. "Allowed."

She holstered her pistol, spurring Rex's companion to shoulder his shotgun. Doe put her gun away as well. The other men came forward. Dasha and Doe could now see them up close. They were young men of about the same age; the hats confirming the fact. "UAB?" Dasha asked.

"What's that?" Doe whispered.

"Local university," Dasha replied. "UAB Blazers," she smiled, gesturing at the dragon. "Baseball team?"

"That's right!" one of the men grinned. He was African-American and introduced himself as Andre. The other young man, the one with the rifle now hanging off his shoulder, looked Middle Eastern. He introduced himself as Rafik. "We were at least, until all hell broke loose," Andre informed her. "Now we are shoppers for our group."

"We are too," Dasha said. "But we call it Supply Runners."

"That's way cooler!" Rex commented. "Like Han Solo."

"Where y'all from?" Andre asked.

Doe tensed, putting her hand on Dasha's shoulder, hinting she shouldn't say too much. But Dasha laughed and told her, "Anyone who asks *where y'all from* is definitely an Alabama boy. I think they are all right."

Andre's grin widened. "That's a bad ass fade you got going on the left," he said, pointing to her hair. "I should get you to be my barber. That's the one thing we don't have at home."

Dasha grinned, appreciating the compliment. "Where is home?"

"Our group settled in one of the UAB Hospital buildings," Rex answered. "Got plenty of room if y'all need a place to stay."

"We must all look out for each other now," Rafik added. "Until we neutralize those aliens, at least."

Tilting her head curiously, Dasha asked. "Aliens?"

"That's what Professor Journer thinks they are," Rafik told her. "He taught biology at UAB. Says whatever life force burrowed itself into those humans who've turned, must be extraterrestrial in origin."

"Interesting," Doe replied. "How sure is he?"

Rex shrugged. "How sure is anybody about what happened? Sounds as good an explanation as any other."

Rafik added more context to his assertion than Rex seemed willing to do. "Journer says if it were a virus, any of us who encountered one of those things would have caught it. Nobody in our settlement has transformed into one. Have you ladies known anyone to turn?"

Dasha shook her head. "I haven't heard of any."

"I wouldn't know," Doe supplied without further explanation.

The guys looked at her strangely, but Andre spoke next. "Whatever happened, seems to change human DNA. Don't know of any earthly virus that can do that. Even in zombie movies, people don't change unless they die first. Gotta be aliens."

Rex removed his hat, his overly long sandy blonde hair fell over his eyes. Scratching his sweaty scalp, he pushed his bangs back under the cap. "Well, let's divvy up this food, everybody."

Dasha led him to the storeroom, showing him the pallets of dry goods, cans, cereals, cookies, chips, and soaps. There was more than enough to share. More than even both their groups could take.

"I have an idea," Andre suggested. "Dasha, why don't you pull your van around back, and Rex, you grab ours. We can open these loading dock doors and slide it all in way easier."

It was a good idea; made even better when the three strong young men gallantly loaded the ladies' van when they did their own. The girls played their part too. While the boys were pushing crates and boxes into the Vernon van, Dasha and Doe cleared the frozen meat department out, dividing everything evenly into shopping carts for both settlements. When they rolled the carts to the loading dock to share with the guys, Doe had something on her mind.

"Rex, what made you guys come so far out of town for supplies?" she asked.

"We can't find anything near us anymore. Every place we go is cleaned out." His eyes widened a moment, then he blushed with embarrassment. "Has that been you guys?"

Dasha chuckled. "No, *even we* can't move that quickly. But Doe here was on a run a few days ago. She witnessed the creatures pulling everything out of a store. Everything. Our thought is that they are trying to eliminate our ability to gather supplies."

"Shit," Rex huffed, then flushed red again. "Sorry, ma'am."

"I really am going to hit you next time, Rex," Dasha teased. "We are in the Lakeview, Avondale area. If you guys are seeing the same thing near UAB, that means the creatures are culling greater Birmingham of anything humans may need."

"Starving us out?" Andre asked.

"Most likely," Dasha nodded.

They continued loading provisions into their respective vehicles until there was no more room in either. It was time for the two groups to say goodbye and part ways, but it was harder than they expected. Making new friends in this world was rare, but Dasha thrust her hands assertively on her hips, and declared, "We need to keep our communities connected. You're in a hospital. If one of our people needs serious medical attention, or if your group needs something from us, we should be able to communicate with each other."

Rafik leaned against the back of their van, folding his arms across his chest. Dasha couldn't help but notice how big his biceps bulged. "She's right," Rafik told his friends. "Not only might we require help from one another in the future, but our groups could share new insights we discover about our common enemy."

Dasha's head nodded, but her eyes still locked onto his powerful arms. *I bet he used to throw a mean baseball.* She blushed now at her own thought. Then she realized she was the oldest person in the group. Maybe Doe? But her age was hard to determine, and she certainly didn't know it herself.

"How do we get messages to each other?" Andre asked.

A thought hit Doe suddenly. "Do you boys have a shortwave radio at the hospital?"

The guys looked at each other, but it was clear none of them knew the answer. "That's a little World War II, isn't it?" Rex remarked. Then his face lit up with an idea. He dashed back into the store, returning a couple of minutes later with two colorful windsocks from the seasonal aisle. "If you ever need to come to our community, fly this on your vehicle and we will do the same if we come to yours. Then our people will know we have friends approaching."

"That is a good idea." Doe smiled.

With the mutually agreed-upon plan established, the two groups said their goodbyes, both feeling better now to know they had friends across town. They were not completely alone anymore.

Dasha watched the boys drive away ahead of them before starting from the parking lot herself. She was relatively silent when she turned onto the stretch of highway going home. Doe could see distracting thoughts dancing in her friend's eyes.

"His arms were amazing, weren't they?" Doe said, biting her lips together to keep from grinning. She could see Dasha's cheeks flush at the mention, as she added, "Like tree trunks."

Dasha looked her way, succumbing to the playful ribbing at her expense. "I would love to climb that tree."

Doe howled, slapping the dashboard with her palm. "I knew it! I thought you seemed all glued to that boy's arms when he crossed them."

Dasha shook her head in exasperation. "*Boy* is the word here. He is a boy!"

"An adult boy," Doe corrected.

"He's a child! He's nineteen."

Doe twisted sideways in her seat, enjoying Dasha's discomfort way too much. "Dasha, I don't think you have to worry about public opinion in a world that has no public. It is a brand-new world, my friend. You can hook up with all the college boys you want."

CHAPTER 12

A SOUVENIR

Having been a sous chef at one of Birmingham's upscale bistros before the world went insane, Dillon knew exactly where to find the wholesale restaurant supply warehouse. It was a little treasure those outside the food industry would never have known about. He sat in the passenger seat while Rylan did the driving, with Allie perched on an overturned bucket between them. While Dillon rattled off vague directions he assumed everybody could figure out, Rylan squeezed the steering wheel to keep from choking his beloved spouse.

"I don't know what *the Chevron by the Vet Clinic past that gym we quit* means!" Rylan squawked at him. "Give me a street name!"

"Nobody knows street names!" Dillon shouted back, equally frustrated. "I told you to let me drive."

"You drive like Helen Keller!" Rylan scoffed. "I still don't know how you ever had a license."

Before Dillon could craft a comeback, Allie slapped both her hands over their mouths. "Go left at the next intersection," she told her brother. "*Even I know* what he means when he says *past the gym you quit.* The two of you wouldn't shut up about it for a month!"

Dillon folded his arms with indignation. "Those assholes started giving married couples a special rate but wouldn't extend it to us. Backwoods, bigoted, homophobes! Rye and I were the only monogamous couple at that goddamn gym. Every husband and wife there was screwing around with somebody else in the tanning rooms, and everybody knew it!"

Despite Dillon's less-than-helpful navigation—marked by two separate instances of "No, not that left, the other left!"—Rylan eventually pulled into the cracked asphalt of the forgotten warehouse.

"I am going to tattoo an 'L' and 'R' on your hands one day." Rylan muttered as he threw the van into park.

As they got out of the van by the front doors, Allie let out a long, disappointed sigh. "We can't get in. There are gates behind the glass."

Dillion strolled towards the entrance, unconcerned and undeterred by the store's security. "Those were always there. This place used to sell expensive equipment, as well as food. But..." his fingers tapped against the numbered keypad mounted on the cinderblock wall beside the door. "They assigned members their own code."

The barred doors pushed open, whereupon Dillion presented a bow, waving them inside. Someone had already pilfered the massive storehouse, as evidenced by the torn-open bags, scattered boxes, and discarded items littering the floor. But as Dillon had suspected, no one had taken *everything.* The shelves still held enough valuable inventory to make the trip worthwhile.

They each pulled a flatbed cart behind them as they explored. Dillon led them directly to the staples he couldn't recreate from Vernon's football field garden. "Rice, noodles, mac and cheese," he instructed his team. "Rice especially. I can make pasta if I have no other option, but I can't replicate rice."

Once they'd loaded a cart with sacks of rice and another cart with noodle boxes. Rylan noticed instant mashed potato flakes on the highest shelf. "I guess other people took what was down low, but I can climb up there and grab those."

Using the heavy metal shelving like a ladder, Rylan hoisted himself higher until he could reach the upper shelves. As he tossed down boxes for Dillon and Allie to catch, he observed something even more exciting in the next row. "Allie! There are boxes and boxes of sealed precooked bacon packages! I guess nobody bothered to look up top before us!"

Allie scurried to the next aisle and crawled up the shelves. The boxes were nondescript from the sides, explaining why no one else noticed before. But the tops of the boxes were cut away, revealing the bacon packages within. She lifted a package out to inspect it.

"Guys!" she shouted excitedly. "These are still good! It says use or freeze by next February. We can still eat these and freeze the rest."

"How many are there?" Dillion called up to her.

"Each box has 30 packs. Each pack has 60 strips. And I think there are probably 12-15 boxes up here!"

She started shoving them down like an avalanche, while Dillon loaded a fresh cart. It was clear they'd need more carts. He sprinted to the front of the store, returning with reinforcements just in time to see Rylan and Allie leaping across shelving units, knocking down more hidden treasures.

"If you two are done playing parkour," Dillon called up, "Maybe one of you can come down and help me!"

"Dillion!" Rylan's voice rang out from several aisles over. "They have *Blo-Pops*! And *Spree*!"

Dillion dashed out of his aisle, searching the rafters for his husband. "Rye, where the hell are you?"

Rylan waved from four rows away, shoving boxed candy to the floor.

"How did you get all the way over there?" Dillon cried, rushing to snatch up the candy.

"Guys!" Allie's sharp voice cut through their antics. "Necessities! Remember."

"Uh, *Blo Pops* and *Spree*, bitch!" Rylan scoffed at his sister.

Suddenly his smug expression faded, replaced by something wide-eyed and primal. Allie caught the change as she looked up at him. He seemed like an animal in the wild that had just glimpsed a predator in the field. Rylan flattened himself down on the top shelf, dropping a hand down to wave her back. Allie crossed swiftly but quietly to the next row of shelves where Dillon had been. She found him crouched low near the end, pulling a case of green beans forward to place on the cart. She lifted a single finger to her lips, signaling silence, then tugged at his arm, pulling him back from the edge of the aisle. Dillon didn't need words. The look in her eyes was enough. Something was in the warehouse with them.

Two rows away, Rylan still lay prone atop the highest shelf. Except for the sweat gathering on his brow, his body was still. From his elevated vantage point, he could see two of the creatures slithering into the warehouse from the back. From afar they could have been mistaken for humans; their misshapen heads and mutated flesh made less pronounced by distance. It was how they moved that gave it away. Like two shadows learning to walk, each step of their elongated legs was slow and careful. Their heads moved in a scanning motion, surveying their surroundings.

Rylan didn't think they knew humans were there. The beings seemed to enter unfamiliar territory the same way Rylan and Allie usually did, scoping out the terrain, gauging potential threats, before deeming it safe. He kept perfectly still on the top shelf, even as the sweat building in his hair and running down the bridge of his nose dared him to lift his hand and wipe it.

Below, Allie and Dillon remained with their backs pressed against the shelving, on alert and awaiting direction from Rylan's lookout. Rylan waited to see if the two monsters were truly alone, or if more of their hive were going to swarm in to perform their assembly-line dance of stripping the shelves bare. But no other entity followed. There were only the two creatures. At least that offered a fighting chance. His eyes glanced down at the strewn candy boxes, worried they might give away that someone was there, but it looked no more alarming than the rest of the debris through the store, so he wasn't too worried.

The grisly monsters moved further into the warehouse, their pace increasing after incorrectly assuming they had the store to themselves. Rylan could see them better now, unobstructed by distance, and it did not ease his fear. Their nearly human legs possessed muscle and flesh but bent weirdly like the hinge of an insect. Their torsos heaved with breath as they stepped over whatever mess hindered their path. Their heads continuously rotated side-to-side, canvassing each new section of the warehouse to ensure the area was clear. They had long, narrow skulls, which were covered in translucent, glistening blue skin that varied iridescently under the light. Twice Rylan observed them communicate using their mouths—split too far back across the jaw—by making brief clicks and guttural grunts. They were too far away to hear adequately, but Rylan's ears registered the sounds as like how it sounded when his fork scraped across his teeth.

They split up. One creature veered down the far aisle nearer to Allie and Dillon while the other turned into the aisle directly beneath Rylan. For a moment, he feared that maybe the monsters had known humans were in there. Peering over the edge of the shelf, Rylan could get a good look at it now. He'd never been so close to one without having to run. He studied it now as he'd never been able to do before.

The monster moved directly under him. Rylan fought his war against panic and waited to see what the monster would do. It wasn't taking anything from the shelves, yet it didn't appear to sense Rylan's presence higher up. Seeing its skin up close now, Rylan couldn't help but think of multiple shades of blue and gray paint being poured into water. It had dark, blackish veins running exteriorly over its body like a macabre relief map.

The heat inside the warehouse was becoming unbearable, especially up top, under the tin roofline, where the air stagnated like the inside of an oven. Rylan was drenched with sweat that was now pooling just under his chin on the metal shelf. Sneaking another fast glance down to see if the creature was moving away, a few sweat droplets fell from his face to the concrete floor just beside the creature. *Shit!* He tried to shift his head back so that his perspiration would drip back onto the shelf and not over it. But his whole body was slick with it now, and he couldn't control the overflow much longer.

Unable to track where the second creature went in his limited line of sight, Rylan could only account for the one directly beneath him. And he was going to have to deal with it. He lifted his hand, contorting as best he could to keep the sweat soaking his arm from dripping off onto the floor below. His fingers found his gun tucked in the back of his jeans and readied it to fire. As he brought the gun up, a rivulet of sweat found a fresh path, rushing down his arm and releasing off the tip of his elbow. Like a dam springing a hole, a stream of compiled sweat plummeted down, striking the back of the creature's thick neck.

Its head jerked upward, its pupil-less eyes locking in on the man hiding above. But Rylan was quick. The creature thrust its arm behind itself as if to grab at something, but Rylan's bullet tore through its jaw! The second bullet, aimed with precision, burst the monster's face apart like a melon dropped from a rooftop. A sickening spray of tar-like blood splattered outward onto the lower shelves and inventory. The creature staggered backward, its head little more than a pulpy crater, and sank against the shelves like a marionette who'd just had its strings snipped.

Rylan quickly scurried down, jumping the last three shelves to the hard floor below. He had to get to Allie and Dillon before the other monster reached them. He rounded the corner but stopped short. The second creature was there, face to face with him. As if in mourning for its fallen comrade, the monster released a shriek that sounded like tearing metal just before it lunged at Rylan, bearing its razor-sharp claws.

Rylan leaped back, his foot slipping in the pooling black blood seeping under the shelves from the next aisle. The slip was advantageous, bringing Rylan crashing to the floor just before being eviscerated by the razor talons. The enraged monster tried again, advancing forward as Rylan army-crawled backwards to get away. Then something hit Rylan's cheek. For a breathless second, he panicked the creatures could spew acid—images of melting flesh from too many alien movies. But the liquid didn't burn; it was greasy.

The monster, distracted by the wave of liquid, turned from Rylan to confront something else. It was now that Rylan saw Dillon standing at the other end of the aisle, two empty bottles of lighter fluid gripped in each hand.

Demonstrating he'd seen just as many of those movies, Dillon bellowed, "Don't fuck with my husband, bitch!"

Allie stepped from behind the end cap, a long butane lighter ignited in her hand like a magic wand. She touched it to the stream of fuel on the floor and disappeared from Rylan's sight as a wall of fire shot up between them. Flames engulfed the creature. It howled, screeched, and thrashed against both sides of shelving on the aisle. Rylan watched the burning monster, transfixed, until Allie and Dillon sprinted around the aisle to drag him away from the flaming, flailing mass.

The store itself did not catch fire. Metal shelving and concrete floors all made for a relatively safe little inferno. The hideous thing burned until it ran out of fuel, leaving behind a charred and putrid corpse. They stood watching, mesmerized, because none of them knew exactly what sort of being they were watching die.

"It has to be alien," Rylan declared. "That weird skin. It's got to be some sort of alien infestation. They are changing us into them."

"It looked demonic to me," Allie noted. "Something straight out of hell."

"There is no such place as Heaven or Hell," her brother scoffed.

"But big clawed purple skinned aliens," Dillon spouted sarcastically, "Those are *totally* for real."

"Whatever they are," Rylan replied. "Or were. They can die. That's good to know."

Rylan crouched over the unburned creature, inspecting it thoroughly so that he could report back to Vernon on its composition. He touched his finger to its grisly-looking flesh. It was soft, and its veiny ridges were only moderately firmer.

He assumed Allie and Dillon were behind him until he heard shuffling sounds nearby and saw they were not with him at all. He jumped to his feet, pulling his gun again as he rushed into the open. "What are you two doing?" he asked.

Dillon let go of the cart he was pulling towards the front door and turned around. "We are not leaving here without all this food. Or those fucking Blo-Pops!"

Rylan left them to their scavenging mission, while he returned to study the monsters' bodies. In one of the back sections of the warehouse, he found boxes of industrial-strength garbage bags. He carefully wrapped the creature in thick bags and loaded it onto a rolling cart.

He found his husband and sister by the van, finishing packing up their haul when they turned to see Rylan coming from the warehouse with the body. "What the hell do you think you are doing?" Allie scoffed.

"Bringing home a souvenir to study."

Dillon shook his finger in Rylan's direction. "My darling, we are not riding home with the dead alien corpse in our van."

"There isn't room anyway," Allie stated. "And feeding the community is priority."

"We will tie him to the top," Rylan suggested. "The more we know about these entities, the better prepared we will be."

CHAPTER 13

SKY FLASHES

All of Vernon buzzed with the rumors that Supply Runners might come back with more cows, a bull, and possibly even a few pigs to graze on the baseball field-turned pasture. Penn had worked night patrol and was still in bed when Farrah came in midafternoon with the news that Decker, Shane, and Terry had left in the early morning to raid a farm.

"You look all fresh and clean, and drippy headed," he commented, sitting up in bed.

She hadn't done a good job of toweling her hair. By the time she walked back to their room from the girl's locker room, her wet hair had dripped onto her shoulders, soaking her T-shirt. "Just got off work and showered. The garden was hot today."

"I swear we are ships passing in the night these days," Penn remarked with a disappointed frown as he got out of bed and dressed. "Next week I go to day shift, so we will have our nights back together."

"That's something, I guess," Farrah answered with a pouty frown.

"Where are you off to right now? Your shift doesn't start until dark."

He explained he wanted to spend a couple of hours giving the radio another try, then asked if she'd like to go with him. Sitting in a dank office listening to static didn't sound very exciting, but it did offer them some time together, so she joined him.

It began again as it had before, with Penn roaming the frequencies like a fisherman casting a net. While he tried to reach someone, Farrah sat beside him catching him up on the status of the vegetables growing in the football field and a few comical tales of Mr. Andy, once again, forgetting he knew her and reintroducing himself at the most inopportune times.

"He actually asked me if I was interested in joining the garden team while I was right in the middle of wrapping pea vines up and across strung wire!" she let out a hearty giggle. "There I am, up a stepladder, hands above my head curling vines, and he asks if I am interested in gardening. Miss Ashley finally came over to tell him—again—that he knew me and I've been working with him for almost two weeks."

"Poor guy," Penn grinned, then spoke into the microphone again. "This is K4RGT in Alabama. That's Kangaroo Four Rabbit Gorilla Tango in Alabama. CQ CQ CQ can anybody hear me?"

The signal whined and hissed as before, frustrating Penn, but he persisted. "If anyone can hear me, I am in Birmingham, Alabama. Are there any others listening?"

Crackle. Hiss. Crackle. Then came the hint of a fractured word. Farrah grabbed Penn's knee in excitement. His entire demeanor lifted as he sat straight in the chair, a huge grin on his lips. His heart pounded in his chest as he tried once more, turning the dial until he saw the needle jump, indicating a rise in connection strength.

"This is K4RGT in Alabama. My name is Penn. Are you there?"

He released the button on the mic and waited. A few seconds of static rattled, but then a faint voice sprang into the air in fractured pieces. "W6S...iego...Carlo...there are you? Over."

Penn looked confused, but his heart still beat with excitement to hear another man's voice across the air. "Sorry," he called back into the microphone. "You broke up. Over."

"...squelch knob...doesn't work, try...frequency down."

Penn felt frustrated, unsure what to do.

"Penn, I think he said squeeze the knob and if that doesn't work..." she paused, guessing at the last part. "...shift the frequency down?"

He rotated the squelch and volume knobs and slightly decreased the frequency back one click. "Are you there? This is K4RGT. Over."

"Hello K4RGT. This is W6SBU in San Diego. Over."

Penn jumped from the chair, hugged Farrah quickly, then plopped back down and pressed the transmit button on the mic. "Hi! My name is Penn. P.E.N.N. I am so glad to hear you!"

"You also...Penn. I am Carlo. How many of you are there?"

"I'm not really sure," Penn said back. "Fifty or sixty."

Farrah tugged his shirt. "Vernon has fifty-seven people. I learned that in garden orientation."

"We have fifty-seven people," Penn corrected. "But it is only me and wife here on the radio."

Farrah tugged at him again. "Over!" she added into the mic.

Penn blushed and grinned back at her.

"Big number Penn," Carlo remarked. "We only have six. Few dozen others scattered around San Diego we either know or have seen out and about. Over."

The information, though comforting to know there were survivors elsewhere, the number itself was shockingly low. "Carlo, we don't know a lot down here about what is happening anywhere else. Do you know anything?"

A long pause flowed between communication. Penn was about to turn the dial back another notch in case they'd lost connection, but as his fingers reached for it, Carlo's voice came back over the speaker. "I talked to a fellow in Maine months back. Said the capital got hit hard—day one. Some hid and made it. The guy there had heard from a Marine who was trying to get answers, but then I lost touch with Maine. Over."

"Lost touch? How? Could I try? Over."

Carlo came back with a grim prognosis. "You can try. Call signal was K1PNE. I quit trying. Figure the Unmade got him. Over."

"Unmade?" Farrah repeated. She leaned forward and pressed the transmit button. "Hi, Carlo! This is Farrah. Penn's wife. Did you say *unmade*? Over."

"Hello, miss!" Carlo greeted chipperly. "That is a name some of us made up for them. The unmaking of man. Over."

"Fits," Penn whispered to his wife. "Carlo, have you heard how this all started? Over."

"God, maybe..." Carlo's voice fell into somberness. "K1PNE told me once that Reboten claimed they seen sky flashes last year in the sky over the beach. Many sky flashes. That's all I ever heard though. Over."

As if it were nothing more than a casual phone call, Carlo told them that though he enjoyed meeting them, his wife was calling him and he must go. They promised to attempt contact again in a few days. As Penn shut off the radio, he looked at Farrah with bewildered eyes.

"Where did he say that happened?" Penn asked.

Farrah shrugged slightly and answered, "I think he was trying to say Rehoboth. That's in Delaware and has a beach. I used to go with my parents as a kid. They always had a big, fun Halloween costume parade and festival."

"By sky flashes, I guess he was saying spaceships?"

"Or meteors, possibly," she suggested. "I told you about the book I read in the library. The scientist who wrote it talked about how some space rocks carry bacteria and contagions." She pressed a finger to her chin, thinking for a moment. "I wonder if there were any meteor showers around that time. I wish we still had the internet."

With it nearing time for Penn to begin his patrol duty, there wasn't much else that could be done. Farrah offered to make notes of the entire transmission with Carlo for him while he worked that night. As he kissed her goodbye to begin his job, Farrah dashed up to the main building to find Marian, the lady who oversaw the supplies stored in various classrooms. If she could get Marian to give her a notebook and pen, Farrah would get right to journaling their communication with San Diego.

* * *

Hunkered down in the library with a notebook and the books she'd previously read many days ago, Farrah made copious notes about the conversation with Carlo. A woman who paid meticulous attention to details, she not only recounted Carlo's claims but added footnotes about the information she'd read substantiating any clues he recalled. Her idea was to log anything they learned, however circumstantial or irrelevant, into the journal and then notate any credible books or sources backing up or discrediting it.

Farrah was head down, lost in her transcriptions and searching in books to help make sense of it. Shane saw her at a table as he strolled into the library. "You are a woman on a mission," he commented, looking at the many open scientific journals spread out before her. "Determined to figure this plague out?"

She glanced up, her thumb clicking the button on her pen repeatedly. "What brings you in here?" she asked. "For a man who has been wrangling cows and bulls all day, I'd think you'd be exhausted."

Shane gave his thigh a slap, replying, "It sure wasn't a stroll in the park. Forget tennis elbow, I've got heifer hamstrings." He glanced around the library, then asked, "Got any idea if they had any books on care for farm animals?"

Farrah couldn't help but laugh again. "Need to find out how to get cows and bulls in the mood?"

Shane pulled up a chair and sat down. "I need to learn lots of things. What temperatures can they withstand outdoors, what to feed them besides the lawn, and how to deliver babies if we get lucky enough to get them in the mood."

Farrah pointed towards the bookshelves in the science section. "I saw some animal husbandry volumes back there when I was in the biology shelves. Look for the 4H sign."

"Thanks!" Shane said, rising from the chair. But he sat back down as his eyes read some of her notebook page. "What's this? Did Penn get that old transmitter to reach somebody?"

She told him about the communication and showed him her research corroborating some of it—at least in theory. Shane appeared very interested, perhaps more than he was in his own research project. He lifted one of the books she had nearby and skimmed the open page.

"You think a bacteria caused all this?" he asked. "One from space?"

Farrah looked a little embarrassed. "Not exactly," she admitted. "But it is a remote possibility. Well...that and a bevy of other possibilities."

Shane did a poor job of suppressing his sarcastic smile. "Guess that rules out my zombie notion! Too bad too. I've seen, like, a million zombie movies."

"You may be joking," she said. "But even a zombie infestation— under most accepted tropes in movies—is, in itself, a virus. Usually, it's from toxic waste or some experiment gone haywire. So, it fits both the bacteria and virus model, and theoretically either of those could have been preserved inside a bit of rock from a long-ago dead planet that was broken up and been hurling our way through space as an asteroid or meteor."

Her knowledge caught him by surprise. Shane hadn't known Farrah well or long, but he hadn't expected her to be such a thorough researcher. "You impress me, Farrah. Keep those wheels turning. You may actually solve the mystery of Earth's latest extermination!"

The word made her shudder. "Extermination is strong, after all, we are still here."

"Yeah but consider all those who aren't anymore." He rubbed his leg again, proving he wasn't kidding about the hamstring. "If it's up to us survivors to repopulate the world, it isn't a world I'd be willing to bring a kid into."

Shane left to find his books on animal care, leaving Farrah sitting with his offhanded proclamation. As a man, he'd merely been making commentary, but as a woman his words left an impact. Farrah had already lost her entire family as far as she was aware, so did she even dare to consider children? Could she, in all good conscience, bring a child into this leftover desert of a world?

CHAPTER 14

THE CREATURES AMONG US

Penn walked the fence line around the school property. Equipped with a rifle, binoculars, and walkie-talkie, his path tonight was counterclockwise, while his counterpart on the ground went clockwise. They passed usually twice before a full rotation around the campus, but Clinton wasn't much of a talker. Not that the few seconds they had while passing was enough to get to know one another. But Penn had Clinton pegged as one of those husky, faux-tough guys who had probably been a bully in high school, the type who would have gone into law enforcement for the power trip—had the world not gone to hell. Instead, he was here, trudging in circles along a fence line, same as Penn.

Penn didn't mind night duty but did look forward to when he'd have a day schedule. Nights felt more sinister. As if the darkness swallowed every sound before it could travel. Daytime had far more community activity buzzing around the property.

So far, his new position at Vernon was proving dull. Penn knew patrolling the compound was of vital importance, but it didn't make it any *less* boring. All he'd seen so far was the distant glow of headlights moving along far-off streets. He'd hoped it was Rye and Ale coming back, but when the lights disappeared into the horizon, he knew it had to belong to other survivors existing somewhere out there on their own.

Normally, the walkie-talkies were not to be used during the shift as a social grapevine. However, as it had grown closer to sundown, all of Vernon had been on edge that Rye and Ale hadn't returned. Of course, it was Dillon causing the anxiousness. Though everyone at Vernon liked the brother and sister team, it was the Chef no one wanted to live without. Penn's position at ground level put him at a disadvantage in knowing when a vehicle was drawing near. The monitors on the roof were the eyes in the sky. Penn, along with several others on the frequency, had checked a few times for updates, and practically all of Vernon erupted into cheers when Patrice finally rang out over the speaker, "Their van is heading this way! I see it!" Of course, her next words had sent chills. "Ya'll. One of those things is riding the top of the van back to Vernon. I don't think they know it's even up there holding on."

Stuck on perimeter duty, Penn missed all the action when the guards at the gate stood armed and ready to blast the hitchhiking monster, until Rylan let them know it had been dead for hours.

Patrice kept him informed of what was going on as Corinne packed up some equipment and moved to the armory to study the find. Augusta ordered that Allie, Rylan, and Dillon stay quarantined in the armory until she could be sure they weren't infected.

Penn was rather eager to hear his friends recount their adventure and how they managed to kill one, but he suspected it would be days before anyone could see them.

He was crossing the old school parking lot when Patrice's voice called out again over the walkie-talkie. "Floodlight on at the fence. Baseball field. The outfield behind second base."

"On it!" Clinton radioed back.

Penn started sprinting toward the field to help when Decker, who must have seen him, chimed in over the speaker, "Penn, no! You stay on perimeter watch! It could be a distraction. Forces are already deployed to baseball."

The order confused him because he thought that what was happening on the baseball field was more important than continuing to walk circles around the fence. But when he came around the building towards the baseball field, he understood what Decker meant.

The bright glow of the outfield motion lights illuminated a chaotic scene. Now, several men and women were on the field, too far away for Penn to identify anyone personally, except Terry Hogland—due to his size. The group clustered together at the fence, but when they backed away and spread out, Penn could see two men had pushed the spiked football sled through the fence, now drawing it back. A body clung to the board, held in place by the spikes. As the sled pulled from the electrified fence, the fence pushed back against the body, sparking like a freshly lit firecracker. The body continued to sizzle until it fell from the withdrawing spikes to the ground behind the fence.

Penn's attention was focused on the field, and he didn't hear Decker coming up behind him until he shouted. "Penn!"

"Shit!" Penn jumped, touching his hand to his heart. "Warn a guy next time, man."

"Sorry," Decker replied. "I need to go down there and assess the situation."

"Is it a creature?"

"Looks like it," Decker said. "Sometimes we get a coyote or bobcat trying to get in and eat our livestock. But Terry says this is one of the monsters."

"Haven't you had those monsters attempt to break in before now?" Penn asked.

"Yeah, but the electric fence was enough to shock them back

before." Decker looked worried now. "This one doesn't seem to have been bothered by it. If they're adapting to daylight, maybe they are adapting in other ways too."

"What do you want me to do?" Penn asked. "Should I go with you?"

"Naw, man. But thanks." Decker answered. "You stay on watch. There may be more of those things coming. Stay sharp."

Decker left Penn on his patrol and walked downhill towards the baseball field. Terry was heading his way already when Decker passed the dugout and they met on what once had been the diamond, now sectioned off for pigs and cows.

"I'm gonna take a couple of guys and step outside the gates and haul that thing in for study." Terry told Decker.

"Is it worth the risk?" Decker said, sticking his hands in his back pockets as he stared out towards the fallen creature.

"He's pretty dead," Terry snuffed, spitting on the ground, not realizing the irony of their being on what once was a pitcher's mound. "It's not going to hurt anybody."

Decker nodded, "I don't mean that, Terry. I mean contamination."

"I just thought it could be good if Doc got to examine it along with the one Rye brought back. See what we're up against."

Decker stood a moment thinking. "Let me check with Gusty. Keep your walkie-talkie on, and I'll get back to you in a few. But Terry," Decker cautioned with a firm grip on his arm. "If you venture out there tonight, drive a car around to it. That is too far a walk from the gate for you or your men to make in the dark."

* * *

Penn's shift ended an hour later. He entered the gym hoping to take a shower before heading to bed. The gym was empty except for a single elderly man standing on the parquet basketball court. His eyes seemed confused when Penn looked into them. Almost afraid.

"Hello," Penn greeted him politely. "Do you remember me, Mr. Andy?"

"No," the frightened man blurted. "Was it you I saw outside?"

"We met at the school meeting a few days ago. My name is Penn. My wife, Farrah, works with you."

Penn's extended hand hung in the air as the man looked at it with some confusion. Then, as if sparked by some flash of ingrained manners, the old man took it and shook. "What is this place?" he asked Penn.

Startled by the question, Penn said slowly, "It's the gym. Are you alright, sir?"

"I thought I was in the strawberry patch."

The gym door swung open and Miss Ashley rushed in. "There you are, Mr. Andy!"

Jogging towards them, she offered an apologetic smile to Penn. "He got out of our room without my knowing." As she linked her arm around Mr. Andy, she introduced herself to the newcomer. "I am Ashley. Mr. Andy is my father-in-law." Lowering her voice to a mild whisper, she added. "Alzheimer's."

Penn nodded. "Yes, we *kind of* met once, briefly. My wife is Farrah. She has told me how much she is learning from you."

"Farrah is a dear!" Miss Ashley replied. "We are lucky to have her. Now if you'll excuse us..."

Penn stepped aside for her to lead her father-in-law back to bed, but as they passed Mr. Andy clutched Penn's forearm and said, "There was a strange man outside the garden fence. I saw him. He doesn't belong here."

Ashley presented another sorrowful smile and led him away. It was clear by her reaction that Mr. Andy's faculties were in a state of decline; she had sadly become used to it. Penn watched them exit the gym and started for the men's locker room to have his shower, but as he lifted his arm to switch on the light inside, he saw dirt. It hadn't been there before. It was the imprint of a dirty hand—Mr. Andy's hand—when he'd grabbed him.

Penn bolted from the gym back into the darkness outside. Decker was at a distance observing Terry's retrieval of the monster's corpse outside the perimeter. Penn sprinted towards him.

"Decker!" he cried, startling the man. "I found Mr. Andy in the gym. He told me he saw a strange man outside the garden."

Shaking his head, Decker answered. "Unfortunately, most men are unfamiliar to Andy Sims these days. I wouldn't worry about it. He probably meant you when you were on patrol. Besides, the garden is closed this time of night."

Thrusting his soiled arm out, Penn replied. "He may not be all there mentally, but his hands were dirty. He's been out digging somewhere."

Decker's expression shifted. "Think it was the monster he saw?"

"He said *a man*."

"Probably nothing," Decker said. "But we should check it out anyway. Could be raiders from someplace else."

The men took off to the fence line, alarming the motion sensor lights while they inspected the area outside Vernon's fences. Nothing seemed suspicious along the border leading to the football field. Decker instructed Penn to continue around to the front of the school while he searched the garden. "Those rows are narrow and the vines thick," he explained. "I know my way around in there in the dark."

Penn left him at the garden gate and followed orders. He made his way up to the school's original entrance, which was no longer how anyone came in anymore except Supply Runners dropping their goods at the auditorium. Still, nothing appeared out of place until Penn walked across the former parking lot. As the mounted floodlights flashed on, Penn's eyes caught sight of a large four-door truck parked on the road before the school. He remembered Decker telling him how they'd booby-trapped the main road long ago. On second glance, Penn saw that all four of the truck's tires were indeed flat. Then he saw something else.

The light from the overhead floods was bright, but even so its reach did not extend far enough into the road to see adequately. Penn's eyes only caught a few quick, jerky shimmers of some light blue thing reflecting dimly. Squinting to see as he lifted his gun, he saw movement again. Whatever it was, there was more than one, and they were surrounding the truck.

"Who's out there?" he shouted into the darkness. Only the sound of shuffling and muffled taps or clicks came as an answer. "Whoever you are...whatever you think you can do here...it's not worth dying over."

A shot rang out from behind him! Penn ducked and turned, only to see Decker running at him, his pistol pointed towards the night sky. Penn understood now. Another lesson in on-the-job-training. The shot alerted the watcher on the roof, and suddenly a bright spotlight beamed from the top of Vernon High School aimed towards the truck.

Penn saw them now. Fast, slithery, iridescent under the white light reflecting from their pearlescent skin. Three figures...monsters... scurrying across the road into the depths of darkness provided by the abandoned neighborhood opposite the school property. Penn fired rapidly at them, joined by Decker. A high-pitched screech filled the air, signaling they'd hit at least one. But nothing was visible in the blackness.

"Probably came with the one we got earlier," Decker said. "Maybe we killed at least one of those others. But I doubt his two friends will try again tonight."

"Mr. Andy said he saw a man," Penn reminded him.

Decker gestured with his pistol toward the truck. "I'm sure he did. Whoever drove down this road probably tried to get our attention so we could let him in before those things got him."

"Think he's still out there?"

Decker lowered his head solemnly. "With four of those bastards after him. Doubt it. If it'd been anybody but old Andy he tried to flag down..." Decker holstered his gun and clapped a hand onto Penn's shoulder, guiding him back to the school. "We're the lucky ones in here. Most everybody else out there can only pick where they fall."

* * *

The remains of the creature Rylan had hauled back from the warehouse raid lay secured inside Vernon High School's armory. The former ROTC facility was the perfect place to research the specimen as well as to sequester the possibly infected to ensure the safety of the community. The thick walls, steel doors, and iron bars of the armory made it the safest location to store something no one yet fully understood.

No one really believed the corpse would spring back to life, but stranger things had happened—like several months ago! Discovering the method of contamination might be crucial to human survival. Was the transformation from human to monster viral? Bacterial? Or even worse, something unknown in all mankind's science.

A patrol monitor stood guard outside the armory door while another inside watched the door of the room holding the monster. No one was allowed in to see the creature other than Doc, or the ones who'd already been exposed—namely, Allie, Rylan, and Dillon. Risk of infection was a genuine concern. Half the world had contracted the "virus" after all. But for Dr. Corinne Chambers, taking the risk of observing and studying the body was worth the odds. To be the very first known person to analyze the physiology of such a life force was not only groundbreaking, but it was also a historical milestone. Not bad for the little black girl people used to laugh at when she told them she wanted to be a doctor when she grew up.

Rylan and Dillon had already fallen asleep for the evening in the little room a few doors down. There were cots for all four of them, but the guys had pushed theirs together to replicate the feeling of their own room rather than the holding cell they were in. Allie wasn't sleeping. She'd heard through the armory intercom speaker that another body was headed their way. A second creature had been killed only a little while ago outside the fence.

Corinne and Allie stood back at a safe distance when the armory doors unlocked and opened. As Terry and Clinton entered the armory, dressed in makeshift hazmat suits. It was obvious they'd duct taped garbage bags around their limbs and torsos, sealing out any contamination before venturing out to fetch the body outside the gates. Over their faces they wore medical-grade masks under baseball helmets, which had been sealed with clear plastic wrap from the kitchen, fogging up under every exhale of breath.

Coming in lugging the monster's multiply stabbed body between them, Allie let out a chuckle hearing the multitude of plastic folds crinkle with every movement. "We ain't taking chances of becoming one of them things!" Clinton's muffled voice muttered beneath the sheaths of protection.

"Wish we'd thought of that," Allie smiled, showing them the way to the quarantine room.

Corinne already had a folding table set up for the creature, and as the men laid it down, they saw the body of the one Allie's team brought in earlier. It was decomposing but enough of it still resembled the fresher one.

"Here you go, Doc," Terry said, backing away from the monsters. "Learn anything about them yet?"

"Some," Corinne replied. "But this new one will be fresh enough to offer more answers. And it has a head! At least one that hasn't been shot to pieces."

The men dropped the specimen onto the table and hurried out as Doc shouted, "Thank you, boys."

The men left the armory, leaving the doctor to her work. Corinne seemed rather excited to start. Though she'd marveled at the earlier specimen as well, having another on her examination table gave her the chance to compare them for similarities and differences.

Allie remained at Corinne's side, equally curious to learn more about these beings plaguing the earth. "Same blue-like flesh," she observed. "Black blood, like oil clotting within those stab wounds."

The doctor pointed to the thickened, raised dark veins across the arm of the latest specimen. "And their almost external blood supply system is strange. In most places, their veins run similarly to humans, but look at this section..."

Allie followed Corinne's finger to the area on the uppermost section of the creature's arm. "Why are the veins more prevalent here, Doc? It's like they come together on the arm?"

"I'm not sure," Corinne answered. "The other specimen didn't have these markings. It looks a little like a map of a congested overpass. I've never seen arteries and vessels converge this way."

Allie examined it again before suggesting, "Maybe that's important to fighting them. What if their upper arm is equivalent to our jugular?"

Corinne shined a flashlight over a few of the puncture wounds from the impaling. "Inside, I see muscle, tissue, organs. Like its counterpart over here," she said, gesturing to the dissected specimen brought in earlier. Structurally human—molecularly, at least."

"What causes the external change?" Allie asked curiously.

"I'm not a scientist. Just a regular old general practitioner." Corinne lifted back a bit of tissue around one of the deeper wounds where the spikes ran through. "But if I am guessing, it could be a disease of the blood. Septicemia can cause skin to turn necrotic, which could explain the discoloration." Corinne lifted a jar of blood she'd taken as a sample from the first monster Allie's group brought in. "If it starts there, that would account for the viscosity and coloration of their blood being different from ours. Their blood pumping through a human body could account for the external shifts."

"But their insides aren't affected?" Allie asked.

"Certain genetic disorders have been known to thicken skin into armor-like plates. Basically, due to rapid tissue destruction. But somehow this doesn't fit any representation I've ever seen of that. Blood infections don't modify bodies at a cellular level."

"But what if this is alien?" Allie offered. "I know it sounds absurd, but something caused our world to turn the population into monsters!" She paused for a moment, considering things. "Or maybe we only believe these creatures were once human. It's possible the humans are all dead, and these things were alien from birth."

Corinne sat the jar of blood down and peered into the vacant, lifeless eyes of the newest specimen. "It isn't an outlandish theory. Dasha and Doe met some people from another settlement today. They told her they have a professor among them who believes this outbreak is alien in origin."

"Do you think he may be right?"

Folding her arms as she looked down at the body, Corinne sighed. "I just don't know, Allie. If this were a simple virus, I would see evidence in the creatures' tissues. But there is no sign of infection, no cellular breakdown whatsoever. These things have claws, raised veins, shifts in skin tone. Known viruses do not alter body structure like this. And any bacterial cause would attack internal organs first."

Allie bit her thumbnail nervously, thinking for a moment. "Doc, what do you think the chances are we could get in touch with that professor? If we could get him here to examine these bodies before they deteriorate further..."

Corinne gave her an approving wink and rushed into the old ROTC office, buzzing the principal's intercom.

"Gusty, I need Dasha and Doe to pay a visit to their new friends tomorrow."

CHAPTER 15

CHECK THE SKIES

Dasha and Doe took one of the smaller, faster cars for their neighborly call on UAB—easier to maneuver, easier to abandon if it came to that. The drive wouldn't be long, but that didn't make it safe in this post-collapse Birmingham. Normally, Dasha's routes consisted of more open roadways where hazards or menacing presences could be seen from a distance and evaded. Driving through a city where high rises flanked each road and where cross-streets capped every block, preventing her from seeing around them, made things more treacherous.

The tall buildings downtown gave the city an eerie feel of a graveyard. Each lifeless structure felt like a headstone marking where civilization once lived and died. Not that highways didn't have their fair share of perils; abandoned cars or various obstructions to veer around. But the city was different. In the city, sidewalks and multi-storied commercial buildings left little room for dodging obstacles.

It was the first time Doe, as far as her limited capacity could recall, had seen the dried trail of slaughter Dasha had long grown accustomed to. Cars, either shed in a panic or smashed against a building in failed escape, now scattered along the streets with the bloodstains of their former owners crusted like spilled paprika around the asphalt, gray sidewalks, or hardened like ossified paint against the twisted metal or brick.

They drove slowly to avoid the hazards along streets where sunlight barely reached around the headstones. The shadows laid out before them felt like something colder than shade. Doe's eyes glazed across the scorched battlefield that had once been downtown. Doors ripped from their hinges. Glass storefronts left broken like the bared teeth of a predator at them. There was no shortage of blood splatter against the brick-and-mortar buildings, flecking away now in the wind and rain like a chalk painting. Sometimes her eyes could see inside the entrances where pools of red seemed more prominently preserved from the elements. But of all the gruesome visuals assailing Doe's eyes, the lone half-rotted stuffed animal glued to the curb with congealed blood was the hardest to see.

"These poor people," Doe almost wept as her eyes scrolled up one of the high rises they were passing. Dasha was rolling at a mild pace, having to steer around debris, when necessary, as well as take a cautious look across intersections when they passed them. When Doe clutched her arm suddenly, Dasha jumped.

"I saw something bluish in a window back there!" Doe gulped. "I think it was on the third or fourth floor."

Dasha swallowed hard. "I guess these buildings are a good place for them to hole up and build their nests." She could see Doe's fearful expression and patted her hand. "Remember, they can't stand sunlight."

"Do you see any sunlight down here?" Doe scoffed. "And Shane said they are adapting, remember?"

"You have a point."

Continuing forward, Dasha made a concerted effort to scan her rearview mirrors every couple of seconds. After another block, they figured the creature hadn't planned on coming outside to attack them. Yet it was on this new block that they went past a well-barred former pawn shop where a figure burst into view behind the filthy glass. It was a woman waving wildly to them. Doe tensed as Dasha tapped the brake.

Her hair was matted from nearly a year of going unwashed and unbrushed, but her hands pressed against the cage-protected glass as her muffled voice tried its best to call out to them. Vanishing from the window, she reappeared in the doorway, pulling back the first layer of protection to shout at them through the bars. Doe rolled down the passenger side window a few careful inches to hear while Dasha kept her foot hovering over the gas pedal, just in case it was a trap.

"They drop things on you up ahead!" She didn't wait for them to reply, shutting her metal door closed and shrinking back behind her fortress.

Doe turned to Dasha. "What the hell does that mean?"

The answer presented itself two blocks later when a thunderous clang ruptured the silence as a massive object slammed into the pavement only a few feet ahead of them. Dasha gasped, yanking the wheel left. Tires squealed as the colliding metal of the object shrieked against the pavement in two disintegrating rolls.

"Shit!" Dasha yelped. "I think that was a washing machine!"

Doe twisted in the seat to look out the side window as they shot around the exploding tin, copper, and plastic shrapnel. As she turned forward, her eyes saw the next threat—a silver block hurtling toward them from an open window above.

"Bank right! Bank right!" She screamed, already reaching for the wheel as Dasha's fast reflexes obeyed the call and dodged the falling missile. The air conditioner unit smashed onto the asphalt where they'd just been a breath before. Above, the city had come alive with the noise of grating metal, breaking glass, and the whistle of projectiles cutting through the air.

"Goddammit!" Dasha screamed.

"Step on it!" Doe yelled as she took the wheel in her own hands, weaving across the road away from the bullseye range of each expected collision. Dasha stomped on the gas just as a microwave caught the back corner of the trunk, causing a horrifying crunch, but not enough to render the car undrivable.

"Shit-shit-shit!" Dasha chanted after jerking her eyes upward to see the foam green Lazy-Boy recliner tumbling end over end through the air. Even the most experienced race car driver can't avoid every hit, and the recliner would have landed directly onto the cab had it not miraculously smacked into a second-story ledge and like a gymnast slamming into the pommel horse, knocked itself off course landing beside the car and not on it.

Dasha gunned the gas, shooting the car down the avenue at 70mph. The road, still littered with mild debris, bent to her will as she sailed over everything in her way until Doe finally calmed her down enough to relax her foot. Nothing had fallen for several blocks, and they felt safe slowing back to a gentle crawl the rest of the way to the hospital settlement.

The car, worse for wear, rolled its grating wheels with bent rods under the portico of the UAB Women's Pavilion. But they had survived the short, albeit cantankerous, journey. Stepping out of the car, both pairs of eyes immediately caught evidence of one projectile they hadn't even known about during the frenzy of evasive dodging. Dasha reached her hand onto the roof of the cab and lifted the object away from its mild crater on the top of the car.

"Really? A blender?" she groaned. "Wonder if it still works?" she quipped, tossing it into the backseat.

Behind the reinforced doors to the hospital lobby, two armed men stepped out, their weapons resting in their hands, but ready to raise at a moment's notice. Their confused and anxious eyes immediately saw the windsock tied to the side mirror.

"Friends of Rex?" one of them said, lowering his gun.

"Yes, as a matter of fact," Doe said, approaching them. "Is it possible for us to see him?"

Dasha joined her, acknowledging the men with a nod, before adding, "Or Rafik." She then seemed a little flustered and quickly added, "Or Andre...It really doesn't matter. Whoever is free."

Dasha forced herself not to look over at Doe. She could feel Doe's eyes burning with silent laughter. *Or Rafik...* She was not going to live that one down.

The men ushered them inside, securing the doors from the dangers of the world behind them. Inside the hospital, a city hummed. Corridors bustled with civilians engaged in their normal routines, while an upper mezzanine showcased lush handmade planters, bathed in sunlight from the glass ceiling rotunda. The scent of earthy soil competed with the decades-old scent of antiseptics saturated into the walls, but neither overpowered the sharp tang of brewed coffee and a faint aroma of food roasting somewhere nearby—causing Dasha's stomach to rumble.

The ladies were escorted up the gently winding staircase to the second floor of the rotunda and down a short hall to a small lobby to wait. An abandoned counter recessed into the wall had the words SURGURY CHECK-IN above. Within ten minutes, Rafik burst through the door with his infectious smile. His eyes found Dasha, then Doe, then centered on Dasha again.

"My friends! How good it is to see you again so soon!" he beamed, moving in for a hug before hesitating awkwardly, thinking perhaps the gesture was too forward. Doe met his embrace, then shot a suggestive look Dasha's way as if to tell her, *I opened the door, now go through it and hug him.* Which she did.

. "I apologize for Andre and Rex being absent to greet you as well," Rafik explained. "Presently, they are occupied with the children. They asked to please tell you to stop in to say hello before you leave."

"Children?" Doe asked, surprised.

Rafik nodded. "Yes—many. One of the first things we did when securing this place was send a rescue team over to Children's Hospital. We saved nearly 70 children before...well, you know."

"And they are all here now?" Dasha replied.

Rafik's face fell a little as he confessed, "It was our misfortune not to be able to save some of the more vulnerable. However, the children with recoverable injuries or illnesses survived and live among our community here."

Dasha felt her heart sink. "Not once during this entire year of scraping to survive, did I think about what happened to people in hospitals. Especially at Children's Hospital. I'm glad someone did."

They sat down in the reception chairs, where Dasha and Doe explained how their group had two dead monsters in their facility which Vernon's doctor had examined. Rafik found the information fascinating and asked what they had learned from studying the specimens.

"Unfortunately, our doctor—though great with human ailments, isn't a scientist. We were wondering if the professor you told us about would come back with us and examine them."

Rafik rubbed his chin between his fingers, considering the idea. For a moment they didn't understand why the request seemed so complicated, but then he explained it to them. "I trust you," he finally said, pressing a hand to his chest. "As do Andre and Rex. Naturally, we told our group about running into you."

"Did that not go over well?" Dasha asked.

Rafik seemed puzzled. "*Going over well?*"

Dasha blushed, reminding herself that not only was Rafik young—so young—he was also not completely fluent in all the American ways of speech. "Was your leader upset over your befriending us and opening up communication between our colonies?"

Rafik chuckled, understanding now. "No, no, not at all. What I mean to say is that I would go with you in an instant—"

I bet you would, Doe laughed to herself.

"But the decision cannot be mine to make," Rafik explained. "I am not important to our community in such a way as Dr. Journer. If he agrees to visit your settlement, it would have to be brief, and only if he can be spared a few hours."

"I don't understand," Dasha replied.

Rafik explained that though his settlement was housed inside a hospital, it didn't have a multitude of medical professionals living there. Despite having been a scientist and a professor in his former life, Dr. Journer was only one of three medical doctors there.

"This was the University of Alabama's Women's Hospital in Birmingham," he said. "When our early residents secluded here to escape outside, there were patients in residence needing care. Those who were infected by the outbreak ran out in madness to the streets to do harm. The ones who did not change—many still require care. As well as some of the children."

His explanation made sense now. With only three doctors and numerous sick people, Dr. Journer's absence would leave them at quite a disadvantage. However, when Rafik took them to the professor's makeshift lab, Journer seemed exhilarated by the chance to examine the entity up close, without fear of being killed by it. Even so, he had reservations about leaving UAB, even if only for a few hours.

"You must understand my position, ladies," he began. "The boys might feel you are a benign neighbor..." his professorial tone took hold as if he were lecturing critical thinking to his former students. "However, as you are both strangers to me, I require some insurance before I would risk going anywhere."

Dr. Journer's little insurance policy didn't seem unreasonable. In fact, Doe could tell Dasha was very much in favor of it. "So...one of us stays here," Doe stated in compliance with the doctor's request. "And the other drives you to Vernon. Then once you are safely returned to UAB, whichever one of us stayed here may leave."

"Precisely."

Doing her utmost to suppress her enjoyment of seeing the girlish glint in Dasha's eye as she tried to remain cool and collected, Doe asked her friend, "I don't mind taking Dr. Journer home, if you'd be okay staying here...with Rafik."

Dasha made a mental note to call Doe out later on just how much she was enjoying this situation. "Fine with me," she answered much too casually. "But Doe, do you think you can get back to Vernon on your own? You are kind of new, remember?"

"I can get back," Doe promised. "We only made a few turns, and it's still daylight out."

Dr. Journer presented a questionable look at them. "Is there a problem, ladies?"

Doe was upfront with their new alliance, briefly explaining her situation. While Dasha feared the new insight might give pause to Journer's willingness to go with Doe, the good doctor surprised them both. "I find your condition fascinating, Miss...Doe. I would be willing to teach you a few psychological exercises that may boost your recall. Of course, after I examine the specimens."

"I'm game!" Doe replied.

"As for any directional challenges which concerns you...Dasha, is it?" He awaited her nod before continuing. "I ended up at this facility because my classroom at the college wasn't far away and I had been routinely here visiting a professor friend of mine having treatments for ovarian cancer." He paused slightly, his eyes betraying him over his friend's outcome. "All this to say, my house was—or still is, I suppose—not far from Vernon High School. I know the way even if Miss Doe gets lost."

Within the hour, Doe and Journer drove away in the car, which had been surprisingly patched up by generous mechanics living at UAB's hospital tower. It wasn't exactly as good as when Doe and Dasha ventured out that morning, but it would get Doe and Dr. Journer safely back to Vernon. Not only that, but after Doe recounted the appliance torpedoes they might experience driving back through the city, Dr. Journer took the wheel, knowing a much safer route to avoid the skyrises.

* * *

Dasha walked alongside Rafik as he led her on a sweeping tour of their facility. Welded cage protections fortified the entire lower floor of the hospital, along the windows and all lower exits. If anything prowled the streets at night, it wouldn't get into their tower. Like Vernon, the power grid still worked, but routine brownouts and occasional temporary outages were common.

"This is why we do not use the elevators." Rafik pointed out as he led her to the fire exit stairwell. "I find it a great source of cardio."

Dasha chuckled lightly, trying to cover how out of breath she was. "This is a 15-story building. That is a lot of cardio."

Rafik laughed back in agreement. "That's why we only use the first six floors."

They wove through the communal areas. The scent of cooked food drifted from a repurposed cafeteria, where the kitchen team worked in efficient sync, making the most of rationed supplies.

"How much of a problem is the food supply here?" she asked, noting no space for a garden and no natural light to grow one other than under the rotunda below.

"We are holding steady for the moment," he admitted. "On the rescue mission to Children's Hospital, our people also pilfered its food stores and freezers. You would be surprised to learn how much frozen food a hospital keeps on hand."

"That will run out eventually."

"True," Rafik replied. "That is why we have begun converting our roof space into a large garden. Of course, sometimes a heavy wind will topple a few of our crops."

Turning onto another corridor, the laundry station buzzed with activity. Hand-washed clothes hung from strung lines that crisscrossed the room and outer hallway like a life-sized spiderweb. Dasha's shoe slipped once on the slick floor, damp from drip-drying laundry. Rafik caught her around the waist, saving her from a fall. For a few seconds longer than necessary, they lingered that way until his modesty and her insecurity split them apart again.

I think I could be his mother, she scolded herself. *If I had him at 13, maybe.*

Moving again into the stairwell, they climbed to the Children's Ward. They were met with the glorious roar of children's laughter and enthusiastic voices when they came in. Andre and Rex were conducting a reading session with some of the older children. A chorus of animated voices brought the shared story to life, entertaining the kids. The moment the young men spotted Dasha, their faces lit up.

Rafik leaned close to her ear. "You made an impression on all of us, you see."

She smiled back at him, teasing, "I tend to have that effect."

He laughed—but she wished he'd say something else in her ear. His warm breath against her neck made her shiver.

Finished with the group story, Rex called the children's attention to the door, introducing Dasha as a special friend from another settlement of humans. The children were fascinated to meet a new person from another place.

He continued his tour of the ward, showing her sleeping quarters for the children. "The older children help look after the younger ones at night."

She suddenly felt like crying. He hadn't said it, nor did he have to. Older kids taking care of the younger ones could only mean one thing...their parents were dead.

Upon entering the common room, Dasha noticed several children on the floor playing board games in groups. But one solitary child sat alone at a table drawing. While the other children laughed and chatted away in their fun, that little girl remained to herself, not even looking up from her coloring once to notice anything else.

"What's her story?" Dasha asked. "Is she a loner?"

Rafik frowned solemnly. "That's Trudy. She keeps to herself mostly."

Dasha moved to the table, peeking at the crayon drawings scattered across the top. They were horrifying. Twisted figures with sinewy limbs covered in bulging dark veins. On one paper, the thing's coal-black eyes stared out like the slitted eyes of a snake. These weren't creations of the imagination; they were Trudy's memories. She'd captured them with vivid realism except for one conflicting detail...she'd colored her monsters red.

Rafik saw the concern on Dasha's face as they left the child to her drawings. "She witnessed the plague-walkers come into her home and murder her parents. Trudy managed to escape through the back door."

Dasha shuddered at the image. Then her mind picked up on his terminology, *plague walkers*. Vernon usually referred to them simply as creatures or monsters. It was interesting to hear someone else's way of describing these beings whose origin was still a mystery to everyone.

"This was at the beginning of the outbreak," Rafik elaborated. "Police took her to Children's Hospital because she was in shock."

Rex and Andre were nowhere to be found when Rafik and Dasha circled back to the common room. She wondered—or rather hoped—Rafik's friends knew he liked her as much as she wished she didn't like him. *He is a child*, she told herself. *Rafik is 20 years old*. He showed her the other wards along the five floors the settlement used. As they re-entered the stairwell, Dasha opened up about herself when he asked.

"I played guitar for a band called Razor Station," she started. "I was the only girl, but I could shred those strings better than anyone else."

"Were you famous?" he asked with wide eyes.

"No. Not at all," she laughed. "Ironic thing is, we had just cut an album. Even had one of our songs make Spotify's *Fresh Finds: Rock*." Dasha groaned, pushing her hands over her scalp. "At least I got to go out with a win!"

Rafik gently took her hand. "Any family around?"

She shook her head. "Not here. My mom died years ago. Dad started over—new wife, new kids. It was just my sister Dodie and me until she moved to Knoxville. I spoke to her two days before the world ended. I don't know if she's alive or not."

"I am sorry," he said. "I do not know about my family either. There has been no way to get in touch back home."

"Where is home?" Dasha asked.

"Jordan," Rafik answered. "Amman, Jordan. My father is a cardiologist, and my mother is a chemistry teacher."

"What brought you from Jordan to Alabama of all places?"

"Baseball," he laughed. "And medicine. UAB is a leading medical university, but I could also play American baseball for the Blazers! I have always loved watching baseball and dreamed of coming to America to play."

She suddenly felt great empathy for the young man. They had a bit in common after all. Neither knew if their families still lived. Both had truly loved something they traded much of their life for, and neither was useful anymore in this apocalyptic world.

"I wish I could look up your song," Rafik remarked. "I miss my playlist. And I *really* miss Google."

Dasha laughed and leaned her head against his shoulder. Rafik turned her towards him. His large brown eyes carried so much depth and tenderness. She struggled not to kiss him. For a moment she thought he might be about to kiss her, but Rex interrupted the moment by sprinting up the stairs behind them. "Guys! We gotta get to the roof!"

"What's happening?" Rafik exclaimed.

"There is a plane!"

The three of them raced up the stairs. Flight after flight towards the roof. Excitement mixed with dread at the prospect of what a plane could mean. No one had seen an aircraft moving across the sky in nearly a year. This was a significant moment, and one they couldn't be certain was positive or negative.

On about the tenth floor, the trio were tiring out with five more levels to go. As Rex's hand reached up to grab the railing to drag himself to the twelfth-floor landing, his eyes caught sight of Andre perched over on the next flight—his hands on his knees, heaving for breath.

"You okay, man?" Rex asked between breaths of his own.

"Yeah, man," Andre gasped. "How are we so out of shape?"

Feeling as though she were going to vomit herself, Dasha choked out, "Because it's 15 floors!"

Rafik, who had his hand resting on Dasha's back while she dry-heaved, stood up suddenly, smacking his head. "We are so ridiculous! The elevators *do work*, even if we do not use them regularly."

"Shit!" Rex yelled. "I totally forgot we could have ridden to 15 and then climbed up to the roof."

"Well, we are nearly there now," Andre yelped. "Let's just keep going."

The rooftop already had spectators. Other residents who probably had the sense to use the elevators. They clustered together between the rows of vegetables, staring upward into the sky. Dasha followed the guys down a row, careful to keep her feet in the dirt between the plants and not crush anything.

The airplane was a two-seater, the crop-duster kind. It had already passed their building, but the back of it was still visible against the blue sky. The buzz of the motor, however, may have been the sensory experience from the old world they'd missed most. Just hearing it in action across the horizon felt like a miracle taking place before their eyes and ears.

"I wonder if this is how people felt the first-time anyone saw a plane in the sky?" Rex mused with a satisfied smile. "What is it doing?"

He cupped his hand against the glare of the sun to watch while something fell from the open cabin. "Is that paper?"

It was a question easily answered by simply looking down at their feet. The plane scaling across the Birmingham skyline was indeed dropping leaflets to survivors. Dasha now noticed that the other people on the roof were already holding a few. She reached into the corn crop and pulled one trapped between stalks.

REGIONAL UTILITY UPDATE

FROM: Alabama Power & Sewer & Water

We're doing what we can with limited staff, broken supply lines, and no outside support to keep things going behind the scenes.

Many of us who have lost our families are staying on-site at pump stations and substations to keep power flowing and water clean. We're running on backup systems, old tools, and sheer grit.

The grid is fragile—every little bit of conservation helps. Boil tap water if it smells or looks strange. Don't leave lights, appliances, or heaters running longer than needed. If you have backup solar or generators, use them to reduce strain.

We can't promise how long we can keep it all running. But for now, we're still here. We're still working. And we're doing it for you. However, we need food, medicine, and basic necessities. We cannot spare people to go out to scavenge. Anyone who has anything to spare, please drop off at main power plant, west gate.

Keep safe. Keep your head. Conserve what you can.

– North Alabama Utility Workers

CHAPTER 16

ALIEN INFESTATION

Upon entering the armory, Dr. Journer brushed off Corinne's concern and declined protective gear before examining the specimens. His arrogance was off-putting—but after a long, brilliant career, it was at least earned. In a world overrun by predators, Corinne decided she could live with a little ego. Allie, Rylan, and Dillon stood back, giving the renowned scientist a respectful distance, but were eager to hear his findings once he examined the creatures in the back room.

Before going to the makeshift morgue in back, Dr. Journer began a cursory inspection of Corinne. Checking her eyes, arms, and pulse, he then placed a stethoscope against her chest, listening to her lungs. "Heartbeat normal, lung function good. You are not infected, and I doubt your three patients in quarantine are either. Of course, I will examine them before you release them back into the general population."

Rylan, Allie, and Dillon stepped over for the professor to look over, finding them uncompromised as well. "If there were a risk of contamination, you'd have seen symptoms by now," he explained. "I wouldn't dream of usurping your role in your community, Dr. Chambers," Journer said to Corinne after. "But I see no further need for quarantine. None of you has contracted anything from your exposure."

Corinne smiled brightly. "Well, that will make our people very happy." She patted Dillon on the shoulder and admitted, "Dillon is our cook. In his absence, his assistant Trisha has done the cooking. The difference has been...noticeable, to say the least."

"Well, your cook may return to his kitchen now."

With glee on their faces, the trio left the armory to resume their normal pursuits as Corinne led Journer to the back room. As she opened the door and the professor saw the two specimens laid out on a table under the harsh fluorescent lights, she could see that even a man of Dr. Journer's credentials was not immune to awe.

"Fascinating," he murmured, running his fingers along the thickened veins, which ran like a relief map over the more recent specimen. She watched him lift its abnormally long arm, inspecting its joint structure before laying it down again.

Corinne gave him space, holding a respectful distance, but finally offered, "I wanted to believe this was an advanced progression of necrotizing fasciitis, or erythropoietic protoporphyria due to the sunlight sensitivity they first exhibited."

He gave a curt nod. "Astute initial thought, Dr. Chambers. I would agree with you except neither condition can account for such rapid physical aberrations."

"These specimens show no internal tissue damage from bacteria or viruses," she added.

"Yes, I can see that," Professor Journer replied, peeling back the incision she had made along the torso. His fingers parted through layers of muscle, exposing the rib cage and organs beneath. "Organs all reasonably normal in size for human beings."

Dr. Journer hovered over the creatures, scanning every anomaly with an intensity bordering on reverence. "There is no precedent for this outbreak," he confided. "No bacteria, no known neurotoxin. Nothing to explain such a full-scale transformation like this." The pause which followed struck an eerie feeling in Corinne. She sensed the brilliant scientist suspected the same cause that her mind always strayed back to.

"This is not earthly in origin? Is it Dr. Journer?"

The professor's face bore an understanding he wished he did not know. "When you consider the rapid external transformation, it suggests a nanotechnology beyond our human intellect."

Corinne reached out and clutched the back of his hand—an intimacy neither expected, but both somehow needed in the face of the terrifying facts. She whispered the word, despite how hard it was to truly believe, "Aliens?"

"I believe so," he answered grimly. "I can find no other worldly explanation. We are at war with an alien life force. One which has the capability to inhabit our bodies and alter our physiology, evolving—or devolving—us to them."

"Then what we've suspected is correct," she stated matter-of-factly, trying her best to contain her anxiety in front of the esteemed man. "They infected human beings until they had an army, and now they are wiping us out."

Dr. Journer shook his head, clarifying the remark. "It is not an infection. It is an *infestation*...but yes, they made enough to finish the job."

* * *

They spent the drive back to the hospital largely in silence. Doe swept across the roads back through the city without asking questions of the professor. Corinne had shared his findings with her before they'd departed Vernon, leaving her virtually speechless. It was a hopeless kind of speechless. After all, what was there to talk about now? This wasn't a sickness any cure would fix. It wasn't a virus someone could avoid with a little determination. They were all out of their league now.

A couple of miles away from the high school, just as Doe entered the city, both noticed the papered trail along the streets. A mild wind tousled and tumbled white paper across the empty lanes, sweeping under and behind Doe's car as she drove over them.

"What are those?" She eased off the gas to slow down, but just as her foot moved to brake, Dr. Journer pointed ahead.

"Don't stop. Look!"

The leaflets were proving not to be the only things prowling the streets. Up ahead a block, a small group of survivors clustered in the intersection, examining the mysterious papers. Drawn from their hiding places, away from their fortified sanctuaries, they'd come out to see what news had fallen from the sky. So transfixed on the papers, they stood exposed and oblivious to the death surging towards them.

Doe slammed her hand on the horn.

"LOOK UP!!!"

The survivors snapped to attention at the horn, staring now at the car rather than what Doe was trying to show them. "Run!!!" she screamed from the window.

But there was no time for anyone to do much of anything, except die. The hostile invaders swept over them like a grotesque wave, drowning them under their elongated limbs and reptilian-like bodies. Dr. Journer turned away as the horrific screams reached the car. Doe had stopped too far away to see details of the carnage, but gunfire erupted from somewhere beneath the scuffle. It did little good. By then, the air filled with gut-wrenching cries mixed with sounds of ripping tissue. Doe and Journer looked out helplessly as, one by one, human limbs flung from the cluster of blue figures. The monsters were tearing them apart.

With their prey exterminated, the alien intruders turned towards Doe's car, stampeding their way like a pack of hideous animals fighting for their territory.

"Hold on!" Doe yelled, thrusting the screeching tires into reverse, fishtailing backwards until meeting an intersection. She slammed the gear into drive, peeling off down a side street. The monsters were fast, making the turn in time for Doe to catch their pursuit in her rear-view mirror, but their powerful feet were no match for the speeding car. Block after block, Doe barreled through the city like a mouse in a maze, losing their pursuers among the patchwork of the city grid.

No danger appeared in sight when Doe pulled up to the hospital portico. The guards worked fast to unbar the double sliding doors, motioning for her to pull the car inside the entranceway. Thankfully, she'd driven a small coupe rather than the hulking van. Doe got out of the car as the guards re-secured the entrance.

Doe and Journer learned about the message from the utility companies, and warned, "Those killing machines have been in the streets since, striking anyone who came outside to read it."

Journer advised Doe and Dasha to stay overnight at UAB and start back to Vernon in the morning when things had died down.

Andre came downstairs to escort Doe up to the large waiting room on the third floor, where Dasha, Rafik, Rex, and several other residents were lounging and playing cards. Dasha was relieved to see her friend, moving quickly to offer a hug. "We were worried," Rex admitted with a satisfied grin when he saw her enter. "We watched from the roof for hours as those horrible things came out, killing innocent people."

Dasha finally let go of Doe and exhaled. "Those poor people, all they wanted was to find out if help was coming. Those papers did more harm than good, I think."

"At least we know how the power still works and why it's unreliable." Rex commented. "I think from now on, whenever any of us go out for supplies, we should shut down the electricity and water at any place we find abandoned."

"Good idea," Andre replied. "Any reduction on the grid helps our communities."

They sat together in a private huddle away from the other residents to discuss everything Dr. Journer had learned. "Basically, it's alien," Doe told them. "He and Doc," she paused, realizing only Dasha knew who she meant. "The doctor at Vernon," she explained to Andre, Rex, and Rafik. "Her name is Corinne, but we just call her Doc. Anyway, Doc let him examine the two creatures we killed, and he believes only an alien technology could have caused this infestation."

"I just wish they could restore communication..." Rafik began with a tone of hope. "I'd give anything to speak to my family."

Rex pitched forward, his hands on his knees now. "Same here. All my folks are in Raleigh. I wonder if we can get the satellites back up?"

Rafik appeared a little sunken in spirit, murmuring, "Raleigh is a lot easier to reach than Jordan. I may never know about my family."

Andre pulled his fingers into a tight fist. "I feel you guys. I got folks right here *in town,* and I don't know what happened to them. I was living in the dorm with you two when we had to run."

"If your family is in Birmingham?" Dasha questioned. "I mean—you do have access to vehicles on supply runs."

Andre frowned. "We did that. First day out hunting for food, the guys and I swung by my family's house, but no sign of them."

Rex slapped his hand across Andre's leg in support. "But we didn't find bodies either, man. That means they got out."

"Yeah, but what happened after they got out? They could just as easily have been any of those people we saw get wiped out from the roof today."

They sat silently for a while before Rafik realized it was time for dinner. As they started down the stairwell, Doe suddenly had an idea. "Andre," she began. "We make supply runs a couple of times a week ourselves. What if Dasha and I, and the same goes for you guys, whenever we go out on a run, what if we leave notes posted wherever we go? Something like *Andre is at the Women's Pavillion at UAB.* If your family is part of a community...someone might see it."

"That's a great idea!" Andre exclaimed. "Why the hell have we not thought of that!"

"Women are smarter." Dasha said flatly, receiving a wink from Rafik.

As they ate a mediocre dish of macaroni and cheese, both Dasha and Doe made eyes at each other. Though not ungrateful to this host community for feeding them, they each knew without boasting openly about it, Vernon was damn fortunate to have Dillon. He could make even the most mundane meal pleasing to the tastebuds.

Andre appeared more uplifted after Doe's suggestion, spending some of his time over dinner sketching out different ways to write his message. Crossing out a few overly complicated attempts, he landed on a simplified statement, passing it to Dasha for approval.

My name is Andre Wilson. If you know the whereabouts of my mother and sister, please let them know I am at The Women's Pavilion at UAB.

Dasha narrowed her eyes disapprovingly. "You might want to put their names on here too. I doubt anyone is going to poll their community to find out who knows Andre Wilson."

Andre smacked himself on the side of the head, scribbling a new message while Doe and Dasha mouthed "athletes" to each other with a grin. Andre pushed it back to Dasha for inspection. Dasha glanced at it again, then with her mouth dropped open, she crumbled the paper into a ball.

"Well, that was easy," she quipped. Turning to Doe, she shook her head and laughed. "Patrice and Lakeisha."

CHAPTER 17

MRS. YARDLEY'S THEORY

Everyone had noticed the change in Farrah enough to mention it to Penn casually. He'd felt something was off as well but dismissed it as the normal stages of grief. Like everyone had, Farrah had lost every family member and friend she'd had in her old life. Not to mention losing the world as she'd known it. But now even Rylan was bringing it up while they were in the men's locker room shaving at neighboring sinks.

"I don't know, man. She just seems kind of down. Lost inside herself." Rylan told him. "Patrice thought she heard her crying in your room last night while you were on patrol. She asked me if you guys had been fighting before you left for work."

"No, we hadn't fought at all," Penn said. "But don't you think it's natural for her to be depressed? She lost her parents, her sister, and our friends. I think the shock has worn off now that we are settled here. She's finally grieving it."

"I don't know, man," Rylan replied, wrapping his upper lip over his teeth as he scraped the blade under the tender part below his nose. "You and Farrah were alone in that cabin for months. Seems like that would've been when she processed everything. Didn't you?"

"I guess," Penn replied. "I haven't really thought about it. But yeah, probably." He nicked himself just above the lip and winced. "Hell, I mourn actual razor blades more than some people I knew. These straight blades are shit!"

Rylan grinned, remembering how long it took him and Dillon to get used to using the old-timey blades, not to mention sharing them with all the other men in the school. Most guys went for beards they could trim, but Rylan, being blonde, grew splotchy, uneven facial hair.

"You need to talk to her, Penn," he advised. "Something is on her mind, and with your conflicting schedules, you may not see just how depressed she really is."

"Maybe I'll ask her at breakfast."

Rolling his eyes as he toweled his face dry, Rylan quipped, "Yeah, ask her in front of everybody at breakfast. That's a brilliant plan."

* * *

Trisha, the assistant chef, likely didn't deserve the residents' lackluster response to her cooking while Dillon was sequestered. But the fanfare he received when he returned to his post was as if he were a returning war hero.

"So glad to have you back, Dillion!" shouted Billy, walking away with his pancakes and scrambled egg.

Taking his first bite of his bell pepper omelet, Andy Sims declared with a fist in the air, "Flavor is restored!" His daughter-in-law, Ashley, held her head down in embarrassment for poor Trisha, who was staring across the cafeteria from her place behind the counter.

Glad to be free from quarantine, Rylan and Allie took their usual table, enjoying their first meal cooked by Dillion's capable hands.

More than once, Rylan felt a pat on the back of a passerby proclaiming, "Your husband has been missed!"

Rylan frowned, turning back to the serving counter where Trisha continued filling trays with her big spoon. He could only imagine what comments she was hearing in line. "Poor Trisha. I hope her feelings aren't hurt."

"If she knew how to use salt, maybe there wouldn't be so many complaints," Decker cawed, taking a seat beside his girlfriend. "We are all beyond thrilled to have Dillon back at the stove."

Rylan smiled proudly. "Tonight, he's making chicken parmesan!"

"With real chicken?" Decker exclaimed.

"Yes, partly. We don't have enough live chickens to spare, but Dillon says he has enough frozen nuggets to simulate something close."

"Sounds great to me!" Decker beamed, gobbling up the last of his omelet.

Allie squirmed a few inches away from him. "You weren't this happy about me getting out of quarantine."

Decker put his arm around her shoulder, snuggling his scruffy cheek against hers. "Baby, you know I missed you like crazy. But a man's got to eat."

Penn and Farrah joined them, both devouring their meals with as much gusto as the rest of the dining hall. With Rylan and Allie back in the cafeteria after a two day sequester, many people approached on their way in or out to ask questions.

"Man, what were those things like up close?" Billy asked Rylan with awe in his eyes.

"And by that...," Maddie, Billy's sister, huffed to Allie, "My brother means, we are so glad you guys are okay and weren't hurt."

"Well, yeah, that too!" Billy nodded, gesturing as though that part should have been obvious. "But Rye, you touched one of them! What was it like?"

"Pretty gross, to tell you the truth." Rylan answered with a minor shudder. "They looked like blue lizards or something."

"With tails?" Maddie cried.

"No, no tails," Allie replied. "But they had these weird vessels running over their skin."

By now it had spread all over Vernon that Dr. Journer declared the creatures to be terrestrials from another planet. The verdict sparked much debate about how long they might have been here and what their endgame could be.

Marian, head of supply storage, popped over to ask, "Did they have helmets, or masks? Aliens wouldn't be able to breathe our air, would they?"

Nearly half a dozen residents had questions they expected Rylan and Allie to answer and left disappointed when they couldn't. When Mrs. Yardley came over to the table, she was the last person they'd have taken for a curiosity seeker. But whatever she wished to ask, she wanted to do it privately. "Rylan, would it be possible for you and me to have a private chat after lunch?"

"Sure, Mrs. Yardley," he replied. "I can go with you now if you'd like?"

She shook her head, refusing the kind offer. "No, finish your breakfast with your friends. Just come to my room after."

With that, she walked away and disappeared through the doors into the main hall. The others exchanged curious glances together as to what her great private chat might be about.

"I'll head over to see her in a few," Rylan said. "I don't really know her well, though. But she always seemed like a nice old lady."

"We have the room next to hers," Penn said. "She is nice. She sweeps the walkway in front of our rooms every day, all the way down. Pretty thoughtful."

Allie sighed, mostly to herself, thinking. "Imagine what it must feel like for her. Working at this very school all those years, then a decade after she retires, she's forced to come back to the same place to live, just for safety."

Farrah smiled a little. "I bet it comforts her." Her eyes drifted across the room to the large, frosted windows on the outer wall. Though she couldn't see out, the sunlight against them let her know there was an outside world still there.

Penn leaned into his wife with a hushed voice. "Are you okay, honey?"

"I was just remembering how happy we all were as kids when the school bell rang, and we could go home. Now, school is home." She wiped a stray tear from her eye. "Sorry," she said to the group. "I wandered down memory lane for a minute. But all those old friends are gone, and the families I grew up around...mine too."

* * *

Penn offered to walk with Farrah down to the garden for her shift, but she insisted she was alright, reminding him he should rest for his patrol later. Allie sensed something off with Farrah and walked with her when she left. "Is all this really about your family?" She asked once they were alone. "It is understandable if it is, but I get the feeling there's more."

"What makes you say that?" Farrah asked, doing a poor job at acting casual.

Allie flushed a little, uncertain how to phrase it. "Well...to be honest, everyone here has had to accept the harsh truth about their loved ones. You don't strike me as a girl who is only now processing that. You and Penn spent months on that mountain. Surely, you have grieved your losses by now."

"I guess."

"So, what is it really, Farrah? Girl to girl."

Farrah stopped as they turned down the path between the portable classroom buildings. No one was around, so she leaned against the vinyl siding and opened up. "I'm never going to be a mother, am I?"

"What?" Allie exclaimed, not expecting that to be what was bothering her.

"Do you think about that ever?" Farrah asked. "How can we possibly bring babies into a world on the verge of being wiped out?"

Allie could see now that Farrah was legitimately upset. This wasn't a frivolous fear, but one she'd been holding inside a while. "I am ashamed to admit," Allie answered. "I've been so busy living in the crisis of each moment, I haven't even thought about babies."

Farrah teared up. "I always pictured my son or daughter running around my old backyard. My mom pushing it on the swing. My kids swimming in the same pool I used to swim in. But that's just not a possibility anymore, is it?"

Allie pulled Farrah into a hug. "I see now. Of course, this is what you'd be thinking about. One of the reasons people get married is to start a family. You got married and then the world pulled the rug out from under you."

"Penn always wanted kids. He talked about it all the time before."

"Oh, honey, if you want a baby, then don't let a little thing like the end of the world stop you!" Allie exclaimed, her hands pressing Farrah's wet cheeks. "Yeah, it won't be like you imagined. But that doesn't mean it can't still be wonderful." Allie pulled back, eyeing Farrah seriously. "Are you pregnant now?"

Farrah laughed through her tears. "I don't know," she admitted. "If I am, there's no way I can rationally go through with it. I just don't want to get rid of the dream yet."

"Then don't!" Allie said supportively. "And you don't have to get rid of it, Farrah. If you decide to have a baby, I will personally find you the best crib I can steal. Right now, dreams are all we have to keep us chugging along. Don't erase any of yours. They can all still come true. It'll be different. But it can still come true."

* * *

Rylan walked with Penn down the outer walkway at the back of the school. Penn was going to his room, and Rylan was stopping next door to see Mrs. Yardley. "What do you think she wants?" Penn asked him.

"No clue," Rylan remarked. "Mrs. Yardley isn't a small-talk kind of woman."

They were about to part ways outside her door when Mrs. Yardley opened it and invited Penn to join them if he wanted. Her room, like Penn and Farrah's, and everyone else at Vernon, was sparsely furnished. She had a narrow bed, a plywood-covered milk crate for a nightstand, a chest of drawers, and a small bistro table with two mismatched chairs. She invited them to take the chairs as she perched on the edge of her bed.

"What can we do for you, ma'am?" Rylan asked politely.

She studied them quizzically for a moment, as if assessing them in her mind. The guys felt as if they were about to be given a test they hadn't studied for. "Boys, the two of you have seen these things up close. Because you have, I would like you to hear me out no matter how strange my notion."

"Hear you out?" Penn replied. "About what?"

She spoke matter-of-factly, beginning with a recap of her former life, although how it related to her subject was still unknown. "I lived in a small apartment complex not far from here before the trouble began. A retired teacher must live frugally."

Penn sneered at the truth in her words. "I never thought it was right how little teachers earned while billionaires got all the tax breaks."

"As an apartment dweller, one lives among a variety of people," she went on. "My neighbors were diverse. From all walks of life and backgrounds." Her voice softened as memories pulled her back to the past. "I used to open my windows to catch the scent of other cultures cooking. Soul food, tacos, curry...it was beautiful. On Sundays, a teenage girl from the apartment below mine would teach me Spanish while I taught her English." She let out a girlish giggle. "I must confess I was a far better teacher than I was a student."

Penn and Rylan listened silently. She was building to something, but they didn't know quite what. "But the harmony had fractures," she continued. "One of the white families stood apart in our complex. They were loud and aggressive in their views. They displayed a Confederate flag sticker on their truck and one in their living room window. It caused quite a stir, as you can imagine, especially with families of color."

"I bet it did," Rylan frowned.

Mrs. Yardley looked at the men with all seriousness in her next observation. "I trace the catalyst to our last election. You could feel a shift of darkness in the air. Animosities ran high, not only in my neighborhood, but everywhere it seemed. Racial injustices. Women lost the right to terminate unwanted or life-threatening pregnancies." She directed her next statement to Rylan. "All the strides of the gay rights movement became overturned."

Rylan's jaw tensed as old anger flooded back. "The right wing did everything to turn their base against anyone different from them. Tearing away all advancements society had made in half a century."

Penn stretched his hands behind his head and growled. "Don't get me going on that. Farrah and I went round after round with her family. She was raised Conservative, and I was a radical Liberal in their eyes. The only reason we didn't fall out completely was because we were all trying to keep the peace before the wedding."

"Same with me and Dillon," Rylan confessed. "Having a gay son was a slap in the face to his parents' religious beliefs—or so they claimed. The big rift didn't happen until I asked Dillon to marry me."

"That's tough, man," Penn said. "I bet that hurt Dillon a lot."

Rylan's reddening cheeks showed his residual anger over it. "In the beginning he thought they'd learn to accept him...and by extension me. After all, a parent's love is unconditional, right? Well, theirs wasn't. He asked them to come to our wedding, but they refused. Claimed it went against their moral beliefs."

Mrs. Yardley placed a gentle hand over her heart. "I am sorry. That kind of rejection leaves permanent wounds."

Rylan's voice cracked with quiet fury. "And then they had the audacity to vote for the man who was the worst example of humankind. No morals, flagrant adultery, a pathological liar, and a champion of white supremacy. He didn't just ignore inequality, he endorsed it. And he fed it all to them as God's will. It was too much for Dillon. He cut his parents out of his life."

"Mrs. Yardley, are you saying that our country's election started all this?" Penn asked. "That it was politics that brought on the infection?"

"No," she replied. "That wasn't the infection. *It was the trigger.*" The guys stared at her, not understanding her meaning. She looked back at them, her wise eyes shimmering with something almost too complex to name. "I think the real infestation began long before anything fell from the sky. The hate. The division. The paranoia. It began with us."

"Us?" Penn repeated. "I don't understand."

"These creatures, this horror," Mrs. Yardley explained. "They used it against us. Whatever this is, it fed on us. It didn't cause our collapse. It harvested it."

"But that doesn't explain an extraterrestrial species killing off our planet." Rylan argued.

"They didn't kill it at first," she corrected. "They harvested our hate. One day the world changed. Division turned to violence. The neighbors I told you about a moment ago—the black man smashed the Confederate flag out of the white man's window. The Hispanics got involved, and from my locked apartment I watched until every member of those families had killed each other on the lawn."

"The day it happened everywhere," Rylan nodded.

"Farrah and I witnessed something similar in the mountains," Penn added.

A silence followed. The old woman, with her years of learned wisdom, gave them a moment to fully consider her thoughts. Penn stared at the floor while Rylan stared blankly ahead, neither fully comprehending the vastness of her theory. "Division, boys, is the most powerful weapon ever made. It took only a pointed finger and a cry of 'witch!' in Old Salem. Centuries later, the Nazis described the Jews as vermin and monsters. They said it enough that eventually their people believed it."

"I don't follow." Rylan said. "Are you saying the aliens were behind all that? That they've been setting us up for years?"

Mrs. Yardley made an indecisive shrug, not typical of her to appear uncertain on a subject. "I am simply pointing out there have been other snapshots in history where the same thing occurred." She patted the history book at the edge of her bed. "I was a little girl during the 50s when the Red Scare swept the nation. McCarthyism devastated Hollywood. Esteemed directors, actors, writers all squashed into professional oblivion as whispers took to the air saying, 'He's a communist!'"

"Yeah, but why would aliens care to plant those ideas in our minds?" Penn questioned.

Mrs. Yardley's eyes appeared even more troubled than they had before. "You keep saying aliens. I have not suggested the word at all. Be it outside forces or an enemy government on our very own planet, it matters very little. Divide and conquer, gentlemen. It is so much easier to kill something you no longer view as human."

"Like how everybody got up in arms over trans people," Rylan said grimly. "Or immigrants. Blacks. Gays. Name your pick! The playbook never changes. 'They aren't like us. Don't trust them."

Penn sat back in his chair, his head resting against the wall. It was a muddled and outlandish idea. Yet it made sense in a way. "Once you have two or more factions of people divided by ideological issues, all you need next is one scientifically advanced contagion released on them..."

"And it's Armageddon," Rylan finished.

"Something like that," Mrs. Yardley nodded. "If this is a toxin that an enemy nation or terror group has released on us, I believe our military and whatever able-bodied citizens remain, stand a chance to fight against it."

"But what if it isn't earthly?" Rylan asked. "What if it is like that professor from UAB said, and it's alien?"

She simply bowed her head, answering, "If this is warfare waged by some otherworldly species, there would be little hope."

"I wouldn't say that," Rylan argued. "Those things can be killed. I proved that."

"Those things, yes!" Mrs. Yardley replied. "But those things, if alien engineered, were created by an advanced intelligence, using human DNA forged with their technology. I doubt the *real alien beings* are anything like what's stalking us now. They would be far more dangerous. Perhaps unstoppable."

CHAPTER 18

EXPECTATIONS

Allie was already in a foul mood when Penn cornered her outside the gym. She'd just taken a shower, where several other women had been doing the same. Between Allie's shower head, Marian's, and Trisha's there was no hot water and, even worse, the cold water was at a trickle, making it take much longer to rinse off the soap.

The moment Penn asked her the question, Allie's hands mounted to her hips in frustration. "Penn, I don't know what you think I can find out that you can't."

"Well, being another woman, she might confide in you what is bothering her."

"Even if she does, Penn, *confiding* means trusting a person to keep a *confidence*. I wouldn't tell you. If you suspect your wife has a problem, then ask her what that problem is."

Penn rubbed his face between his palms in frustration. "I'm sure it's nothing. Like I told Rye, she's probably finally processing everything and everyone she's lost. I should just give her space to adjust."

"Don't ask Rylan for advice on anything!" Allie cried, smacking Penn's shoulder. "Why do people still think gay men are some magical mix of male and female insight? My brother's gay, not psychic—and trust me, his take on women is just as useless as any straight guy's. Even less because he's got zero experience!"

"Then what should I do, Allie?"

"Jesus Penn! Go talk to your wife and ask her."

His face turned pale, almost afraid. Penn was always such a together guy, it seemed unlike him. As he turned to go, Allie grabbed his arm. "Penn, have you ever had a truly serious talk with Farrah before?"

"Of course, I have!"

She sat down along the edge of the curb just outside the gym, patting the spot beside her for him to join. "Why are you so nervous about asking your wife what is bothering her?"

He balled his hands into fists, lightly pounding his knuckles together. It wasn't aggressive, just annoying. Allie put her hand between them to stop it. "Oh my God, why can't men just talk? Penn? Are you scared to ask her?"

She certainly got her wish as Penn suddenly ceased to be afraid to talk. In fact, he practically gushed sentences. "She acts so sad, Allie! What if this isn't only about losing people we've loved? What if she's looking around now at this Armageddon and thinking she's stuck in it with me now! I am all she's got left in the world! How am I enough to cover losing her mom, her sister, her best friends? I must be everything now...and I want to be...I'm trying to be. But what if I'm just not enough? It's just me. Me! And the way she's acting...Allie, it's obvious I am not making this new life okay enough to be in."

Allie didn't intend to burst into laughter. It was only that Penn's confession was the very last thing she'd expected from him. Here she was, believing him to be a shallow, skin-deep fellow when in truth he was petrified of failing the woman he loved. Allie laid her arm around his shoulders.

"Oh, honey, no. That isn't what is wrong."

"How can you know?" he asked.

She shot him a sharp look. "I know."

"Know what?"

"I know you are not what is bothering Farrah, and that is all I will say. Anything else, you need to get from her." Allie patted his back and pushed his head to her shoulder. "You are way sweeter than I took you for. But buddy, you can't carry the weight of being Farrah's everything. And you cannot allow yourself to think that she'd rather have everyone else back than be in this afterlife with you. Farrah loves you, and you are enough."

Penn nodded his head, fighting back tears. "Okay. Okay. Thanks. I should go find Farrah."

"Yes."

He stood up, and he gave Allie a hug. "Thank you so much, Ale." Then as an extra show of gratitude, he added, "You are so much wiser than your brother."

* * *

The sheet over the window held back most of the afternoon sun from the room, but at the sides where the sheet didn't quite cover the window, two bright lines shot golden light against the flimsy sheet-rocked divider. The former classroom, now split into four sections, was part of the duplex division of Vernon. Dillon had popped into the quarter he shared with Rylan for a brief rest before beginning the meal prep for dinner. Rylan was sitting on the bed, lost in his thoughts, as he absentmindedly traced his finger over one of the threadbare splits in the bedcover. He hadn't even noticed Dillon coming in.

Dillon entered with his usual confidence, kicking off his shoes before he flopped onto the bed beside his husband with a sigh. He stretched his legs out with an exaggerated groan. "What has you so deep in thought?" He didn't wait for an answer, rubbing his tired eyes. Rylan was familiar with the cues. The question hadn't been asked to be answered. The question—properly translated between husbands—meant, "Whatever is distracting you from me and my needs isn't important."

"I am beat!" Dillon continued without prompting. "People kept coming in for seconds asking if we had more chicken parmesan. I don't know if we'll have a full cafeteria tonight for dinner; most people are too full from lunch. So, I just made a few vats of soup to simmer."

Rylan still hadn't felt like saying anything. He did, however, understand the subtext, and began massaging Dillon's tired feet. His thumbs kneaded into the arch with practiced familiarity. He knew the pressure points to hit and where the knots usually hung out. Usually, they'd talk during these moments, but so far Dillon was the only one to speak.

Finally, after the silence became uncomfortable, Dillon asked, "Rye, what's up with you?"

Rylan let go of Dillon's foot and rolled onto his side, so they were face to face. He told Dillon everything Mrs. Yardley had said, from her unsettling historical comparisons to her convincing interpretation of what was really happening in the outside world. He began the retelling in earnest, but as Rylan finished, his tone had switched from one of openness to dismissive. "But the more I think about what she suggested, the more ridiculous it sounds."

Dillon's face didn't reflect Rylan's opinion. "Sounds like a brilliant tactic to me."

Rylan shot him a condescending look. "Dillon, you aren't serious. What a stupid, roundabout way to start a war."

"No, it isn't!" Dillon scoffed. "Remember back when we used to go dancing at that club in Lakeview? They had those drag shows on Saturday nights that lasted till midnight, and the bar closed at 2 A.M. leaving almost no time to have fun."

"How can this possibly relate?"

"If you listen, I will tell you." Dillon continued with the story. "That DJ we liked—Malcolm, or Roland, or..."

"His name was Hal."

"Oh, that's right! Well, Hal saw how Saturdays brought in less and less people. Then he told the drag queen, Nell Salon, that customers wished her set were longer. He then informed the other drag queen, Willie Flucker, that he had heard Nell brag she was going to run over into Willie's time from now on."

Rylan wrung his hands in frustration. "The point! Any point, Dillon!"

"Well, Nell and Willie were enemies from then on. It was nothing but trouble until the owner got so tired of it, he fired them both and gave DJ Hal the whole night to spin dance music. Divide and conquer."

Rylan shook his head. "Oddly enough, I see how your asinine story fits. But are we expected to believe some enemy has been seeding our animosities, our cultural differences, our prejudices all our lives?"

"Is that any crazier than what we've seen with our own eyes?" Dillon challenged. "God, Rye, you fought one of those things yourself." Smiling, Dillon traced his finger across Rylan's forehead and the bridge of his nose. "You were so brave that day."

"Me?" Rylan grinned. "I'm not the one who doused one of those monsters in lighter fluid and torched him!"

Now tracing his thumbs over Rylan's eyebrows, Dillon teased, "I couldn't let that thing hurt you. What if it marred this handsome face?"

"I do have a rather striking face, don't I?"

Rolling his eyes, Dillon teased, "Well, I have wanted to strike it a few times in our marriage." He then gave Rylan a peck on the cheek. "But seriously, Rye. I don't know if I believe the whole alien thing."

"Really? Why not?"

Dillon made an awkward face, the kind he usually made whenever he wasn't even convinced himself about his own assumptions. "I just remember a couple of things about that day I thought were odd even then."

Propping up on an elbow, Rylan asked, "Like what?"

"Well, for starters, those creatures were not looking for humans. They were looking for supplies too."

"Yeah, and we know why," Rylan countered. "Dasha witnessed them stripping that pharmacy. Their plan is to starve out the rest of us before they move in for the final kill, then take our planet."

"Maybe," Dillon said. "Or maybe they need to eat too. Aren't we just assuming they're trying to starve us out? What if they are just as desperate to survive as we are?"

"Wouldn't they have thought of that before coming here, Dillon? I doubt an advanced life form, capable of traveling the solar system, took a road trip unprepared."

Dillon folded his arms judgmentally. "They don't seem to be doing very much."

"They sure have killed a bunch of fucking people!"

"But why?" Dillon challenged. "To get us out of the way for their big plan? What plan? The creatures aren't terraforming our land. They aren't mining our minerals. They aren't draining our lakes and oceans. Except getting rid of people, I don't see a reason they've even come here."

Rylan laughed sarcastically. "I'm sorry that we've been invaded by the laziest form of alien life! Maybe they'll get some gumption and do a little more damage to please you."

"I'm not saying we aren't at war, Rye," Dillon replied. "I am not even saying there isn't something sinister at work here. But what if this isn't an alien invasion? And what if it isn't some rogue terrorist group waging chemical tricks on us either?"

Rylan looked incredulously at Dillon. "What do you think? That we're hallucinating all this. People are dead, Dillon! Millions of people are dead."

"Do not take that imperious tone with me, Rylan James Daily! All I am suggesting is chemical warfare is remotely possible. Some kind of super-amped LSD, sent by a hostile nation right here on Earth. What if all we are experiencing is mass hallucination."

* * *

Penn found Ashley Sims hunched over a potting table when he stepped through the waist-high fence surrounding the football field. With two plants lying end to end, and a scalpel in her hand, Ashley looked as if she were dissecting the roots of both.

"Good afternoon, Penn!" she said over her shoulder. "Do you want to see Farrah? Her shift ended an hour ago, but she's still here working!"

"Please, if I can," he replied. He leaned in closer to watch what she was doing. "May I ask what those roots ever did to you, Miss Ashley?"

She acknowledged his joke with a half chuckle, keeping her eyes carefully tuned in to her work. "I am crossbreeding carrots to grow a much larger hybrid. Imagine how much food we could store for winter next year if I can expand our produce."

"Wow," he remarked. "That's pretty sciencey!"

She rose, wiping her brow with the back of her hand, leaving a smudge of dirt. "I don't think it's working though. Some root systems don't blend with others like you hope they will."

Penn didn't respond. He walked down the long rows of growing vegetables while the blistering sun beat down on his neck. A sudden thought struck him as his arms grazed tall, leafy plants budding with their yield. Farrah likely had her hands on every one of these plants at some point in their lifespan. She helped ensure every single day that the people at Vernon could eat. He found her in the next row tying new strands of pea vine to the support wires running through the bed. She glanced at him, shielding her eyes from the sun with her hand.

"Talk to me."

* * *

Corinne found Penn and Farrah waiting for her in the infirmary when she returned from the supply closet. The concerned look on their faces worried her. Farrah looked as though she had been crying, so Penn started the conversation and the reason for the visit.

"We always assumed we'd have children one day," he began. "But honestly, from our honeymoon until arriving here, we lived in survival mode. The thought never crossed our minds. Besides, neither of us felt very...except once or twice."

"I understand," Corinne offered. "And now you are worried you're pregnant?"

Farrah burst into tears again. "How can we bring a baby into this? Nothing is the way it was supposed to be when we got married. I'm terrified. What if the aliens find and kill the rest of us? What are they even here for? Are they going to leave? I can't have a baby."

Corinne placed a calming hand on Farrah's leg, and it did seem to restore normal breathing before she'd started hyperventilating. "Farrah, we have no idea why the invaders have come," the doctor said calmly. "Or what they plan to do now that they have eradicated so much human life. But from what I hear, Penn, you are actively trying to discover that information with radio transmissions. Perhaps you will arrive at some answers."

"I try a little every day," he replied. "Sometimes I have luck, but usually all I get is static."

"Well, trying is at least doing something proactive." Corinne addressed Farrah now. "I cannot tell you with any certainty that humans will survive this. But I also wouldn't have been able to assure you that you and your baby wouldn't have died in a car accident on the way to a pediatrician appointment. But what I can tell you, Farrah, is that if you are pregnant, everyone here at Vernon will do everything we can to ensure your child's safety and long life."

"But what about complications?" Farrah exclaimed. "What about diseases? Tetanus, measles? Any baby born would live in the equivalent of the dark ages again."

Corinne broke into a smile. "Not exactly as primitive as that, Farrah. But I understand your fear. All I can say is that humankind did survive the dark ages, and we appear to be making our way through this latest world crisis too. If you have a little faith in the human species, I'll do all I can to take care of the rest."

The doctor withdrew a pregnancy test from a cabinet. "We will be back in a few minutes," she told Penn as she led Farrah by the hand to the girl's bathroom across the hall.

Penn waited. His mind spinning with worries. All of Farrah's reservations were ones he shared, yet despite the odds against two people beginning a family under these circumstances, he prayed the test would be positive.

Corinne returned with a teary Farrah still clutching her hand. "You're going to be a dad."

He wasn't sure how he should respond. He wanted to be happy, but if Farrah wasn't...then he saw her smile. It was small, but it was real. Penn swept Farrah into his arms, kissing down her neck. Corinne closed the door behind her, leaving them alone to embrace the moment or express their fears. Or both.

CHAPTER 19

HOME IS WHERE THE LOVE IS

Patrice Wilson froze just outside her own door. She'd been on her way to get Lakeisha from Rylan and Dillon's room, where she'd slept the night before, and was probably now with her math tutor. However, all thoughts of her daughter drained from her head when her eyes caught sight of a mirage that could not possibly be real.

Three figures, too far away for her middle-aged eyes to decipher, were walking her way. Patrice suspected two of them were Doe and Dasha, but the third figure was unclear against the bright morning sun casting in her eyes. Patrice's heartbeat increased as her soul seemed to scream a miracle her heart had long given up on.

"Mama! Mama!"

Even as she heard his voice ring through the air, she still couldn't permit her heart to trust it. If she were wrong...Patrice couldn't go through that pain a second time. Then the figure yelled it again, causing her to turn around just to see if someone else was behind her.

"No, Mama! I'm calling to you!" the figure cried, closer, and nearly out of the glare of the sun. Patrice knew it was a man now walking between Doe and Dasha. As his face hit the space just under the blinding rays, she knew it was not imagination.

"Annndddrrreee!!!!!" Her lungs burst with his name like a trumpet announcing a king. Patrice jumped the rail between the walkway and the asphalt, breaking into a run towards her very much alive son!

Andre was weeping as his legs carried him to meet his mother's arms. He seized Patrice around the waist and fell into her.

"Dre, is it really you?" she pulled back to examine his face. With her eyes so full of tears, she couldn't properly make him out even at such close range. Patrice swiped them away, staring into his beautiful bronze features. "My baby is alive. My boy is alive." She pressed him into her again with the intensity of someone trying to merge. From her periphery she noticed Dasha and Doe coming closer. Patrice let out a sharp cry over Andre's shoulder. "You found him! You found my son!"

"Damn, Mama!" Andre flinched. "That was right in my ear."

Both laughed and pulled apart so they could inspect each other thoroughly. The women were beside them now, hearts swelling from the happiness on Patrice's face.

"Where?" Patrice gasped at them. "How?"

"Would you believe Andre is one of the guys we met on that supply run the other day?" Dasha grinned.

"Then why didn't you tell me?" Patrice asked.

"Oh, we only figured it out an hour ago," Doe chuckled.

"And now you are home," Patrice beamed into her son's face. "And I am not letting you out of my sight ever again!"

As she pulled him into another embrace, he shot a look at Dasha. Neither said anything, but they both knew that Andre wasn't planning on staying in Vernon. His home was UAB, and Dasha was to drive him back in a couple of days.

No one had noticed Lakeisha. Coming back to their room after her math lesson, she'd seen her mother running towards a man. It did not take young Lakeisha Wilson nearly as long as it had her mother to recognize him.

With her eight-year-old hands on her hips, she shouted with moxie, "Andre Wilson! Where the hell have you been?!"

* * *

Trisha caught Dillon coming out of the linen supply classroom with frustration written across his face. She waited for a couple of people to pass by before asking, "Rough afternoon?"

"Everyone has gone all weird today," Dillon huffed. "When I took the kitchen inventory to Gusty, she wanted to go over every single item, line by line, asking ridiculous questions about what we have or don't have, and what we really need and can do without."

"Well, she does make the supply lists based on things we need," Trisha defended. "That isn't so crazy."

"For her, it is!" Dillon remarked. "She's never questioned me before. I just hand her the list and that's that. But today she wanted to discuss practically everything. Then, when I finally got out of there, Maddie was losing it in the hall, acting completely hysterical because someone had gone into the linen classroom and knocked over the towel and bedsheet stacks."

"Who would do that?" Trish gasped.

"Beats me!" Dillon replied. "But you know how methodical Maddie is. She was practically in tears until I promised to help her refold everything. Then I had to help her reorganize by color. Now I've got to get back to the kitchen before we end up serving dinner late!"

Trisha smiled knowingly. "No rush. Dinner is already prepped and ready for cooking. But there is a shelf in the pantry that came loose and spilled flour everywhere. Can you fix it before we start?"

Muttering obscenities under his breath, Dillon disappeared down the hall unaware of the setup. Both Maddie and Augusta peeked from their doors to see Trisha give them a proud thumbs up!

Moving practically at a march towards the kitchen, Dillon was in no mood for any more setbacks. But just as he turned the corner behind the stoves, he saw yet another mess awaiting him. He paused, looking down at the floor. It wasn't so much a mess as a trail. What he'd at first mistaken for drops of dough or batter were tiny petals. It looked as if someone had crumbled hydrangea blooms in a line. He followed it to the dry storage pantry door. Pulling it open, expecting to find a shelf half askew from the wall and flour spilled everywhere, his eyes saw something else entirely.

"Happy Anniversary, my beautiful love."

There, dressed in a slightly too large suit borrowed from Marian's men's clothing stash, sat Rylan. He'd arranged a small folding table draped in a floral sheet. Two mismatched candles flickered between glasses of what looked like champagne. A plate of chocolate-dipped strawberries completed the tableau.

"What is this?" Dillon gasped, utterly caught off guard.

"Today is our eleventh anniversary," Rylan smiled, gesturing to the second chair across from him. "This is just a little way for me to commemorate the day—with the help of a few friends."

There were very few times in life when Dillon Daily was at a loss for words, but this was absolutely one of them. Slowly, he took a seat and reached across the table to hold Rylan's hands. They didn't say anything for a moment, simply looking into the face of the person they loved. Then Rylan lifted his hand, the silver wedding band catching the candlelight. "Even at the end of the world," Rylan tearfully smiled. "I've never been happier or more lucky. Thank you for cuffing up with me."

Cuffing up with me. Dillon couldn't help but laugh at the memory as he raised his own left hand and tapped his ring to Rylan's. This was their way of toasting—and sometimes how they ended fights. It had symbolic meaning, special only to them.

From the beginning, Dillon had been expressly against the idea of marriage and said so within their first few dates. It was a bit of a shocking declaration for Rylan to hear considering how long and hard gay people had fought to win the very right to marry. Dillon's adamancy had been off-putting until Rylan knew him well enough to understand.

"My mother loves my father," he'd once explained to Rylan shortly after they began dating. "And Dad loves her too, I'm sure. But Mom lost herself in their marriage."

"How so?" Rylan had asked.

"Dad had big aspirations, and they left little room for Mom to be her own person. I always thought of their marriage as if she'd been handcuffed to a policeman. He made the rules, and she followed them. And she liked him well enough not to fight against him, but she'd long lost whoever she'd once been. Now she's a programmed robot copy of him. She has no individuality at all. I never want to be that."

"Why would you have to?" Rylan countered. "That was your mom, not you. Marriage doesn't always mean losing yourself. Sometimes it means gaining someone extra to challenge and enhance you."

Dillon had stared him directly in the eye and replied, "I don't like to be challenged either."

That certainly proved to be a truthful statement over the years. But as their relationship grew and their love expanded into depths neither could have imagined, being merely together wasn't enough for Rylan. He wanted a marriage. Dillon's family would have nothing to do with them, forcing Dillon to make a choice. When he chose Rylan, Rylan wanted to show him he would never be sorry.

The day Rylan had proposed, with his sister Allie and all their friends watching in shock at the Memorial Day barbeque, he told Dillon as he fell to his knee, "Maybe to you, a ring is a shackle. But Dillon, there is nothing I want more in this world than to be shackled to you." He pulled the ring from a little black box and asked, "Will you cuff up with me for the rest of my life?"

* * *

Still together after all those years, Dillon lifted the champagne glass from the little table in the pantry and asked, "Do you remember what I said that day?"

Rylan smiled as his eyes brightened. "You know I do. You said, 'Okay. But only *the rest of your life*. I get a few years before I promise eternity."

Dillon beamed as they clinked their glasses together, as they had their wedding bands, then downed the champagne. But it wasn't champagne, and Rylan had failed to warn him of that. It was gin and a dash of lemon juice. After a round of harsh coughing, they ate their strawberries while they held hands.

"This isn't chocolate," Dillon muttered as the berry went down.

"I don't know how to make chocolate, and I didn't want to ask you. It's Nutella."

"No, it's not." Dillon said.

"Well, homemade Nutella." Rylan frowned. "Peanut butter mixed with some old packets of Swiss Miss Hot Chocolate."

"You are an idiot."

"An idiot in love," Rylan grinned.

And for a few moments, the world beyond the small pantry of a high school kitchen didn't exist. There was no death, no apocalypse. Just two men, eleven years into something real, sharing bitter gin, strawberries, and stale hot chocolate powder...and a little eternity.

* * *

Several things plagued Penn's mind now. Mrs. Yardley's interpretation of things was certainly intriguing and paired well with Dr. Journer's declaration of an alien invasion. However, the newfound knowledge that Penn and Farrah were going to be parents lit a fire under him to seek answers and find them fast. If his child was going to grow up in an alien-compromised environment, Penn needed to know everything he could about the state of the world.

"This is K4RGT in Birmingham. Can anyone hear me out there? Over."

Penn sat in front of the HAM radio, hoping to reach someone else who might have more to impart than Carlo from San Diego had. He continued moving along the dial for almost ten minutes until a clear and sharp voice burst from the speaker.

"Hello K4RGT. This is G7TJM Cornwall. Your call sign and voice aren't British," the woman said with a thick English accent. "I assume you aren't Birmingham, England? Over."

"No," Penn answered. "Alabama. My name is Penn. Over."

The clarity of the transmission was much better than California had been a few days ago. He could only assume that the time of day made the difference. "What has you calling the U.K. so early—or I suppose late, for you, Penn?" she emitted a short laugh before adding, "So sorry to be rude by not returning my name. I am Portia. In fact, you are the first person I have heard come across this device...oh, right. Over."

Penn nodded his head in understanding, although he knew she couldn't see him. "I've had that trouble myself, Portia. Must be a dismal sign of our losses, right? Over."

The transmission went silent for a moment. He thought he had lost her. "Are you there, Portia? Over."

"Portia?" he called again, louder this time. "Are you okay, Portia? Are you alone? How bad is it in England? Over." He waited. Nothing. "G7TJM in Cornwall, are you there? This is K4RGT in Birmingham. Over."

Static and hissing met his anxious voice over the ocean. Penn was just about to give up when suddenly Portia's voice broke through the static again. She sounded afraid. Panicked. "I can't continue now," she whispered into her microphone.

"What's happening, Portia?!" Penn yelled. "Are you under attack?"

"I must go," she whispered. "Goodbye, Penn."

* * *

He sat for a while imagining what terrible fate his brief friend might be scrambling to survive at that exact moment. Penn's mind raced with questions, the most burning one being whether it was his fault. Had he broken through some cloak of protective silence in this woman's home and been overheard by the monsters? His fingers hesitated to try another frequency. The last thing he wanted to do was endanger someone else. Still, he had to talk to someone and find some answers.

"This is Pete," a new voice, male, called back. "Damn, wait. Okay, it's written on it. This is K3LSW. In Athens."

"Greece? Over." Penn asked.

"Naw, man. Georgia," the guy replied. "And I don't know much about all this. Let's just skip the *over and out* shit, okay?"

"Okay, Pete. I'm Penn. How's it going in Georgia? I'm next door in Alabama."

"Everybody's dead, that's how it's going," Pete said in defeat. "I ain't seen hide nor hair of anybody in over two months. Course, I live kinda out by myself. This was my grandpaw's radio. My daddy had it. But Grumblers got in and ripped him up but good before I made it outta Florence and got here."

"Damn, man. I'm sorry." Penn answered back. "Do you know anything about what's happening in the world? Is the government still operating?"

Pete let out a forced laugh, although it might have only been the static. "I heard from some guy in Maryland who said he got one of those morse code things saying some gas bombs got dropped on us."

Penn sat up straight in the chair. "Really? He said that? So, this is a manmade situation? A foreign enemy?"

"That's some bullshit right there!" Pete yelped. "My daddy was Air Force. You wouldn't believe some of the fake stories he said the government sent out to cover up shit they didn't have answers for."

Penn took a chance on sharing Vernon's theory. "We killed two of the things and had a scientist tell us they are alien. What do you think of that idea, Pete?"

"Fuck yeah, this is some outer space shit!" Pete cried. "My daddy saw some crazy motherfucking shit up in the skies when he flew. Said the higher-ups made up cover stories, and nobody ever said anything about it again. What else could do this kind of fucked-up shit to Earth?"

Pete was clearly not the most educated contact Penn had reached over the HAM radio, but his opinion of events stood out to Penn as the most plausible. Which begged the question once again, why were beings from outer space here? What was their plan? Pete was as lost for an answer as Penn. However, before he cut transmission, Pete said one rather peculiar thing.

"I gotta shut down now, Penn. Those burned-looking motherfuckers like to come around at night. I gotta stay quiet and blow out my lamps."

Pete was gone. There had been no time to ask him what he meant by *burned*. Had someone injured some of them? Set them on fire the way Dillon had at the warehouse? Penn wished he'd been able to ask. It also sounded as if Pete didn't yet know the creatures had overcome their light sensitivity. Penn had come down to the armory for answers but left with even more questions.

* * *

Up in their room, Farrah quizzed him relentlessly on every detail of his transmissions with Portia and Pete, only breaking her seriousness to laugh over the *Penn, Portia, Pete* irony. But if there was one thing his wife was, it was thorough. While Penn drifted off to sleep beside her, Farrah furiously scribbled everything he'd shared into her notebook, including Pete's calling the creatures *Grumblers* and hinting that the ones he'd seen appeared burned. One of these days, these bits and pieces of random information would come together and make sense. She just had to keep logging them down long enough.

CHAPTER 20

THE GALLERIA MALL

The once-thriving Riverchase Galleria Mall had been a shining symbol of mass consumerism in its day. Now it had been transformed into something more vital: a fortress city, shielded from the chaos and carnage of the outside world. The refugees within the mall's impervious cinderblock walls had found a rare sense of safety. It was something few places could offer anymore. The mall appeared to have been designed for an apocalypse. Each entrance came with a steel-reinforced security gate, sealing out the roaming threats plaguing the less fortunate souls left to fend on their own out there.

Inside the mall, the central promenade ran like a town's main street, crowned by a second-story mezzanine. Above, a vaulted atrium of steel and glass bathed the avenue in natural light, nourishing the makeshift garden now running through the mall's center in the ribbon of raised planters once used only for decorative plant life. Now repurposed for sustainability, the nutrient-rich soil housed a rotating crop of fresh vegetables to assist in feeding the population.

A center court, once a stage for fashion shows and live music, now operated as the town square. From this raised platform came community announcements by the newly formed government, while on Sundays it became the pulpit for Reverend Tucker's sermons and the hub for the population's worship.

At the inception of this enclosed and highly fortified colony, those who took immediate charge acted swiftly. They stripped shopfronts of their elaborate displays and emptied them of their contents, repurposing all 156 stores according to the colony's new social blueprint. Each space was restocked with essentials—clothing, tools, books, batteries, first aid—based on its assigned function. The presentation wasn't very polished, and most items were secondhand, but between the mall's existing inventory and nearby scavenging, the community assembled a generous bounty fit for survival within their necessary confinement.

City "Searchers" who braved the outside world, recovered what they could to prolong survival. Moving expeditiously through the ruined landscape beyond the Galleria's walls, they took everything they found. Nothing was inconsequential. Every raided store, home, or junk drawer had something the colony could use, from flashlights to clothing, to the groceries in cabinets, refrigerators, and freezers. Even old toys or television remote controls provided batteries which might one day power light sources if the electricity, miraculously still operating, went out.

Perhaps the most remarkable feature of the Galleria settlement was its living quarters. When the mall was built in the opulent 1980s as an upscale commercial hub, the architects added a bold nod to excess by including a luxury hotel at its center. Now, the eight-story tower served a more functional purpose, offering enough rooms on its second and third floors for every colonist to have a living space. It was a small dignity in an otherwise dismal existence.

Over the course of its first year as a self-sustaining refuge, the

Riverchase Galleria had withstood countless assaults—both from violent marauders and the inhuman horrors devouring the world like locusts. It had remained impenetrable by both, protected not only by its architectural strength but by the will of God—a conviction shared by the citadel's residents and the shepherd who tended their faith.

"The wretched souls who came scratching at our gates," Reverend Elias Tucker often reminded his flock, "clawed and wailed like the damned who pounded on the sides of Noah's ark as the floodwaters rose. But Noah stood firm. He understood the Lord's plan. Only the righteous and the worthy would be spared. And our colony is no different."

From the beginning, when Reverend Tucker first looked out across the mall's huddled, frightened people, he gave them the peace of mind they were so desperate for in those early days.

"Providence, my friends," he explained. "Providence has spoken. The unseen hand of your maker guided each of you here that day. He had prepared a home for His children and called you to it."

* * *

If Reverend Tucker had accepted his role as spiritual leader, the rest of the mall's government seemed equally predestined from a Divine hand. Franklin Collins, former esteemed mayor of nearby Homewood, along with his wife Linda, had been at the mall on the day the world crumbled. His election as leader of the colony, with Reverend Tucker's support, was an easy choice when forming the new government. From there, a small council assembly was chosen to make necessary decisions, guiding laws, and systems of enforcement to ensure the new community thrived peacefully.

During the many months of life within the thick walls of the Galleria, most days passed with little deviation from the last—except for Sunday worship. But that all changed after the papers fell from the sky. High above their heads, in the atmosphere of pitched glass, an overhead plane stopped everyone below in their tracks. It had been nearly a year since anyone had seen anything other than sun, rain, or birds in the daytime sky. As the papers rained down onto the atrium, a buzz of excitement rolled over the mall plaza like a tidal wave.

The mall offices on the third floor overlooked the Galleria's center through one-sided mirrored glass. The city council, summoned to an emergency meeting after the plane went overhead, stood at the glass observing the people it served below.

"Why are so many people still looking up?" Bill Wicker asked. In the Old World, he had owned the largest auto dealership in the city, but it was his longtime friendship with the mayor that landed him a council seat.

Dorothy Maxwell stepped away from the lookout window, retaking her seat at the table centered in the room. "They are looking to see if another plane is going to come by."

Abandoning the lookout as well, Mayor Collins settled into his chair with a slow exhale of breath. "My fear is that they are trying to read what is written on those papers, despite the height above them."

"Why fear?" Dorothy questioned.

Collins narrowed his eyes. "Because we should know the contents of those papers first."

The remaining council members at the window, Bill Wicker and Reverend Tucker, took their seats at the table. "False hope can be a dangerous temptation," Rev. Tucker suggested. "To maintain the tranquility we have been blessed with so far, we should decide what our people know."

"We should send a Searcher outside to retrieve one," Bill proposed. "It might be a set of instructions on how to send the demons back to Hell."

The conference room door opened as former attorney and final council member, Corbin Hartley entered waving a paper in his hand.

"I have it here!"

The others met his entrance with surprise and curiosity, except for the mayor, who appeared annoyed. "How did you get your hands on one of those, Corbin?"

"I went outside and grabbed one from the parking lot."

With consternation in his eyes, Mayor Collins replied sharply. "Who let you out? The door guards have strict orders. Only I can decide who enters or exits that door."

Corbin chuckled unapologetically. "Under the circumstances, I think a thing like this supersedes normal adherence to policy."

Unhappily, the mayor remarked, "That is your opinion."

He took the paper from Corbin's hand, reading it silently before allowing the others to pass it around the table. "Did you show this to the guards or anyone else?"

"No," Corbin answered. "I came straight here."

"And the guards asked you no questions?" Reverend Tucker inquired as he finished reading and passed it to Dorothy.

Corbin grinned slightly. "They were busy securing the door back. I was out and in quick."

As Bill's eyes scanned the document, he placed it on the table. "There are people manning the power stations and waterworks."

"That would explain a lot," the mayor argued. "Thank goodness for them."

Dorothy pulled the piece of paper towards her again, taking a second look at what it said. "We certainly owe those people our gratitude. I think we should gather some food crates and basic necessities and deliver them to their hubs."

The reverend stood up once more, returning to the lookout window where he could evaluate the colonists' reactions below. "That would be quite a mistake, I'm afraid."

"How so, Reverend?" Dorothy asked. "This note says they need help, and after all they are doing to keep the utilities going—"

"Others will help them, I'm sure." Reverend Tucker's words came as a shock. "I think the mayor will agree this bit of insight is best kept to ourselves."

Mayor Collins immediately agreed in gesture, but his eyes clearly revealed he was just as unclear about why. It was Corbin who pressed the reverend for an explanation. From the expressions on Dorothy and even Bill Withers' faces, they too were curious about this proclamation.

"My dear council, surely you see that our faithful here in the colony attribute our fortunate circumstances of basic electricity and water supply, albeit unreliable at times, as God-given."

"I don't see the harm in them knowing about the utility workers," Corbin commented.

With a genteel pat to his arm, Reverend Tucker insisted, "In these dark and tumultuous times, our people need to believe their Lord has them in His hands. I see no use in stripping them of one of their miracles. And suffice it to say, if the brave men at the power company are providing us with this gift, it is surely only by the guiding hand of the Lord."

Though he seemed slightly uncomfortable with the decision, Mayor Collins sided with the logic. "Then it is settled. We do not share the contents of the note. Of course, we must tell the people something. Everyone saw the papers fall from the plane. Suggestions?"

"I don't know when truth stopped being the best suggestion," Corbin continued to argue. "I, for one, take great peace in knowing there are enough surviving communities out there that someone thought it important to let us know what they are doing to help us."

Leaving no further room in his tone for discussion on the matter, Reverend Tucker replied, "We have built a fine settlement here. Fully protected and filled with the faithfully chosen. Any colonies beyond our walls are doomed to fall once the demonic forces at work outside locate them. Let's not muddy the already treacherous waters on which our ark floats."

Once Withers sided with Tucker and Collins, there was nothing left to say. They posed the suggestion of implying the note was nothing more than an accounting of how deadly the outside world had become. This, they felt, would cement the colonists' gratitude and reverence for their mall sanctuary.

* * *

Dorothy left the mayor's office after the meeting, biting her tongue on the decision, and stood by the small rail of the third-floor stairs looking down. She couldn't help but peer below at the citizenry going about their lives without knowing how in the dark they were so often kept. From her vantage point, Dorothy could see her family on the lower level across the plaza. Calling it *her family* was a broad statement; in fact, it was her sister Leslie's family who oversaw the tool department. Leslie's husband, Joe McNab, along with their son, Scotty, and daughter, Renee, were responsible for keeping track of all the tools and hardware collected throughout the mall or brought in by Searchers. Although the job was mundane, it was essential for the community.

Dorothy had no family of her own. She had never married or had children. Leslie, Joe, and the kids were all she had in the world now. It was quite a different existence from how it had been before, when Dorothy had been the successful one. Working her way up the ranks of the realty company until she was a full partner by the time the world collapsed. In those days, Joe and Leslie had been betas to her alpha.

A mechanic at a chain-brand garage, Joe often struggled financially. Always hit with a fresh crisis—Scotty and Renee's births, overdue rent, a broken appliance, dental bills. Dorothy had stepped in every time, even co-signing the mortgage without hesitation, never making them feel indebted. It was just what family does for each other. But when the world crumbled into anarchy and monsters crawled out of the earth to slaughter humankind, Dorothy's wealth and status became meaningless. The tables turned, and the new world had little use for a realtor. Men like Joe, with more practical abilities, fell into favor. Joe's family not only managed the city's tool supply, but he also helped to keep the automobiles used by the Searchers and the Strike Force operational.

While Searchers scavenged for necessities, the Strike Force was the only other group allowed external access from the mall. Their job was to actively seek out and destroy the demonic forces ravaging the land within a few miles' radius of the mall. This team comprised of four, rotating alphabetically in monthly shifts. Only men were allowed to serve, and it was deemed a privilege—a mandatory privilege.

Dorothy, being unable to join either rank, found herself subjugated to serving a mere storekeeper role in the tool department with the rest of her family. The one consolation gained from the former currency her name had held in the pre-Armageddon community was her place on the Galleria's city council. But like the others she served alongside, Dorothy knew her power was tenuous, held only by the mayor's favor.

Of course, she understood what no one else dared say aloud. Mayor Collins was a figurehead. The actual power rested with the one who controlled the masses—masses starved for guidance, salvation, and hope. They clung to every word that dripped from Reverend Tucker's lips, as if God himself had slid into his DMs.

"Funny, isn't it?"

The voice startled her as she stood lost in her thoughts.

"All that down there," Corbin said, joining her at the railing. "This monument to consumerism is now our sanctuary. Sometimes, I think it's a blessing, and other times, it feels like a prison. But it is all we've got left."

"Unless the government gets a handle on this crisis," she offered.

Before the demons arose from hell, as Reverend Tucker so often espoused, the face of Corbin Hartley was plastered across dozens of billboards throughout the state. "The Lawyer with a Hart" was practically a household name in Alabama, and some parts of Tennessee, Georgia, and Mississippi.

"Do you really believe our government will ride to our rescue?" he smirked. "They couldn't even get their act together before the world ended. Half the country's taxes went to entitlements and welfare of those too lazy to work, and the rest covered the tax credits given to prop up billionaires who did not even need half the money they had."

"It was indeed a mess, that's for sure." Dorothy remembered. "I pray that if anything is left of the government, they have enough force to remove these monsters and finally pull society back together to be one nation under God."

Corbin chuckled slightly. "I wouldn't hold my breath."

CHAPTER 21

HOW WE SHOW WHO WE ARE

Corbin and Dorothy parted ways on the second-floor mezzanine. Neither had noticed with the bright midday light streaming down from the center atrium spanning the promenade, that another brownout had occurred. If the outage continued until night-fall—or Heaven forbid, the electricity stayed out permanently—the solar panels scattered atop the roof would soak up enough sun to power the generators. Those generators produced just enough juice to operate the few emergency lights along the mall and run the ovens for the cooks. And the refrigeration units would stay cold until the sun rose tomorrow, if no one opened the doors that is.

Corbin was noticing now as he made his way to his family's store-front. Whatever light filled the center plaza of the mall did not fully reach into the facing stores. Though power drains were always a point of concern for colonists, they'd learned to expect them here and there. So much had changed since Corbin and his family realized they would never leave the mall a year ago.

He and Genna had been celebrating their son Colin's tenth birthday at the mall's Dave & Buster's when the bedlam broke out. Colin and his best friend James had been locked in a heated game of Skee-Ball, laughing and shouting, while pop music pulsed overhead and arcade machines blared around them. Cutting through the arcade's usual noise came a curious sound. Corbin and Genna strained to hear it against the backdrop of bells, buzzers, whistles, and dings. Exchanging puzzled glances, they edged closer to the mall entrance. Something had shifted. Beneath the music and machine noise, another sound was rising—shrill, frantic, and growing louder...or was it *closer*?

"It sounds like it's in the mall," Genna had whispered to Corbin as other parents in the arcade also began noticing. Several followed Corbin and Genna toward the exit.

Just as the small group of parents reached the arcade's exit, the Dave & Buster's manager yanked down the security gate with a thunderous crash, sealing them inside. From behind the barrier, a nightmare unfolded. Ordinary suburban shoppers—families, teens, retirees—had turned on one another in a haze of madness. Cutlery from the housewares department became weapons; box cutters, likely wrestled from the hands of stock clerks, were now dripping with blood. Gunshots cracked through the chaos, fired by mall guards, off-duty cops, or armed civilians who'd dashed to their cars for a glove-box pistol. Improvised tools of death joined the fray—umbrellas used like spears, shattered bottles wielded like daggers, and small appliances swung by their cords, crashing into skulls like a medieval mace.

Corbin and his family stood frozen at the gate, the scene searing itself into their memories like third-degree burns. Now and then, someone hurled themselves at the barrier, only to bounce back from its loose give, like a body flung against a trampoline net. Rage, or something darker, contorted the faces beyond. Corbin tried to shield the boys' eyes, but they pulled away, mesmerized by the sight of the world tearing itself apart.

Corbin had stood as stunned as the rest, transfixed on the carnage beyond the gate. Only when Genna screamed behind him did he whirl around to see the crazed look on the manager's face, wildly swinging a bar knife. Two adults already lay on the floor, grasping their sliced throats as the last of life seeped out of them. Whatever infection had come over the crowd outside, had gotten to him too. Genna swept the boys out of his path, taking refuge behind an air hockey table as Corbin lurched to fight the man off. The knife sliced Corbin's forearm, but the wound was not fatal. Drawing on years of once-weekly Tae Kwon Do, the lawyer blocked the second strike and countered hard, sending the manager crashing to the floor. It happened in a blur of seconds. When Corbin stepped back, his heaving chest catching its breath, he saw that he'd buried the knife into the neck of the manager during the struggle.

The shock of it—of taking a life with his own hands—left Corbin momentarily dazed, but the pandemonium in the mall left no time to process it. Something had to be done. Corbin and a few others who had been watching from safety swarmed into the mall to assist those fighting. By the time the last attacker was killed, it was Corbin who suggested that they secure all mall exits by lowering the gates. The arcade manager had at least shown him that trick before dying.

With the mall sealed off from the outside world, and the internal threats neutralized, the bloodied and frightened masses clustered together, tending wounds and comforting grieving survivors. Around them, mall television screens, cell phone feeds, and emergency broadcast systems revealed the fate of the world. The bleak dawn of understanding settled onto them. Loved ones at home were likely dead. And any who had fled the mall to take their chances outside would soon be dead as well. A collective storm of panic swelled within the remaining mall patrons. Then, like Moses on the mount, Reverend Elias Tucker climbed onto the mall stage at center court and delivered a message of hope and guidance.

"The Devil has raised his demons to penetrate our world, brothers and sisters," Reverend Tucker thundered, his voice bouncing off the glass and tile. "We are witnessing a possession the likes of which God's faithful have never seen. But fear not, for your Heavenly Father has upheld you." His arms raised upward and out as if encompassing all before him. "Each of us was brought here tonight by Divine intervention. The Gospel of John rings now with new meaning. *In my Father's house are many mansions...*" Tucker's hands pointed across the many storefronts surrounding his new flock. "*I go to prepare a place for you.*" Reverend Tucker's calming voice, filled with unquestionable assurance, set the course for a new world. "Brothers and sisters, God brought us here tonight because He foresaw Satan's uprising. He brought us to the place He has prepared. This citadel shall be our home. Our new Eden. Let us bow our heads in thanks and prayer."

His words delivered calm when it was needed most. By morning, more people arrived—loved ones fortunate enough to be reached and told of the protected city. Then, once cell towers fell, the mall doors sealed permanently, leaving those left outside forced to skirmish for water, food, and first aid. Genna did her best to reach poor James' parents, but no one ever answered. They had known where the Hartley's had gone that dreadful night when the world fell into cataclysmic ruin, and Genna did leave messages about the mall being safe and secure, but they never came. Every day for a week, Genna watched poor James stand at the upper rail looking down on the plaza. His eyes searched every face allowed in. It must have seemed like the animals boarding Noah's ark in twos from his young perspective, but his parents were never among them. Corbin and Genna Hartley knew James was their son now, and at least he and Colin had each other.

Now, nearly a year later, the Hartley family—primarily Genna—managed one of the quieter shops in the mall: a boutique for high-end women's dresses. With little need for such refinement, she rarely had any "sales."

As Corbin neared his family's "store" after the council meeting, he passed by the book depository Martha Lowell ran. Martha appeared rather busy boxing things up, which was unusual considering that normally everyone's job was putting out new items brought in by Searchers.

He stopped to inquire out of random curiosity. "Good afternoon, Martha. You look like a woman on a mission."

"Mission?" she repeated, tightening the silver bun at the back of her head.

"I saw the books being packed up and thought maybe they are finally moving you to a larger space?"

Her expression turned sour. "Most of what they bring back is filth," she hissed disapprovingly. "Romance novels, murder stories, and then there are the even worse ones. Some of them were already here when this was a real bookstore."

"Worse books?" Corbin asked.

Martha cringed as if the words themselves disgusted her. "You know what I mean. Books for or about homosexuals. Race-baiting stories meant to make us regular folks feel guilty for things that happened 200 years before we were born." Martha was a severe woman on a good day. Her weathered face, etched deep with frown lines, crow's feet, and furrowed crevices above the brow, looked as if her entire life had been lived in one frozen expression of condescension.

Corbin's stomach often knotted at her open disdain for much of the written word. He wondered why she'd even volunteered to oversee the community's reading material until he realized she'd quietly positioned herself as *decency czar*. The attorney in him took umbrage at any kind of censorship. Politically, Corbin always considered himself a conservative man. He had his own gripes over society's push toward liberal agendas, but erasing history and silencing marginalized voices had never seemed to him to be moral guardianship, but unconstitutional tyranny.

"And this?" he said, lifting a copy of *The Diary of Anne Frank* from the box Martha was packing. "I remember this being required reading when I was a boy."

With a disapproving look and biting tone, she remarked. "That was struck from libraries long before the devil took over the world. It's about Jews, and we have no Jews here. This is a Christian colony."

He left the subject, as well as the store and its warden, alone, continuing his way to the store Genna ran. He found his wife sitting in the chair she'd taken from the Sears home furnishing department, working a crossword from a book of puzzles she'd undoubtedly gotten from next door. Corbin kissed her cheek as she looked up. "Slow day?" he asked.

"Always is," she smiled. "Nobody wears dresses anymore except for Sunday service."

"Maybe you should run a sale!" he teased.

"How do you have a sale when everything is free in the first place?" Genna laughed.

"Fair point."

Genna gave him a peck on the cheek as she left him to close the store. She had her Tuesday night prayer group to get to at the other end of the mall. Corbin wanted to tell her what the note from the sky said but knew he couldn't. And she would never ask. Genna was accustomed to most council business being private. If there was one thing she knew the committee enjoyed, it was deciding what was best for the entire group without bothering to ask them personally. It didn't bother her. She had everything she required for their little life in the Galleria.

Corbin had known since the day he proposed to her that Genna was a perfect spouse for him. She'd been right at his side, helping him through law school, then cheering him from home as he climbed the corporate ladder. As a mother, she never complained about his workload or inability to help as much as fathers with less demanding careers might. When it came to routine socializing, she was a poised, charming wife who never once gave him any reason to be embarrassed the way some of their friends' wine-swilling wives could. She was extremely active in the community, spearheading charities and various fundraisers. In business-related environments, Genna operated as the perfect partner, talking up her husband's strengths, finding opportunities in his weaknesses, and leaving clients and law partners charmed and bedazzled. But it was when the world collapsed that Corbin Hartley understood, without a doubt, he'd placed his ring on the right finger. Genna had proven herself worthy more than once, sometimes causing him to consider if perhaps he was worthy enough of her.

"We need to be thankful each day, Corbin," she'd reminded him at the beginning. "We are so lucky to be alive and safe here. It could have so easily been us out there receiving the fate that poor James' parents got. But we were here, and we made it!"

Then, when he worried this new life was such a letdown from the whirlwind of activity and bounty they'd once had, Genna surprised him again. "Are you kidding me?" she'd laughed. "Don't misunderstand, Corbin. You provided us with a glorious life before we came here. But I don't miss it at all. All the obligations. All the dinner parties to woo and appease clients. The inner office in-fighting with your colleagues. Those long court cases occupied your every waking minute. You, me, and the boys have so much time together now. I really am very happy, as crazy as that must sound."

And then there was James. Corbin had fallen in love with his wife many times throughout their marriage, but none was as strong as the night he found her at their son's friend's bedside, holding him in her arms. "You cry as much as you want over your parents, James," she'd said without knowing Corbin was in the door. "But cry for them because they were wonderful people you will miss. Do not cry because you are afraid you are alone. I can never replace your real mom in your heart, but you will always be my son in mine."

***

Dorothy Maxwell had gone in the opposite direction when she parted from Corbin after the council meeting. As she walked through the mall, she passed by the Tool Center, where her sister's family worked. Leslie was not on duty, but her son Scotty was and looking every bit as energetic as a robot with a low battery. The open can of mineral spirits on the table was overpowering, but at least it masked the usual odor of rusted metal and dirt.

"Well, you look thrilled with your work," his aunt remarked.

Scotty was fifteen years old, lanky, with sandy blonde hair and a pale-yellow t-shirt. He answered his aunt's comment with a weary groan while scrubbing at a socket wrench with an oily rag. "I hate this job. The only good part is I get a little high from the fumes."

Dorothy chuckled, "Yes, in the old days I would never have expected you to be de-rusting tools for a career." She glanced around the shop. "Where's your mom?"

"Where else?" he muttered. "It's Tuesday."

"Ah yes, the grief group."

Scotty gave an exaggerated groan. "As if she grieves anything. She only goes there so she can recline back on all that designer furniture!"

Dorothy squinted at him with disapproval. "Now Scotty, she lost people too. I'm sure she had friends. Besides, it's a prayer group, and Leslie loves a prayer group."

He threw his head back against his neck and groaned in frustration. "I am so sick of this place! You can't walk three feet without somebody praying. It's like they've all just drowned in the blood of the lamb!"

Dorothy twisted the laugh overtaking her face into a sympathetic frown. "You shouldn't say such things. But listen, I know all this is tiresome, Scotty. At least your mom has found something to do in a world where none of us have anything to do."

"I hate it all so much, Aunt Dottie."

She checked over her shoulder, making sure no one passing through the mall overheard. "I know. So do I, but this is what we've got, honey." She tried to smile. "Beats being killed outside."

"That's...subjective," he muttered with an eye roll. He had eyes far older than his age. Eyes that carried a depth his parents didn't. "I wouldn't mind taking my chances out there. Anything is better than this. And tonight is *Asian Wok* night. I'm so sick of noodles."

She patted his hand in solidarity but assured him they were the lucky ones out of Earth's survivors. Safe, fed, and with friends and family around.

"For you, maybe," he argued. "It's not just the food. It's...everything. These forced daily prayer meetings. Wednesday and Sunday mandatory church. Me having to clean tools, loan tools, inventory tools. Aunt Dottie, I don't even know what half these things are for!"

"I know this has been difficult for you, Scotty. I wish it weren't so... in opposition to your interests."

Dorothy had always been a freethinker, and because of that, she'd been considered somewhat of a black sheep in her family. Though in youth, she'd had a few romances with men, she had never met a man she deemed husband-worthy. She had made her own way, and it had been a successful way indeed. Not that it stood for much anymore. But despite all her rebellious thinking, Dorothy was also pragmatic. This society did not look generously upon nonconformists, which was why she'd hidden herself among them as a council member, taking tiny strides for advancing conditions in the colony, but ruffling no feathers. Of course, so far, her largest contribution to progress was convincing the council to allow a woman into a Searcher role. It had been a huge win for women in the colony...until that woman never made it back.

"You've seen Gavin again, haven't you?" she guessed from his present return to dissatisfaction.

Scotty set aside his work, his face brightening. "Last night."

Dorothy's eyes widened with concern. "How did you sneak out? The

Moral Police don't play around!" She remarked, using the nickname uttered only by the more careful colonists. It referred to the Safety Guards stationed each night in the hallways of the hotel; their real purpose was to hold everyone accountable and to dissuade unmarried colonists from sinful rendezvous in the night.

Scotty smirked, folding his arms together with pride over his brilliant solution to the problem. "Didn't you hear? The sink pipe broke in Renee's bathroom." He seemed very delighted with himself as he noted with a wink, "I do know what *some* of these tools can do."

Dorothy stifled her impressed grin. "*That's* why you gave her your room! Your room was between hers and your parents."

Scotty laughed, "Which meant I needed a new room assignment?"

"Let me guess," Dorothy replied. "The third floor had a vacancy. But that still doesn't explain how you can evade the guards."

"Oh, but it does!" her nephew winked mischievously. "The room next to Gavin was empty and shares a connecting door with his."

Placing her loving hand on Scotty's shoulder, Dorothy cautioned him to be careful. "You know how your parents feel about homosexuals. You've been able to stay off their radar so far. And now...here..." she looked out of the store to the greater mall beyond. "With Reverend Tucker and his scaremongering sermons on how all this is demonic aggression..."

"I know. And Gavin knows." Scotty assured her. "Everyone here is so embroiled in righteousness...so afraid of the devil...they'd *kill us* if they found out. We are very careful. Most people don't even think we know each other."

* * *

A year ago, some women would have been too intimidated to enter the Slate & Frame furniture store. If the ultra-modern sleek style of the products didn't make them feel unworthy, the accompanying top dollar price tags would have. Of course, that was then. Now, women from all walks of life came in every Tuesday night for a grief prayer and support group. The showroom where designer labels such as Urban Luxe, Cassina, Muuto, and Roche Bobois once stunned the visual senses was now simply a gathering place for those Galleria colonists still mourning the loved one's lost to the end times.

Sofas, chairs, chaise lounges, and ottomans which only the wealthiest could have afforded, existed now as mere places to sit rather than the artistic pieces of home décor they once had been. The end of the world turned out to be the great leveler. Fine furniture didn't feed the hungry. It couldn't fortify weak spots in a barricade. And if anyone happened to still have a home of their own, they certainly had no visitors to coax envy from. The end times had leveled many areas of life, including trauma.

Whether rich or poor before it all fell to ruin, everyone was seemingly equal now, and everyone had experienced great losses. It was for this reason that Linda Collins and Genna Hartley started this support group, to help others cope with all the world had taken from them. No one ever declared that the meetings were specifically catered to women, but women were all who ever attended. Men knew how to handle any residual sadness stemming from loss. They didn't require talking openly about it. At least that was the general assumption since no man ever strolled down to Slate & Frame Tuesday nights.

"How is everyone feeling this week?" Linda started off by asking. "I know last week was rough on you, dear Jennie. I hope things got a little better."

A younger woman, early thirties nodded. "I appreciate you praying with me, Mrs. Collins. It really helped. And Reverend Tucker stopped by a couple of times as well. I appreciate you sending him to me. It seems so silly for such an insignificant thing to set me off again." Jennie glanced around at the other ladies, an embarrassed smile on her lips. "Of all things, for my brother-in-law's birthday to trigger me to break down after so many months."

Genna Hartley, who was sitting next to her, placed her hand on Jennie's knee. "It isn't silly at all," she told her. "Your brother-in-law's birthday reminded you of him, which naturally reminds you of your husband. It has only been eight months since he was killed on his Strike Force tour. Give yourself permission to mourn him whenever the loss hits you again."

"And it is a loss we all share with you, Jennie," Leslie McNab said. "He was out there hunting those evil savages, trying to make things safer for all of us." She then couldn't help herself from adding, "I pray every night that when my Joe heads out on his upcoming tour that God will bring him back to me safe and sound."

The members of the group voiced their shared hope for the safety of Leslie's husband, as they did for all the men who ventured out when it was their time. Leslie enjoyed the nods her way in appreciation for her Joe's upcoming bravery. It never dawned on her she'd just stolen focus from Jennie's actual grief, not to mention that by saying she hoped God would bring Joe home safe again, hinted at possibly Jennie's deceased husband might have purposefully been knocked off by the Lord.

Ever the diplomat's wife, Linda Collins took back charge of the conversational direction, addressing the group, "I feel it is important that we all, not only Jennie, give ourselves permission to live in our sorrow when it strikes us, for only by allowing it to be heard can it begin to soften some of the pain."

"That's what I keep telling James," Genna replied. "He has processed the loss of his family, but sometimes I still think a part of him holds onto hope they will show up at our door one day. It holds him back from fully letting his grief out."

"I'd say that's probably to be expected," remarked a woman seated across the room. "Most of us here in this group physically witnessed the deaths of our loved ones. Your young adopted son did not. He was here, in this very mall with your family. A part of him must still live in a fantasy where the world is as it was outside, and his parents are at home as he remembers them."

Martha Lowell, a typical sour woman on a good day, chimed in. "I know one thing for sure, that boy is certainly fortunate to have been with your family that night Genna. Otherwise, he'd have met the same grisly fate." Her pauses were usually followed up by veiled criticism or a sort of friction-laced insinuation. This would be no different now. "That boy isn't acting out with you is he? I'd think he'd be thanking the Lord under every breath that he has you and Corbin."

Genna maintained her smile as she tossed water on her storefront neighbor's incendiary spark. "No, Martha, James is a kind and courteous boy. In fact, I suspect sometimes that what he perceives as sadness over his parents is really guilt over how smoothly he has blended in with us."

Linda steered the conversation into another lane, digging into other types of reflection that correlated well with her planned prayer exercises for the night. "All of us have lost someone in life, even well before this dark age we've entered. Some of us lost our parents to old age. Some had friends who unexpectedly died." Linda then pushed into more personal territory. "Franklin and I lost a son many years ago. His birthday is coming up," she smiled at Jennie. "We all have our triggers."

The mayor's wife opened her Bible, signaling the others to do the same. "After the clock ran out for Earth, and the Devil's hand of death reached up through the cracks, there is not one of us who hasn't felt the pain of losing nearly everyone we know. So, tonight, I want us to spend time thinking quietly to ourselves about those we lost, who perhaps didn't leave a lasting anguish. Neighbors. Co-workers. Physicians. The person who groomed your dog. The kind lady working the checkout counter at the market. Loss is larger than only the ones that broke our hearts." Linda opened her Bible. She didn't instruct the others to turn to a passage or scripture. Instead, she said, "Place your hand on a page. Any page. Close your eyes and picture one of those acquaintances from the sea of friendly faces who once filled the background of our lived days. Let us bow our heads and pray for the peace of those individuals. Then flip the page and do it for the next who comes to mind. With each page, let's honor the nearly forgotten smiles of those we didn't know well, but who leave a space by their absence."

This was what Genna liked best in this new community—this new world...this Ark, as Reverend Tucker called it. The unexpected generosity of love that her old life lacked. Thinking back on it now, there were so many individuals who helped brighten her days back then. She found herself recalling forgotten moments of small conversations, cheery waves from joggers running by her kitchen window, kind office workers who always remembered her name and asked how big her son was getting. Many times, it had been those interactions that had helped her through a bad day. It was nice to pray now for those people's peace.

Several seats over, Leslie followed instructions, enjoying this unique exercise in mindfulness. Praying for people she barely knew had never occurred to her until now. Linda Collins was a role model for Leslie. She hoped to be more like her in time. Every few seconds, Leslie peeked out to see how far Linda had gone in her Bible. How many pages had she turned? She checked the other women around her too, each one concentrated in prayer. But Leslie's hand stopped after a couple of pages. She strained to bring someone else to mind. Anyone. But no face appeared in her thoughts. *I didn't ever run across as many nice people as they did,* she thought. *But I guess people are nicer to you when you're rich.*

CHAPTER 22

WHAT DOES IT ALL MEAN?

The light flickering across the arcade in neon was a sickly sweet cocktail of fuchsia, lime green, orange, and hot pink. It stretched the shadows of the abandoned games around the two boys huddled together in the corner. The games, once portals to recreation and digital distraction, now stood like silent sentinels in the near dark of the arcade. Colin Hartley and his friend James Whitlock often came into the Dave & Busters to get away on their own—the last place where they remembered truly being children. They didn't remember the lights being as unstable back when the place was an active gaming haven for kids. Then again, none of the lights in the mall were very reliable these days. But the arcade was still a refuge, no matter how changed. The large game center was by no means dark, and the games still worked as long as only one or two ran at a time. Of course, it wasn't the same as it used to be when a cacophony of digital tunes, ringing score bells, and hi-ho sounds of "game over" had filled the air.

Besides the epileptic lights around the perimeter, the air hung low with the haunting scent of stale pizza, chicken wings, and fries, mixed with the nauseating odor of old oil, none of which was around anymore, but all of which left their imprint in the carpet fibers long ago. There were a few other imprints staining the carpet in a few places too, bloodstains. It was a memory the boys never shed and one forever tainting the anniversary of Colin's birth. He could never quite process the knowledge that another entire family who'd been in the arcade with them, as well as the manager who had murdered them, all died on his birthday. As for that, it was likely James' parents had as well. In fact, most of the world all died on Colin Hartley's birthday. Somehow, he rather hoped that when it rolled around again in a few days, they could avoid commemorating it altogether.

Colin and James sat against the wall with their knees tucked towards them, talking now while Colin absently played with one of the stray medallions that operated the games. His fingers were rolling it back and forth on its edge into the grooves of the worn floor covering while James chewed nervously on a chipped fingernail. He knew if he continued pulling at the nail with his teeth, it was going to tear to the quick and hurt for a couple of days, but he couldn't leave it alone. It was much the way the boys couldn't leave alone the subject they discussed, despite the painful thoughts it dredged up.

"I don't know," Colin said to his friend, sweeping a tuft of his almost white blonde hair from his eyes as his other hand stayed with the coin. "Reverend Tucker says they're demons, and I heard my mom say it a few times."

Worry nearly always shadowed James's bright young eyes, but it was even more noticeable now. "Doesn't it scare you?" he asked Colin. "How can people stop demons from getting in here?" James looked anxiously at his pal. "I mean, *they're demons!*"

Colin shrugged his shoulders, his finger almost shifting off the edge of the coin as he circled it around the swirl in the carpet. "They haven't gotten in so far. Maybe it's like the preacher says, we're all good. We got the Lord in our hearts, so He protects us in here."

James rested his chin on his propped knee, staring at the floor. "What does that even feel like? How do we know God is in our hearts when my heart doesn't feel any different than it used to?"

The coin got away from Colin, rolling out of his fingers and behind the old Dig Dug game. He crawled over to it, stretching out on his belly so his flattened hand could slide under the machine to retrieve it. "I don't know either," he told James. "It's like how we're all Saved. I don't know what that is supposed to feel like."

"Weren't you Saved in church that time? I was there. Then you got baptized."

"Maybe," Colin answered. "I dunno. I remember wondering when I was supposed to feel God saving me, but nothing ever felt different. But my mom and dad and grandmother all kept talking about how God would save me one day...so...I just went up to the front of the church like I'd seen other kids do. Reverend Tucker was our preacher then too, and he patted me on the back and said the Lord saved me, and then we prayed."

"Then are you saved?" James asked.

"Sure, I am!" Colin exclaimed as if the very question was ridiculous. "I'm here and I'm alive. No demon got me, so I must be saved. You are too probably."

A beat of silence passed between them a few minutes before James spoke again. "My parents were good people," he began. "We went to church every Sunday just like your family. But why couldn't we find them? Nobody answered their phones. If the demons got them, does that mean they were sinners?"

Colin sat back up, looking at his friend and knowing he was trying to keep from crying. "Hey, man. I think your mom and dad were really nice. Demons may have killed them. I don't think they were part of those people who turned into demons."

"You don't?"

"No," Colin exclaimed. "My grandmother was good too. I think she got killed, but I know she didn't change into a demon."

"Yeah, but everybody is saying God is punishing the wicked out there."

Colin leaned back against the racing game, still on and still sounding its tiresome little melody. He reached behind him and flipped the switch to OFF. "The devil sent his evil angels up here to possess and kill people who weren't Christians. Your parents were. That means if they got killed, they must be in Heaven now."

Rising to his feet, Colin extended his hand down to James, pulling him up from the floor. It was time for them to get back. Nobody was supposed to come into the arcade on Sundays, and they'd lied to Colin's parents about where they were going. But it was getting late, and they had to get back to their hotel room before the watchguards took their positions in the hallways.

* * *

Across the mall's dim alleyway, two older boys followed the people ahead of them towards the hotel. Scotty McNab and Gavin Tanner moved in tandem yet kept a wide enough distance from each other to give the impression they were not together as they strolled into the lobby. They took careful pains not to make eye contact when they mingled into the population trickling into their lodgings for the night.

Scotty slowed when he saw his parents—Joe and Leslie McNab— seated on one of the lobby's worn couches. His father was deep in conversation with another man, Ben Noland. Ben was an ex-marine and built like a military tank himself. He towered over most men at six and a half feet tall, with a broad chest and arms like men in those muscle videos Scotty used to watch online before online stopped existing. Scotty joined his family with practiced nonchalance, as his eyes trailed after Gavin, who disappeared through the stairwell door by the elevators. Joe's voice pulled Scotty's attention back to his family.

Joe McNab was doing his best to appear formidable; almost on his toes with his shoulders reared back so that his chest looked more pronounced while he talked with Ben Noland. It took only a few seconds for Scotty to understand why his father was presenting his most imposing self. The men were discussing their upcoming tour with the Strike Force.

Tour was what the men called it. Four men on a one-week stint outside the walls hunting demons, reclaiming territory. It could be a death sentence or a hero's odyssey. And Joe and Ben's names were among the next to go tomorrow.

"Man, I've been waiting for this!" Joe said much too enthusiastically to the ex-marine. "Time to show those devils they shoulda never climbed up to the surface."

"Well, we get our chance in the morning." Ben said, slapping Joe's shoulder firmly.

Scotty noticed his father wince as the powerful hand made contact. Scotty noticed something else as well and had for the weeks leading to this...his dad was petrified. It was nothing Joe showed by any means. His wife and young daughter wouldn't have picked up on it, both brimming with certainty that this was the day he'd been counting down to. Scotty was sure of it too, but not in the way they believed. He could see the fear hiding in the backs of Joe's eyes. Only another male who has lived in equal fear could ever recognize it. Scotty had spent every day of his life in such fear. Fear of being found out. It was a minor comfort to know even his father could be a coward on the inside sometimes.

The alphabetical lottery pulling the McNab name to the front was responsible for the extra dose of theatrics to Joe's normal swagger, and his son saw right through it. It was the same sort of camouflage Scotty sometimes exhibited himself when caught in the company of his father and other men like him. He'd spit in a planter or spread his feet a little wider than his normal stride when he walked. It didn't matter the affectations one improvised to conceal their truth; it was all the same act.

Joe wasn't in the minority when it came to trying to impress Ben Noland. It'd been that way since Ben, and his wife Stacie had shown up at the mall door a month after it had been sealed tight. Ben's brawn, when viewed over the security camera at the door, was the only reason he and Stacie were permitted in. Mayor Collins knew just the sight of Ben walking through the mall plaza would instill a sense of safety for the colonists. After all, he had survived outside for a full month. Having him join the Galleria could only boost morale. Mall rules stated newcomers must pass a kind of test before being admitted to the settlement, but somehow Scotty doubted they asked Ben to take any tests.

Personally, Ben was too much of a man for Scotty's comfort. The teenager avoided Mr. Noland as often as possible because he feared the marine could smell Scotty's gayness from 20 yards away. Stacie Noland had been nice though. Scotty remembered liking her a lot. She wasn't like her husband and had obviously been a compassionate person because once she'd caught Scotty and Gavin kissing in the Sears lawn care department and never told a soul. She'd promised she wouldn't when she'd wandered in and seen them. The boys had felt safe meeting up there as it was one of the few areas in the mall that hadn't been stripped of its supplies. In a civilization living inside a shopping center, how often could the need for a lawnmower come up? Gavin and Scotty had secluded away in this forgotten corner of a practically emptied anchor store for weeks without a single disturbance.

But Stacie had walked in mid-kiss on them. The boys felt certain she would out them to their parents, or at the very least tell her husband. But a full day went by, and she didn't. Two days went by, and still no trouble. Sunday came, and she barely made eye contact with either of them, proving her word was golden when she gave it. Sadly, Scotty and Gavin's secret ally didn't survive long in the colony. Much to the chagrin of her husband, Stacie lobbied the council to let her be a Searcher, basing her argument on having survived on instinct and skill before finding the colony. It was a blow to all when the mall's first and only female Searcher died during her first outing when a band of demons cornered her in an abandoned market. Ben Noland hadn't been the same after, and demanded no other woman ever be permitted outside the walls again.

* * *

As the colonists continued making their way upstairs to the second and third floors of the hotel, Joe, still upselling his bravado over his tour of duty in the morning, turned to his son and exclaimed, "This time tomorrow night I bet I'll have sent twenty or more of those things back to the fiery hell they belong." Mimicking Ben's earlier shoulder slap, Joe passed it along to Scotty. "Bet you wish the council didn't have that 18-year-old rule, don't ya boy? It'd be me and you out there showing 'em what we're made of."

Forcing a smile as his family looked at him, Scotty said, "Yeah, Dad. We sure would."

On the second floor, Scotty's family split off from him through the hall door to go to their rooms, his aunt Dorothy shooting him a brief, amused look. Scotty continued up two more flights to his new floor. The separation from his family's quarters had been a much-needed reprieve from their constant scrutiny. There was peace in those few hours now away from their suffocating expectations, a peace which he hadn't even realized he needed.

* * *

The pale apricot paint on the hotel room walls had peeled near the top corners where it met the ceiling. Scotty was on the bed when Gavin slipped through the connecting door from his room, locking Scotty's side behind him. Gavin moved to the bed with a satisfied smile, then straddled Scotty's lap, kissing him with the kind of fierce passion only young love ignites. Scotty happily gave in to the kiss, pausing only to swipe back Gavin's bangs falling between them.

It was an intense passion they shared, made more pronounced by raging hormones and the excitement of a clandestine rendezvous. By day, they were forced to play strangers—at best, acquaintances. During meals when their families sat only yards apart in the food court, Scotty and Gavin learned to sit with their backs facing, both knowing theirs was a passion they could not conceal.

"It is so hard to see you across the mall court at church when you're dressed up in your tight blue suit." Scotty teased, kissing Gavin's neck. "You wear those tight pants just to drive me crazy."

Gavin laughed, unable to fuel the fantasy. "No, I wear them because we live in an apocalypse, and all the other available pants were too big."

"Well, I enjoy it anyway."

"My dad almost caught me looking at you," Gavin warned. "We have to be careful."

"Yeah, and I got a weird look from Ms. Lowell?" Scotty admitted. "Reverend Tucker was ranting about Satan opening the gates of Hell to slaughter the wicked, and that bitch turned and looked right at me!"

Gavin seemed nervous at the admission. "That hateful woman at the bookstore? Why? Does she know?"

"That I'm gay? I don't know," Scotty replied. "I think she did it because I asked if there were any John Grisham books. She tried to give me a new Bible instead."

"What did you say?"

"I told her I have one. Read it. Prefer John Grisham." Scotty answered.

They both burst into laughter, but Gavin swiftly regained composure to warn him. "You can't keep pushing like that, Scotty. If anybody thinks you're a blasphemer, or begins to suspect us..."

"I know, I know. They will put us out, and we'll be dead out there before the sun even sets."

"Or..." Gavin cautioned with a chilling reply. "They'll just kill us inside here. Reverend Tucker, the mayor, and even our folks...they really believe people like us are why the world ended. They'll kill us, Scotty."

"Maybe we are supposed to be outside," Scotty commented. "What if we are part of the wicked God is punishing? I don't feel evil, not just because I love you. But if everybody else believes it, and the world *did end*...is that supposed to have been us too?"

Gavin was shocked to hear such a thought out of Scotty's mouth. "You can't really think that?"

Scotty raised his hands in confusion. "Everybody says people like us are evil. Deceived. Lured to the devil." His eyes seemed truly troubled as his young mind did what it could to make sense of the truths he'd been raised by. "I don't feel wicked. I still love God. But I love you too. I don't see how love is a bad thing."

"It isn't, baby," Gavin wept, kissing Scotty's cheek. "God made us this way, and just because they don't understand why He did, doesn't mean it's us who are wrong. I don't understand why we have mosquitoes, but they exist, and they aren't evil."

"I don't know," Scotty grinned. "I really hated mosquitoes."

Scotty plopped back onto the mattress, folding his hands behind his head as he stared up towards Heaven. "I hate feeling like something is wrong with me," he confessed. "I used to try to pray it away. Then, when everything went crazy and we were all in this place, everybody talked about how God saved us all by leading us to this mall. But inside, I felt like He'd made a mistake and didn't notice I was here too."

Gavin lay down against him, gently running his fingers along Scotty's forearm. "Then you saw me," he picked up. "And..."

Scotty grinned, wrapping his arms around him. "And I just didn't see how God could make *two mistakes*."

"Because He wanted us both here together, Scotty. I believe that."

"How?" Scotty asked. "It's making me question if God was ever real. I mean…if I love God, I can't be evil. But if I love you, I can't be right with God. So maybe God is a fairy tale they have lied to us and themselves about."

Gavin sat up, taking his boyfriend's face in his hands to stare right in his eyes. "Or… God is real, Scotty. And they are the ones disappointing Him because they won't accept some of His children all because they don't understand our purpose. Personally, I don't think God makes mistakes, and I know I don't have the devil in my heart. That pretty much proves it's them who are wrong, not us."

"I dunno," Scotty shrugged. "Maybe you're right."

Gavin pulled Scotty into his lap, staring down at him with tears welling up in his eyes. "Don't question your faith, Scotty. Don't make yourself believe you are bad just because they say you are."

Scotty laughed a second. "Maybe you're right. My dad is a bigoted idiot anyway, and I've always known that. He'd be just as outraged if he found me in bed with a black girl."

"Speaking of being in bed with me," Gavin said with a sexy smile. "Why are we talking?"

Scotty grinned, lifting Gavin's chin to meet his lips as he slowly stroked Gavin's soft face with his hand. Flinching, Gavin pulled Scotty's hand away, staring into it. "You have calluses. That scratched. Please file those things down or never give me a handjob."

They both burst into laughter, muffling the sound with pillows. In that fleeting moment, all the fear and fire of the outside world melted away. Inside the cracked walls of a forgotten hotel room, they were simply two boys in love—fragile, resilient, hopeful.

"What if we left?" Gavin asked suddenly in all seriousness.

Scotty sat up. "Are you serious? I've never heard you speak like that before. *Me*, yes. *You*, no."

"If it comes to it," Gavin vowed. "I will face down the demons of Hell to stay with you."

CHAPTER 23

TOUR OF DUTY

As the sun began its afternoon descent, the mall was buzzing with excitement. It was time for another tour of duty. Time when men ventured outside to hunt and kill the demons plaguing the earth. Most of the Galleria citizens turned out for the procession—an increasingly patriotic occasion. People working in upper-level shops lined the railings while those on the first floor stood shoulder-to-shoulder on each side of the plaza. The brave men began the long walk in what might have been a military parade of decorated war heroes for all the pomp and circumstance involved. Joe McNab, Ben Noland, Marcus Nabors, and Curtis Jackson accepted the cheers and hurrahs as they marched towards the mall exit where the mayor awaited. Clad in makeshift combat gear: cargo pants, army fatigues, multi-pocketed vests, side arms, and ammo slung across their chests. They looked every bit the war soldiers they were pretending to be.

To the mall colonists watching the parade, the four men appeared brave—almost eager to get out and fight. But within each man swelled a dichotomy of emotions. Fear was seeded inside all of them, for even the most courageous man would know missions can go wrong. Ben was the most courageous of them, but lingering underneath that valor was a deeper understanding of what they faced outside. He had, after all, come late to the Galleria. He and his former wife had seen far more beyond those concrete walls than the rest had, and Ben wore that insight in the form of a smirk; like a man possessing secret knowledge none of the others knew. Joe wore a different smirk on his face. One of hubris—the unearned kind—slightly jaundiced by a fear he hoped no one could see. His eyes found his family in the crowd. Leslie clapped proudly, while his children watched with somber faces and forced grins. As his eyes caught Scotty, he felt exposed, almost as if Scotty saw the yellow streak down his back. It made him angry at his son despite having no actual proof Scotty was thinking such things. But Joe was. Marching towards the mayor and the vehicle to leave, Joe knew he would never have received this much fanfare or adoration in his old life. These people revered him now only because their necks depended on his team hunting down as many demons as possible.

Mayor Collins stood at the steel gate, keys in hand as the men climbed into the Jeep idling at the doors. With another quick check at the security camera mounted outside, Collins unlocked the first barrier, the pull-down gate, which guards rolled up into the ceiling. Next, Colins switched on the automatic glass doors, which drew open immediately. Collins unlatched the outer steel doors, which the men slid back quickly. The last barrier no longer existed. These such exits were the few times the mall ever stood vulnerable for a few seconds. The Jeep sped through the opening as guards re-secured each barrier to refortify the colony.

None of the men had been outside in nearly a year and found themselves a little startled by the strangeness of it again. Unfiltered sunlight glared through the windshield at them, striking the forgotten sensation of solar warmth and the need to squint. Birds chirped from passing trees, and a warm summer breeze carried scents of nature. Curtis sneezed in succession several times, having forgotten the effects of pollen. Ben gripped the wheel tightly in his massive hands as his eyes took in the changes now taking him by surprise as he drove off mall property onto the adjoining highway.

He was a man of few words but not few thoughts. The ex-marine did not offer his observations to his comrades, but Ben noticed the changes. *The Chick-fil-A is gone. Looks burned down.* Suddenly the irony struck. *It's a Christian business, even closed Sundays. Of course, the devil breathed his hellfire breath on it.* The scenery passing behind the Jeep's windows was normal, considering. Even though the place looked abandoned, ransacked or torched in places, the landscape wasn't exactly decimated as an end of the world scenario would have brought to mind before one actually happened.

There were some fallen trees occasionally, a few limbs along the roads which Ben had to dodge. It looked like storm damage. It struck him as funny. With hell's gates releasing its wrath on the world, no one had given any thought to weather still occurring. Nature had retaken the earth in little ways. Weeds and stray grass had found their footing in cracked asphalt, where few cars now passed to tamp them down. Occasionally, a discarded vehicle — sometimes several—littered the streets. A random skeleton, or fragments of one, was still visible in some seats or had fallen just outside the open car door. People who had tried to make a run for it and failed.

Along the roadside, makeshift barricades sometimes caught the men's attention. Sheet metal, bars, and, in a few cases, long sharp spikes encircled whatever hovel desperate humans had plucked together to survive within. Occasionally, a human face would look out at the passing Jeep from a slit, crack, or secured window in one of the fortresses.

Beside Ben in the passenger seat, Marcus fidgeted nervously at every hollow storefront. He seemed to expect monsters to ambush the vehicle at any moment, and he might have been right. There were many suspicious dwellings around, but Ben felt confident he could maneuver through any attack the hellspawn might wage. As the Jeep drove into more residential areas, where remnants of apartment buildings stood like eyeless ghosts with their shattered windows, the visuals grew more gruesome. Stray bodies lay bloated across medians or just outside their former homes, all in varying states of decomposition. The putrid odor of rotting flesh or muscle tissue still clinging to some bones seeped through the vehicle's air vents, nauseating the men. Smears of dried blood coated sections of the road where human beings hadn't made it in their escape attempt. Ben didn't alert the others to what his war-experienced eyes picked up. Some patches of dried blood clung not merely to the ground but to the tops of high weeds overtaking the street. That meant the kills were fresher than the decaying corpses suggested.

None of them, not even Ben, had served on the Strike Force before now. Their only understanding of it came from the men before them who had survived. The actual experience was proving far more unnerving than the tales.

"How do we know where to look?" Marcus asked, attempting to sound more casual than his voice conveyed.

Joe spoke up from the back seat beside Curtis. "Mayor briefed us on the places the Searchers hit for food, clothes, and medicine. I guess any place that ain't those."

"And let's not forget that the mayor also said if we discover a new resource for the Searchers, we should make note of it." reminded Curtis.

"Just keep your eyes peeled, boys." Ben advised. "What we've learned from the men on tour before us is this is the time of day those devils go back to their hiding places. If we can spot one and follow it, it'll lead us to their nest."

Ben Noland did not seem afraid. Maybe that was the Marine in him, or maybe he was better at closing off his emotions. But Joe admired him for it. Curtis and Marcus were practically shaking with fear, and

Joe wondered what Ben must be thinking of them. Joe was frightened too, but knew he was doing a much better job of not showing it. To a man like Joe McNab, fear was something shameful. He'd never backed down from a fight in school, never held his tongue when he felt he was right, no matter who he was arguing with. Joe was determined that once this tour was over, his teammates would only tell stories about how fearless he had been. One of his biggest fears about his son was that Scotty seemed weak. Joe always planned to force him to join up with the military when he turned 18—make a man out of Scotty. But now...maybe Strike Force could do that for him one day.

"Look over there, Ben!" Joe cried, pointing at the novelty sex shop down the hill in a strip mall. The sign said *Love Stuff*.

"You see one going in there?" Ben asked from behind the wheel.

"No," Joe answered, "But if there's one place a disciple of Satan would go, it'd be a damn sex shop. Let's try there."

They all knew the place, although none of them had ever been inside. When it opened a couple of decades ago, there was quite a stir in town. Churches spoke out at city council meetings; Sunday School groups wrote protest letters and led demonstrations by the roadside, shaming the store and its customers. However, it didn't close, and society did not fail just because the adult store opened. In fact, many of those very protesters became customers in the ensuing years; their once indignant aversions caved as it became a fun boutique for gag gifts at bachelorette parties. Ben turned onto the access road to the specialty shop. The men got out, all mimicking Ben's bravery, who, every inch the soldier, slung his rifle over his arm and strolled towards the door. The others followed with their firearms ready.

The bell over the door jingled as the men came in, startling them a little, as it had been a very long time since they'd walked into a store with a bell. *Love Stuff* appeared unpilfered upon entering, which seemed logical—after all, it wasn't a destination one would go to for life-sustaining supplies. The men's eyes quickly went to the two mannequins on podiums at the front of the store.

"What in the name of decency..." Joe groaned, as his eyes locked on the male figure.

The male mannequin was naked except for a red leather harness strapped across his chest and a matching red jockstrap. Joe blushed with secondhand shame at the thought of a man having so little pride in himself that he would wear something like that. His gaze drifted to its female counterpart. The lady mannequin wore a tiny red G-string bottom and a leather corset with holes for the nipples to poke out from.

"Well, this one, though..." Joe remarked with a gregarious laugh. "I wouldn't mind seeing this walking around...on the right woman, that is."

Ben grunted in response, but Joe couldn't tell if it was one of approval or one of condemnation and not knowing made him feel embarrassed for saying anything. Joe moved slowly through the racks and shelves of dusty erotic toys and risqué lingerie, touching nothing, as if the very action would stain his soul by association.

Curtis and Marcus wandered through the aisle, whispering and snickering like teenagers. Lingering a little longer than natural by the erotic toys shelf, Curtis was trying to figure out what the objects were used for, when Marcus gently tapped him, urging him forward.

The men moved forward in relative unison towards the center display counter. Picking up no sign of demonic activity, Marcus called out that they were wasting their time. Curtis let out a playful laugh, commenting, "Well, at least I can say now I saw what one of those sex places looks like. Let's get out of here."

Joe didn't laugh. His eyes locked on Ben, who had paused at the side of the U-shaped counter. Something was off. Joe knew from Ben's stance shift—his hands tight on his rifle—that his skilled combat senses had kicked in. When Joe saw Ben heft the rifle to his shoulder, he followed suit.

Marcus, being the first to move around the counter, saw it before they did. A staircase shielded behind the display, leading down under the shop. The shout came quickly, erupting from Marcus' lungs, breaking the silence like a siren as three grisly creatures rushed up from their subterranean hiding place into the store. More followed directly behind, surging up the stairs!

"Demons!!!" Ben roared as the muzzle of his gun exploded, spraying shots at the stairs.

The glass countertop exploded against the barrage of bullets tearing into the ascending monsters. Waves of black blood shot from their bodies, splattering against the windowless framework of the counter and dripping down the treads of the basement steps. Ben had taken out the second batch before they reached the top, but the original three were now in the store somewhere, obscured from view behind the tall shelves and mannequins.

Another scream from Marcus filled the air somewhere nearby—out of view—trapped in a corner. One demon had found him. Marcus tried to unholster his gun, but his shaky hands betrayed him as the creature neared. Its scorched red flesh gleamed like molten rock as the vessels running along its outer body pulsated like rivers of black lava. Spikes that resembled stalactites crowned its head, and its eyes flicked like a cobra's. Marcus wedged back against, and into the shelves, pushing its inventory through the back as the hell beast raised its clawed hand.

The movement was quicker than the eye, only evidenced by the warm spurting of Marcus' own blood pouring down his neck into his shirt. His severed vocal cords, no longer capable of sound, struck new panic within him as he recognized he could not survive the wound. The pressure against the shelf gave way under his weight, toppling Marcus backwards. His hands instinctively grasped at anything. A rack of lingerie slammed sideways across him, which he shoved away pointlessly.

Curtis followed the commotion around a mirrored support beam to find Marcus' body choking out its final seconds with delicate lace unmentionables of black, red, and pink stuck to his blood-soaked body.

"Marcus!" he yelled, paralyzed by the sight before him.

"Go!!!" Joe bellowed, emptying his rifle into the monster before it could climb over the debris to get to Marcus.

Joe's frenzied shots covered a wide spread, many missing the creature, riddling surrounding displays, but the volume of his bullets covered the shortfall, mortally wounding the demon and collapsing him half on Marcus and half on the ground. Its dark devil-blood spilled into a macabre spiral with Marcus' like a melting red and black checkerboard.

Joe ran for the exit, shooting blindly behind him in case the other two monsters followed. Ben walked backward to the exit, making sure of his aim. Curtis got out first, rushing to the Jeep to start the engine. One of Joe's untargeted shots clipped a second demon in the hip, slowing its pursuit. Ben's steady control over his own rifle took the beast out with a single headshot, then did the same to its friend closing in behind it.

Retreating from the sex shop, now layered in the sickening scent of spent casings, blood, and synthetic fruit-fragranced lubricant, the two men jumped into the revved Jeep where Curtis peeled away from the deathtrap they'd fallen into.

No one knew where they were going. Perhaps they were merely trying to outrun Marcus' screams echoing in their heads.

* * *

Further down the road, they passed several locations that raised suspicion as other likely dens for the hell monsters, but Curtis didn't stop. The eerie shells of empty gas stations, crumbling warehouses, and abandoned eateries could be checked later. They needed a moment. Up ahead, a burned-out sporting goods store stood as only an open-air charred stick structure, perfectly transparent from front to back. Curtis pulled into the flat, vacant parking lot and stopped the vehicle.

The men got out.

"We gotta be smarter, fellas," Ben warned. "All eyes scanning for any surprises or blind spots. All ears tuned in to any sound not coming from us."

"Ben's right," Joe said. "Things might have gone down differently back there if Marcus hadn't spoken so loud. We've got to assume every place is full of those damn things."

What Curtis had seen and been through had visibly shaken him. He wasn't sure how he could last a solid week like this. But he kept his inner dialogue to himself, knowing there was no choice.

Ben retook the wheel as the Jeep began a slow descent down Highway 31 into the Vestavia Hills district. He hadn't intended to find their next strike immediately after their last disaster. Already, they were down a fourth of their team. But the setup was too perfect to pass up. He eased the vehicle to a crawl so that he could observe what was going on down the hill, below the overpass. A flash of crimson skin broke through the green leaves of the tree limbs in the distance. Two goblins, grotesque and hunched, skulked around a glimmering chrome tank. Behind the tank stood an apartment building. On closer inspection with his binoculars, Ben saw more of the red-skinned monsters weaving in and out of the building, crawling across the balconies like insects nesting in a corpse.

Ben steered onto the exit ramp, circling under the highway, bringing them to a stop in the shadow of concrete pillars under the bridge. Quietly, he motioned for the guys to follow as he stepped to the side of the last support column where he pointed downrange.

"Check that out, boys. See what I see?"

Joe squinted as the setting sun reflected off the chrome tanker in the distance. "Is that a fuel truck?"

"It is," Ben sneered. "Ain't that a gift from the Lord."

Curtis leaned between their shoulders, his distance vision not what it used to be. "That's right beside the building," he commented. "It'd be a suicide mission to try and steal that thing."

Ben shot him a grin over his shoulder. "Who said we're gonna steal it?"

He went back to the Jeep, grabbing his rifle and Joe's, then returned. "Curtis, you keep the Jeep running. Be ready to floor it like you did last time if things go sideways."

Moving with deliberate caution, Ben stepped only on solid earth, avoiding twigs, pinecones, or gravel—anything that might emit a sound beneath his boots. Joe followed his exact footsteps until they both reached a patch of trees and brush where the road turned into the apartment parking lot. They now had a much better view of the complex and a far shorter range to hit.

It was a bustling hive of evil. Dozens of them were now visible in the broken windows, doorways, or stalking around the building.

"No telling how many more are inside we can't see," Joe whispered.

"Probably hundreds," Ben sneered.

"Why would they need a gasoline tanker?"

Ben let out a low grunt. "Keep us from getting it. Gas is a limited resource now. Steal the gas, cut off the enemies' mobility."

A little confused now, Joe asked, "So...we do need to steal that truck?"

"Nope." Ben grinned. "We're gonna blow it up."

Ben gestured for Joe to aim his rifle as he now did, lining the scope to the tank. "One shot, Joe. Directly at the tank. Don't waste ammo. It'll just take one and between the two of us, we should hit it at this range."

The crack of gunfire split the air. There was no time for the enemy to react. The tanker erupted like an atomic blast! A swell of orange and yellow burst upward and outward, the pressure of the explosion lifting the tank several feet before dropping it back down like a firebomb. The shockwave punched the hillside, bouncing back into the men like a physical echo, knocking them off their feet. The fireball roared into the dusky sky, carrying a mushroom of black smoke billowing out over the flame-swallowed apartment building. The torrid blaze surged into and through the structure, engulfing it entirely. The demons who'd been outside scurried wildly, trying to extinguish their fire-coated figures. From within the inferno of the apartment complex, a chorus of howls and high-pitched shrieks rose into a crescendo of unfathomable torment before dying out like a hellish choir finishing the hymn. Within seconds, the cries of incinerating bodies disappeared under the roar of the furnace.

Ben and Joe howled in celebration, high fiving each other as they watched the devouring inferno send the demons back to Hell. Walking back to the Jeep where Curtis stared in astonishment, Ben slapped Joe on the back and declared, "I'd say that was a fine day's work, boys!"

Next on the agenda was finding a secluded location to eat and rest, resuming their mission once the sun was fully down. The original Galleria team—the ones who went out on that very first tour to find and destroy the monsters—had faced overwhelming odds. They had been vastly outnumbered then, but one of their returning team members had lived to tell an important detail. Nighttime was safer.

The demons tended to retreat to their nests after sundown, becoming less active as darkness fell. From that first brutal tour onward, every mission followed the same strategy: move out in the late afternoon, try to find a creature to follow home, and strike under cover of night. Ben's team had been too cavalier when they'd gone into Love Stuff. A rookie mistake and not one they would repeat. The apartment explosion had been the godsend they needed to put their heads back in the game. Now, after a short rest, they'd really get started taking the Lord's world back.

CHAPTER 24

RED MONSTERS

The Galleria Mall colony always adhered to its successful structure of doing things. Everyone had a purpose. Everyone stayed in their lane. So, when Joe McNab suggested to his Strike Force team they should detour to the Walmart on the outskirts of town, Ben Noland reminded him *that's Searcher territory*.

"What if there is ammunition left in their sporting goods department?" Joe argued.

"We have ammunition," Ben countered as he drove the Jeep under the starless night.

Joe dropped the subject, reluctant to say anything further. The last thing he wanted to admit to Ben and Curtis was that he'd lost two boxes of shells. He hadn't even noticed himself until they were a significant distance from the park. He'd been so shaken when they stopped to rest, though he tried to hide it. Not even a day into their tour, they'd already lost Marcus. Joe's mind was reeling. After consuming his meager meal, he sat against a fencepost, closing his eyes to rest his mind and nerves. They all had taken the opportunity for a brief rest. When Ben tapped Joe's shoulder to wake him, Joe had been a little disoriented—it being his first time outside in a year. They hurried back to the Jeep, eager to make a real dent in the population of demon predators. But then five miles away from the park, Joe realized his careless error. An error, he had to admit before his omission endangered one of his teammates' lives.

"When we took our break at the park," he said with a childlike guilt on his face. "I'd pulled a couple of boxes of bullets out of my pockets... to get comfortable..."

"Shit," Ben said, pinching the bridge of his nose. "You left them, didn't you?"

Joe felt humiliated. To make such an amateur mistake in front of a man like Ben—a man's man—was a blunder someone such as Ben would have never made.

"Let's just go back to the park," Curtis suggested.

"No," Ben said. "We'll hit that Walmart. This is a remote part of town. Doubt many survivors have come looking for supplies this far."

The automatic doors, which in better days opened quickly to greet customers, now hung askew, making it impossible for them to retract anymore. What remained was a groaning electronic whine when it tried. The broken glass made for easy entrance despite the off-kilter frames. The three men stepped inside with a crunch of glass under their boots. Dust and pollen drifted under the few fluorescent bulbs still operational, but the broken doors had allowed summer humidity to overtake the place and undoubtedly overworked the A/C system to failure.

Contrary to their earlier assumption, the store had been raided. Whether by humans or the spawn of Hell, they couldn't tell. With guns drawn and their wits about them, the men made their way through the store prepared for combat.

Ben led like a predator; his shoulders squared and braced for action.

Behind him, Joe still felt the sting to his ego over his stupid mistake, but he tried to channel some of Ben's bravery. The smell of mildew and rot filling the space stung his nostrils, but he refused to wince.

Curtis trailed behind; his nerves nearly shattered after seeing the way the demons killed Marcus. Curtis wasn't like the others. Not a fighter. He possessed neither the self-assurance of Ben nor the drive for excellence of Joe. He was out of his depth on this mission and knew it.

Ben whispered to Joe and Curtis. "In and out. Let's get to Sporting Goods, take what we need, and go."

The picked-over condition of the store left little hope there would be ammunition, but they'd come this far, and the answer lay only a few aisles away. Ben's ears picked up on something he couldn't quite decipher. At first, he'd thought it was voices, but that wasn't it.

Overhead fluorescents, dimming from a drain on the power grid, or compromised by humidity, made sizzling noises, clouding the quiet. Whatever Ben thought he heard was coming from across the store in the old grocery section. It might have been people. It could have been animals. Or it was something worse. Every hidden space was a gamble, and if that space was emitting noise, it was a gamble whose odds he needed to know. He signaled his companions to keep going, while he turned, switching direction. With easy, careful strides, Ben moved towards the peculiar sounds echoing from the farthest reaches of the store.

He made his way towards the refrigeration aisle, where the noises grew louder. If it was speech, it was not language as he knew it, but a succession of growls, clicks, and hisses. The language of Hell. There was another sound, just barely audible, like trickling water. As Ben reached the aisle, fresh bloodstains marked a section of glass on the long, short-circuited refrigeration units. Just under that, a streak of blood disappeared around the corner. Again, fresh. Red. Human.

The long wall running next to the aisle had once been the dairy and cold cut section. It was along those shelves that Ben found the root of the trickling sound. Two bullet holes had pierced a jug of rancid milk and a carton of spoiled orange juice, releasing the last thin strands of their contents to the shelf below. This had just happened; otherwise, both containers would have long emptied by now. It must have been right before his team arrived.

Ben flattened himself against the last cooler in his row, his weapon at his shoulder, ready to strike. Whatever was there was one row over from him. Stilling his breath, he made a quick dart of his head into the adjacent aisle before pulling back. Two human bodies lay dead several yards away on the adjacent aisle. Though he still could not see what was on the other side of his row, he knew it had to be demons who'd killed those people. Gearing himself up for a fast approach, Ben was about to act when breaking through the silence rang the inexperienced voice of Curtis Jackson calling out from nearby, "Ben, we found some bullets! Where are you?"

With not a second to spare now, Ben sped onto the connecting aisle and around the corner to the next row where he saw two of the blazoned-skinned devils targeting the sound of Curtis' voice. Ben glimpsed them only for a brief second before they twisted out of sight. He opened fire, clipping one of the swift beasts in its upper back. It howled, but did not fall, stumbling after its partner in pursuit of the dimwitted human stupid enough to announce his presence.

Rounding the corner, Ben saw them closing in on Curtis, who stood frozen, paralyzed by terror, unable to react. In the distance, from the middle of the store, Joe sprinted forward, his pistol aimed and ready if only Curtis would get out of the way. Joe yelled at Curtis, and Ben shouted to both, as the two creatures shrieked to each other in their indecipherable devil tongues.

Ben advanced on them fast, landing another shot into the one he'd wounded, but this time his shot struck the demon in the back of its horned-rimmed head! The impact sent the monster skidding into shelves, raining down loose packages of dried raisins and apricot slices as it tumbled lifelessly to the floor.

The other demon had pounced onto Curtis, who flailed his arms out frantically to defend against the bellowing creature. Joe, still holding his gun up, did not aim it at the demon attacking Curtis, but at Ben. Ben stopped in his tracks when he saw Joe's gun directed at him. Instinctively, Ben raised his own rifle at Joe, but his moment of stunned surprise had stolen valuable seconds. Joe's gun exploded in a wisp of smoke and sparks as a bullet whizzed past Ben's shoulder. A shrill cry sounded just behind him as Ben whirled around to a spurt of blood on his face. The woman behind him, hit in the shoulder by Joe's bullet, fell. Ben's arms reflexively sprang out to catch her. They fell to the ground together, her head smacking with force against the hard store floor.

Her dazed eyes appeared panicked as her lips curled into a scream. "Dasha!!!!!"

Doe fought against the blue-skinned alien, but her head was spinning. The shock of the bullet or the sustained blow to her head was sliding her into unconsciousness. "Shane..." her weakening voice tried to shout. "Run..."

Ben held the woman in his arms as she mumbled indiscernible words before passing out. Joe's astonished face stared at Ben in disbelief. His gun still poised for another shot, Joe stalked forward, bypassing Curtis's struggle with the other demon. Joe was now over Ben and angled his arm to press the nose of the gun against the red demon's temple. Before Joe released the trigger, Ben flung his arm into Joe's, knocking off the bullet's trajectory.

Joe's bewildered face looked on, utterly speechless at Ben's actions.

"She's human!" Ben roared. "Can't you see that?"

Joe shifted his eyes from Ben to the demon in his arms. His vision was blurry somehow, probably from the adrenaline. But then his vision cleared. Ben was right! It was a woman! Joe had nearly killed her. In the frenzy, he must have mistaken the figure running up behind Ben as one of the demon creatures.

"Where did she come from?" Joe gasped. Then immediately he remembered Curtis, twisting back to help their teammate. But Curtis was gone. And so was the other demon.

"Where did they go?" Joe exclaimed, stalking back to the end of the aisle to search. But there were no signs of either.

"Joe, help me get her up. We must get her back to the colony."

"We can't!" Joe cried. "Mayor Collins would never let her in! We don't know who she is or where she comes from."

"Yes, we do!" Ben argued, looking up at Joe with a rare grin of joy. "Don't you recognize her?"

Joe glanced at her once more. Her blonde hair had grown out a bit since he'd last seen her, but now he did recognize her face. "Geez! Ben, that's—"

"Stacie," Ben smiled. "My wife, Stacie. She isn't dead."

CHAPTER 25

BLUE MONSTERS

The alien lifeform had been easier to subdue than Shane expected. It seemed weaker than others Shane had run into before on supply runs, which explained his ability to overpower it and knock it out. Had the struggle with it not sent Shane's gun skidding off under a shelf, he'd have shot the damn thing instead of dragging it off a few rows and zip-tying it. But at least with it hogtied, it couldn't resume the fight, giving Shane time to go back for his gun and try to save Doe.

He rushed back to the scene and located the gun. It hadn't strayed far, just under an end cap. With his weapon back in his hand, he scoured the aisles looking for the other two aliens and Doe, but they were nowhere to be found. His worst fear set in, they'd taken her. He couldn't grasp why the aliens would have taken Doe, but they did. Maybe because they believed he'd absconded with one of their own and it was a retaliation, he wasn't sure. The one and only spark of hope was that there were no signs of them having killed her.

Not like Dasha…

It hit Shane all at once as his adrenaline subsided. They killed Dasha. He knew he had to go back to that aisle. He owed her that much. He owed her a lot, in fact. She'd not only been his scavenging partner all these months, but she'd also become his best friend. Some at Vernon even whispered they were lovers, but they weren't. Shane wasn't her type. There had been a time when he wondered if any man was her type, until he overheard Doe giving her a hard time over some kid at UAB. Apparently, Dasha's type was much younger guys of the Middle Eastern persuasion. Not that it mattered now.

With reluctant steps, Shane found her body.

Blood pooled around her head, clinging to the stubbled side she kept shaven. Her longer hair on the other side drifted like seaweed in the crimson pool. The bullet had entered cleanly and passed cleanly, thank goodness. Shane could not have taken seeing her head mutilated from the impact. He wanted to bury her. Give her the dignity she deserved. But the world didn't allow for such things anymore. Humans couldn't risk the luxury of standing out in the open for too long. He said a silent goodbye, forcing back the tears he would have to shed later when time allowed.

Shane went back to the creature he'd left restrained and dragged it out to the van. Just touching its scaly blue lizard skin made him uneasy. He'd already hoisted it onto the back alongside the earlier finds he, Dasha, and Doe had collected before he asked himself why he was bothering to take it back to Vernon. Why not just kill it as its friends had Dasha? He couldn't explain his reasoning. Maybe he thought a chance would present itself to trade it hostage for hostage and get Doe back? It was their only leverage. For whatever reason, its counterparts had not killed Doe. Strange as it was, they almost appeared captivated by her. But why? Were they taking human prisoners now? *If so*, Shane thought. *We've got one of their own now too.* It was ridiculous implausibility, but for whatever reason, he was taking it back with him.

The darkness of night awakened an even deeper level of dread inside him. The space monsters liked to do their hunting at night, but Shane had to risk it. He had to get back to Vernon before this monster woke up again. Maybe by capturing a living specimen, Doc could figure out its weaknesses, maybe even how to communicate with it. If that were possible, and if these aliens shared a connected telepathy or communication capability...Shane might be able to trade prisoners and get Doe safely home.

Driving back along the blackened streets of Birmingham, headlights bouncing off broken glass and debris, Shane's mind replayed everything that led to the tragic turn of events. It was supposed to be Doe's final training ride along. Next week she was to go out with a partner of her own, increasing Vernon's supply teams by a third. Doc had requested them to be on the lookout for blood pressure medication and blood thinners. Mrs. Yardley and Mr. Sims were nearly out of their meds. It was for this reason Dasha suggested hitting the old Walmart they'd pilfered before.

"That pharmacy is fully stocked," she reminded him. "Remember, the security gate was down over it. No one had raided anything out of there."

"Doesn't mean they haven't by now," Shane argued.

"Who the hell has time to cut through all those panels, Shane?" Dasha said to him sharply. "It's way too dangerous to linger that long."

"But now it isn't?" he asked.

Doe popped her head forward from the back seat and yelped, "Yes, but now there's three of us! You can pry open the gate while Dasha and I keep lookout."

He should have known that would be their plan. He'd be the one with the bolt cutters clipping through those thick metal bars while they only held back leisurely to rob it. The girls had wandered the store for any items Vernon could use that may still be leftover in the store, while Shane went to work. And it had been exhausting work cutting through such thick posts. He'd just finished opening a hole big enough to pass through when he heard gunshots ring out at the back of the shopping center. Shane broke into a run to find them when he heard Dasha's voice call out.

"It's okay, Shane! Only two aliens and Doe and I took them down!"

Pitched over, hands on his knees, catching his breath, Shane shouted back. "Okay! Great! I'll go back and load up the drugs! It's virgin territory, so I am taking everything I can crate up. If we don't take it now, it'll all be gone next time with this hole I cut."

He went back to work, loading bottles of pills, syrups, syringes, and whatever he could into crates. He didn't even have to go get his own from the van; the pharmacy had plenty stacked in a corner. Doe came to assist him while Dasha was busy in the storeroom loading up things former raiders had missed.

Once Shane and Doe had cleaned out practically everything the pharmacy had to take, they began loading the van. Dasha met them at the van herself a few times, packing in her own discoveries before heading back inside to the storeroom. As Shane and Doe carried the next-to-last crates of medicine outside, they noticed the sun had gone down.

"Damn," Shane moaned. "That gate took a lot longer than I thought. We need to get out of here."

"You go find Dasha," Doe said. "I'll go grab the last two crates and meet you both here."

Shane went back inside, where he found Dasha coming from the back room with the last two giant packs of toilet paper. "You look as exhausted as I am," he said, wiping his brow in the hot sticky air of the store. "But I dare anyone to get sick at Vernon now and not have medicine for it!"

Dasha grinned, continuing to lean against a freezer door, which had ceased to be cold in ages. "I'm tired too. This has been a long damn day."

"Longer than you think," Shane frowned. "It's dark already."

"Have we been here that long?" Dasha cried, a touch of concern in her tone.

"That pharmacy took a while," he answered. "Doe's waiting for us at the van."

She gave him a thankful wink and summoned the strength to traipse through the superstore once more on the promise of leaving. Shane was a few steps ahead of her when suddenly she reached for his arm, pulling him back with her finger to her lips. She mouthed, "We have company."

They crouched low, listening to the sound of heavy steps crossing the middle section of the store. They were too far on the left side to see the middle, but Dasha slowly maneuvered to the end of an aisle where there was a less obstructed vantage point across the way. That was when she saw the ghastly beings stalking towards the back. Too far away to hear them well, it wouldn't have even mattered considering their garbled language.

"Three of them," she whispered to Shane. "I wonder if they're looking for their friends that Doe and I shot earlier?"

"Stay back, head down," Shane advised. "Let's try to get out of here without being seen."

But one monster had split off from its team. The sound of its clumping steps approaching them warned Dasha and Shane to get ready for a fight. A fight Dasha didn't walk away from.

* * *

The van was almost to Vernon now as Shane wiped the tears from his eyes. He couldn't imagine living in this world without Dasha. His partner in crime, his best friend. Maybe the hope of rescuing Doe would get him through; after that, he wasn't sure how he'd face the days. He still couldn't understand how Doe ended up behind them all in the store. She must have left the van when Dasha and Shane didn't immediately return. Doe must have seen the creatures coming in. She had to have sneaked back in and tried to come up the long back wall where the dairy cases were. Had she not, Shane was certain he would be lying dead beside Dasha right now on that laminate floor.

The gates at Vernon opened quickly, admitting the van before swinging back shut to keep the community protected. Shane called from the driver's side window, "I captured one of the aliens. It's alive. I am going to lock it in the armory cell. Somebody tell Doc! Then I'll bring the van back for unloading."

He knew the question was coming from Terry Hogland's lips, but he rolled the window up, pretending he hadn't heard it. Shane couldn't bring himself to say the words. Coming in so late, they knew something bad had happened. How could he utter the words, "Dasha is dead."

The armory was dark as Shane parked in front of it. He swung the van doors open staring in at the lizard-like devil, zip-tied and unconscious. Word of Shane's arrival and what his appearing alone might signify, must have spread like the wind through the hallways of Vernon because he had only just hefted the monster onto his back when Corinne, Rylan, Penn, Allie, Dillon, and Augusta came shuffling down the hill.

Penn and Rylan darted over to relieve Shane of the burden of the heavy beast. As the creature lifted from his back, Shane sank to the pavement, burying his tear-stained face in his hands. The weight of the creature, combined with the emotional gut-punch of his loss, left him utterly drained.

Decker came rushing forward with the keys to the armory lock, pulling open the heavy iron door for Penn and Rylan to enter. He rushed in after them, switching on the light before opening the thick barred cell.

Someone had tucked a few dusty crates of ammunition away in back, but Dillon and Allie worked quickly to clear the makeshift jail cell. Within a few minutes, the unconscious alien lifeform lay locked behind an impenetrable cage of stone and steel.

Shane had composed himself and come inside. He didn't say anything. He only stared with bitter hatred at the monster. Augusta hurried in with Doc and Terry behind her. She placed her two gentle hands on the sides of Shane's tear-stained face. "We are grateful at least you made it home," she said with a kiss to his cheek. He fell into her comforting arms, weeping once again.

"It was so fast," he said. "I don't know how it happened so fast."

Augusta tried to quiet him. "Shane, you do not have to relive it again. We know if you could have saved them, you would have. You owe no one an explanation."

Shane shook his head. "No, I do have to tell you…it's why I brought this thing back with me. The aliens killed Dasha, but they *kidnapped* Doe. They just *took her*, and I don't know why. I panicked and brought him back with me. Maybe we can use one of their own to get her back?"

Penn steadied him by the arm. "That was a good idea, man. We can study it. Maybe figure out how they live and operate. And just maybe trade him for Doe. That was smart."

Corinne motioned to Augusta to come closer. "I want to give him a sedative. Shane is in shock and needs total rest."

"He lives in the men's dorm with me," Terry reminded her. "I'll keep a look in on him."

"There's medicine!" Shane suddenly remembered. "A ton of it in the van!"

Corinne nodded, smiling. "Yes, I saw. Billy has already taken the van up to Marian to inventory. You don't need to do anything now but rest, Shane. I will be up soon with something to help with that."

Dillon and Rylan helped Shane up to the school's main level to his dorm. Terry remained behind with Penn, Decker, and Allie. The four of them all stared at the alien on the floor behind the cage. "Anybody know what we do about him?" Terry asked, more than a little apprehensive to have one of those monsters among them, and alive.

Penn folded his arms and reared back on his heels. "Decker? You want me to skip perimeter tonight and sit with *the thing from Mars*?"

Decker forced a chuckle. "Yeah, that would be good. I'll pull Patrice on perimeter, and I'll come relieve you around 2am." He put his arm around Allie, taking her with him as he turned to leave, then stopped and added. "Penn, keep a gun always loaded and ready. If this thing wakes up and tries to get out, kill it. If you feel strange in any way, like it has some kind of mind control or is waging a subliminal attack, kill it. Take no fucking chances."

CHAPTER 26

UNRECOGNIZABLE ENEMIES

Her eyes flicked open like a light switch turned on. Her head was swimming in an ocean of unanswered questions that her mind was far too foggy to grasp. She was staring at an unfamiliar ceiling—the drop kind with Styrofoam tiles. *Am I in a store?* The foreign surroundings made her uneasy as she searched her brain to remember. Then suddenly she did, which was even worse than not remembering. Dasha!

Images of her friend, murdered at the claws of the alien monsters, replayed in her head. Doe sat upright on the wooden-framed cot, catching her breath. This was the second time she'd awakened on an uncomfortable cot in a strange place. Surveying her surroundings, she discovered she was in fact in a store. A metal security gate stretched across the wide doorway; the kind stores used to shutter up at night. Empty shelving ran sporadically across the walls at even levels, matched by podium boxes at equally mismatched heights across a lower counter. *This used to be a shoe store.*

She stood, wincing from the pulsating pain in her shoulder. She looked down and saw that someone had wrapped it tight. Though woozy, she at least had minimal use of her injured arm. Doe walked to the gate over the entrance. Through the security bars she could see she was inside a mall—one which appeared to be open...or at least inhabited. It required little deduction to understand the locked gate was meant to keep her in, so she searched the back of the empty store and found a backroom. The dust-covered shelves still housed a few leftover shoe boxes. There was a back door, most likely leading to a service hall, but of course, it was thick metal and securely locked.

Suddenly the gate up front rattled. Someone was rolling it up. Doe went back to the showroom, peering around the corner to see the broad-shouldered man stepping inside. She had no memory of him, yet she knew she was afraid of him. The fear didn't stem from this immediate captivity. It went deeper; like the face of a man from an old bad dream she couldn't quite place.

Ben saw her lingering in the back. "You're awake!" The man smiled pleasantly, but something inside her warned not to take it at face value. "What do you remember?"

His voice sounded garbled to Doe's ear, most likely the result of the bump on her head. She could make out only a few words. It was as if he spoke English with a mix of some other language she'd never heard before. Ben took a few steps towards her, seeing her flinch at his approach. The reaction took him aback. He'd expected a more joyful reunion, but Doe felt a little like an opposing magnet against another. The closer he came, the farther pushed back she felt. Her brain, compromised well before this night, must have sustained more bruising from her fall because the man's image kept coming in and out of focus, sometimes even appearing to be one of the blue aliens stalking at her.

"Who are you?" she asked.

Ben's eyes met the question with disappointment but maintained his smile. "You don't know?"

"No."

"What *do* you know?" he asked.

His response was garbled, gravelly, as if he had a mouth full of rocks. She touched her head as if disoriented. "Did you ask me what I know? Your voice…it's hard to understand."

He nodded. "You have a concussion, I think."

"Seems to be a pattern with me," she said, almost amused. "I was on a supply run…"

"Yes, I know," Ben said. "But that was a long time ago."

She could hear him a little clearer now, but his statement made little sense. "No," she explained. "It was today. Or yesterday." The images replayed, almost like seeing them for the first time. Those ghastly alien things. And Dasha. One of them must have stabbed its claws through her because Doe remembered the blood projecting out from her when she'd been struck. "There were two monsters there when we arrived, but Dasha and I took care of them. But then… suddenly there were others."

Ben confirmed her account with a nod. "My friends and I came in for ammo. I heard something on your side of the store. I saw your two friends' bodies near the back, before I found you."

"Two?!" Doe repeated mournfully. "They got Shane too?"

"I guess," he replied. "There were two bodies. We fought off the demons but in the chaos, my teammate mistook you for one and shot you in the shoulder."

She looked again at her bandaging. "I seem to attract chaos."

"You always did." Ben approached her slowly, looking into her face, straining his eyes as if hoping to awaken something in hers. "You really don't know who I am?"

"Should I?" Doe asked, recoiling slightly again. He was a strong, rather good-looking man, which made her revulsion to him more alarming. "I had an accident weeks back. Lost my memory. But are you saying you know me?"

He hesitated a moment, weighing the importance of telling her now or waiting. He chose to wait until she was stronger. She needed time to adjust and recover. "My name is Ben," he told her. "You used to live here."

"Here?" she remarked with an upturned nose.

"No, not here in this room." He tilted his head towards the walkway beyond the gate. "You were a member of this colony. We are in the Galleria Mall."

"Wow," Doe replied. "Must be a nice settlement. Why would I leave?"

Ben stroked his beard with his fingers. "You were a Searcher. Someone who goes out for supplies."

"Same job I was doing at my other place."

"Doesn't sound like you're very good at it," Ben remarked, attempting humor.

"You have a point."

She couldn't help but notice the way he cast an occasional covert glance at her, as if scanning her right down to her hands. She was on the verge of asking him why when he cut her off, asking, "Where was this other place?"

"A little high school," she answered. "Not sure where. Vernon."

Ben grunted, then asked. "Wouldn't you even like to know your name?"

"My name is Doe," she said.

He didn't appear impressed; he even looked a little offended. "Your name is Stacie."

Doe furrowed her eyebrows and sneered. "I don't feel much like a Stacie. Better just keep calling me Doe."

He didn't like the reply and didn't hide it well either. "I'll leave you alone to rest. Later I'll bring some food up once the kitchens have breakfast ready."

"Am I a prisoner?" She asked as he went back to the gate, beginning to lower it again behind him. "If not, I'd like to get back to my people."

"We are your people, Stacie," Ben told her, leaving little room for argument. "Rules say you must be kept separate from the population for a few days until we are sure you haven't been converted or possessed. After that, you will settle back into your real life in no time."

The gate slammed locked, and Ben disappeared into the mall. His statement had been aggressive. She couldn't pinpoint it, but something alarmed her about him. She didn't have to remember him to know that she didn't like him. For the moment, she didn't mind this enforced quarantine. Vernon had done the same thing. Of course, they'd used the word "infected," not "possessed."

* * *

No matter how Joe McNab tried to spin it to his family, his son Scotty and sister-in-law Dorothy knew it was less Joe's cagey instincts that kept him alive on his tour and more basic luck. He'd grandiosely retold the scene of his...his...bullet ripping into the fuel tank and obliterating the demons in a hell storm of napalm, steel and brick. Leslie fawned over her husband's bravery as their daughter Renee ran off to brag to her friends.

"Ain't you proud of your old man, boy?" Joe asked his son, when his reaction had seemed tepid at best.

"Sure, Dad," Scotty answered. "But I don't get how setting demons on fire does anything to them. Don't they live in a lake of fire in Hell anyway?"

Dorothy turned her head to hide her smile. It wasn't only amusement in her nephew's comment, but how her brother-in-law and her sister stared, flummoxed by it—as if the contradiction was lost on them.

"That's gratitude for you," Joe snapped. "Got a boy here who can't even be proud when his own dad saves the world."

Scotty almost said, "*Saves the world* is a bit of a stretch," but he kept quiet, having already angered his father.

"It's real easy to sit and be a smart ass while the real men go out there and provide the very blanket of protection you sleep under!" Joe said cuttingly. "You better man-up boy and focus on how you're gonna prove your worth one day. It ain't gonna be with sarcasm, I can tell you."

Scotty hadn't meant to ignite his father's ire, but it seemed like that was all he ever did these days. Still, just like with the *save the world* comment, it took everything within Scotty not to call his dad out on basically just restating Jack Nicholson's line from *A Few Good Men*. Scotty hadn't even seen that movie, and even *he knew* the quote was copied.

* * *

Linda Collins carried the little tray of lemonade into the old tie store, now converted to a game room where people—mostly men—gathered to talk, play checkers or chess, or occasionally backgammon. She placed the tray on a small table beside the checker set, pouring both her husband and Reverend Tucker a glass.

"Well, Sister Linda, this could be like the old days, sipping lemonade under a shady tree with good friends."

She blushed, apologizing. "It won't be as authentic as all that. Just some water, and a couple of packets of artificial lemon juice I found in the condiment closet. But I thought it might be nice."

The mayor's wife left the two men alone with their checkerboard. Mayor Collins lifted his glass to toast, "To miracles. Mrs. Noland certainly outran the hounds of hell this time. It's by God's good grace she made it back alive."

The Reverend raised his glass, a little begrudgingly. "She was spared, yes. But maybe the Lord didn't perform this miracle for her sake. I recall Stacie Noland as having been somewhat resistant to our little

Eden here. Maybe her return is the Lord issuing a warning."

Mayor Collins moved his red checker diagonally to a side square for protection. "You think this was a warning?"

The minister leaned forward, his voice low. "I consider it providence. That girl caused quite a stink until we allowed her to venture out on a man's task. And what happened? Nature corrected her, casting her out to survive on her own and nearly dying because of it. She was brought low before God; humility returned. Maybe now she will be thankful for her place. And perhaps the others will understand what can happen when you stray from God's plan."

The mayor rubbed his temples, remembering himself how Ben's wife had stirred a few of the women to want more of a role than minding a store. "I'll not let it happen again, Reverend. I'll say that plainly. No woman will step outside this city again. Not until the Lord tells us it is safe."

Tucker noticed the opening left on the board by the mayor's clumsy move, jumping two of his pieces with his black checker, receiving a crown for the play. "It will be a new world, Franklin. Stripped of the messiness and the distractions from before. When God tells us we may leave this Ark, the new world will grow from a solid foundation of scripture. We know how a house should stand and the roles its inhabitants should follow beneath its roof."

Mayor Collins took another sip of lemonade as he eyed the board for a way to salvage his game. "I wonder if that's how we should spin Mrs. Noland's narrow escape to the others among us here. Stacie's survival...not an inspiration, but a cautionary tale. Let the women see: she wandered, she suffered, and she returned to the fold."

"Just another example of the Lord's merciful grace," the preacher said. "Let us hope Ben's wife learned the lesson. There is nothing more disappointing than those who reject the path chosen for them."

Tucker noticed the crestfallen expression on his friend's face. "Franklin? Did I say something wrong?"

The mayor waved his hand, dismissing the notion. "No, not at all. I am reminded only of my own disappointment." Franklin began anxiously tapping a couple of checkers he'd captured together. "The anniversary is in a few days."

"I remember very well that terrible time in your life," Reverend Tucker frowned. "I hope I was of some comfort at least to you and Linda after your loss."

"You were a good friend then, as now."

"Losing your only son," Tucker said mournfully. "Especially at the fault of his own choices. God got you through then as He will move us all through now, to a new kingdom."

Mayor Collins leaned back in his chair, staring at the board he now had no way of claiming victory over. "Let us hope that Stacie Noland makes better use of her gifted grace."

CHAPTER 27

BRIMSTONE

With every seat in the Galleria mall's central court filled, Reverend Elias Tucker stood on his makeshift altar to deliver his Sunday sermon. His voice began low and mournful as he lamented the deaths of Marcus and Curtis, calling them martyrs to the Lord's holy cause. From sorrow, he rose into fire and brimstone—his thunderous voice booming through the high atrium, each word sharpened with righteous fury. Then, as always, came the silence. A deliberate pause. The calm before his final descent into a gravelly cadence that whispered of judgment, obedience, and total submission.

"They were soldiers of Christ," Tucker declared, pacing the stage like a general before his troops. "They gave their lives in service of God's war. Make no mistake, dear Brethren, this is a war. Satan and his demonic creations have risen to consume us...but we, the righteous, shall prevail!"

The congregation answered his guiding call with a chorus of "amens" and "hallelujahs" as Reverend Tucker's eyes swept the room. "This is God's land, brothers and sisters, and has been since time began.

And since time began, the Devil has tried to lay claim to it. He's crept into our books and music, through the screens of our televisions and movies, luring us with the belief that we have power over the lives our Heavenly Father gave us. Satan has told us we can choose our own identities—tell God what our sex is! The Devil tricked men to lie down with men and women to lie down with women."

The minister paused, allowing his congregation time to roar, applaud, and shout their agreeing voices to the rafters. Scotty's eyes locked with Gavin's across the aisles. Both boys stiffened. Each cheer exploding around them felt its own dagger stabbed into their hearts. The swell of approval was like a wave of hatred aimed directly at them, and neither boy understood why. Why was their kind so repulsive? Why did their private sexual side matter to these people? Did it erase the boys' kindness? Did it strike out every cheery hello or offer to help carry something heavy for a neighbor? When Scotty and Gavin looked at each other, they didn't see anything evil. They saw nothing that would make God ashamed of them. Their attraction to each other shouldn't have altered their innate goodness any more than if Scotty's mother preferred to be on top, or if Mr. Reynolds liked his wife to wear a cheerleader outfit. Did God think those things were shameful? Why would God even care about such private and passionate matters? Jesus said to be good to each other. Love each other and do not judge one another. Wasn't that basically the only rule?

However, Reverend Tucker had not finished his emphatic revision of what offended God. He was only getting started, as if the Lord Himself had texted him a list before going on stage. "They called murdering babies 'healthcare'. They let criminals overrun our shores and called it 'immigration'. They said our punishing criminals was 'racist.'"

Another roar from the righteous. Another fervent wave of applause. Tucker lifted his Bible as if it were a holy sword, sweeping it across his stage at the crowd. The men and women swayed with it, as if the book had manifested an invisible tidal wave from the Holy Spirit. Scotty remained still. If this was worship, perhaps these people were the ones the Devil had corrupted? Maybe the entire argument was backwards. He suddenly felt that if Jesus were here among these parishioners, He would have remained just as silent and just as motionless as He witnessed His words shouted back at Him, drained of all their meaning.

"The left-wing radicals, the feminists, the atheists, the gays…all pawns in Satan's grand deception. But we didn't fall for it! We stayed with God. And God shielded us from evil and rewarded us with survival! One day soon, we will rebuild His world into a place of purity."

Once more, the congregation roared in approval of Tucker's message. Some people stood pressing their hands to their hearts. Some raised both hands to an unseen presence in the sky. A few chanted in tongues, a holy language which never seemed to sync up with the person next to them. And others cried, sobbing in their righteous conviction.

"We are God's warriors," Reverend Tucker assured them. "And we will send the demons back to hell—one by one!"

The final cheer was deafening, and if Heaven were listening, it must have shaken from the sound. Scotty wanted to leave. He wanted to run as far away from this display as possible. He loved God too, but God never moved inside of him the way He appeared to pull at other people. Unless it was all imagined. Unless these people were faking their cries and gestures; overcompensating for feeling as alone and scared as Scotty felt himself. He glanced at Gavin across the room. Perhaps he shut his eyes in prayer—or maybe just to avoid witnessing—and joining these theatrics. But when he opened his eyes again, his head turned immediately to Scotty, and in an instant all was clear. That message from God—that thing people called being saved—they both understood it now. And it wasn't this spectacle.

The boys now understood fully what God wanted, and it was for them to get out of here. This wasn't love. It was division. It was "Us" against "Them" …and this warped interpretation of Jesus' legacy was indeed the influence of the Devil.

* * *

From her cell on the mall's second floor, Doe heard every venomous word dripping from the sermon. Though her barred gate kept her confined, it felt more like mercy than a precaution. She remembered them now. Ben had told her she'd lived there—that she'd been a member of their community. But he'd been only partially right. She'd never been one of them.

Stacie Noland had sat among those people below, in those seats, her head bowed—not in prayer—but fear. Stacie's life flashed through Doe's mind like a kicked puppy who'd only ever wanted petting. Her father died shortly after her fifth birthday. Her mother died when Stacie turned 18. Ben Noland met her, wooed her, and married her all within a month. She moved on base and lived under stalwart conditions. Stacie lost two babies in her first trimester under Ben's aggressive and punishing dominance over her. When she'd gained a job as Searcher in this new world, it was her opportunity to get free. Even if it meant her death in the outside world, it was better than her life had been.

And now she was back. The bastard stumbled into a Walmart and found her. Maybe he did save her from the aliens, but she'd rather have died with them than come here.

"I remember you," a voice called softly to her, startling Doe from the disturbing memory. She saw him standing on the other side of the gate, sealing her in. "You were friends with my mom. You're Stacie, right?"

"I used to be," Doe replied, a little suspicious of the kid. "Are you supposed to be up here talking to me?"

He shifted on his feet. "Probably not. I'm Gavin." He pressed his face into the slats, his voice lowering a bit. "What's it like...outside?"

"Kid, I don't feel like playing post-apocalyptic tour guide."

His face flushed pink. "Sorry," he said as he started to move along.

"No, wait!" she called to him. "Sorry. I didn't mean to sound like a bitch."

Gavin laughed, covering his mouth so no one would hear. "Nobody cusses around here," he informed her, then with a teenage roll of the eyes, added. "God might hear."

"Gavin, why do you want to know what's outside? You've got it pretty cozy in here."

At the mention of his name, his eyes lit up. "Do you remember me?"

"No," she confessed. "But you told me your name already, remember?"

The admission deflated him a bit, and he turned to go, realizing he was bothering her.

As if it had been timed perfectly, an image flashed through her mind. "Gavin, hold on," she urged. He stepped back to the gate, innocently clutching his fingers through the cage. Doe moved to the cage, standing very close to him now. "I saw you," she revealed in a low whisper. She could tell by his widening eyes she'd hit on something. "You and another boy."

Her sudden memory sparked a hushed conversation between them. He confessed his relationship with Scotty and their growing fear of what might happen if caught. He also let her know how much it meant to him and Scotty that she'd never betrayed their secret all those months ago.

"I heard that preacher," Doe said grimly. Her fingers reached through the slats and touched him. "You do know there is nothing wrong with you or Scotty? No matter what these fanatics here say."

"We know," Gavin smiled. "But we must get out of here. I was hoping you could tell me what to expect. What to look out for. How to stay alive outside."

"I could," Doe grinned. "But wouldn't it be better if I simply showed you?"

* * *

That night, after Gavin said goodnight to his parents, he locked the connecting door between their rooms and sneaked through to Scotty. Scotty was already waiting on the bed for him when he came in. After sharing a kiss they'd longed for all day, Scotty's hormones started taking control, but Gavin made him slow his engine. "We need to talk first."

After listening to Gavin catch him up to speed, Scotty sat back in awe. "The woman they brought back is the same woman who knew about us?" Scotty gasped.

"And she doesn't want to be here anymore than we do," Gavin revealed. "She wants to go back to her settlement, and she says she will take us with her if we help her escape."

Scotty's eyes grew bright with hope. There was a way. It had been one of the motivating reasons he'd gotten himself moved to the hotel's third floor. His only hesitancy had been what would happen once he and Gavin escaped. But now...if this woman meant what she said...

* * *

Doe was almost asleep when she heard the gate rise. Impetuous as teenage boys could be, she doubted it was Gavin so soon to spring her. She sat up, finding Ben coming towards her in the dark.

"Don't be afraid of me, Stacie," he said. "I'm not here to hurt you. I wanted only to check on you."

"Thanks."

He was looking at her hand again. It wasn't the first time she'd noticed him doing so. "Is there something wrong with my hand, Ben?"

He frowned, lifting it into his. "Your ring is missing."

"My ring?"

He turned his hand over onto hers. "I still have mine."

Doe's eyes stared at him, unblinking, widening by the second. "I don't understand?"

Doe understood very well. But allowing Ben to know she was

remembering might inspire him to take liberties with her—liberties he'd never minded taking against her will in the past.

He nodded his head. "You are my wife, Stacie."

She pretended to be surprised. Pretended to hear him out with bated breath. She listened while Ben Noland recounted a vastly different rendition of their marriage than Doe remembered. But with every word, she listened attentively, as if hearing it all for the first time. She even asked, with a feigned tone of hope, "Do we have children?"

"Sad to say, we haven't been lucky there yet," Ben frowned. "But maybe now we can keep trying."

Doe wanted to punch him in his lying, twisted face. He'd beaten the babies out of her during her only two pregnancies. But she pretended to look upon him with a shared sense of loss. He touched her cheek with his rough, calloused hand. Doe pulled back, but respectfully.

"I'm sorry. I don't remember." She gave it a good three-second pause before sprinkling in enough hope to keep him waiting a while longer before trying anything with her. "Maybe we can start over...if you can be patient with me. I guess I need to get to know you again."

"You'll be out of here after tomorrow night," Ben informed her. "If you haven't shown signs of possession by then, the rules say you can get out of this old store."

"That's twice you've used the word possession," she noted.

"Because that's what we are up against here, Stacie. I can't believe you forgot that too. You had to see those demons out there while you were on your own."

"Demons?"

He looked at her strangely, as if suspecting she might be infected after all. She quickly tried to cover. "I did see the creatures," she confessed. "Those monsters killed my two friends."

"Well, they are from Hell," Ben told her. "Those damn things crawled right out of the mouth of Hell."

Not aliens. Demons. Still...it was only semantics. Doe suddenly understood the aliens might have been called a great number of names by those who hadn't yet learned their true origin. But as the next words trickled out of his mouth, she knew to keep quiet.

"Those red skin, spiked-head devils!" Ben sneered. "But we're killing them little by little. I took out a whole building of them the night I found you."

His words stayed with her long after he said goodnight. He had said virtually the same thing the night he murdered her best friend. She'd been next door at Cassie's house while Ben was on duty. The world had fallen into havoc somehow—people killing other people for no understandable reason. Stacie had gone to stay with Cassie while Ben was away from the house. It was for mutual protection in case any of those crazies tried to break in and hurt them. But the only menace that night had been Ben, who'd never liked Cassie anyway. Cassie had patched up Stacie's wounds one too many times, and it bothered Ben the way she looked at him when he was around.

He'd burst through the door, gun extended, spouting at Cassie as if she were a monster. "That's not your friend!" he had shouted to Stacie. "Can't you see? It's all burned and disfigured." He unloaded two shots into Cassie's stomach before he snatched Stacie from the house.

At first, she had believed him, despite Stacie having never seen her friend any differently than before. But as time went by, and she and Ben moved from abandoned house to abandoned house, she saw enough of Ben killing the real red demons which she herself could see, that it left questions whether Cassie's death was really just something he wanted to do and used the demonic infestation as the excuse.

Now Doe was left bewildered. Are they aliens? Are they demons? Or is there more than one deadly peril to evade outside these walls?

CHAPTER 28

AN ANNIVERSARY OF LOSS

Franklin and his wife Linda rarely found time for a quiet meal together anymore. Even before the world ended, when Franklin served as mayor of Homewood, civic duty inevitably pulled him away or ran him late getting home time and time again. Now in the year after the fall of civilization, serving as mayor of the Galleria colony had changed very little in regard to his time constraints.

But tonight was going to be different. It was an important occasion for Franklin and his wife—their son's deathday.

Linda had made a special request of the cooks in the Food Court to make something special just for herself and her husband. Although a juicy steak would have been preferable, meat was a rare treat these days. A golden brown, extra-cheesy broccoli casserole would have to make do.

She pulled the small hotel room table, with its two chairs, to the center of the room, and spread a floral-print bedsheet across it to act as a colorful tablecloth. She'd procured a candelabra and three stubby candles with some life still in them from the candle supply unit, as well as two official ceramic plates and forks from the dinnerware supply.

When Franklin stepped inside and the door shut quietly behind him, the dancing candlelight illuminated the tearful smile on his face. Linda rose from her chair to embrace him, then they stared at one another gently for a few silent moments.

She vaguely resembled the woman she'd been when he married her. And Franklin knew he bore very little resemblance to the man she'd married. Wrinkles had replaced the softness of her skin and the light that used to shine from it. She looked older than her years, but stress, fear, and heartbreak will do that to a wife and mother. His own face looked even older than hers, and she at least still had her hair. His hair now grew only at the sides and was forced to pull double duty combing over to disguise the empty top.

Their age-worn faces reflected the life they'd lived together. All its struggles, all its suffering, all its stresses and rewards were in those lines. It was those lines, not their former glory, that preserved their love now. A shared life bearing the scars they earned together.

Franklin pulled out her chair from the table, then took his own across from her. Each smiled over the candlelight, both recognizing the sadness they weren't speaking aloud.

Franklin lifted the covers off the plates and looked down appreciatively at the meal. "This is nice," he grinned. "Thank you."

Linda winked and took her first bite of the casserole. A memory flooded back to her; one that made her smile. "Remember how tough it was to get him to eat his broccoli?"

"I remember the stubbornness," Franklin chuckled. "That night we all sat up at the table until midnight waiting for him to clean his plate."

"Then you finally gave in and called it quits," his wife laughed quietly. "And a week later, he claimed to love broccoli because he'd eaten it at his friend's house."

Franklin hung his head over his plate. "I miss him. I miss his voice.

I find myself strolling back in memory to the happy days...before he succumbed to his sickness."

"I miss him too," Linda whispered, reaching her fragile hand across to his. "It is still hard for me to imagine how our handsome, kind boy could have become so lost in the vices he chose to pursue. How many nights I prayed for his soul and his mental health, only to lose him in the end."

"Our prayers were not enough," Franklin sighed. "It was he who needed to pray for help. If he'd only turned it all over to God, his hunger for things poisoning his soul would have ended."

Linda swept tears from her cheek, then sat straighter in her chair, summoning her resolve. "Even though we lost him. I don't want to think about our son's demise. I only want to remember those couple of decades when we had a beautiful family."

Franklin rose from his chair and walked over to the dresser, pulling something hidden from beneath the few pitiful clothing items he had. He carried the small wallet back to the table and removed a photo to show his wife. Linda's eyes welled with tears.

"I thought we'd lost everything when we weren't able to go back home again," she wept. "You've had this all these months?"

"Tucked in my wallet along with our wedding photo," Franklin smiled. "I didn't even think about it until this morning." He gazed down at her as she gently touched their lost son's face. "He was a handsome young man, wasn't he?"

"Until that wicked disease took him over."

* * *

There was nothing left to say on the subject. Franklin and Linda Collins commemorated their son's death as they did every year, by honoring the parts of his life they were proud to remember. Each was long past the days of regret—when they would mull over his choices and their reactions, as well as their choices and his reactions. He was buried now, and so were any misgivings they might have had about how better they could have helped him.

They'd spent the following years deepening their spiritual journey, using his unfortunate fate as a mantle to help others avoid it. Linda had counseled many mothers going through the same agony with their children. Franklin had fought the courageous fight legislatively when he could. His friends in the state senate pushed any reform or mandate Franklin supported forward to save other families the same pain. Of course, the world was very different now. For the Collins's, the world was now only as large as a shopping mall—but it was still a civilization. And if the good Lord planned to build the world over again, Franklin and Linda were determined to model the future on this little Eden. Family would prevail. Under their example, and Franklin's leadership—accompanied by Reverend Tucker's teachings—the new dawn of man would never again see a parent lose their child to vice, addiction, or destructive indulgence.

CHAPTER 29

SNEAKY BUSINESS

There hadn't been a woman in the dress shop for days. Genna Hartley was consumed in her crossword puzzle book when she heard a feminine throat clear next to her. She jumped at the sound, then laughed politely when she saw Dorothy Maxwell and her sister Leslie McNab standing there.

"Oh my gosh, ladies!" Genna blushed with a smile. "You scared me. I'm so sorry I didn't see you come in."

"That's alright, Genna," Leslie replied. "I know it's a rare day when you get any women in here. Our tool shop is just across the way, so I see how little traffic comes by."

Setting aside her puzzle book, Genna stood up and waved her hand across the store. "Not much call for dresses these days when women don't have razors to shave their legs."

Leslie, who was in a dress, grinned proudly. "I'm just grateful my husband uses an old-fashioned straight blade. And it stays sharp thanks to the grindstone machine we have in the store. I've become quite adept at using it myself." Even as she said so, Genna could still see a few nicks and scabs on Leslie's legs.

Dorothy, who wore slacks, admitted she wasn't brave enough to try the blade. "But the Searchers who came in yesterday had a case of razors they found in a backroom of a warehouse. While I have the opportunity, I thought I'd pick a nice dress to wear for a few days."

Genna looked hopeful, pulling Dorothy's arm to bring her close as she asked, "Are there enough razors for everyone?"

"No, but I sneaked you one." Dorothy looked around to make sure no one else was near and slid a disposable razor in her hand. "One of the perks of being on the town council."

Leslie began looking around the store. Colony rules stated colonists could only take what they needed from any supply department; however, being that no one ever took any dresses out, Leslie did not feel guilty selecting a new one whether or not she needed it. Besides, her husband was something of a hero at the moment, helping her feel even more entitled to a treat.

Her sister Dorothy didn't bother browsing, and quickly picked a navy-colored dress whose formality suited her position on the council. However, Leslie seemed determined to examine every bit of Genna's stock.

"I'm a little surprised you never ran for council, Genna," Dorothy admitted. "I recall you being very active in the community back before... well, before this mall was the community. From what I used to hear around town, you had your hands in every organization, museum board, Junior League..."

"I did," Genna said with a faint, nostalgic smile. "I had fun. But between Corbin's work and mine, we were rarely home together. The housekeeper had Colin in bed usually before I even came home. But here everything is different. I have time with Colin and James now. We talk. We play games. We eat all our meals together, and we bow our heads to pray as a family every single night. I don't miss the old me very much."

"Oh, Genna, Dottie will never understand what you are saying!" quipped Leslie, now perusing a rack of dresses nearer to their conversation. "My sister was a wheeler-dealer back in the day. The very thought of domestication is as foreign to her as Latin is to me."

Dorothy looked grim as she replied to Leslie's comment. "I am afraid in this new way of life; I am a relic. As the world rebuilds itself, motherhood, home, and hearth seem to be far more valuable than a female with ambition."

"Here, in this new way of life," Genna explained. "I have enjoyed embracing a more traditional role, which I used to think was antiquated. I have time with the boys, friends, and community. No home stands without a foundation, and every roof needs rafters. I find I prefer being a support...not a partner."

Dorothy offered an understanding smile, although she didn't understand how Genna could be so contented. Dorothy found nothing was better in this new world. When she laid the dress across the checkout counter, Genna opened her ledger and logged its removal from the inventory and to whom it went. "And I'll take this one!" Leslie called out, tossing her pale green gown over her sister's dress. Then with a conspiratorial wink, added, "I really liked this one too." Leslie placed a second dress, crème-colored, over the other. "I don't suppose you could bend the rules for me this one time?"

Maintaining her patience and grace, Genna answered, "Just this once."

* * *

Scotty had been sharpening wire cutters, garden shears, and saw blades when she stepped out of the tool store to go with Dorothy to select a dress. With his mother in the dress shop, Scotty used the time alone to his advantage. He set his work aside and crossed to the far wall of the store, where a bin of bolt cutters was kept. There were only four in the box, all previously used. He found the strongest of what was available and took it to the grinding wheel. Although his knowledge of most tools and their uses was limited, he used bolt cutters once when he'd lost the key to his bicycle lock. He knew the cutters were more a matter of being strong enough to press through a bolt rather than literally cutting it. Still, a little edge to the blades helped.

Giving the bolt cutter a rudimentary sharpen to aid performance, he then checked the outer mall to see if the coast was clear. It was. No one was coming his way, and no one inside any nearby shops was looking out. He left the tool shop and slipped down to the space a few doors down. There was a planter there. Once it housed decorative palms and Hosta plants. Now, it was a space growing red, yellow, and green Chile peppers.

Checking his surroundings once more, Scotty worked quickly to bury the bolt cutters under a bit of loose soil. The peppers weren't ripe for picking yet. No one would find the cutters.

He hurried back to his family's store and went back to his mundane task. His mind raced with the possibilities he had just helped put into motion. His hands stayed busy, doing the maintenance on the tools that his father instructed him to do that morning, but his eyes kept scanning outside the store into the mall causeway.

Leslie returned after a while, very elated by her two new dresses. It wasn't long before her friend from the choir popped over chattering away about Wednesday night's musical selection.

Scotty's eyes remained steady on the outer mall, waiting for the second phase of the plan to come to fruition. It was about half an hour later when he saw Gavin coming through the mall. Scotty's boyfriend never glanced his way, careful to keep up the pretense that they barely knew one another. Gavin disappeared on the other side of the tool shop doorway, but Scotty knew where he was going.

Gavin lifted the bolt cutters from the soil and kept himself hidden behind the planter box until he tucked them into his pants under his shirt. The steel mouth of the tool was cold and sent chills over his skin as it touched his stomach. His gait slowed a little now with the concealed, but heavy cutters wedged into his pants. But he didn't have far to go.

Reaching the holding area where Doe was waiting out her quarantine, Gavin made sure no one was around, then he shoved the cutters through the slats of the security gate. "We'll be here after dark," he whispered.

Doe grabbed the tool quickly, rushing it into the back storage room of the former shoe store and dropping it into one of the remaining shoe boxes on the shelves. When she returned, Gavin was already gone. She knew it was dangerous for him to be seen lurking near her cage, but she had wanted to ask him just how he and Scotty planned to get out of their rooms that night without the guards in the halls seeing them.

CHAPTER 30

STUDIED IN CAPTIVITY

His cheek felt cold and scratchy, as if pressed into grit. Opening his eyes, he saw he was face down on a cement floor. He attempted to get up but found he couldn't. It was then that he realized his wrists were bound behind his back. Trying to rise using only his feet was of no use either, as they also were bound. He tried lifting his head to look around, but three inches of range didn't provide a clearer assessment of where he was. He could tell by the bars rising from the floor that he was in some sort of jail cell. He didn't recall how he got there.

The last thing he remembered was being attacked by one of the demons. That red-skinned bastard had ambushed him just as he was running to tell Ben how he and Joe had found ammunition in the sporting goods department. He understood now that his mistake had been yelling across the store, but he'd believed they were alone in that Walmart. Shots had fired. Joe got hit. And Ben looked like he was wrestling one demon to the ground. That was when the other demon rushed Curtis, knocking him to the ground.

Shifting against the floor, trying to turn for a better look, his eyes caught sight of movement beyond his cell. He could see a pair of boots walking away. "Hello?" he called out to whoever was leaving. "My name is Curtis. Curtis Jackson. Can you help me?"

A heavy door closed somewhere he could not see. It reverberated through the stone facility. Curtis shut his eyes and panicked. Who bound him up and kidnapped him? Where were Ben and Joe? Had they been killed in the battle? Silently, he prayed for the Lord to protect him and help him get free.

The heavy door opened again, and the boots returned. With them came a pair of sneakers. A piece of fabric swayed near the top of the sneakers. It took him a moment to realize it was a lady's skirt. "Boots" had a woman with him.

"My name is Curtis," he said again. "I'm not dangerous. My team got attacked by the devil creatures."

The man with the boots stepped from view while the sneakers lady remained where she stood. Without warning, Curtis suddenly felt himself dragged by an invisible hand across the floor toward the bars of the jail. He cried out, asking what was happening and repeating that he meant no harm, but no one responded. He struggled against the straps binding him and broke his legs free! Before he could balance his way to standing without the use of his arms, he felt himself jerked backwards towards the bars. His hands popped free! Curtis whirled around to face his captors and couldn't believe his eyes. Whatever tricks his mind had played on him at ground level disappeared. There was no man in boots or a woman in a skirt. All that stood before him on the other side of his cell were two grotesquely seared demons.

Decker and Corinne stood facing the cage as Decker folded his pocketknife closed and slipped back into his pocket. The alien creature howled at them from the enclosure. Agitated and hostile, its elongated hands wrapped around the bars menacingly.

"I shouldn't have cut the zip ties," Decker said firmly. "That thing is dangerous."

"The cell will hold," Corinne told him. "The bars are buried deep in cement above and below, and the cinderblock walls are two feet deep," she said. "It won't escape."

"Still," Decker worried. "Better safe than sorry, Doc."

"Yes, but I need to study it fully if we hope to understand how it functions and what they want."

Decker tucked his hand back behind his head, staring at the revolting monster. "Should I let Shane know it's awake?"

Corinne shook her head. "Shane is too raw right now from losing Dasha. He might try to kill it."

"Doesn't sound like such a bad idea."

"Not if we hope to learn about these things and possibly get Doe back." Corinne warned, placing a motherly hand on Decker's back. "You have been here all night with this thing, Decker. Why don't you get some sleep and send Penn in to relieve you."

Curtis couldn't tell what the wicked devils were planning. They communicated with a language of grunts, hisses, and clicks—like Morse code. It must have been the trauma to his head that initially caused him to believe they were people, or the grimy floor obscuring his vision. He saw them now plainly. No boots, no sneakers, no skirts. Just two demonic monsters from Hell. Their burned skin glistened red under the harsh lighting of whatever place this was. It looked military, which did not foster any encouraging hope for rescue in Curtis. If the devils had overtaken the military and were using their headquarters as a nest, then no one was coming to rescue him.

One of the monsters lifted its ghastly claw to touch the other one, likely to give instructions, because the second demon left the dungeon. Curtis stared at the remaining monster. This was the first time he'd been able to really get a good look at one of them when he wasn't fighting or running for his life. It was evil personified, for sure. Charred red skin, like a terrible burn victim you'd see in a medical journal. Its outer vein system pulsed as it carried its black lifeblood across its body. How Curtis wished he had a long, sharp knife on him to slice one of those arteries.

Corinne had seen the corpses of these beings before, but never a living specimen other than the ones she fled from when originally coming to Vernon to live. Its body was very much like the others she studied. The same iridescent blue skin, almost like a lizard or chameleon that could shift hue under the right conditions. Its long arms and hands were most disturbing, and this one did have claws. But it was the conveyance system of blood flow that fascinated her now. With the deceased specimens, she hadn't seen their circulatory systems in action. With this living creature, the doctor saw how its external veins pulsed with coursing black blood across its alien shell.

Another one of Satan's minions entered the dungeon, or it could have been the same one from before—there was no actual way for Curtis to tell. Each one looked so like the others it would be like trying to differentiate between ants crawling over their mound. The only suggestion that this creature might be new was in how it approached the cell with what looked like curiosity. It seemed to inspect Curtis in a way the others hadn't before. The monster, who had not left the room, began growling and hissing with the other one now. Then it disappeared through a doorway in back. The remaining demon stood in the center of the room, a sentry, as if its job was to be on guard.

Penn studied the creature as it stalked back and forth within the confines of its cage. It acted as if it were looking for any weak points in the cell that it might use to escape. Corinne had gone to her makeshift office at the back of the armory to look over the notes and drawings she'd made of the deceased aliens. Now that Clinton and Terry had burned their remains, her sketches were all she had to compare with the living specimen. Alone with the alien while he guarded it, Penn was curious to capture his own images of the monster. He pulled out his own phone and began snapping pictures. He then took video of the alien as it stalked within its cage. These images might come in handy when talking to people on the HAM. Besides, Farrah would want to see it in action herself. She was one of the few humans who had never had the misfortune of being in close proximity to one of those things.

"This is a phone!" Penn shouted at the alien. "At least it used to be. Thanks to you assholes, all it's good for now is a camera." He thrust the screen forward near the cage to show the strange animal creature. "See? That's you! That's you on my phone now. It's called taking a picture."

Curtis did not understand what the demon was doing. It had manifested a light from its hand, which pulsed outward suddenly. For a second, Curtis was sure his life was over, that the evil thing was sending a fire burst to incinerate him. But when nothing happened, and he looked back at the monster, its hand now shimmered into a translucent surface, and on that surface, Curtis saw himself. His own image!

"What have you done?" Curtis shrieked. "Did you just steal my soul!!!"

Corinne returned from the back just as the entity began screeching a high-pitched cry. "Well, that is an unpleasant sound," she commented.

Penn flashed his screen towards her. "I took its picture and made some video. It apparently doesn't enjoy being filmed."

She let out an amused chuckle. "If it does anything unusual, record it for me to study tomorrow. I am going to grab a bite at the cafeteria and go to bed. Tomorrow, I will need my brain fresh to start tests on this thing." As she crossed to the exit, she made one last safety check. "Penn, you do have your walkie-talkie on you?"

"Yes, ma'am."

"That's good. But I'd feel better if you had a partner down here with you."

Penn grinned with satisfaction. "I don't think our buddy here is going anywhere."

Curtis focused on the ghoulish firewalkers outside his cage. Whenever one made its strange sounds, the other followed suit, making him think they were communicating with each other in this manner. Curtis also now noticed a device clutched in one demon talons was a cell phone. The monster hadn't magically materialized a replication of him in the ether; it had recorded him on a phone. Curtis didn't know why he hadn't realized it immediately. Perhaps his fear was too great. Or maybe it was simply because he hadn't seen a phone in ages. But what he could not comprehend was why a disciple from Hell would carry a useless cell phone, much less want to snap Curtis' picture.

CHAPTER 31

ESCAPING THE ARK

Saying goodnight to them in their room, Gavin Tanner entered his quarters where he closed and quietly locked the deadbolt between his room and his parents. Alone now, he took a deep breath with his back against the door. That hadn't merely been a "goodnight," it had been a "goodbye". Part of him wanted to cry. He would never see his mother and father again. Despite knowing his decision was the best thing for him, it still came at quite a cost. Gavin reminded himself that this was not his fault. He didn't want to live in a world where the choice between his heart and his family was necessary. It was a world they'd helped construct even before the end days arrived, and it was just as locked into this new society as it had been before. They'd left him no alternative but to strike out on his own, without them.

He stuffed his few pieces of clothing into a pillowcase and moved to the door on the opposite side of the hotel room. The boy's mind dredged up the passage from Genesis: *"Therefore a man shall leave his*

father and mother and be joined to his wife, and they shall become one flesh."
Perhaps Scotty wouldn't exactly be *a wife*, but the meaning still held.
Gavin no longer belonged to his parents. He and Scotty belonged to
each other.

He slipped into Scotty's room, locking the door behind him. Scotty
was ready and smiling hopefully at him when he crossed through...
the first step to a new life together.

"You ready, baby?" Scotty asked in a hushed voice, his own eyes
nearly mirroring his boyfriend's mix of emotions.

Whatever trepidation lurked in Gavin's eyes disappeared when
Scotty wrapped him in his arms for a kiss. "Yeah, I'm ready," Gavin
beamed. "The sooner we're out of this place, the better."

Scotty lifted Gavin's chin with trembling fingers. "Are you sure?
Be sure, Gavin," he warned. "Once we leave, there is no coming back.
They wouldn't let us back in if we tried. And we don't know what's
out there. Hell, we might not make it a mile."

"But we will be together," Gavin answered. "It's worth trying for."

Scotty nodded, then after a deep breath, moved to the second
connecting door on the wall opposite Gavin's room. He twisted the
knob, pushing it open. The door creaked slightly, causing him to wince,
glancing back at Gavin.

"You actually did it!" Gavin whispered excitedly. "How long did
it take?"

Scotty grinned with accomplishment. "Just about every night since
I moved into this room. Ever since we started talking about leaving,
I started picking locks and prying latches."

Gavin noticed now the scuff marks on the inner doorframe. "And
you got them all?"

"Don't look so shocked," Scotty teased. "I'm not completely useless,
you know."

"I'm just impressed, that's all."

The boys moved through the pitch-black room next door, guided only by the knowledge that the connecting doors were all placed in the same location. Using any light to maneuver through was not an option with the guard posted in the hallway corner. Even the faintest shimmer under the door of an unoccupied room would draw attention. Room after room they moved swiftly, but quietly. Their only company was the faint scent of old furniture and dank, uncirculated air. Scotty's prior handiwork with the locks made the escape down the corridor, unseen from the hall, a brilliantly orchestrated scheme.

"This is the sixth room," Scotty whispered in the dark. "The hall turns here, so the next door won't be straight ahead."

Gavin took hold of Scotty's hand, allowing himself to be led by the only one of the two of them familiar with the layout. It wasn't without its hazards, however. Gavin smacked into the side of the bed when his boyfriend made a sharp turn without warning. Thankfully, no sound reached the hall as they moved ahead to the next door.

From there, they continued as they had originally, moving directly across the unobstructed path to the next connecting door. Somewhere near the center of the adjacent hallway, Scotty stopped his detour. Guiding Gavin to the hotel room door that exited into the hall, he whispered. "I didn't go any further. Nobody lives on this side, so we can sneak out to the stairs from here."

With breath held, Scotty pulled the door open as slowly and quietly as humanly possible. He opened it just wide enough for Gavin to slip through, then himself. Once the boys were in the hallway, hidden around the corner from the guard, it seemed like the closing of the door behind them was scariest of all. Hotel doors always made more noise closing than opening as the steel locks glided across the doorjamb into the strike plate. It was something Scotty hadn't given thought to. The guard might still hear the click echo down the silent, empty corridor.

In fact, this was the primary reason for the guards. In the very beginning, Reverend Tucker had decided that the best way to protect his flock's virtue was to place a security watch in the colonists' sleeping quarters. He said it kept morality easier to adhere to and the sanctity of the family protected. Scotty could still remember his parents talking about it months and months ago. *"Even the most virtuous of the faithful sometimes need a guardrail to keep their moral compass straight."* Just remembering how his mother spoke made him so glad they were getting out of there.

While Scotty's mind was flashing back, Gavin's was strictly in the moment, pulling a sock from the pillowcase on his back and shoving between the door and the frame, so that it could not fully close.

Scotty winked at him with pride. Only a few more steps to go. The stairwell lay only three doors down at the end of the hall. All they had to do was slip through without making a sound to alert the night guard in the opposite hall parallel to them. The boys moved quietly to the end where Scotty, his back pressed against the wall, sneaked a quick look around it. Mouthing the word "Dammit," to Gavin, they knew they would have to wait. The guard had moved down to the other end of his protected area. Seconds dragged by before the sound of movement came again. Scotty checked around the corner, spying the guard walking back to his original post, rubbing at his calf as he went.

Scotty held his breath and moved with steady, patient ease. As if it were made of dynamite, he edged open the stairwell door only enough for them to squeeze through. Again, closing it presented an issue, but Gavin was already on it, pulling out the mate to his earlier sock, wedging it in the frame behind them.

The danger wasn't over yet. The boys still had to get down three floors, six flights of stairs, unseen by guards on the other floors. It was a slow-going descent, each step in danger of reverberating off the long rectangular walls and alerting a guard who might be very near a door. The second floor posed a bit of a concern, it being a floor fully inhabited by colonists—which meant a guard on constant patrol around the hall perimeter. He would not be resting in a corner. Scotty edged close to the door, peering as best he could peripherally through the slotted window into the hall.

The guard was approaching, absentmindedly whistling to himself while he trudged along what might easily have been his hundredth circle around the floor. The boys waited until he passed the window, then waited a beat longer for him to turn the corner before they started down the next set of stairs.

Once they reached the hotel's main floor, they emerged from the stairwell into the dark lobby. There was not a soul in sight—which was a relief. They'd known about the floor guards, but neither boy had any knowledge of what lay beyond the hotel rooms. Finding no guard positioned in the lobby was a welcome surprise. They crossed to the mall entrance, tucking themselves behind the wide arch as they scoped out the opening into the mall. Peering around the corner both ways, Gavin noticed a lone guard sitting on a bench at the end of the mall colonnade. His head sagged to one side, while his arm lazily draped along the back of the bench. He appeared to be sleeping. They decided to chance it.

Crouching low, the boys tiptoed across the mall's tiled floor and pressed themselves against the center garden planters. On the other side, a second patrolman passed by. He was fully awake, as evidenced by the soft click of his shoe heels. Thinking the coast was clear, Gavin veered toward the non-operational escalator a few yards away, but Scotty stopped him, shaking his head. He held his hands out, palms up, shaking them slightly. The escalator treads wobbled underfoot and would surely be heard in the quiet of night. They needed to keep moving ahead against the high planter boxes until they reached the actual staircase in the center of the mall.

The massive glass atrium running overhead through the mall provided a little light from the cloudy sky above, but it was an excellent amplifier to gauge the patrolman's footsteps against the tile in the empty, silent mall. He was far away now, nearing the end of the main plaza. Gavin leaned in and, barely above a breath, whispered in Scotty's ear, "He's at the end. He'll turn the corner any second."

Gavin crawled ahead, moving through a break in the planters to cross to the far side of the mall. Scotty followed his lead, and they continued moving through the mall, but now switching sides with the guard, allowing planters to shield them. They kept together in succession until the tall staircase jutted from the middle of the upper mezzanine, stretching down in two flights to the first floor. They waited for the patrolman's footsteps to move past them and fade into the distance before they started for the stairs.

They scaled the staircase softly but swiftly to the second tier of the Galleria. They crouched at the top, surveying the area until it seemed safe. From the looks of it, guards must have felt as if patrolling the lower level was enough to keep order and security. No guards patrolled up top. This made things far simpler than they had initially imagined. As long as the boys stayed clear of the railing, they could move unnoticed through the upper mezzanine.

Making their way silently to the empty shoe store where Doe was serving out her protective quarantine, the boys soon saw that whatever work they'd been through to get this far was nothing compared to what Doe had been doing. As they approached, she was removing the last few sections of the gate that she would have to squeeze through. The sweat on her brow and the white blisters forming in her hands proved she'd been industrious. She'd mapped out her best options for removing enough of the cage with the least noise to get herself out. She'd cut through each of the metal wires with the bolt cutters across the bottom in a two-foot section, then up on each side until only the top remained. She hadn't wanted to risk any metal falling after a cut, deciding the smartest way would be to push the severed panel out like a dog door. Smiling proudly at the boys, she carefully pushed at the loose panel. But it did not budge enough for a person to squeeze out. Attempting to force it would rattle the security door and draw attention. Scotty took the cutters and went to work on the top section—not cutting through the bars, but crimping them enough to force a bend. The boys pulled the flap out until Doe edged her way to freedom.

"Okay, boys," she whispered with a grateful smile. "Now what?"

Scotty, with a smug but reluctant grin, whispered in response, "Now, comes the hard part."

* * *

They tiptoed back to the stairs. Scotty held up a finger, signaling to wait while he tracked the guard below. Once the footsteps faded again, he led them down the stairs and back to a crouched position by the mall planters. Fear crawled up their backs as a second set of footsteps rang out just behind them. Luckily, the curvature of the planters widened at this area, continuing to obscure their presence from the second guard—now awake from his nap—and patrolling the other side.

The boys led the way in a slow zigzag across the mall, depending upon where the closest guard was, until finally they reached their destination. As Scotty directed them into the Dave & Buster's, Doe asked in a whisper, "What did you mean now comes the hard part?"

Pulling them through the maze of long-abandoned games and electronic entertainment towards the back, far from the mall entrance, Gavin explained. "Every door in the mall is welded shut, except for the one the mayor holds the key to."

"Then how do we get out?" Doe asked. "I promised to get you guys to my community, but if we can't even escape this mall—"

Scotty put his finger to his mouth and let her know there was no reason to panic. He led them across the shadowy floor, illuminated only by random neon bulbs overhead or against the walls. As they came to a gray swinging door, leading to the kitchen, he showed them inside.

"Okay," he announced. "You two need to stand right under me and take everything I hand you carefully and place on the floor without making a sound." Scotty's expression intensified. "And that part isn't going to be easy."

Gavin knew about the plan already but could see from Doe's face that Scotty hadn't informed her before tonight. He climbed up onto the stainless-steel countertop, his feet depressing into the metal to make a slight "wong" sound. He winced at the noise but didn't figure the guards in the mall heard it. They were, after all, in the kitchen of an arcade against the exterior wall of the building. The guards were far away in the central mall court. Even so, they had to be careful. Metal is loud if struck or bent or dropped.

"Hand me the socket wrench," he told Gavin. Doe watched with amazement as Gavin sifted through the pillowcase of clothes. "It's in my Talking Heads T-shirt."

Gavin found the shirt and unraveled it, producing a rusty wrench. Scotty put it to the bolts under the stove range but shook his head. "Bigger socket. The sockets are in the pockets of my gray cargo pants."

Dazzled by the cleverness of the boys, Doe stood back until needed, watching as Scotty worked to unfasten the bolts while Gavin handed him tools with the skill of a surgeon's assistant. Once all but three bolts were removed, Scotty looked down at his cohorts. "When I take these final ones out, this thing is going to start to fall. We have got to keep it held up until I get all the bolts out. Then we have to move it without making noise."

It was a dance of strategy, an intertwining of bodies and limbs and delicate maneuvers, but once Scotty had a mouth full of bolts, he lowered himself with extreme care to a squatting position on the countertop while Doe and Gavin struggled to hold up each side of the heavy hood. Scotty slipped his legs out, landing with a thud on the counter with his rear. They all stopped in place, assessing how loud it had been. But when no one came to investigate, Scotty slowly scooted himself off the counter while continuing to hold the hood in the center. Doe on the left and Gavin on the right worked with Scotty in unison to slide the hood onto the countertop as Scotty ducked from under it. It made a few screeching sounds, enough to run shivers through their bodies, but the guards had not heard it.

"So how does this get us out of here?" Doe asked.

"Like this," Scotty grinned, standing on the counter again and pushing the large cylinder of aluminum tubing out of the hole. "This vents to the outside. Now we just crawl through."

Crawling through the muck of the kitchen exhaust vent felt a little like worming through the intestines of some long-dead beast. Every shift and tug smeared decades-old grime on their hands and clothes and assailed their mouths and nostrils with the taste and odor of grease and filth. With a grunt and a forceful kick, Scotty knocked the exterior vent panel off the side of the building with a metallic rattle. He dropped from the grimy duct to land in a crouched position on the concrete six feet below. Then he stood back for Doe and Gavin. The three escapees inhaled the fresh air like drowning rats. It was a celebration of triumph for the three adventurers...when they weren't about to hurl from the nausea. They leaned against the outside wall of the mall alley, breathing in the fresh air of freedom and feeling wind on their faces.

Doe squeezed the boys' shoulders in awe, and said, "Okay. Now it's my turn."

CHAPTER 32

TRICK OF THE EYE

Doe moved around the corner of the alley like a cat searching for mice. Both Scotty and Gavin assured her no guards from the mall patrolled outside, but still she made them wait until she assessed the situation. When she came back for them, she reported the coast was clear.

"I told you there wouldn't be guards," Scotty said.

"Guards aren't our problem anymore," she told them with severe seriousness. "You two have been living in a fortress all this time. The dangers out here are nothing you're used to. We stay alert. We stay together. And if I tell you to run, you run and don't look back."

"Well, this seems like a fine idea," Gavin quipped. Then, looking over at Scotty, he grinned. "Whatever is out here is worth it, to be with you."

Scotty squeezed his hand. Doe laughed, nudging Gavin in the arm. "You two can kiss now, you know. Nobody out here cares."

The further they moved away from the enormous mall, the more they felt like Jonah must have, escaping the whale before it digested him. Everything now was unknown. The next meal, where to sleep, where to take cover under rain. The boys couldn't even be sure they would live through the night if the demons came crawling out, but one look behind them at the oppression they'd just escaped, bolstered their courage to face anything.

The parking lot looked like an empty desert of asphalt and tall weeds finding their way through the cracks. Doe squinted into the darkness, searching for a reflection of moonlight against a windshield or curved roofline of a forgotten car, but there was nothing. As far as her eyes could see, there lay nothing that might be of help to get them to Vernon. But with the disappointment of finding no means of travel, came the relief of there also being no immediate danger presenting itself...at least for now.

Moving on was the best thing to do, putting as much distance between them and the mall as possible. The highway was up ahead, ghostly and silent under the cloud covered night sky. Ransacked gas stations, abandoned storefronts, and hollowed out fast food restaurants stretched along the far side of the once bustling street. They kept moving, quickening their pace away from the mall's imposing shadow. This had once been a busy place, often overcrowded with impatient travelers, shoppers, and freight trucks. The six-lane highway ran empty now, like a long black river between the decay and destruction. Doe and the boys walked down the center of the street, feeling like they were walking to the edge of the world. Scotty wondered how many times he had ridden in a car down this very highway to and from whatever he was being dragged to by his family. Not once had he ever imagined walking down the center on foot.

Shopping centers lining the road on either side looked more like desolate tombs than the retail spaces that once thrived. Dense cloud coverage left little of the moon's light to see by, but their familiarity with where they were made navigating the way easier. This road was

Highway 31, or used to be. It was the primary thoroughfare, connecting towns like Chelsea, Pelham, Hoover, Vestavia, Homewood, and into Birmingham. The businesses along the extensive road were looted long ago, leaving now a wasteland. If there were any hopes of finding resources, they would need to get off this road.

The idea of venturing off the main road gave Doe pause. The very thing that made this street useless also made it safer. With nothing left for scavengers or monsters to take, who would bother coming this way? Any of the deadly creatures creeping about would most surely be onto fresher finds than this used-up and spit-out region of town. She kept going the way they were, making sure every step was toward Vernon, no matter how far they still were from it.

"What makes this other place so much better?" Gavin asked. "Are you sure they won't just think Scotty and I are *sinners* corrupted by the devil like the folks back there would?"

"Vernon isn't anything like what you've experienced." Doe explained. "If you like to pray, then you can pray. And there's somebody else around who'll probably pray with you. If religion isn't your thing, nobody cares, and no one is interested in forcing their beliefs on you."

Scotty, trailing a few steps behind, perked up and caught up to them. "And they'll be okay with me and Gavin? You know...being together?"

Though they couldn't see it in the dark, Doe was grinning at them. Happy for them. "No problem at all. There's another gay couple there. Rylan and Dillon. And they are beloved by the community."

"Wow," Gavin sighed with joyous relief.

Something caught Scotty's eye suddenly, interrupting the conversation. "What's that up there? Aren't those cars?"

Doe caught a glimpse as the rolling clouds uncovered a bit of the moon's light for a second. "That's a car dealership! The old Buick place, I think!"

They sped up their pace a bit, but Doe's mind drifted off to things other than transportation. *How did I know that?* Then it hit her like a slap. *Ben bought a car there once.*

"You okay, Doe?" Scotty asked, marching beside her. "You got really quiet."

"I keep getting fragments of memory back."

"Really?" Gavin cried. "Like your whole life?"

"Some, I guess," she said. "I remember getting a car from that place. I remember Ben. And some flashes of our life."

Scotty suddenly stopped walking, his blood running cold. "Are you having second thoughts? Do you want to go back now that you are remembering him?"

She turned sharply his way, her tone emphatic and hard as steel. "That would be the last thing I would ever do."

They continued along in silence for a while, each step drawing them nearer to the abandoned car lot ahead. Gavin was holding Scotty's hand in the darkness. Partly for support and partly to express his love. And Gavin realized Scotty was probably as unsure of what to say to Doe now as he was. But eventually she spoke again, breaking the uncomfortable silence.

"I know why I left now. Why I fought so hard to become a Searcher." She stopped walking for a second, turning to put her hands on each of their shoulders. "Boys," she began. "You are young and in love, and I hope that lasts for you, I really do. But if it doesn't...don't turn on each other. Don't *hurt* each other."

"Hurt?" Gavin echoed, startled by the word choice. Did she mean *hurt* or *hit*.

"You are both guys," she said. "Full of testosterone and ego. Don't unleash your anger on each other. Never raise a hand to each other. Stay in love. And if you can't stay in love, leave each other better than you found him."

"Did Mr. Noland hurt you?"

She sniffed the air. It was too dark to see if she was crying, or if the odor of old grease was still clinging to her nostrils. "He did. He came back from the military angry. Stacie was weak. But she was also smart and found her way out.”

Nothing more was said about Ben, or her old life with him, and before too much longer they had made their way to the car lot. The sky had cleared a bit, enough to see their way around without bumping into cars. “Do either of you boys know how to hot-wire a car?”

“What is that?” Gavin cried.

Scotty tapped him and replied, “Something old people used to do when they stole a vehicle. But cars don’t even operate like that anymore.”

Doe rolled her eyes. He was right, though. Although she didn’t exactly appreciate being lumped into the old people group. They explored around, checking doors and looking for keys under the mats or visors or glove boxes.

“Nothing!” Scotty scoffed.

“Yeah, I don’t see any way to get one of these running either,” Doe agreed.

“What about you, honey?” Scotty asked. He waited for an answer, but none came. “Gavin?” He spun around, seeing him nowhere. “Gavin? Where are you?” Starting to panic, Scotty ran to Doe. She reached into Scotty’s knapsack and dug until she found a long screwdriver, which she armed herself with like a knife.

“Gavin!” she screamed.

The sound of feet pounding the pavement frightened them for a moment, Doe pulling Scotty behind her. Then the sound grew closer, coming from behind. Doe spun around with her screwdriver poised to strike. It was Gavin, bright faced and excited, but out of breath. “Where have you been?” Scotty scolded.

“Just grabbing some keys!” he smiled, opening his hands to reveal a collection of key fobs.

“Where did you find those?” Doe exclaimed.

“In the showroom office,” he answered as if it were obvious. “You don't think this place just sold a bunch of keyless cars, do you?"

He clicked one fob, and a yellow flash of light emitted across the lot. Jogging down to see the car, Scotty pumped a fist in the air and cried, "Yes! A convertible!"

"Which has been rained into numerous times," Doe pointed out. "And probably won't start. Try again."

Gavin clicked another fob, sounding out a short horn blast and flash of light several rows over. Making their way to it, they saw it was a rather suitable sedan. Gavin opened the door and got into the driver's seat until Doe shook her head at him.

"I can drive!" he announced.

"Not this thing," she said, pointing to its location. The car was surrounded on all sides by other vehicles. "Let's try to find one on an end row that isn't blocked."

They made several more attempts, each leading nowhere. One car was indeed free from obstruction, but the tires had dry rotted. Another looked acceptable, only the engine wouldn't turn over. After another raid on the office, Gavin came back with more options, one finally resulting in success. It was one of those luxury models, four doors, all the bells and whistles, and it cranked. The boys loaded their pillowcases and themselves as Doe pulled the four-door luxury town car off the lot and headed towards home.

She remembered the area now, far better than before when she rode along with Dasha. *Dasha*. She couldn't permit herself to think about her now. Not Dasha. Not Ben. Not the bruises. Not the mess she'd made of her life. But it was hard to shut out the many memories of her sad and frightening life, which continued unpeeling in her mind like an onion. So many layers led her here with these boys tonight. The death of her parents. Her downward spiral into depression and loneliness. That night she met Ben Noland and believed he was her Prince Charming. Stacie was ripe for the picking. Vulnerable, submissive, starving for love. But Doe wasn't Stacie—not anymore. Doe wouldn't take the back of any man's hand. Doe was no one's victim. Doe was a badass. And right now all she wanted to do was get to Vernon. To go home.

"Stop!" Scotty warned suddenly a few miles down the road. "Shut off the headlights."

Doe brought the car to a slow stop in the street and cut the lights. Uphill, something was stirring. Under the wavering patches of moonlight, between the quick flashes of passing clouds, light from the night sky hit like strobes, illuminating something terrifying in the dark. It was an attack in progress! Doe glanced around to get her bearings, and her guess was right. They were in the Vestavia Hills district, and the attack was happening at the former YMCA directly off the highway.

The building looked as if it was being swallowed by the aliens. Doe watched in horrified fascination as their sickeningly blue-gray slimy skin reflected under the strobing wisps of light. They were at every boarded window, every sealed door. Clawing and tearing their way in. Screams erupted from behind the walls of the YMCA as Doe and the boys saw the creatures smash through their barriers and crawl inside.

"Jesus!" Scotty muttered. "Those poor people who've been living in there. Those damn red demons are tearing the place down around them."

"We have to help," Gavin whispered.

"There's nothing we can do," Scotty warned him. "If we try, they'll see us. We've come too far tonight to be ripped apart by those red hell monsters. Keep driving."

But she didn't keep driving. Doe kept still on the road, far enough away to not be seen by the hive, but close enough to recognize she and Scotty were witnessing two very different things.

"You keep saying red," she pointed out. "You said it twice."

"Yeah," Scotty answered. "Their skin—it's all red and burned looking."

Doe froze, waiting for the current cloud cover to roll by. When it did, she cried, "Look now! What are you seeing?"

Scotty exchanged puzzled glances with Gavin, then answered. "Like I said. They're burned. Like charred red skin with black, bubbly scorch marks."

Doe whispered softly, her eyes laser-focused on the monsters invading the settlement. "I see blue."

"Huh?" Gavin exclaimed. "Blue? No, those things are definitely red."

It was the same as Ben had described the aliens to her. Red skin? Doe grappled with how they could appear so differently to other people. Unless there could be more than one kind of them. Humans came in varying shades, so why shouldn't extraterrestrial life? But that wouldn't explain what she saw right now. She saw blue.

Before she could reason it out, the scene up the hill turned more gruesome. The monsters who had made their way inside the building were coming out again, and with them they dragged the people under attack. Their long taloned fingers stabbed into their victims, ripping them apart in a spray of blood and agonizing screams. The boys shielded their eyes, but Doe watched. It was an awful thing to witness, yet she couldn't turn away. Because when she looked at the creatures, her eyes registered them as blue. But then suddenly, they didn't. For a split second, she saw red monsters just as the boys did. The chaotic scene was happening too fast and under too little light to be sure. As her eyes strained to see against the night, a horrifying thought came to her. One her untrustworthy eyes thought they were seeing at that very moment. Blue monsters. Red Monsters. Both. There were two breeds. She slammed on the gas pedal, peeling the car away from the scene.

A DOE IN HEADLIGHTS

Nothing would scrub the images from Doe's mind. The YMCA. The screaming. The tearing. The blood. But what else she saw—or thought she saw—haunted her more than even those horrors. She'd kept her observations to herself, choosing not to tell the boys. Not yet. Maybe not ever. Not until she could trust herself. It had been terribly dark, and the car was at least forty yards away. The light had been unreliable as well. The moon kept slipping behind the clouds as if even it couldn't bear witness. But still. What if there was more than one kind of creature attacking Earth?

They were driving in silence now, each digesting the traumatic massacre they'd witnessed. Or perhaps the boys were contemplating their decision the closer Doe brought them towards Vernon. She wondered whether they had regrets now. Had Scotty and Gavin's desire to be together overshadowed the reality of leaving their families? The boys were walking away from everything they'd ever known in life, for each other. And that was quite a burden to place on one person.

She hoped they were wise enough to know that. Was it brave of them? Yes. But that kind of bravery, which feels so bold in the moment, can sometimes leave you empty after the adrenaline wears off.

In all the hurried planning to escape the mall, Doe never once considered what panic a car pulling into Vernon so late in the night might stir. This wasn't the same as a supply run caught after dark. Supply runners, even if returning late, still would be expected. No one was waiting for a strange Buick to pull up to the gate. Especially this late at night. When it did, the automatic perimeter lights brought immediate attention from Patrol Monitors.

"Stay here," she ordered the boys, stepping from the car.

The astonished face of Terry Hogland pressed against the fence line. Moving quickly, he waved to the gate guards to open as he rushed out into the headlights. "That ain't..." he muttered over the hum of her engine. "You *can't* be...Doe! Doe, is that you?"

She stepped quickly towards him, whereupon he swept her up into a bear hug. "Holy shit!!!" Terry was practically crying. "Dammit, girl, we thought we'd never see you again."

* * *

Doe wouldn't let him wake Augusta, not at this hour. Nor would she let Terry wake Marian or one of the other storage supply managers to get a room ready for the boys. And since she couldn't very well go back to her bed in the ladies' dorm with two teenage strangers, Doe told Terry she, Scotty, and Gavin would sit up in the cafeteria until everyone woke up. Terry was determined to stay up with them, hearing all about where she'd been and how she managed to get back to Vernon.

"You fellas have spunk, that's for sure," Terry grinned at the boys after hearing the story.

Doe put her hands on their shoulders, telling Terry, "It was a pretty fanatical place. They weren't free to be themselves...or together."

Scotty and Gavin cringed when she revealed *that part* of their story to the intimidatingly large man. Their kind of secret usually met with condemnation. Terry's reaction, or lack of one, came as a total surprise.

"Well...you're at Vernon now. And you're welcome here. I'm sure somebody will get you boys settled in a couple of hours and you can get something to eat and rest."

Terry left them to rest, needing to return to patrol duty. Within the next two hours, Doe, Scotty, and Gavin had drifted off to sleep, slumped over the table. But rest, was short-lived as the first reunion shook them awake.

"Doe!!!" Dillon's voice cut through the empty cafeteria like a cannon blast, jolting both Gavin and Scotty from their nap. Before she had time to react, Dillon had jerked her up into another bear hug. "You're alive!!! I can't believe it! We were devastated. How did you get away from the monsters?"

Trisha, a little calmer and not born with Dillon's flair for high drama, gave her a reasonable hug and welcomed her back. "You have been missed, girl."

In a short time, the cafeteria transformed from a quiet, sleepy hall to a hub of celebration. Word spread like wildfire, rousing everyone and drawing all who'd been close to Doe. Rylan, Allie, Farrah, and Penn swarmed her upon entering. But it was Shane bolting through the doors, pushing everyone out of his way, who wept as he swept her up.

They held each other in silence for a moment, both unable to say it aloud, but both understanding what was deeply felt by the other. They'd been through a trauma together, and they'd lost a friend together. Finally, Shane spoke. "I captured one of them." He said as he released her from his arms. "We've got it in the armory. All I could think was maybe we could trade it to get you back."

"You have one here! At Vernon?" she exclaimed. "What does it look like?"

"Like all of them. Blue. Ugly as hell."

Scotty and Gavin looked at each other, mouthing the word *"blue?"* Then Gavin asked Doe, "Is there a second type of demon?"

"I want to see it," she told Shane.

"Later," he said. His eyes glanced around at Allie, Farrah, and the rest of their friends. "Right now, you have a lot of people who've missed you."

"Those things killed Dasha, Shane. Our Dasha. I need to see it."

Rylan told Doe he would get the boys settled in if she wanted to go down to the armory with Shane. Doe thanked him, then told the boys she would find them later. Shane led her down to the armory to let her face the monster.

* * *

"So y'all are *together*?" Dillon asked Scotty and Gavin after Doe had gone.

"Yeah," Scotty said. "How'd you know?"

Dillon let out an amused laugh. "Because I've been behind those uncomfortable eyes before." Then with a smirk, added, "Plus, you're holding his hand."

The boys flushed pink and let go of each other.

"How old are you two?" Rylan asked.

"15," Gavin replied.

"And you both had the guts at 15 to run away from your families to be together!" Dillon grinned proudly. "Good for you! I had to cut my family out of my life too. So much for parents' unconditional love, right?"

"Right," Scotty nodded. "So...it'll be okay if we join you guys here?"

"Of course," Rylan answered. "I'll take you boys to the office to be assigned rooms."

"One room," Gavin corrected.

Rylan furrowed his brows a little in that condescending way that drove his husband crazy. Dillon noticed instantly, shooting Rylan an angry look and a quick shake of the head. But Rylan went ahead with his opinion anyway. "Probably best if we get you each assigned your own room."

Dillon smacked him on the arm, biting back, "Rye, if you tell these two young men, they cannot share a room because they are minors—after all they've been through to be together...Well, you'll be needing a room yourself tonight!"

Rylan looked embarrassed but still argued. "I mean, yes, I of all people understand...but...boys, you aren't adults yet..."

"They were adult enough to escape a prison. *In the dark*. With *monsters* out there," Dillon snapped. "They aren't children."

Gavin mouthed a silent *thank you*.

Rylan escorted the boys to the office. In all the madness, he'd forgotten to warn them about Dolores. "Oh, my stars!" Dolores cried out with exaggerated delight. "Such young men joining our little haven! Welcome to Vernon, Scotty and Gavin!"

The boys smiled appreciatively at her, while Rylan leaned across the counter offering Dolores a fisheye as he said, "And they would like a room they can share *together*."

Dolores clapped her hands together with a giddy glee on her face. "Oh...are you two boys...a *couple*?"

With a touch of anxiety rising in his chest, Scotty answered. "Yes. We are."

Without missing a beat, Dolores chirped excitedly. "Well, then certainly you can have a single room to yourselves!" She ignored the disapproving look Rylan shot her as she went to the far wall above the filing cabinets, tracing her finger over a map of the school. "There is an available room upstairs on the second-floor hall," she informed them.

The front door of the office opened as Augusta came in to meet the new arrivals. Dressed in a navy-blue pantsuit with a long lavender scarf draped under the lapels, she offered a cheery, "Good morning, everyone!" Rylan made introductions, but she waved him off. "No need, Rylan," she said. "I just reunited with Doe! She told me about these young men."

"Hi," Gavin smiled anxiously. "You're the mayor here...right?"

"Well, we don't call it mayor, young man. But yes, I am the elected supervisor of Vernon. But people just refer to me as the principal. And you boys can call me Gusty, if you like."

"Thank you, ma'am." Scotty stammered. His astonished eyes looked upon her as if he were star-struck.

"Is there something wrong, Scotty?" Augusta asked gently, patting his hand.

Blushing now, Scotty fumbled for the words, then wished he'd never found them. "It's just...where we are from, they'd never let a lady...especially..."

Gavin's eyes grew large as he turned to glare at his boyfriend. "*Scotty?*"

"A black woman?" Augusta laughed. "Doesn't surprise me. If they couldn't recognize the value in the two of you, I wouldn't expect anything else." She took hold of their hands and with a tender smile said, "Boys, never allow someone else to decide who you are or convince you that you are without value."

* * *

Shane stood several feet from the cell with Doe. The mutual hatred each shared for the brute was palpable between them. Neither could be certain if this was the exact alien who killed Dasha, but it mattered very little. It was just as responsible.

"I suppose we can kill it now," Doe guessed. "You no longer need it as leverage to get me back." Shane seemed surprised that she knew about that. Doe gave him a friendly wink. "Terry told me last night."

"I was hoping to end its repulsive existence today, but Doc suggested we might want to allow Dr. Journer to observe a living specimen before we do anything. Just in case we can learn anything about them." He offered a disapproving moan. "I think it's pointless myself. We should just kill the goddamn thing."

Doe took a slight step forward—still a safe distance, but close enough to peer in at it better. "You know something odd, Shane? At the settlement I escaped, the things they are fighting are red. At least they say they are." She glanced back to see she'd caught his interest.

"Red?"

"They call them demons," she explained. "It's a very religion-focused settlement. The definition of a fundamentalist theocracy. They believe the aliens are literal demons from Hell."

"Bullshit."

"I don't know?" she admitted. "Naturally, I'm not buying the demon story. However, the boys I brought back with me claim the same thing. They say the monsters have red skin. And last night...I can't be sure. It was dark. But I thought I saw it too. Shane...what if there are two aliens?"

"Two?" he scoffed. "One with red skin and one with blue. That makes zero sense."

"It actually makes the most sense of anything," Corinne's voice startled them as she stepped from the back. "Pardon me for causing you to jump," she said, a little embarrassed. "I had been looking him over myself, then had to use the restroom in back."

"Doc, explain how two aliens make better sense to you?" Shane asked.

Corinne began her revised assessment of the truth. "Our accepted theory is that a species from outer space decided to colonize the Earth. If that is true and its method of eradicating us was to infect our people with something that rebuilds our DNA into something more like their own," she now gestured to the cell. "It would make sense that a majority of the things we would find would be those now-transformed former-humans."

"Then what are the red ones?" Shane shot back.

Corinne's expression turned darker, more frightening. "I would surmise that if red ones are now being spotted, those are the true alien race. And our friend here in the cell is a rather cobbled-together facsimile of them mixed with us."

Doe grabbed Corinne's arm. "If you are right, and the actual aliens aren't like these guys...is there a chance to cure it? To restore our people back to human form?"

Corinne shook her head, scoffing at the notion. "Even if our world still had scientists, laboratories, and the resources we did before, our limited knowledge is light years behind theirs. We could never reverse what they've done."

"But even if we can't reverse it," Doe posed. "Is there at least a chance to tap into their humanity? If we can get these blue ones to remember."

"What good would that do, even if it was possible?" Shane asked.

"For starters," Doe suggested. "They are stronger than we. They used them to take us out. Who says we couldn't do the same?"

Shane shared none of her optimism. "Ladies, if any of this is real. The master extraterrestrials would never have come here unless they were certain their blue worker ants had wiped out enough of us to ensure it was safe for them. Either way, we're fucked."

CHAPTER 34

REPERCUSSIONS

No one ever thinks about what happens in the minds of the other fish in the tank when two seemingly insignificant fish disappear. But at the Riverchase Galleria Mall colony, the entire aquarium was abuzz with panic and speculation—and oddly enough, it wasn't the *little* fishes causing the stir...yet.

On the first day after Scotty McNab and Gavin Tanner escaped, almost no one noticed—except maybe their parents. Even then, the McNab's and the Tanners never dreamed their sons were gone, only off somewhere shirking their duty. They certainly didn't expect they were together. Both families were unaware they were even friends, much less a couple of co-conspirators. They were so in the dark about Scotty and Gavin's connection that neither set of parents knew the other kid was also missing. Joe and Leslie McNab, long accustomed to Scotty's falling short of their expectations, dismissed his absence as his goofing off somewhere in the mall. Joe even quipped to a friend at breakfast, "That boy probably found some girl around here he's chasing after."

He'd said it with false pride, fully aware he was lying to himself as well as his friend. Of the two or three girls in the Galleria near Scotty's age, Joe had never once seen him speak to one. The Tanners were no different.

While the parents of the *small fish* distracted themselves with denial, it was the disappearance of a big fish that jolted the colony into alarm. Stacie Noland—Ben Noland's wife—was gone, again...for the second time. Somehow, she'd cut her way free from her quarantine cell, and the news spread like a flood across the mall. The city council quickly met in its third-floor conference room to discuss the fallout.

"Our men have scoured the mall," Bill Wickers told the mayor nervously, catching himself before he ran his anxious hand over his bad comb over. "She is just gone."

Mayor Collins was furious. "The only means out of here is through the main exit, and I possess the only keys to that exit."

"I don't know what to tell you, Mayor," Bill muttered. "She's either found a way out or somebody is hiding her very well."

It was Corbin Hartley who asked the obvious question to Ben Noland, who'd been called in for this meeting. "Ben, why would your wife want to run or hide? I'd think she would be grateful and very relieved to have been found again."

Ben shifted uncomfortably on his feet, a nervous reaction which was very out of character for him. "Can't say. You know how women are." He paused, glancing at the only female council member. "Nothing personal, Dorothy."

"Wives usually like being with their husbands," Dorothy commented. "Obviously, yours didn't. Why?"

Ben appeared angered by the question. "You trying to say something, ma'am?"

Mayor Collins quickly intervened. "The interpersonal goings-on between a man and his wife are not pertinent to our problem." Collins pressed his hands firmly onto the conference table, addressing his council with all seriousness. "Somehow, a person has managed to escape this colony. It is highly doubtful that someone is helping her hide. Such a feat couldn't go on indefinitely in a sealed environment."

"Not to mention," Bill added. "Her quarantine wasn't up, and it's unlikely any of our colonists would risk contamination."

"Exactly!" the mayor cried. "We cannot have our people believing this might be a place they would wish to leave!"

"So what! If someone chooses to leave, let them." Corbin answered. "This isn't a prison. Is it?"

"Of course it isn't!" Reverend Tucker bellowed, slamming a fist onto the table. "But we are building God's city here! It will fall to us to repopulate the world, just as Adam and Eve did before us. Just as Noah and his family did after that! You see, this is not the first time our Lord has hit the reset button. But this time He chose us to start things over. The very idea someone would prefer *out there* to in here...it is blasphemous!"

Dorothy cleared her throat. "Has anyone checked the doors we welded shut in the beginning?"

"Yes," Bill said. "Not a single one has been touched. I am telling you there is no way out of this place."

"And yet my wife is gone! Again," Ben growled.

Dorothy sat with her thoughts for a moment, debating whether to mention her nephew's absence. Her sister and brother-in-law didn't seem terribly worried, each saying he'd show up by dinnertime. But Dorothy couldn't help but think back to her recent talk with Scotty. He had hinted at wanting to leave. Did he find a way out? Was that secret boyfriend of his with him? Dorothy knew mentioning Scotty's absence might jeopardize his escape—and his life—if he were still in the mall. She chose to remain silent.

But Dorothy's silence bought little time. By evening, when neither boy had shown up for dinner, rumors swept the mall once again. With two teenage boys now missing on the same day as Stacie Noland, there was little doubt in anyone's mind they must be together. It didn't take long for concerned mall colonists to seek answers from the man who routinely assuaged their fears...Reverend Tucker.

The preacher found himself surrounded at his table in the food court by worried members of his flock. A few tables over, the McNab's and the Tanners sat watching stone-faced and nervous. There was little denying now their boys had run off...together. Dorothy sat beside her sister Leslie, watching the flicker of emotion in her eyes. It wasn't a sadness at the loss of a son. Leslie's tears were for her own shame and embarrassment because people were finally connecting the dots...and letting their imaginations run with it.

"That boy of yours, Tanner," Bill Wicker shouted over the amassing crowd and cacophony of competing voices asking their questions to the mayor and the reverend at once. "I always had my suspicions about him. What was his name, Gaylon?"

"Gavin," Tanner bit back.

"Just as sissified," Bill remarked, garnering some laughs from the court. "Reckon your boy's kinda light on the feet there too, Joe?"

Joe McNab jumped from his chair and grabbed Bill by the collar. It took Ben, Reverend Tucker, and a few other men to pry him off.

"My son ain't no faggot Bill!"

"Then explain why two boys the same age, with rooms right next door to each other, haven't come back home for supper with their families and haven't been seen since yesterday."

The remark sparked something in Mayor Collins's mind. "Yes! Their rooms! Has anyone checked the rooms?"

Leslie raised her hand timidly. "I looked in Scotty's room. He wasn't there."

"Let's look again," Reverend Tucker suggested. "I am curious about something."

A procession up the hotel stairs, led by the minister, brought the McNab's, the Tanners, the mayor, and the council members up to the third floor. Inside Scotty's room, his mother gestured, "See. He's not here."

Reverend Tucker walked to the connecting door to Gavin's room and opened it. "The McNab boy's side isn't locked. Only the Tanner kid's door."

"That proves what they're saying about my son isn't true!" Gavin's father exclaimed. "Gavin's side is locked!"

"Actually, it proves the opposite," Reverend Tucker declared. "Gavin relocked it once he came into Scotty's room."

A hush fell over them, all except Joe, who shouted furiously, "My son ain't no damn fag!!!"

Leslie burst into tears. Dorothy didn't console her. She simply stood by herself in her position as a council member. Had her sister truly been mourning her son, her reaction might have been different. But watching Leslie carry on with such despair only angered Dorothy, because none of it was over losing Scotty. All Dorothy cared about now was that Scotty and Gavin would get away.

Reverend Tucker moved now to the other connecting door into the empty room on the left. "It opens," he showed them. "And this lock has been jimmied." He turned to Ben. "Check all of them for me."

Ben slipped into the vacant adjoining room, then the next, through the entire chain of doors. When he returned it was through the door to the hallway, startling the others in Scotty's room. "They made a loop around the floor to the stairs. Guards wouldn't have seen them at all."

Leslie crumpled in on herself. Mrs. Tanner just stared blank and numb. But Joe's face flushed red, his temples throbbing. "That boy ran off with another boy! They're queers!" He looked at Dorothy, making her very uncomfortable. "He was queer? Did you know?"

Nervously, she answered with a lie. "No. I wondered sometimes, but no."

The preacher's expression darkened, almost sinister, his voice like thunder. "Dorothy, if you had any inkling whatsoever that we had a

Sodomite in our midst, you owed it to God and your community to bring that to our attention!"

"To do what?" she asked. "Throw them out to the demons?"

His eyes shifted into a menacing slant as he replied. "The demons would not have harmed them because they are already in their camp. Homosexuals are not God's chosen, Dorothy. They belong in hell with the other monsters."

"What do we say to the people?" the mayor asked in a white panic. "How do we explain their escape? Or why they'd even want to?"

Reverend Tucker lifted his chin piously and pronounced his righteous assessment. "We tell them the devil claimed his own. We say those boys were here to contaminate our colony. To put a stain on God's chosen people. But we could not be corrupted and so they left to tempt another community."

"Isn't that overdoing it a bit?" Corbin commented. "Two boys and a woman ran away. Big deal. People will talk for a few days and then forget."

Tucker addressed him with unquestionable authority. "Our explanation is real. The boys and their temptress demon Stacie have been removed. We are the vessels with which God will build a new world. There was no way they could remain."

Ben began pacing like a caged animal, his fists tightening, his teeth gritting. "It makes more sense now." He turned accusingly towards Joe. "Your boy gave Stacie the bolt cutters to free herself! And he stole what he needed to wedge all these doors open. And somehow, somewhere in this mall, he made a door out!"

Joe stood stunned by the accusation but did not deny it. It was true. Scotty had disgraced his father, his entire family, and damned his soul to Hell. Joe hoped his son would burn forever in the lake of fire. And by the remotest chance Scotty might still be somewhere in the mall and found...Joe might just kill him himself.

CHAPTER 35

A PICTURE IS WORTH…TWO WORDS

The boys folded into the Vernon population with ease. Within a few days, it seemed as if they'd always been there. It pleased Doe to hear them rave over the community as they sat down together for breakfast.

"This place is like a dream!" Gavin exclaimed. "Everybody is so nice!"

"It's really more than we imagined," Scotty said gratefully. "Thank you, Mrs. Nol—thank you, Doe."

Farrah was still giddy over Doe's safe return home and even giddier that Gavin was joining the ranks of the garden crew. Scotty had already asked to work in the kitchen as Trisha's assistant, but when Trisha realized that meant her having to work more in sync with Dillon she decided to stay in her position as potato peeler and vegetable slicer—pushing Scotty into the assistant spot.

"I think a Patrol Monitor job would be less dangerous than working under Dillon," Penn laughed.

"No, thanks!" Scotty replied. "I'll take my chances with a moody chef over fighting those demons any day."

"There is that word again," Doe scoffed. "I should take you down to the armory and let you see that thing. You'll see it's way more alien than what Reverend Tucker forced you guys to believe. Unless we are talking about two different beings."

Scotty shuddered. "I'm not getting near one of those things. Not after what I heard it did to the two men on tour with my dad."

Smiling proudly, Penn whipped out his phone. "I can show you right here! I recorded the freaky thing a few nights ago to show Farrah."

He opened his photo gallery. The video of the alien was easy to find, being the last thing he had recorded. The boys were more fascinated by seeing a cell phone again after so long than by a caged monster. "Man, I miss my phone," Scotty whimpered.

"Here," Penn said, thrusting his phone in front of the boys.

Scotty and Gavin's gazes locked on the screen, then wide-eyed, looked up at each other. "Where did this come from?" Gavin gasped.

"I told you," Penn repeated, pressing play. "I took it the other night after Shane captured it."

Cracking a smile, Scotty asked, "Is this a joke?"

"Yeah," Gavin added. "How would you even come across video of him?"

Doe, Penn, and Farrah were now the ones with puzzled expressions. "What do you mean, Gavin?" Penn asked. "I already said I recorded it in the armory a couple nights ago."

Gavin took the phone and stuck it back in Penn's face. "Don't you see him? Can't you hear him?"

Farrah lifted the phone and held to her ear as if it might uncover something she'd missed before. "I can't hear anything but the thing yapping in its weird alien language."

Doe took it next, listening closely. It wasn't making any sounds now, so she swept her finger across the screen, restarting the video. When the gurgles from the monster started again, she raised her brows and told the boys, "I don't hear anything but noises." Despite what her own ears told her, Doe could tell from the boys' faces they heard something else. "What do the two of you hear?"

Scotty clutched Gavin's leg under the table with a cautionary squeeze and answered. "It's like you guys said...it's just noise."

"Yeah," Gavin said. "We weren't sure if you heard it. But I guess it's the way you said, that's how it speaks."

He cued his boyfriend with a look, whereupon Scotty smiled nervously, and said, "Well, I need to go back to training in the kitchen."

"Me too," Gavin replied. "I start my garden shift soon. See you all later."

The boys rose quickly, taking their trays to the washing area. Penn and Farrah went about their breakfast while Doe's eyes followed the boys. If Scotty had to return to the kitchen, why was he walking out into the hall with Gavin?

Doe quickly excused herself and caught up with the boys, who were huddled in the hallway whispering. "What is going on?" she asked. "What did you see and hear on Penn's recording?"

"Same thing you guys did," Gavin muttered anxiously.

"You aren't a good liar, Gavin," Doe replied.

Scotty checked their surroundings to make sure no one was around. "Look, Doe, we just got here. These people don't know us. You don't even really know us. We don't need trouble."

"Or everybody looking at us with suspicion," Gavin added. "We didn't come here just to feel as *othered* as we felt there."

Doe could tell they were afraid, but of what?

"What is on that footage, guys?" she asked again. She took their anxious hands in her own. "I will believe you. I saw a blue entity. Did your eyes view it as red?"

"It isn't a creature," Gavin whispered. "That wasn't a clip of a demon or one of those aliens you guys talk about. It's a man."

"It's Mr. Jackson," Scotty specified. "From the Galleria. He went on that mission with my dad, but he never came back."

"He was even yelling his name to Penn on the video!" Gavin exclaimed. "But none of you can hear it."

Doe's face, frozen in shock, did not know what to make of their claim. But she knew the boys were telling the truth, as their senses understood it to be. "Come with me to the armory."

"No!" Scotty answered. "I do have to get to the kitchen, and Doe…we aren't getting involved in this. Nobody here would believe us anyway, and we just want to blend in and feel safe."

Nothing more was said on their part. The boys rushed off to their own duties, leaving Doe alone in the corridor, unsure what to do next or if she should tell anyone what they'd said. She found herself walking down to the armory alone several minutes later. Though she'd already seen the alien prisoner once, she needed to see it again.

* * *

Doe adjusted her eyes to the dim barrack lighting as she went inside. She saw instantly she wasn't alone. Rylan was sitting across from it in a chair against the wall—his rifle laid across his lap in case their captive tried anything.

Doe met him with an upturned brow. "I thought you were a supply runner?"

Rylan grinned, patting his gun. "We're all pulling double duty with this thing in our jail." He nodded his head towards the cell, getting out of his chair. "It doesn't do much. Just stares at you and sometimes grunts out sounds, but it's mostly stopped that now."

Doe approached the cell stiffly, her body tense, saying nothing. Quietly, she tried willing herself to see something other than what her eyes saw. She blinked a few times. Squinted more than once. Then, stared without blinking as though the monster was one of those puzzles with a hidden figure within it. But her perception never shifted. All she could see was a terrifying life form from another planet. It was undeniably alien. Nothing Earth's evolution could have spawned. Its slick, iridescent skin shimmered under the fluorescents—shifting into bluish purples, greens, and smoky gray.

"You okay?" Rylan asked concernedly. "You look...disturbed, maybe?"

Doe wasn't going to tell him. After all, there wasn't anything to tell other than what the boys told her...and no one would believe two adolescent strangers. Cautiously, she took several steps closer to the cell.

"Doe, not too close." Rylan warned, coming closer with the rifle. "You want to stay as far away from that thing as you can."

Doe brushed off the warning. "I was face-to-face with those things when I disappeared. Why didn't they kill me?"

"You said it yourself," Rylan reminded her. "Men from that mall settlement rushed in and saved you."

"Did they?" she muttered absently. "I wonder."

Puzzled, Rylan asked, "You wonder if it was them who saved you?"

Doe took another step closer to the monster's cell, noticing the way it stared at her as if it were just as perplexed by her as she was by it. "I wonder what they thought they were saving me from. Maybe I was never in any real danger at all from either side."

"Huh?"

"Maybe...just maybe...both sets of *creatures* knew me. Maybe I was the only non-creature in the entire store."

"You aren't making sense, Doe," Rylan said, raising his voice. "And you're getting too close to its cage!"

Her mind poured over the muddled facts from that day. Her perception of how things went down, and how Shane's account matched her own up to a point. Ben's version, and what Scotty recounted from his dad, matched Doe and Shane's nearly perfectly with one difference.

The color of the monster. There was no way to account for it. Even if two alien forms existed in red and blue, it still wouldn't sync with how things went down at that Walmart. It was the same story on both sides…

"Depending on your POV," she muttered, closing the distance with the last step to the cage. She heard Rylan protectively cock his rifle behind her as she clasped her hands around the bars and studied the alien's eyes looking back at her. "Curtis…Curtis Jackson," she said with a whisper. "What did we look like from your point of view?"

"What did you ask it, Doe?" Rylan called over her shoulder. "Did this thing kill someone else besides Dasha?"

Her eyes remained fixed on the monster. It, too, stepped a little closer to the bars. Its elongated fingers seemed to tremble as its hands reached to clutch the bars as Doe had.

"Get back!" Rylan called. "It's going to grab you!"

"Wait!" Doe cried, pushing down his rifle. "Give it a second. I think it wants to touch, not grab."

"What are you doing, Doe?" he exclaimed.

Doe was quite calm, even breaking into a slight smile at the creature, as she told Rylan, "I think…it's human. Or used to be."

The creature's long fingers shifted down the bar slowly, stopping only when grazing Doe's. Doe slid her hand up the bar and over the strange blue fingers, closing her hand over his.

Curtis couldn't make sense of what the devilish duo were doing outside his cell at first. Perhaps the demons were deciding the best way to kill him. Or worse, drag him down into Hell, where he would be trapped and tortured for all eternity. Those red-skinned monstrosities, who reeked of sulfur and burned flesh, spoke to each other in their hissing, clicking tongue. But one of them stood out, drawing nearer to his cell, watching him intently. Every step it took nearer made him frightened. But then the red devil extended its talon-crowned hand as it made more noises—almost as if it were speaking to him. Curtis couldn't understand it at first, but then suddenly he could.

"Curtis...Curtis Jackson..." The sound cracked like shredding metal, but he'd heard it! The syllables were unmistakable. Curtis stared mesmerized at the seared gremlin. Did it really know who he was? Did the demons in Hell know the names of the people on the earth?

"Doe, what the fuck, girl!" Rylan shouted, taking new aim with his rifle to defend her. "Step back before he slices you with those claws."

"Curtis?" she said again carefully. The monster strained its head her way, its black empty eyes cutting into her. "Was your name Curtis Jackson?"

"This is insane!" shouted Rylan.

The creature didn't react at first, continuing to behave as if it were struggling to understand. Then, slowly...almost like a voice under water...the words came in audible snippets and garbled fragments. "Mynne...glammme...izzz...Kaarttezzz."

Doe unwittingly shed tears, squeezing her hands tighter around the being's fingers on the bars. "Curtis...my name is Doe. And this is my friend...Rylan."

* * *

Mrs. Yardley welcomed Rylan and Doe into her room, the urgency on their faces enough to silence any pleasantries. Doe launched into a quick summary of what they'd learned. Rylan, visibly shaken, said nothing until she finished.

"That's why I told Doe we should talk to you, Mrs. Yardley." Rylan shifted in his chair anxiously, noticeably unnerved by what he could not explain. "I think I really did hear him say his name." Contemplating his next words carefully, he said, "Mrs. Yardley, when you told Penn and me that ideological fractures might have drawn the aliens here—do you still believe that?"

Before she could answer his question, Doe cut in. "What are the chances someone contaminated with alien DNA can be restored to human?"

Mrs. Yardley appeared puzzled. "Restored?"

"The Nazis for example," Rylan said. "After the war, how did people who'd been convinced Jews were inhuman, come to see them as human again? What un-brainwashed them?"

Mrs. Yardley nodded, grasping the picture now. "You believe this alien prisoner has somehow accessed his human side again?"

"It's got to be possible," Rylan answered. "According to Doe, the new boys who fled the mall can see the alien's human form. Maybe because they knew him before, or maybe he hasn't fully transformed yet. If there is something left of a man in there, maybe it's not too late."

"If he still understands our language," Doe added, "We might be able to undo whatever they've done to his mind."

The teacher looked skeptical. "You are speaking as if psychology can deactivate some mysterious, and frankly unparalleled, scientific leap in physical metamorphosis."

"I realize we can't undo what has happened to these humans *physically*," Rylan admitted. "But if we can still reach their minds, some leftover humanity…we might stand a chance. We may even get them to fight alongside us."

Mrs. Yardley stared down at her folded hands, flexing her fingers nervously. "It is all so very complicated," she confessed. "The more I think about my conversation with you and Penn, the more I doubt all of it."

"How so?" Rylan asked.

Her eyes drifted to her bookcase—years of history, philosophy, theology lining the shelves like silent sages. "We've tried to make sense of this—alien infestation, mutations, biological warfare, transformations. We try to force puzzle pieces to fit, believing that even if we can't get them all in, it still shows enough of the picture to know what we are looking for. But now with these red aliens...blue aliens... it all feels like noise."

"But you said it yourself," Rylan reminded her. "The red aliens are probably the aggressors. The ones who traveled here to take over. The blue ones are merely the army they built to take us on. Their bio-weapons. Their victims."

"It's the only thing that makes sense," Doe agreed.

Mrs. Yardley shook her head. "We keep forgetting what Occam's Razor has taught thinkers for centuries: the simplest explanation is usually the right one."

Doe's voice dropped. "Then what's the simplest explanation?"

"Frankly," Mrs. Yardley answered with a disheartened fall in her voice. "I am afraid it may be so simple that I can't see it either."

CHAPTER 36

CROSSING CONTINENTS

Something about Scotty and Gavin's evasiveness with the video clip of the captured alien would not let Penn's mind rest. Not wanting to ruffle Dillon's feathers in the kitchen, he bypassed Scotty and sought Gavin out to ask questions. Besides, Gavin seemed more easily swayed to speak than his boyfriend.

Miss Ashley had the boy shadowing her for his first shifts, giving him an orientation on how things worked in the garden. Penn interrupted them in the middle of a lesson about the significance of crop rotation in preserving nutrients in the soil. She didn't mind giving the boy a ten-minute break to speak with Penn, citing the need to check on her father-in-law anyway. Mr. Andy had taken to wandering off in recent days, a side effect of the Alzheimer's acceleration.

Gavin appeared nervous when Penn once again showed him the video footage. "You and Scotty saw something this morning when I showed you this clip. I would like to know what that was."

Gavin attempted to deflect the accusation, but Penn wasn't buying it. "Sir, we just started fitting in here. We don't want people looking at us like—well, like something is wrong with us."

"This won't go further than me, Gavin. Trust me. I just want to know what's going on in the outside world. I'll share something with you. I've been using an old HAM radio to contact others across the country. I haven't learned much more than when I started, but maybe what you saw on this clip could help me figure things out."

Against his instinct to remain quiet on the matter, Gavin told him.

"You mean you don't see a monster at all?" Penn questioned. "Not even a red one?"

"All I see is a man named Mr. Jackson who lived at the mall. Those noises you hear...I don't hear noises. I hear him telling you his name and asking what you plan to do with him." Gavin sighed awkwardly. "I don't see how that helps you."

But Penn did. Penn not only believed Gavin but now allowed himself to consider a few things his mind had rejected early on. He found Farrah a few rows over, harvesting ears of corn into a large wicker basket. As he came up to her, he noticed she looked pale and clammy.

"Are you alright, honey?" he asked instinctively, placing a hand on her stomach. "This work is too much for you in your condition. I'll speak to Gusty—"

Farrah pressed a finger to his lips to quieten his rant. "Miss Ashley has me doing the lightest duty. I am fine."

"But you look terrible!"

There are moments in a relationship when a man wishes he could snatch back the words he chose the second they've left his lips. This was one of those times for Penn.

"Well, aren't you the flatterer!"

"You know what I mean," he replied gentler. "I only want you to take care of yourself and this baby."

Farrah smiled at him appreciatively and explained. "I am perfectly fine. I look this way because I've had a wave of morning sickness. In fact, if you go two rows over, you'll find a black plastic sack I've been throwing up in."

He grimaced. "No thanks. I don't need the full tour."

She assuaged his concern, letting him know she was staying fully hydrated, and that Doc had told her the nausea was perfectly normal for her first trimester. "Now, what brings you out here to find me?"

"Farrah, remember back to that day in the mountains...the day we found out. Remember when we heard our phone messages?"

Her face dropped. "Penn, I don't care to remember any of that."

"It's important," he told her. "You had a message from your friend Jessica...remember?"

"Of course I remember, Penn!" she said, tensing. "I wish I could forget."

"Her family," Penn pressed. "Her family had killed her husband Jim and were coming after her, right?"

"Why are you resurrecting such traumatic memories for me?"

He stroked her arms affectionately. "Just a few more questions, honey, then I'll drop it," Penn promised. "Jessica was really into her church, wasn't she?"

Farrah appeared rather confused by the odd question. "I don't know?" she scoffed dismissively. "No more so than other people, I suppose."

"No, no, I remember you telling me after you had lunch with her the last time, that all she could do was talk about her new church and Bible study group. You said she was almost obsessed with it."

"Okay?" Farrah remarked. "So what? She'd been through a really rough patch after her miscarriage. She needed to cling to something."

Penn began nodding, answering his own questions quietly in his head before he had even asked them. "Jim was just as into it. I remember him telling me when we all had dinner that he had stopped drinking because he had found the Lord."

"Well, that was wonderful, wasn't it?" Farrah shouted, raising her hands. "Who doesn't like God?"

"Yeah, but they got really sucked into it." Penn replied, pieces falling into place. "I remember you talking about how laid-back Jessica's parents were when you two were growing up."

"They were." A smile came over Farrah's agitated face, sparked by an almost forgotten memory. "Her dad caught us smoking weed once. Instead of yelling at us, or calling my parents, he just told us we hadn't rolled the joint tight enough. Then he showed us how."

Penn didn't ask her any more questions. "I'll see you after work."

"You mean at the meeting," she corrected. "There is a school meeting tonight, remember? I will meet you in the auditorium."

"I forgot all about that," Penn said, a little chill running through him.

"It's a big one too," Farrah explained. "Decker says it's to decide if they should kill the alien in the armory, now that Doe's back."

The ramifications plunged into Penn's soul. Killing a murderous alien was one thing. But what if Gavin was right? What if that thing was only a man...a man no one else at Vernon could see for some inexplicable reason. But perhaps it was explicable. Penn was beginning to realize just how plausible it might actually be.

* * *

Clinton was half asleep in the chair on guard duty when Penn slipped into the armory, heading to the back office. Penn flipped the radio power switch and began fumbling across the ranges until he heard a voice crackle.

"This is Felix Hornsby in NYC, radio number W2NYP. Anyone read? Over."

Penn seized the frequency. "Felix, this is Penn Fletcher in Birmingham. K4RGT. I'm so glad to hear someone else over the wire. Tell me, what condition is Manhattan in these days, pal? Over."

"Ransacked. Burned. Barely anybody left here, Penn. Those HCEs have got us nearly wiped out. Most of them moved on across the river weeks ago. Just a few of us left. Maybe a hundred here in midtown. That's all I've been able to count. How about you? Over."

"Jesus!" Penn gasped, unable to fathom New York City's population decimated to almost nothing. "About the same here. A few settlements. Not much." He paused a second, not tossing transmission back to Felix yet until he asked, "Felix...you said HCEs? I don't copy the term. Can you describe your monsters to me? Over."

"Sure thing," Felix obliged. "HCE is Hostile Contagious Entities. News called them that before we lost power. Living off batteries and candles these days. Thank God for stocked bodegas on every corner or we'd have starved to death. Of course, I'm getting seriously tired of beef jerky and potato chips. Over."

"I bet," Penn replied, butterflies rising in his chest. "Can you describe the HCEs for me? What do they look like? Particularly...their color? Over."

"The bluest and purpliest things you ever saw. Their build reminds me of insects, like grasshoppers or a mantis, only huge."

Penn felt some relief from the description. It was the same as he'd seen. He asked a few follow-up questions before wrapping up, but Felix knew about as much as he did. Penn needed new perspectives, something new to glean from the chaos. He searched across more frequencies.

"Ain't you ever seen one of those Hellwalkers?" cried a former rancher from Oklahoma. His family was having an easier time than New York, with cows to eat and milk to drink. But there was still a hint of desperation in the cowboy's voice as they were nearly down to their last of the livestock.

"What color are these Hellwalkers?" Penn asked him.

"Like I said, ain't you seen one? Red as the devil's wife's wedding dress! Got these black veiny tubes running over them too. Straight outta hell itself, I tell you!"

Penn wished Farrah were with him to be recording all of this in her notebook. Penn jotted a few notes for her as he went along. Transmissions were coming in much clearer than usual. Perhaps the night sky made a difference in signal strength without sunspots or ultraviolet rays competing. He made a mental note to transmit only at night from now on. He tried another frequency before he had to get to the auditorium. He took a chance, calling across multiple ranges until he reached where he hoped to reach.

The Argentinian accent was thick as the man tried to confer with Penn in his broken English. "Si, LU8ARG, here. May I be of assistance, senor?"

"Please," Penn shouted across the wire. "My location is in the States. Alabama. I wanted to know what your invaders look like? Over."

"Invaders senor?"

"Yeah, your aliens, or demons, or contagion entities. Whatever your people call them. When you see one...is it red...or blue...what do they look like?"

Silence. However, the Argentinian man still had his finger on his transmission button because Penn could faintly hear him speaking to someone else in the background. "Creo que este es un estadounidense... Me está pidiendo que le describa a nuestros monstruos. ¿Le digo que en Argentina no hay monstruos?"

"I'm sorry," Penn shouted. "I don't understand what you said."

The man didn't hear him. Penn's transmission hadn't gone through because the Argentinian hadn't released the button on his microphone yet. A woman's voice sounded in the distance. Perhaps the man's wife.

"No te metas."

The man spoke back to her, continuing in his hushed tone, "Creo que debería ayudarlo." The woman uttered something else Penn could not quite hear, followed by the man's response, "Claramente no sabe la verdad."

"Sir, please..." Penn begged. "I don't understand."

The man must have released his button because he answered Penn's response. "I am...very sorry, señor. Is clear you don't know... your problems, in United States... they are only happen there."

Penn's heart jumped suddenly. *What did he just say?*

"Are you saying the aliens only landed here in America?" Penn asked back.

Again, silence for a moment. "We don't have them. I am sorry, señor."

As the man abruptly ended their transmission, Penn's mind thought back to the conversation he and Rylan had with Mrs. Yardley. She had mentioned that if aliens had landed only in America, or if this was indeed biowarfare from an enemy nation, then the U.S. might stand a chance.

CHAPTER 37

THE UNAFFECTED

On the heels of the shocking discovery that Stacie Noland and the McNab and Tanner boys had left the Galleria colony, Sunday morning arrived, offering a much-needed call to spiritual action for the people living there. There was a palpable tension rippling through the mall's central atrium as the quiet rustle of the crowd settled into the chairs of their makeshift chapel. Unlike most services, when chatter would echo from the glass above with the chorus of an entire community gathered in one place, this Sunday voices spoke in whispers if they spoke at all.

For the McNab and Tanner families, these whispers were as powerful as if it had been a heated political rally because they knew it was all about them. They had dreaded this sermon, knowing it would be about their sons and the disgrace they'd placed upon their families and the colony. As usual, Mayor Franklin Collins and his wife Linda sat in the front row, flanked by board members Bill Withers, and Corbin Hartley's family.

Reverend Elias Tucker approached his pulpit, putting an end to the hum of whispering gossip. "Brothers and Sisters, we once lived in a world that had forgotten shame." The pause he placed after his opening words gave weight to his meaning, indirectly drawing attention to the missing boys' parents.

"It was a world where the values once cherished as 'good' had become labeled as 'bad'. Believers of the Good Book," he said, patting his hand onto his Bible. "Knew that world could not stand. And so, God—just as He did when he cleansed Eden of Eve's sin, and as He did when sending the flood to wipe away all but the few faithful on the ark—brought His wrath again in our time, by setting the world aflame with the demons of Hell."

He had his congregation's full attention now, emboldening him further. "Our Heavenly Father directed us here," he continued, sweeping his hand across the mall court. "To this majestic sanctuary where we could fortify our safety, spared from the damnation outside these walls. Little did we know that among us..." His eyes drifted to the third row, to the McNab family. Leslie felt herself locked in his gaze and felt stripped bare from it. "Among us, Brothers and Sisters, an egregious sin camouflaged in righteousness. Scotty McNab and Gavin Tanner..."

Joe tensed as if physically struck while Leslie shrank with humiliation, shoulders dropping, as if weighted by the very mention of her son's name. Fighting the urge to look across the court to see what the Tanner reaction was, Leslie kept her head straight ahead—too afraid to catch anyone else's eyes.

"Scotty McNab and Gavin Tanner dwelled in this holy sanctuary as part of us." Reverend Tucker's tone sharpened slightly, "But they were not like us. Somehow the Devil himself snuck in two of *his faithful*. The world, which fell into oblivion a year ago, tried to trick us into believing homosexuality was natural. 'Love is love,' they would say. 'How can love ever be wrong?' they would say."

His next words spat like venom. "But I tell you, dear flock, our Lord told us how in Leviticus 18:22. *You shall not lie with a man as you would a woman. It is an abomination.*"

Reverend Tucker paused now, staring out over the congregation. Scatters of 'Amens' floated through the air, while most remained silent, as if unsure whether to nod or look away.

"They told us acceptance was progress. They said it was all right for boys to become girls and girls to become boys, and we were in the wrong to say differently." He sneered at the idea, sparking amused chuckles from a few. "They told us to open our borders to foreigners and turn a blind eye to the crime and disease they brought on their backs. They said The Church needed to evolve."

Raising his fist as he raised his voice into thunder, Tucker cried, "But none are more evolved than God! And the Word of God does not change! Our Father does not *tolerate* wickedness in His own house!"

His demeanor softened now as he wiped his sweaty brow with a handkerchief. He stepped forward onto the stage and lifted his hand out towards the McNab's and Tanners as if offering absolution. "You did not lose your sons, my dears. You lost the undoing of your salvation. Satan planted among you seeds of destruction. Two moles to burrow in and destroy our righteous walk with God as we build His new world. But their damnation is not your fault, Brother McNab, Brother Tanner. God rejoices in the purification of your family."

Scotty and Gavin's families smiled now, nodding their heads in agreement, no longer frozen in shame or ridicule. They were thankful. Their esteemed minister washed them clean of their sons' sins, and they felt a part of the flock again.

Still looking out at the McNab and Tanner families, Reverend Tucker extended a loving smile to them before saying, "You were tested Brother and Sister Tanner, Brother and Sister McNab. God tested your faith, and you passed."

Leslie cried now, nodding her head vigorously, feeling fully justified now in her piety. But her sister Dorothy simply stared at her, in stunned clarity. She understood fully now what Scotty had tried to tell her for a long time. Leslie did not love her son. Not the way a mother should. Leslie had spent her entire life trying to elicit envy from other women like her—women who had done nothing remarkable with their own lives and resented those who had. Their only chance of acclaim now came through their children's success. The more revered their children, the more credit they could accept for having created such a notable person. If their children couldn't gain adoration for accomplishments, it could come through their Christian values. And now Scotty had shattered Leslie's only means of superiority on both fronts.

"You are not alone, Brother and Sister McNab, Tanner," the reverend continued. "Many of you here today may not know this..." Everyone's attention focused on the preacher and what he might be about to divulge. Attentive eyes would have noticed his glancing down to the first row and receiving a supportive nod from the mayor before he continued.

"I have known Mayor Collins and his family for many years. Frank and Linda are faithful Christians. Salt of the earth. Yet they too had a choice to make once, long ago. Their only child fell down a dark path. Brother and Sister Collins lifted him in prayer each day, but he clung to his ruination. Our esteemed mayor and his dear wife made the ultimate sacrifice to their Lord, just as Abraham was prepared to do on the stone altar. They rooted out the malignancy within their family and cast it out. For not even a mother or father can walk the road of salvation for you."

The crowd gasped and whispered among themselves a moment while eyes saw Linda Collins reach behind to the next row to take Leslie McNab's hand.

"Brother and Sister Collins lost their son to his sinful addiction," Reverend Tucker went on. "But know this...none of us who are cloaked in the Lord, walk alone."

* * *

Colin and James were both sleeping in the connecting room when Genna looked in on them. She closed the door behind her so that she and Corbin could talk privately without being overheard. "You seem very uneasy, Corbin," she said softly as she crawled into bed. "That gathering tonight shook you up a bit, didn't it?"

Corbin scratched at his chin stubble, shaking his head in bewilderment. "Didn't it you?"

Genna hemmed and hawed a little beside him, then answered. "I suppose, a little. But I don't see how it affects us."

Corbin's eyes widened in surprise at her. "Genna Hartley! Back in the day, a speech like that would have put your dander up. Those two boys are being vilified. Worse than that, literally demonized. And all I can see that happened was two homosexual boys fell in love. It isn't their fault. It doesn't make them evil. And knowing they'd never feel safe here, they ran away."

"Without even thinking about what is waiting out there to kill them!" Genna remarked. "They should have stayed here with their parents. They weren't thinking about anything but their hormones. And it has probably already gotten them killed."

Corbin exhaled a long breath, as if trying to cleanse his lungs of the tainted air inside their compound. "I believe they did think. That's the saddest part. I think those boys knew the danger outside, and it seemed preferable to remaining in this stifling, oppressive environment another day."

She could see now Corbin eyed her view disapprovingly. The lawyer in him would always feel compelled to play devil's advocate. "You know I have no problem with gay people," Genna reminded him. "I was wonderful friends with my hairdresser Peter before all of this."

Her husband bit his tongue, making an active choice not to point out how cliché she sounded in reminding him *she once had a gay friend*. A friend whom she never invited to their annual Christmas parties or any of her birthday dinners and probably didn't even know his address. Still, he knew his wife wasn't a bigot—but she wasn't an advocate either.

"Ever since that first night, when we locked ourselves here in the mall," Corbin reflected. "This place has drifted from a place of community and empathy into something verging on fanatical. It makes me nervous."

Genna rested back against the headboard leisurely, signaling she wasn't very anxious about anything. "You're only upset because everyone was so riled up earlier. But Corbin, you've always been a Christian man, and we have always been a Godfearing family."

He flinched at the word. "I have always hated that expression *'Godfearing'*. It used to scare me as a kid. God is supposed to be about love and compassion. Not fear."

Genna laughed at his thought. "Well, those who follow Him don't have to fear Him. The fear applies to everyone else."

Corbin was far too tense to sleep. He flipped the covers away and hopped up. Pacing the small hotel room, he tried making his case again, just like in the old courtroom days. "Genna, don't you see? With that mentality, we will all eventually be at risk of being *othered*. Right now, they are up in arms over a pair of gay kids—completely overlooking how frightened and ostracized those kids must have felt. But what happens when it's over young women who don't want to marry and repopulate the world? Anything might become the sin du jour? You can assign any grievance to sin if you try."

"I think you are getting carried away here, Corbin."

"I don't think so," he argued. "Beware the momentum of closed-minded masses."

Genna reached out her hand pulling him back to bed. Stroking his mussed hair with her fingers, she hoped to squelch his fears and put an end to the silly conversation. "You act as if this is The Lord of the

Flies. We are a faith-based society. We do have values, you know."

"If the rhetoric sounds holy enough, sheep don't notice when the shepherd trades his values for power."

Genna was only now realizing how very much Corbin meant the things he was saying. It was times like these when she had to remind herself that his was a mind trained in observation. Whatever he'd heard in council meetings or seen festering in the greater community must have been troubling him for some time.

"I do understand what you are saying, Corbin," she told him gently. "But darling, this is the world we live in now."

"Devolved to," he corrected.

"Regardless," she continued. "None of it applies to us or to our boys."

"We don't know that," he countered, a sense of urgency in his eyes. "Colin and James are close. Best friends. What if one day one of Reverend Tucker's minions points a finger of accusation at them? And what if it were true? What if one of them turns out to be gay?"

Genna scoffed at the notion, dismissing it with the wave of her hand.

"It happens, Genna. And it wouldn't be within those boys' control. Is it truly a better world if everyone is the same? If we allow people to become targets for a few voices who know how to get a crowd to echo them...aren't we culpable in endorsing division?"

She placed her delicate hand upon his cheek, turning his face to look into her eyes. "Corbin, my sweet crusading husband, it is best for our little family if we do not become involved in the colony's little controversies. It isn't our problem."

Genna clicked off the lamp and tucked into her pillow for sleep. Corbin sat up for a long time, weighing his conscience against her argument. It was best for his family to stay out of it. The controversy over the Tanner and McNab boys really wasn't their problem...but it was somebody's problem. It had been those boys' problem. And once, not too long ago, Corbin Hartley had been a defender of people like those boys—both in court and in theory. Turning a blind eye to social injustice was not the path he wanted a new world to found itself upon. Because when it came down to it, wasn't injustice always *someone else's* problem? Until it is you.

CHAPTER 38

SCHOOL ASSEMBLY

Farrah waited for Penn to join her in the auditorium. More people were filing in, and still there was no sign of him. When he finally rushed in only minutes before the meeting began, she scolded him. "Where have you been?"

Keeping his voice as low as he could, he quickly filled her in on his latest HAM radio transmissions. When he finished, she stared at him with a combination of amazement and confusion. "You see," he said after. "Mrs. Yardley may be correct. Maybe the United States was hit first. That would mean there's still a chance."

There would be time to talk more about it later. With all the Vernon residents in the auditorium, Augusta stood at the front to call the meeting to order. "We have much to discuss tonight," she began. "But before we do anything else, I want to take a moment of silence for a fallen hero."

Everyone knew who she meant. Vernon's unified spirit brought the auditorium to a hush as every head bowed in respect. "The job of a Supply Runner is one of the most dangerous we ask of our people," Augusta continued solemnly. "And Dasha was fearless. Because of Dasha and others like her, our people here in Vernon have never gone without a meal. We have always been able to tend our sick and injured. Outside our fence lies a landscape fraught with danger. Every road is a landmine. Every building is a potential death trap. Dasha was our champion, and she shall not be forgotten."

Augusta waved to someone in the crowd.

The audience turned to see Lauryll emerge from the back of the auditorium. In her hands, she carried a large canvas covered with a dark blue tablecloth. She made her way down the center aisle as Augusta continued. "Our own talented artist, Lauryll, has ensured Dasha shall live on—not just in memory, but as a permanent beacon of inspiration in this school."

Augusta lifted the tablecloth from the canvas to the cheers and applause of the entire community. As onlookers viewed the portrait for the first time, it radiated with the essence of Dasha. Lauryll had captured and preserved her in the vivid color she had exuded in life. But it was the smile that captured the eye. Unmistakably Dasha's, it was a grin of both mischief and sincerity, with eyes daring anyone to guess. In a post-apocalyptic world, Lauryll's portrait of Dasha might one day become the new Mona Lisa.

"Dasha's loss belongs to us all," Augusta told the audience. "But one person above all deserves the honor of placing her on our wall."

Shane had dropped his face into his hands, overcome by the unexpected tribute to his partner. But when Augusta called upon him, he took the painting from Lauryll, thanking her for capturing his best friend so perfectly, and started down the wall aisle. He stopped by Doe's chair, showing her the painting up close. Her tear-streaked face smiled approvingly at both Shane and the portrait. He moved on to the center of the auditorium, where a nail waited. Shane lifted the canvas, catching the wire on the nail, and gently rested it in place.

In a world with few photographs and no way to commemorate loved ones who came into your life after the world fell, Dasha would always be there now.

Once Shane took his seat, school business became the focus. Clinton started things off by being so exuberant with his point he forgot to be recognized by the principal before standing to speak. "Dasha's death is just another reminder that Vernon isn't doing anything about the monsters outside these walls. We've been here a year now, and the only enemies we have stopped are the ones that have attacked us here, or the few our Supply Runners have run into. When are we gonna take the offensive? Playing solely defense ain't getting rid of the problem!"

There were a surprising number of residents in agreement with Clinton's point, and they made their opinions known with applause. Even Terry Hogland, a board member, was among those who supported Clinton's suggestion.

"I gotta say, I think Clinton is right on this," Terry began. "We gotta start hitting back. Find their nests and exterminate them. We have plenty of weapons in the armory. And our first step needs to be killing the one we got captured."

"But those weapons are for our protection, *here at home!*" Dolores cried with a shaky voice. She wasn't normally one to take part in open forums and demonstrated her anxiety with constant adjustments of her glasses. "We can't possibly take out all the aliens. Trying will only use up the little protection we have."

"She isn't wrong!" Decker shouted from the fourth row. "We have weapons, but not the kind you need to strike enemy territory."

Terry spoke out again, making a valid observation. "We have a couple of test cases right here tonight," he said, looking at Augusta. "Where are the new guys? Scotty? Gavin? Where are you, boys?"

Scotty and Gavin were there, just like everyone else, only they'd hoped to blend into the crowd unnoticed. Knowing so few people, the last thing they expected was to be drawn into the governance meeting.

"Don't be afraid, boys," Augusta called out. "You could be valuable in this discussion."

Reluctantly, they rose to their feet. Doe offered them a supportive wink from two rows away. "Yes, ma'am?" Scotty replied.

"How did your former community handle such matters?" the principal asked. "Did they take the fight to the enemy? Or did they save their resources for home protection?"

Gavin and Scotty shared a brief stare, determining which of them felt brave enough to speak in front of the entire community, then clearing his throat, Scotty answered. "Men went out hunting them. My father had just got back from going out to fight. He got injured, but it wasn't serious."

"One guy died though!" Gavin piped in.

"Tell us about it," Terry said.

"Well," Scotty shifted on his feet. "They called it a tour of duty. Four men chosen alphabetically, go out and hunt demons. They took down a whole apartment building full of them on the last one. Those were the men who found Doe."

"See!" Clinton cried excitedly. "We have to take some initiative out there if we want our planet back! Starting with the one we've got locked up right now!"

A wave of hubris swept the room as people joined in to agree. Some wanted revenge on the aliens for destroying life as they once knew it, while others only wanted to make the area around Vernon safer. Vying to be heard over the gregarious enthusiasm were the naysayers; the members of the community who felt waging war on the invaders would be an act of folly. They took the position that existing under the radar was the safest way to survive.

Mrs. Yardley did not have the strength of voice to be heard above the fray, but the senior resident stood tall and poised, waiting for the chatter to die down. Once eyes fell on her, she spoke. "Before this board takes any offensive action out there, we must have a more crucial conversation about the legitimacy of our perceptions."

"Meaning what?" Terry asked.

Mrs. Yardley turned to face Doe. "This young woman has managed basic verbal communication with the prisoner in the armory. She and Rylan have a working theory—that the creatures, once human, might still retain fragments of their former selves."

The crowd began buzzing at this insight, but Mrs. Yardley wasn't finished. "Dr. Chambers believes the creatures we've seen so far were seeded here as a kind of first wave—an army. But the true aliens have only just arrived... and they look different."

Corinne picked up, corroborating Mrs. Yardley's statement. "It's true, that is a working theory. What is undeniable is that we do not know enough about these beings yet. Killing our only living specimen would be a mistake until we learn more."

Augusta asked Doe to explain what Mrs. Yardley meant by her having communicated with the alien. Doe explained her rudimentary exchange with Curtis, and Rylan backed her up by having been a witness.

"And what do the two of you make of that development?" Augusta asked.

"I'm not sure," Doe answered. "At the other settlement, they only reported coming into contact with red-skinned beings. While we here, and our friends at UAB, have only ever seen blue ones."

Farrah nudged her husband in the ribs, whispering, "I think you should say something."

Penn hesitated, not sure he had enough yet to convince anyone, but stood up anyway once Farrah's urgings attracted notice. He recounted his limited radio contact, citing he'd had confirmations of both reddish and bluish monsters across different regions. Terry backed up Penn's testimony, having joined in occasionally on the HAM radio.

"It's fair to say there are two distinct types out there," Terry informed the crowd. "The red ones might be the real invaders. The blue ones? They could be... I don't know, drones. Pawns."

"But the man in the armory isn't an alien!" Gavin blurted out accidentally.

All eyes landed on him as Scotty shrunk in the chair beside him. "What do you mean, Gavin?" asked Augusta.

"I only saw the video Penn showed us. But Scotty and I don't see a monster at all. We see a man. A man we know. His name is Mr. Jackson."

A stunned silence fell over the auditorium.

Doe stood again, posing a question to Shane. "Shane, the night Dasha was killed, I saw you fighting one of them. And you saw one grab me too, correct?"

"Yeah," he answered. "And the one I fought is the one in the armory right now."

Doe looked around, uncomfortable under the weight of so many stares. "But when I woke up at the mall, the man who saved me said his friend Curtis was fighting a red creature when he pulled me out."

"Your point?" Shane asked back.

The group fell into uneasy silence until Mrs. Yardley raised her hand. Her voice cut through the tension—calm, clear, professorial. "This could be a word problem on a test," she smiled meekly. "One man reports fighting a blue creature while a woman is taken by another. Meanwhile, someone else claims a red creature attacked that same woman, and his friend fought off another red attacker." She looked around at the skeptical faces. "The variables? The color of the creatures. The common factor? The woman."

Shane frowned. "What are you saying?"

Mrs. Yardley folded her hands. "If both accounts are true—if no one is lying—then someone isn't seeing what's really there. Or perhaps... we're all seeing what we expect to see."

She looked at the sea of bewildered faces among her, then clarified it for them. "Maybe the monsters were never monsters at all."

CHAPTER 39

DISSENTION IN THE RANKS

The school board meeting adjourned, leaving the residents of Vernon with more questions than answers and nothing resolved. But behind the scenes, the board members wouldn't be satisfied until they had answers. They required answers, and they wanted them now. Augusta, Corinne, Shane, and Terry directed Doe and the boys to venture down to the armory with them to examine the alien prisoner to determine if any part of what Doe and Mrs. Yardley were claiming was possible.

Gavin and Scotty followed quietly behind the leaders of Vernon as they descended the hill toward the armory below. The boys spoke only through occasional glances, each fearful of being characterized as liars, or worse...double agents sent by their former colony to weaken this one with doubt and suspicion. They hadn't come to Vernon to be test subjects. They came for inclusion and community—a safe place to start over. Yet here they were, taking part in a warped psychological experiment.

Leading the group, Terry and Shane appeared stoic. They did not believe Doe was a liar, but they also didn't believe what she thought was accurate. Behind them, Augusta and Corinne were unreadable. When Terry opened the armory door, ushering everyone inside, the boys felt a mild sense of relief seeing Rylan standing guard duty over the prisoner. Of the people they knew so far at Vernon, Doe, Rylan, and Dillon were the ones they trusted most.

"Come here, boys," Augusta asked, motioning for Scotty and Gavin. Together, the three of them faced the cell.

"That's Mr. Jackson!" Gavin cried. Glancing back at Doe, he added, "Just like that video you showed us."

With no trepidation, Scotty rushed to the cell. "Mr. Jackson! Are you okay?"

"Stop!" Augusta panicked. "It may grab you!"

Rylan and Shane charged after him, catching the kid under his arms, dragging him back to safety. "No, you don't understand," Scotty protested. "We know him. He isn't going to hurt anyone."

With their focus on Scotty, no one had seen Gavin stride forward, even closer than Scotty had gone. Gavin gripped the bars with his hands and made eye contact with the creature most everyone else perceived as a dangerous killing machine. "Do you know me, Mr. Jackson? We've seen each other back home."

Behind Gavin, the adults watched in stunned silence as Gavin's words elicited more of the monster's gurgled responses. In a cascade of clicks, hisses, and snaps, which appeared to be deliberate replies to Gavin's question, it looked as though the monster was answering the boy.

"Boys!" Curtis exclaimed from the cell. "Did they take you too? Have they harmed you?" His eyes glared at the group of hideous red devils surrounding the boy and restraining the other one. Curtis shifted his gaze to Scotty, still in the clutches of the demons who dragged him away from the cell. "You're Joe McNab's boy, aren't you?"

"Yes," Scotty answered. "I'm Scotty."

"It *spoke* to you?" Corinne asked with astonished eyes.

"Yeah," Scotty replied. "Can't you hear him?"

Augusta placed her hand over the boy's arm and answered. "No. We only hear noises."

Rylan and Shane let go of Scotty, allowing him to join Gavin. Though no one yet truly believed this outrageous claim, the boys stood side-by-side like interpreters in a foreign embassy.

"Mr. Jackson," Scotty began carefully. "They believe you are an alien...from space."

"*Alien?*" Curtis shouted. "You mean those demons think we are invading Earth?"

"No, sir," Gavin said quickly. "They aren't demons."

Augusta and Corinne exchanged glances. That word *demons* again.

Curtis turned, pointing through the bars. "But look at them! Look at the red devils!"

The creature's arm darting between the bars prompted Rylan and Shane forward again, assuming it was about to strike one of the boys. But it didn't. It only pointed.

"That's not what they really look like, Mr. Jackson." Scotty tried to explain. "They are people like us." He gestured to himself and Gavin. "We can see them just like we can see you."

Doe came forward now, her eyes fixed on the alien mirage her brain was presenting to her, concentrating as hard as she could to break through the illusion. But so far, she still saw only another species of life.

"Curtis?" she said softly. She was now between Scotty and Gavin by the cage, her eyes locked onto the creature's. "Curtis Jackson. Can you understand me?"

Curtis recoiled from the bars—not in fear but bewilderment. "That demon can speak!" he exclaimed. "It said my name. I heard it!"

"Her name is Doe," Scotty explained. "She's the woman my dad and Mr. Noland found the night you were taken. She's really *Mrs.* Noland.

Stacie? Remember?"

Scotty's revelation was just as much news to the Vernon crew as it was to Curtis. Terry, Shane, Corinne, Rylan, Penn, and Augusta exchanged surprised looks.

Doe took a bold chance and reached her hand through the bars of the holding cell. It hung there a moment, an invitation offered without an acceptance. The board members had expected the monster to tear her arm off at the roots...but it didn't.

"If you understand my voice, Curtis," she said. "Take my hand in yours. Feel that we are both human beings."

Curtis hesitated, taking a step forward, then back again. The idea of touching one of those things terrified him. It might be a trap. Clasping its hand might even imply sealing a deal with Satan, damning his soul. But somehow, he trusted the voice coming from the demon's mouth. It didn't sound especially evil. With another look at the boys, nodding that it was safe, Curtis moved closer, extending his hand. No one breathed. The people of Vernon watched as the blue beast's elongated fingers closed over Doe's hand. But it didn't harm her.

Doe and the alien...and Curtis and the demon...stood staring at each other, eye to eye, seeing one another's beautiful and fragile humanity reflecting, at first, only in the eyes. A humanity so delicate mere mental suggestion could twist it into misperception. As the two locked their fingers together, Doe saw the claws turn translucent in her grip. Curtis experienced much the same vision, as their senses then watched the thick black blood vessels coursing over one another's flesh shrink and fade into nothing but the mere illusion, they had always been.

"Hello," Doe whispered to the bewildered man with a gentle smile.

Curtis blinked in disbelief. "Hi. You're much too pretty for a demon." His eyes shifted to the others. "But they still look the same."

"I think that'll fade in time," Doe told him.

One by one, Doe introduced each of Curtis' perceived devils by name. "This is the leader of our community. Her name is Augusta."

"*Her?*" Curtis said curiously, straining to find a woman within the beastly figure.

"Most people call me Gusty," she said, reaching her hand into the cell to touch the alien creature.

"Gusty?" Curtis whispered, his eyes blurring slightly as the crimson visage evaporated like steam from a boiling pot. In its wake, stood an older African American woman with a purple scarf around her neck and large brown friendly eyes.

Augusta Davis had been a sensible woman all her life. She was not prone to fantasy, nor vulnerable to suggestion. But as the layers of illusion peeled from the alien monster to show the unimposing and shaken man before her, she understood how susceptible the human mind could be and how even she was not immune to it.

"Let's get this man out of this cage," she said to Shane.

Shane didn't budge. "It's a monster. It stays locked up...or we kill it."

"No, he isn't," the principal explained. "I can't say for sure whether Mrs. Yardley's theory is right or not. But I can say definitively, there is a man here. You must open yourself up to the possibility that you've been manipulated."

"I am not manipulated, Augusta!" Shane bellowed like a trombone. "This is an alien species. I don't know how it's managing to hypnotize you and Doe, but I am stronger-minded than it is, and it hasn't fooled me."

"I'm with Shane, Augusta," Terry weighed in. "I don't see nothing but a monster."

Augusta turned to her old friend for support. "Corinne?"

Corinne's troubled face showed the struggle between her loyalty and her own clinical mind. She wished she could see what Augusta saw, but she didn't. "I'm sorry, Augusta," the doctor answered. "I don't see a person."

"Doc!?" cried Doe. "I'm telling you, I see a man there. If you don't believe me, believe these boys," she added with a hand on Scotty and

Gavin's backs. "They immediately recognized this man."

"Doe," Terry snorted with authority. "I mean you no offense. You've been an asset and a friend since Dasha and Shane brought you in. But we don't know these boys at all. I'm not about to question what my *own eyes* plainly see on the testimony of two kids I don't even know. They could be like that thing in there, just disguised to trick us."

"But you know me, Terry!" Doe pleaded.

"Do I?" he answered. "Like I said, no offense, Doe...or Stacie...or whoever you are. But we only met you a few months ago ourselves."

Raising her frustrated hands to her temples, Augusta beseeched them. "Well, you all know me! And I see a human being locked behind these bars, and we aren't going to leave this man in here. I am sure he's hungry and certainly needs at least a glass of water."

Shane stood boldly noncompliant. "I will not unlock that cell, Gusty."

Augusta was astonished at his insubordination. He'd never defied her before. "Shane! I am the head of Vernon, and I say let this man out."

"This monster killed Dasha!" Shane roared. "And anyone who wants to set it free is going to have to kill me first."

CHAPTER 40

LAURYLL'S LAST PORTRAIT

Shane stood rigidly in front of the creature's cell, his pistol hanging at his side, his hand gripping the handle so tightly his white knuckles were going numb. His jaw was clinched, teeth gritted, as he stared down at the sleeping monster. Every fiber within him was screaming at him to kill it. It had killed Dasha, whether by its own hand or the others of its kind who were there. Augusta and the others had left hours ago, defeated in their effort to set the murdering beast free. Shane had not left. He guarded the armory as if he were the earth's last living soldier.

He was on edge for trouble, so when Rylan pushed the creaky door forward and came in to relieve him, Shane was skeptical. "I've got it," he told Rylan. "You can skip your shift tonight."

"It's okay, Shane." Rylan went to the gun cabinet and removed his rifle. "I won't let anyone in, let alone near that cell door."

The assurance hung there a moment, Shane scanning Rylan's eyes for treachery, but finding none. Finally, he blinked, stepping down for a much-needed rest. He took his gun back to the cabinet, then relocked the doors before turning back to Rylan. "What do you think about all this?"

Rylan rubbed the back of his neck. "I don't know. Mrs. Yardley has some valid points. And I trust Doe. But when I look at that thing over there, I just see an extraterrestrial life force. And until somebody shows me otherwise, that's what that thing is."

With a nod, Shane made his way to the door. "Okay. See you in a few hours. If anybody gives you trouble—"

"They won't," Rylan said, patting his rifle. Then, just as Shane pulled open the door to leave, Rylan called out. "She was my friend too, you know. I'm not letting anyone set Dasha's killer free."

Alone with the creature, Rylan's curiosity challenged him to at least consider the possibility Doe and Augusta were right, and they had in fact broken through the spell and seen a living man beneath the monster's flesh.

He approached the cell cautiously, the prisoner watching him back just as suspiciously as Rylan looked at it. "Are you truly a person under there?" Rylan asked the air rhetorically.

Curtis could not understand the demon's sounds as it stared at him through the bars. "I don't understand what you want?" Curtis said with a nervous shakiness in his voice. "Are you trying to talk to me?"

"Those grunts and growls you make," Rylan said to the creature. "Are you attempting to form words? I am trying to see you. Trying to try. But all I can see is a monster."

* * *

The end of Patrice's shift came around ten o'clock, but when her relief took over, she didn't feel much like going to bed. Lakeisha was with Dillon, probably fast asleep by now. She would let her stay there until morning and not disturb her. Sometimes on nights like these,

Patrice would sneak into the cafeteria and pour herself some coffee, then sneak down to the library to read until she got sleepy. But as she climbed the switchback steps to the main hall, she passed the art room. The light was on. *Lauryll.*

"You okay?" Patrice asked, stepping in quietly. As usual, Lauryll was busy at her easel. "You seemed a little upset at the school meeting tonight. Thought I'd check on you."

Lauryll poked her head around her canvas. Her eyes were bloodshot from overuse. Or perhaps fumes from paint thinner. Accidental dabs of color stained her cheeks and chin as her hands furiously worked at the canvas. "It is the last one."

The announcement came as a surprise. "I thought your series was already complete?" Patrice's eyes drifted to the wall where the painting of the creature in the doorway hung, and Lauryll's small grandchildren murdered in the yard.

"It wasn't," Lauryll said. "Tonight taught me that. I now understand with full clarity." Her voice broke. "And it is tearing me apart."

Patrice noticed now Lauryll had been crying by the color of the tears. No one cried green tears, but Lauryll was. Weeping in her work, the tears had crossed the flecks of paint staining her face, resulting in streaks of green and violet.

She started across the room to console her, but Lauryll stopped her with a raised hand, misinterpreting Patrice's intentions. "If you want to understand this last painting, start at the beginning."

Reversing course, Patrice moved to the gallery wall. Many paintings covered it, including two finger paints Lakeisha made. But it was the series of paintings lined together across the long stretch of wall that told Lauryll's story.

She'd seen them before, the progression of portraits of Lauryll's daughter Heather. Ranging from childhood to womanhood, each work reflected Heather's transition through life. The early pieces, with their warmth and innocence, into the later years when, as a wife and mother, the vibrance had dimmed in her eyes, leaving something darker and hollow. Only the gold cross worn tightly at the neck gave any hint of light.

"Religion fills some people with compassion," Lauryll said, startling Patrice as she stood examining the paintings. "Faith can provide a comforting serenity to one's existence if they haven't learned to forge their own." Lauryll held the wet canvas of her final painting turned towards herself, waiting for the coming reveal.

"But your daughter didn't get that from her faith," Patrice said, repeating the story Lauryll had told her before.

"No, it was more like a cloud, fogging up her mind." Lauryll sneaked another private peek at her latest work, still hidden from Patrice's view. "Or poisoning it."

Looking at the second to last portrait on the wall, Patrice could feel it. Despite the cross at her neck, the woman in the painting bore no sympathy or kindness. "Sounds like she missed the point of having faith."

Lauryll nodded sadly. "For Heather, religion gave her a self-appointed permission to cast judgement on the rest of us who she felt had fallen short of the standards *she decided* we should have."

"That couldn't have been easy," Patrice frowned.

Their eyes moved to the last canvas on the wall, the one depicting the deaths of her grandchildren lying lifeless on the ground, and the sinister blue monster in the doorway who'd killed Heather and her family.

"The second I heard the reports, I drove straight to her house." Lauryll's eyes were glossy now. Maybe tears. Or maybe simply too overworked from completing her final installment. "I saw the children first when I drove up. They must have tried to run. I don't think they were even fully dead yet, but there was nothing to be done..."

"And the monster who'd just killed them was staring at you from the porch," Patrice added.

Lauryll nodded. "I had a gun. Always carried one in my purse. When it came charging at me, I shot it. Many times. Then I went into the house. I knew what I'd find...but I had to see for myself."

"Lauryll, you don't have to dredge this all up," Patrice cautioned. "It is best left in the past."

"But it is never in the past," Lauryll cried excitedly. "It is with me every day! There has been no peace for me. No reprieve. And now I understand why."

"If it helps you, then tell me."

"I found my son-in-law in the foyer. He'd probably been getting the children through the door." Lauryll paused a brief second to remember him, then continued. "He was a good man. Generous, funny. More liberal than Heather and he never shared her intense devotion to faith. Seeing him there was brutal. I tried to keep going. I should have gone upstairs, or checked the kitchen. But fear paralyzed me. My heart was broken. I didn't want to see what that thing had done to my daughter. So...I left. I got back in the car and drove around for hours. Carnage was happening all around me, but I don't remember any of it."

"Lauryll, no one can blame you for leaving. Is that what this obsession with these portraits has been about? Guilt for not confirming Heather was dead. You must know she was. It's okay if you didn't see it yourself."

Patrice didn't expect it to be that moment when Lauryll turned the final painting around and hung it on the last nail beside her series. "I did see Heather that day, don't you understand?"

It was the most disturbing portrait yet. The transition from the angelic child in the first portrait to the scaly, slit-eyed, blue reptilian creature was jarring. And shining from the creature's neck hung Heather's golden cross.

"I killed her," Lauryll explained. "It was my very daughter who mutilated her husband and children. And it was I who shot her to death without recognizing my own child beneath the illusion."

"Oh, Lauryll."

"She put the malignancy inside her own heart, but it was I who stopped that heart from beating."

CHAPTER 41

CONFINED CHAOS

No matter how much he tried to dismiss Mrs. Yardley's off-handed comment at the school board meeting, Penn hadn't been able to shake the implication. No one else had paid her theory any serious attention, but it haunted Penn Fletcher. There were too many questions. Too many explanations. Aliens. Demons. Two types of aliens. Foreign influences and chemical warfare. Mrs. Yardley's outrageous suggestion may have fallen on deaf ears, but Penn's ears had listened...and considered the possibility.

"Grab your notebook," he told Farrah just before she turned out the light for bed. "I think we may have a lot to add to your notes. We just may figure this out tonight."

"Are we going to try to reach someone else on the radio?"

"Yes."

* * *

Rylan was still guarding the alien when they came into the armory. His stance seemed surprisingly relaxed, almost amused, as he sat in a chair looking at the thing in the cage. His rifle—no longer in his grasp or across his lap—was leaning against the wall beside the chair. Penn's eyes cut to the cell to see what fascinated him so much. What Penn saw next was unexpected.

"Who...?"

"I did," Rylan said, rubbing his nervous hand through his blonde curls. "The guy hasn't eaten in days."

Farrah now saw what they were referring to, as the monster was sitting on the concrete floor with a tray of food before him. For an alien with such exaggerated hands and fingers, his dexterity with a fork was remarkable.

"Maybe that thing is human?" she remarked to Penn.

Rylan looked uneasy as he made a confession. "I can see him now... sometimes. The alien façade lifts a little when we talk. Call me crazy, but I believe Doe and the boys are telling the truth. I have been able to see traces of a man under all that scaly skin. Kinda like a hologram glowing under it."

"You're *talking* to him?" Penn asked with surprise.

Rylan strolled to the cell. "Hey, Curtis? Is the food all right?"

Penn and Farrah heard a succession of grumbles and snaps, like a tongue clicking against the roof of a mouth.

"He says it's wonderful," Rylan said, acting as interpreter. "He was starving."

"And he didn't try to hurt you when you put the tray in there?" Farrah asked with astonishment.

Rylan blushed slightly. "He is very understanding. He knows Doe, Gusty, and I are trying to help him. I even let him out for a few minutes—to go to the bathroom in back. He put up no fight and even returned to his cell for me."

It was a startling revelation, but somehow not unbelievable. Penn shared with Rylan what he and Farrah were about to do, even allowing him to glimpse Farrah's notebook before taking it back to use in the sergeant's office.

Penn and Farrah secluded themselves in the back, turning on the office lights and revving up the HAM radio. "Will anyone even be awake?" She asked as he flipped on the transmitter.

"Where we will be trying to reach? Yes."

Farrah turned to a fresh page in her journal and sat ready to transcribe as Penn tuned the frequency. His voice called over the airwaves, across the ocean, searching to find anyone overseas listening. "CQ, CQ, CQ. This is K4RGT in the United States. Is anyone outside North America listening? Over."

Only a series of rising and falling swoosh sounds came over the speaker as signals faded in and out. Penn swept the dial across other frequencies, garnering intermittent pops, then squeals, which gave them a moment or two of hope, but it seemed to be only atmospheric noise.

"It was nighttime when I spoke with Argentina," Penn reminded her. "I think night is key for reaching the furthest away."

"But if it's not nighttime there," Farrah pointed out. "Then does it make a difference for them when trying to answer us?"

He shrugged. It wasn't something he had an answer to considering his very limited knowledge of long-range radio. His voice continued calling across the wavelengths, growing more hopeless as he reached the end of the dial's range and had to start back over.

"K4RGT in Alabama here," Penn stated, now with a twinge of desperation. "Anybody out there? Things are bad here. We need some answers. Over."

Farrah nudged him gently. "How about mayday, mayday? Does that make a difference?"

He wasn't sure. He squeezed the microphone again to try it, when suddenly a voice rang through the still air of the cramped little sergeant's office. It was a voice he knew, and it carried an urgency in it now.

"K4RGT, this is G7TJM in Cornwall. I hear you! Please answer back. Over."

Impulsively, Penn jerked the mic towards him, pulling the cable post out of the socket. Farrah quickly stuck it back in as her husband relaxed his tension on the microphone.

"Portia? Portia, are you there? It's Penn!"

"Penn!!!" cried the British voice from across the sea. "I have tried multiple times to reach you since our last transmission."

"I thought something happened to you!" he exclaimed. "You just disappeared from the frequency last time."

"I do apologize, Penn," she said earnestly. "Your questions caught me by surprise. I was ambivalent about responding. It was so obvious you were in the dark over things. Have you learned the truth since?"

Penn and Farrah locked eyes, their expressions frozen. *The truth?* Farrah grabbed her notebook, quickly flipping to the last notation. "Penn! That man in Argentina said *They stay in your country. We don't see them.* Is that what she means?

Penn's words came slowly across the airwaves, so that Portia would understand each one clearly. "Portia. You said you are in Cornwall, England. Do you have alien sightings in the U.K.? Or has anyone reported encounters with... monsters?"

"Or demons?" interjected Farrah into the mic herself.

"That's right," Penn added. "Various people see the entities differently. But are there any strange creatures attacking England?"

When her voice came back over the air, Portia sounded uneasy. "Is someone else there with you, Penn?"

Farrah gave him a curious look, whispering, "She sounds scared. Why would it matter?" She took the mic. "Portia? My name is Farrah. I am Penn's wife. Have there been any sighting of the creatures in England? They'd look like aliens, or big lizards, only without tails. Or they could appear as burned-looking scary things people might refer to as demons? Anything like that where you are?"

Silence. It was much as it had been before when Penn spoke to her. Only now did he realize it hadn't been a frequency issue. It had been reluctance.

"Please, Portia," he called over the wire. "People here are dying. What is happening in Cornwall? Or the entire U.K? How are you handling this invasion?"

Portia's response sounded remorseful. "We have had no such trouble."

Her responses were still far too vague to be helpful. Penn tried once more for a clearer answer. "Cornwall hasn't been attacked? Is that what you mean, Portia? Or in all of England?"

"Nothing has occurred here, Penn."

He exchanged concerned looks with Farrah again. She jumped back on the mic. "Portia, Farrah...Can you tell us if there have been any reports of a foreign government attacking other countries with chemical warfare?"

"I...we are not supposed...we've been advised by the Prime Minister, to stay out of this. I am sorry."

Penn clutched the microphone again, his stomach in knots as his heart raced. "Portia, please. You must help us. We are afraid. Millions of our people are dead." Glancing at his side where Farrah sat with a pen in hand, ready to write down whatever might be helpful, Penn looked down at her stomach. "Portia," he said back into the microphone. "My wife is pregnant. We are going to have a baby. Please, Portia. We need to know what we are facing. Has the BBC reported America having been attacked by a foreign government...or by an extraterrestrial race that has invaded the planet?"

Portia's voice rang with mournful hesitancy, as if she wasn't sure if she should tell them anything or not. Ultimately, she felt she had to. "Penn...nothing has happened. Not here at least. Not anywhere but in the States."

Her words stung their ears. Suddenly, Penn felt somehow foolish. Embarrassed to have even asked. Farrah's eyes betrayed a similar feeling, as if all the world were looking at the United States like a bunch of frightened children afraid of something in the closet.

"Penn," Portia continued. "Europe stopped all flights to and from the United States nearly a year ago...once it became worldwide knowledge of your circumstances."

"What exactly are those circumstances, Portia?" he pressed. "We do not understand what has happened over here."

Several more seconds passed with only silence from Cornwall. But then Portia gave in to her basic human compassion and confessed everything she knew. "Your people began a kind of civil war on themselves. At first, European heads of state attempted to intervene, but it was clear a madness had overtaken the States."

"Madness?" Farrah cried.

"Perhaps it was a virus or a toxin. There is no consensus. Whatever happened there didn't cross the ocean. It is contained in North America."

She cut transmission, fearing she'd said too much or possibly broken international law by divulging what she had. Both Penn and Farrah sat stunned at the controls.

"I still don't understand," Farrah said, flipping through her journal pages. "Is this a virus? A contagion? Invasion from space? We still have no answers!"

Farrah's hand clutched the mic again, transmitting one final plea. "Portia! Portia, if you are still there...please answer one more question for us. We still don't understand why us? Why the United States? Who did this to us?"

A squealing hiss sounded from the speaker, another signal attempting to tune into their frequency. "This is F6PBR, Le Mans calling. I read you, monsieur. There have been no confirmed sightings of extraterrestrials.

No UFOs, no viral outbreaks, no hallucinations spreading. Nothing unusual has occurred here. None of the reports coming from the United States appear to be legitimate. It isn't real."

"Not real!" Penn exclaimed furiously. "Buddy, we know it's real! We've seen people murdered before our eyes by monsters!"

"I believe that *you* believe what you see, monsieur. The rest of the world has seen your chaos spreading online, footage of civilians in panic, even your Congress turning on itself. We witnessed it all, from the collapse of New York to Los Angeles in flames. There are no monsters, monsieur. Your nation has been tearing itself apart. People are only killing people, nothing else."

CHAPTER 42

COMING TOGETHER

Penn shut off the radio. There were no words he or Farrah could say to assuage the gut punch they'd just received. As they stood to leave the back office of the armory, Terry stood in the doorway. His white ashen face reflected the panic they felt themselves. Behind him was Rylan, mouth hanging open in utter shock.

"We heard the last few minutes," Terry told them. "That British woman and that French guy." Shifting on his feet, staring down at his shoes, he exclaimed. "Is this truly real? We have all been hallucinating this nightmare?"

"I think it runs deeper than that," Rylan commented. "It's like Mrs. Yardley tried to tell us, Penn. Once you start thinking of the enemy as inhuman, the next step is making them monsters."

Farrah stood up too quickly, feeling slightly dizzy. She steadied herself with a hand on the desk. "Everyone is dead. Our families. Our friends. Dasha. And there never were any creatures?"

"What do we do, Terry?" Rylan asked.

"We tell everybody."

Twenty minutes later, a small group of weary conspirators and the school board assembled in the outer office. Augusta paced behind the long counter, absorbing the weight of what she'd just heard. Rylan sat on the edge of the counter, waiting for her response. Decker, Allie, and Patrice lined the wall, deep in thought. Corinne and Shane leaned near the file cabinets, exchanging skeptical glances. It was clear—at least two people in the room didn't believe them.

"It isn't that I don't believe you, Penn," Shane explained. "It is the transmission I don't trust."

"I don't want to believe it either," Farrah asserted. "But when you look back on all Penn's interactions, and I have the notes, it seems like Argentina, England, and France basically say the same things. This isn't happening anywhere but here. And the images don't show monsters. Just people killing people."

"I have to agree," Rylan chimed in. "Our prisoner is just a frightened man. I don't know why our eyes are playing tricks, but from what Doe and Gavin and Scotty say, that mall settlement sees us as the monsters."

"Then why do we see different enemies?" Shane snapped.

"Because we are different," Doe exclaimed, tossing her hands in the air. "It is that simple. The leaders of those mall people were Uber conservative in their old life. Naturally, they attributed everything bad to the devil or a war on God. And I'm guessing that anyone there who wasn't conservative originally, got indoctrinated the more it was fed to them. They perceive their enemy as straight out of Biblical Hell."

Rylan understood the implications for their side as well. "Likewise, most all of us at Vernon were more center-minded or liberal. We've been living with each other in a very diverse community. Our minds lean more toward scientific explanations. Like aliens."

Penn had to agree. "There've been some I've talked to on the radio that see them even differently than blue or red. Hostile Contagious Entities."

Farrah flipped quickly through her notes. "A man in California calls them the *Unmade*."

"My point exactly!" Penn remarked. "It's all perception, but it's aligning."

"I'm sorry," Shane argued. "I don't believe any of this. It's too incredible."

Allie scoffed at his resistance. "Yet aliens traveling light-years and landing only in America isn't incredible?"

"I don't believe those conversations Penn had, Allie." Shane maintained. "How hard is it for alien technology to hijack a simple shortwave radio signal and reroute whatever answer they want us to believe?"

Corinne cleared her throat. "I mean...he has a point. Any life-form with the technology to come here can surely manage a simple transmission bait and switch. And that goes for foreign governments attacking us, as well as UFOs."

Patrice sighed deeply, having stayed out of it until now. "Not that I have been asked," she grinned. "But I'm split. Shane makes an excellent point. It doesn't take much for a terrorist organization to hack a simple radio signal. But I must also say, there aren't a lot of people whose instincts I trust—but Rylan is one of them. If he says he sees that thing as a human man...I believe him."

Rylan sent her a look of gratitude.

"Gusty," Doe said gently, "The man in the cell is Curtis Jackson. Scotty and Gavin confirm it. If we return him to the mall, they'll see him for who he is. Then maybe we can stop this by opening communication between us."

"That thing killed Dasha!" Shane roared. "We are not setting it free."

"He didn't necessarily kill Dasha," Doe shot back. "But whoever did, believed she was a monster, the same way we saw Curtis as one. If we can meet with this other settlement and get them to see none of us are monsters—we stand a chance."

"A chance of what exactly?" Shane cried.

"Of stopping this!" Rylan yelled back. "A chance of restoring peace between two opposing groups who have been murdering each other!"

"And if any of that were even true," Shane replied. "How does this help the rest of the country?"

"Maybe it doesn't," Doe cried. "But I don't see how we can continue living this way now that we know underneath every one of those shifters is a fellow man or woman. It changes everything."

Augusta raised her hand, ending the discussion. "Every journey begins with a first small step. Even if all we accomplish is ending a misperception between two communities, that's one less war in our backyard."

The principle made her decision. Curtis would be returned to the Galleria and an attempt at diplomacy would be made. Rylan, Patrice, and Doe volunteered.

"If Rye is going, I am too," Allie piped in.

"Oh no!" Decker barked. "No way. Not happening. If those people see us as demons, they will shoot first and ask later."

Allie whipped her head around so fast her curls slapped him in the chin. "You are not my lord and master, Decker Caldwell! If my brother is going, then I am going."

"If you go…" Decker groaned, as if about to issue a threat, but then stopped himself. "Goddammit! I'm going too."

Penn opened his mouth to offer, but Augusta cut him off. "No, Penn. The others can handle the mission. What I need from you is to get back on the radio. Contact more people. See if anyone else has reached the same conclusion—or at least let them hear ours."

* * *

Dillon was waiting up in bed for Rylan when he came in. One look at his husband's folded arms and scowled expression said it all. "Once again, you are taking an unnecessary risk, Rylan Daily!"

"Geez! How do you even know already?"

"I listened at the door," Dillon confessed. He crawled across the bed and grabbed Rylan by the arms. "This is a bad idea. I don't want you or Allie going."

"Honey, my sister and I have fought these things before if we have to."

"Not a whole fucking city of them, Rye!" Dillon exclaimed.

Rylan's face fell as if a sudden rush of sadness came over him. Or perhaps...shame. "They are people, Dillon. Underneath whatever tricks our eyes play on us, they are people."

His words did not carry the weight he'd hoped for, as Dillon's response illustrated rather coldly. "I don't care. I don't trust those mall people."

Rylan sat on the edge of the bed, his hands folded across his knees, head facing the floor. "Dillon, try to understand. I have killed half a dozen of those things whenever we've encountered one out finding food and supplies."

"Yeah, I know," Dillon answered, unmoved. "I killed one too. And I would do it again because it was trying to hurt you."

Rylan's teary eyes looked upward now, pleading with his husband to grasp the weight of guilt he carried. "We know now those were people. Human beings who were just as scared and confused as we were. Don't you see, honey...if I can get those people at the mall to understand...maybe some of this blood on my hands will wash away."

Ever the pragmatist, Dillon didn't see any reason Rylan should be burdened. "You can live with dirty hands!" he shouted. "Baby, you killed slimy gross monsters before they killed you. Okay! They weren't monsters. But you didn't know that. You were still only defending yourself and your sister."

"And they were doing the same," Rylan explained. "Defending themselves against what they perceived as threats. It must stop Dillon. And if I ever hope to live with my mistakes, I need to be an active part of the solution."

Dillon pressed his head between his hands, frustrated. "I hate when you get all noble. It's not as sexy as you think it is." He grinned now, knowing he had to give Rylan this chance at absolution. "Just be careful. I have a bad feeling about this, Rylan. And I am always right.

"You are not always right," Rylan laughed. "You are usually very, very wrong in your assertions."

"You just don't understand greatness," Dillon replied with an arrogant smirk. "Especially mine."

Rylan pulled him into a hug, kissing the top of his head. "I fully understand your greatness, my love. You are the greatest thing that ever happened to me. Even though you are wrong a lot." Dillon grumbled playfully at him, as Rylan continued. "Correcting the misperceptions is the first step in ending this war and saving lives. And that must start *somewhere*, one settlement at a time. We might make history today. Be the first group to show the enemy how wrong we've all been."

"I doubt the historical first step of world peace is destined to take place in *Alabama*!" Dillon quipped.

"What about the Civil Rights movement? That started here."

"And did that get us anywhere?" Dillon roared. "We still ended up tricking our minds into thinking the other side are monsters. Not a real good example to use when everyone is currently killing each other!"

Rylan took Dillon's face into his hands. "I love you. I am coming back to you. And I will look after Allie, and Decker will too. Someone with outside experience needs to help Doe take Curtis back. He will explain to his people what is happening."

"I am making a strawberry cake with chocolate icing."

Rylan raised a brow and licked his lips. "My absolute favorite."

"I know." Dillon replied with a lone tear welling in his eye. "It's not easy to make now that there is so little chocolate."

"Well, that alone is enough incentive to bring me home to you."

CHAPTER 43

SEEKING REDEMPTION

Leslie and Joe McNab's involvement with their community had been greatly curtailed since the escape of their son with his lover. Though Mayor Collins and Reverend Tucker outwardly washed them free of any stain upon their own names, the others within the mall had not yet been as generous. Day after day, they sat alone together in the tool department, saying nothing to one another for long stretches of time. Their daughter Renee had been ostracized in her own way by the other children in the colony, but only Leslie's sister Dorothy had been aware enough to notice.

"Every day I spend as much time with Renee as I can," Dorothy told them that morning after another solitary breakfast in a food court filled with voices speaking to everyone but their family. "But your daughter needs her parents. She's lost her brother too, we must remember, and she's being shunned by the other kids."

Joe closed his eyes, tightening his jaw in contempt. "That boy has done more damage to this family than any joy he ever brought. Knew he wasn't right the first time I threw a ball at him and he let it smack him right in the face."

Dorothy folded her arms in disgust as she looked down at her brother-in-law and sister sitting idly by the tool counter. "There was nothing wrong with Scotty. Never was. He simply wasn't like you, Joe. But that didn't make him bad."

"Didn't it!" Joe yelled, slapping the countertop hard enough with his hand to make a set of wrenches bounce to the floor. "He's an abomination, Dottie. Do you even understand what he is? What he does?"

"What did he ever do but try to laugh, and enjoy life, and stay true to himself?"

"Staying true to God is what he should be doing!" Joe groused. "Instead of laying down with boys and letting them do...stuff to him like he wasn't anything more than a female."

"Is that the thing stuck in your craw?" Dorothy exclaimed incredulously. "Is that what you cannot move past? Scotty loved another boy. Not boys, plural, Joe! One boy! And whatever they did privately together is no more our business than what you and my sister do behind closed doors."

Leslie erupted now, her beady eyes glaring at her older sister. "Don't throw me in with any of that nasty talk. I'm a God-fearing woman. I follow what the Lord says I should do."

"Does that include loving your own son, Leslie?" Dorothy challenged. "Have you ever loved Scotty? Or did he make you nervous whenever he was around because you knew Joe couldn't tolerate him?"

Leslie jumped from her seat, offended by the comment. "You don't know what's in my heart, Dorothy! I loved my kids. But that doesn't mean I can't be ashamed when they fall from this family's grace."

Dorothy simply shook her head. "Grace is something I don't believe this family has ever had to fall down from. Love shouldn't be conditional."

Joe shot her an angry look. He had to stop himself from rising to his feet. He'd never struck a woman before, and with every second he was reminding himself that Dorothy had been there for him during several rough patches. But her tone was making it hard to remain calm. "Dottie, what the boy has done flies in the face of all our morals. Even you heard Reverend Tucker's sermon the other day. How can you stand here judging us when you heard yourself the Reverend say folks like Scotty and that Gavin boy are aberrations?"

"Because I believe Reverend Tucker is wrong."

To their ears, her admission was astonishing and bordered upon blasphemy. "I can't believe you said that," Leslie gasped.

"I am frightened by how this place has changed the two of you," Dorothy confessed. She kneeled between them, hoping to compel something within them to think for themselves again. "I know neither of you ever had an easy time understanding Scotty, but now you are coming to hate him. It is this place. It's almost medieval in its doctrine. We didn't crawl out of the ruins just to take orders from new kings."

Turning to leave, Dorothy nearly ran into Ben Noland, who'd been standing in the tool shop's doorway, for how long she didn't know. She brushed by him without acknowledgment and left Ben to them.

"That woman needs to be put in check, I'd say," Ben remarked, walking towards Joe. "McNab, I've come to tell you I share your humiliation."

The comment got Joe's immediate attention. "How?"

"Stacie played me for a fool once again. But she will not get away with it." Ben's face was stern, vengeful...and had a plan twitching at the edges. "She probably doesn't even remember what she told me that morning she woke up here. She wasn't aware of who I was at the time. Had no idea she was my wife. She told me about the colony she'd been living with since leaving here. I know where it is."

"You do?" Leslie gasped. "Is that where Scotty would be now?"

"I'd bet anything on it," Ben grinned viciously. "She was taken in by a group living in the old Vernon High School building near Crestwood. If she's there again, with your boy and that other one…"

"But I thought the demons had corrupted them?" Leslie replied. "Reverend Tucker said…"

"Probably," Ben broke in. "But even if it is a group of people there and not another nest of devils…they clearly aren't God's chosen. Not as we here are."

"What are you suggesting, Ben?" Joe asked.

Ben grinned sinisterly. "I think our Strike Force has one more nest to stomp out."

Joe's face suddenly lost some of its color. Perhaps in all his big talk about Scotty, somewhere inside he did not truly believe his son was bad. Or maybe he did, but wasn't sure he had the fortitude to actually kill Scotty himself. And there was also the possibility that Joe McNab was simply terrified to go back out into that dangerous world he had narrowly escaped last time. Ben could see all three possibilities reflected in Joe's eyes, but Ben also knew what words to say to pull him on board.

"It's gotta be me and you, Joe," Ben declared. "We were the only men who knew how to handle themselves out there last time. Curtis and Marcus fell apart. We carried them, and you know it."

"Yeah," Joe nodded, a grin curling at his lips as he heard the praise. "Yeah, we sure did."

"We'll get a couple other guys to tag along with us this time, but it'll be you and me who set this all right again. We will burn that school to the ground and kill every damn demon and abomination in there!"

Joe grabbed at an excuse, reaching a rather flimsy one first. "Doubt the city council will let us go though."

"You kidding?" Ben laughed. "I bet Collins and Tucker are as upset as we are about how this colony got played for a fool. What do you say, Joe? You in with me? It's your chance for redemption. Time to clear your name and take your place as a respected pillar of this community again."

"Redemption," Joe repeated. "I'm in."

* * *

Mayor Collins, Bill Wicker, and Reverend Tucker voted 3 against Dorothy and Corbin Hartley's 2 in favor of a raid on Vernon High School. Both Dorothy and Corbin argued against the menace in attacking a human settlement, stating that the Galleria had never waged war on people before.

"A den of homosexuality, wanton women, and demonic sympathizers are not considered people under God's new order," Tucker bit back.

Dorothy saw her brother-in-law's face while he, Ben, and the few recruits stood before the council waiting for the approval to strike. It was a harrowing thing for her to watch—the hatred in Joe's eyes. Approval was granted and as the men left to gather the guns and reinforcements to take with them, Dorothy ran after Joe.

"Joe, you can't mean this?" she begged. "We are talking about Scotty! Scotty! Your own son."

"I have no son," Joe barked. "Not anymore. I had a devil's disciple wedged inside my own Christian family. But I'll show God just how faithful I am. I will find that blight on my name, and I will send him straight to Hell myself!"

"By killing your own son!" Dorothy bellowed, grabbing her sister's husband by the shoulders and beseeching him to reconsider. "Scotty is a good boy, Joe. He's a good person. What does it matter if he's gay? That doesn't give you the right to kill him for it! Who gave you, or Ben, or anyone else for that matter, the right to play God?"

Joe shoved Dorothy against the wall, his venomous glare warning her not to interfere further. She stared with terror into his eyes, knowing he possessed the will to kill even her if pressed into it. "God gave me the right! By ending this world and ordaining this community to be the new blueprint for the world to follow. I have the right to play God. And Scotty's life is mine to give or take. He was my flesh and blood, and I can rid this earth of him at my choosing. And I choose to."

Dorothy was not normally such a brave woman, yet now she felt she had to be as she spoke words she knew would be heard as blasphemy to her community's ears. "You are wrong, Joe! It's Tucker and Collins who keep saying we are the blueprint. But I haven't heard God say it! You are taking a good deal for granted here. God has told this community nothing! But Tucker has said much. Maybe too much if it has led you to murder your very own child."

She saw his hand rise only seconds before he brought it down on her. But after that, Dorothy saw, felt, and heard nothing until she opened her eyes on the floor with Corbin and Genna Hartley crouched over her, trying to rouse her up.

"What—what happened?"

Genna held a cold cloth to Dorothy's cheek. "We found you knocked out," she told her. "You have quite a swollen eye and lip."

"Joe," she murmured. "I tried to stop him."

"He's gone," Corbin frowned. "He's gone. Ben's gone. A couple others with them. They've gone to wipe out the colony Stacie Noland came from. If she's there with those boys, they are as good as dead."

CHAPTER 44

THE SHOT THAT BROKE THE WORLD

When morning came, Rylan and Allie met Patrice in the armory, surprised to find Doe and the boys already there. Immediately, Rylan shook his head at Scotty and Gavin. "You two are not going."

"Oh, we hadn't planned to!" Scotty offered. "We just came down with Doe to explain to Mr. Jackson, just in case he still can't understand."

Rylan nodded, saying it was thoughtful of the boys to want to pave the way for easier transport. "But I see him now pretty clearly most of the time."

"I can too now," Doe added. "And I think he can still see me."

"He does," Gavin informed her. "He says he can also see that the demon who fed him is really a man."

"But tell them I do know that even the ones I still see as demons are really people," Curtis quickly asked the boys to convey.

Within the hour, Decker had a van outside the armory where Allie, Rylan, and Patrice loaded guns for protection while Scotty and Gavin walked with Curtis to the van. As they pulled away, Scotty put his hands on his boyfriend's shoulders and dared to dream for a moment.

"Wouldn't it be great if Mr. Jackson gets back and tells our folks how happy we are together? That nobody else cares at all that we love each other."

Gavin smiled back at him. "That's a wonderful wish. But highly doubtful."

He kissed Scotty gently. "They may never come around. But we are all we need."

"Or ever will."

* * *

Decker's van turned off the deserted roadway into the parking lot of what used to be the Riverchase Galleria mall. He parked the car near the mall's only entrance or exit, according to Curtis. As they got out and started for the sealed steel doorway, Doe and Curtis warned the others to keep out of camera range while they rang for someone.

"We don't want them to think we are an ambush," Doe explained. "And they probably won't recognize anyone besides myself and Curtis as human people."

Upon seeing the faces of Curtis and Doe, the door guards inside immediately sent for the mayor. Within a few minutes, the voice of Mayor Collins sounded over the intercom. "Curtis! How did you escape from the demons?"

"It is a very complicated story, Mayor," Curtis said into the speaker, grinning with relief to hear a familiar voice. He was only a few feet away from the comfort of home and was eager to get inside.

But then the mayor sounded reluctant. "The woman with you…"

Behind them, tucked out of sight, Rylan whispered to his sister,

"Good, they see Doe as a human."

"Mayor Collins, will you open the door and let us in, please?"

Silence hit the air from the other end, striking worry within Curtis and Doe. But several yards away, standing off camera, Rylan and Allie's eyes flared as their stunned faces mouthed the word, *Collins?*

A different voice came over the speaker now. "Brother Jackson, you must understand our concern. You were reported as taken hostage or even killed by the devil's minions. And to reappear now mysteriously at our door."

"Reverend Tucker!" Curtis shouted. "It's okay! I promise you. Things aren't the way we thought. This lady with me, she is…"

"I know who she is, Curtis," Tucker said sharply. "Stacie Noland, who has fancied herself quite the escape artist from this colony, twice over. You will pardon my apprehension at finding her with you now. I believe the devil may have corrupted your soul and used this Jezebel to do so."

Doe stepped back out of range, whispering to the others, "He's not going to let us in."

"Let me try," Rylan shot forward. "Turns out the mayor knows me."

Allie jerked him back. "Seeing you won't make him more inclined to let us in."

Doe smiled, hand on her hips. "Well…there's more than one way in this place."

* * *

She drove the van around the building to the recessed alleyway abutting the back of the former Dave & Buster's. Exiting the van, Doe showed everyone the access hole where she, Gavin, and Scotty had sneaked out. It was even with the top of the van.

"Just crawl on up, ladies and gentlemen."

Dropping out of the greasy restaurant ventilation system was a lot easier than climbing back into it. Using the person behind them as a stopper, crawling ahead and through was challenging with the greasy path. Once they all crawled back into the kitchen, Doe's nerves were acutely aware she was back inside the prison she had wanted to escape so desperately.

Patrice searched for the nearest towel or apron, anything to wipe the rancid grease from her face and arms. "That was absolutely nasty."

"I think I threw up in the back of my throat climbing in," Allie gagged.

Curtis, who'd had the worst time of them all squeezing through, turned now in all seriousness. "What do I say once we see everybody?" He asked. "Will they see you the way I do now?"

"Doubtful," Allie answered. "You still look like an alien to me, but at least I understand you when you speak now!"

"I don't," Decker growled. "Even coming all this way, I still don't think this monster is human. But I do think it's made you think it is."

Doe rolled her eyes and started out of the kitchen. "Come on, we can get into the mall through the game room."

The others followed, passing through the dimly lit arcade. The flickering neon bulbs sent eerie chills down Allie's spine, but when she glanced over at Decker, he gave her an encouraging wink.

"How do we do this exactly?" Patrice whispered.

Rylan gently took Curtis by the elbow. "I think we simply walk him into the mall and try to speak to whoever we see first. Maybe little by little, we can convince some people in small clusters."

Decker put his hands out to pause everyone. "Okay, we need to be as unimposing as possible." He gestured towards Patrice, Rylan, and Allie. "Guns behind the waistband. Let's not look all attacky."

Curtis led the way, cool and even, from the arcade's archway into the mall's court. The Vernon crew hadn't given as much thought as they should have that, to the Galleria people, they would appear to be large, burned demon creatures. *Blending in* until they could explain the truth was never a possibility. They were spotted immediately.

"That's her!" cried a woman with an accusatory finger pointing in Doe's direction. It was Gavin's mother, Carol Tanner, who recognized Doe and drew the initial attention. "That's the demoness who stole my son from us!"

Doe saw Carol plainly, no longer under the influence of the alien façade. But to most everyone else in Doe's group she appeared as merely another alien jabbering away incoherently.

Another voice rang out among the cluster of "blue monsters" rushing at them. "She's with Curtis! And they have let demons inside the mall!"

"Go get the security guards!" screamed yet another frantic voice.

"Well, this could have gone a whole lot better," Decker scoffed, withdrawing his pistol, readying for a fight.

"We've got to take cover, "Patrice warned as she scanned the immediate area.

"Where's my son?!!! What have you done with my son? Where is my Gavin!!!" Doe tried to defend herself from the onslaught of the raving mother. As Carol lurched forward at Doe, clawing and slapping, Doe landed a punch straight into Carol's face, knocking her to the ground.

Patrice clutched Allie's wrist. "We need to get to safety," she said, looking across the mall at the alien masses charging closer. "I can't even find words for this mess!"

Doe was towering over Gavin's mother now, yelling down at her, as Carol scrambled back across the tile. "Your son got out of here of his own choosing! Had you allowed him to be who he is, he wouldn't have left!"

Now, safely protected by two other aliens helping her up, Carol shouted back, "Yes, because that McNab queer put some kind of spell on him! You and your master Satan damned my son to hell!"

Allie shot Patrice a look and commented on her previous statement. "Well, the word *hysterical* has a nice documentary feel to it."

Patrice snatched her gun from behind her back, edging back under the arch of the arcade entrance, where Rylan had taken cover with his gun. Allie sprinted towards Doe, seizing her arm and pulling her away from the massing crowd. They made a mad dash across the plaza to a long row of planters tall with vegetation. Decker moved right behind them while Patrice positioned herself behind the arch across from Rylan. Everyone was ready to open fire if necessary.

"See the guys with rifles at the far end down there?" Allie shouted to Doe and Decker.

"I only see aliens," Decker yelled back from his squatting position behind a potted palm.

"No, they're men with guns," Allie replied. "Penn was right! All I see now are people."

"Still aliens to me!" Decker quipped.

Chaos was building within the mall, and with it, a rising tension, as if their holy colony had been polluted. Rylan and Patrice shielded behind the arcade arches, tried to wave a stunned Curtis back to them. He stood frozen in place, watching as his own people swarmed through the mall now. He tried to raise his hands to calm them, hoping to reach their rational minds.

"Friends, listen! Listen to me! We have all been tricked! What you are seeing isn't real! There are no demons! I saw them that way too, but they're only people! Our minds have been tricked. Infected."

Corbin Hartley spotted Curtis through the crowd and tried to press his way through to him, but every person blocking the way seemed consumed with rage at Curtis instead of celebrating his safe return. As Corbin scanned the mall, he saw the strangers. Two in the arcade door, and three more behind the planters under the atrium. People! Not demons.

The voice of Reverend Tucker rang out over a megaphone from somewhere behind the wall of colonists surging ahead at Curtis. "You see, brethren! Our Curtis has been corrupted, poisoned by Satan." Curtis staggered back, dumbfounded and afraid. Corbin shouted his name, jumping up with an extended hand to catch the man's attention, but too many people blocked him from view.

"Curtis!" Rylan yelled to him. "Run to us!"

"It's okay!" Curtis called behind him. "I can make them understand."

Patrice and Rylan watched as the animosity in the crowd continued to grow at a fevered pitch. Curtis, too blindsided by faces he knew, couldn't recognize that they no longer trusted him. In the distance, Corbin Hartley tried to get through. With every person he passed, he pleaded, "Don't be afraid of Curtis! He's come home. This is a good thing!"

But no one was listening. The mob fed on each other's frenzy, bolting forward like Trojans into Sparta. Again, Reverend Tucker's voice echoed overhead from his megaphone. "A wolf in sheep's clothing has led the devil's henchmen into the very sanctuary our Lord provided us. He means to destroy us all, he and his demonic friends. Kill them! In the name of God, kill all of them!"

"No!" Corbin screamed, trying to be heard over the stampede of feet and angry cries. "You're all overreacting! They are people! People!"

Someone tugged sharply at his sleeve. "Stop Corbin," Genna urged discreetly, looking to see if anyone had heard his words. "You'll be next. We will be next!"

Corbin grabbed his wife's shoulders, hoping to make her understand. But one glance into her desperate eyes told him she already did. And she was right. It was too late for Curtis. Too late for the human beings he'd led into the colony. Their neighbors had bloodlust in their eyes, and this was one jury Corbin Hartley would not be able to persuade. Genna pulled him back, further and further, until they were well at the rear of the fray.

* * *

Decker moved from the potted palm to the large planter with Allie and Doe. He parted a few stalks of growth blocking his line of sight, whispering down to them. "It's an entire horde of them." He aimed his revolver through the stalks, and said, "I don't see any people here, Ale. Just a fucking battalion of aliens hissing and growling our way."

Through the mob, Mayor Collins was making his way forward. Upon seeing him, Gavin's mother fell into hysteria. "Mayor! He's brought the devil's army with him! Curtis Jackson is in league with the demons now!"

"Wait! Wait!" Curtis shouted, pushing his way through the raging colonists to reach the mayor within them. "Mayor Collins! It isn't what you think it is!"

Curtis had moved too far for Rylan and Patrice to protect now, but at the mention of the mayor's name, Rylan thought of another way. "Mayor Franklin Collins!" Rylan cried out. It took a few times before the mall's voices simmered down enough to hear him. "Mayor Collins," he repeated. "Mayor Franklin Collins! We mean no harm. We brought back your citizen, Curtis. We want to talk only with you. To share the vital information we have learned from Europe. Please listen to us!"

"Demons do not make demands of God's chosen people," Tucker snapped indignantly through the megaphone from the mayor's side.

"Mayor Collins!" Rylan shouted once more. "You know me. You know both me and my sister. She's here too. Our names are Rylan and Allie Daily. Rylan Daily, Mr. Collins… Dillon's husband."

Mayor Collins' eyes grew wide, his face pale. As if drawn by radar, his gaze lifted to the upper mezzanine where his wife Linda stood at the rail. She looked down at him with caged restraint. Linda only shook her head once, but it conveyed the message to Franklin.

Waiting with everyone else amid the silence, Reverend Tucker turned to his longtime friend, passing him the megaphone. "Every man must be tested at least once, Franklin. The Lord is testing you now."

Mayor Collins lifted the megaphone and gave his command. "Kill them."

The Vernon crew felt the shots whipping past as they took cover. Some saw men charging forward with guns; others saw aliens scurrying at them with haunched legs and taloned fingers. The frontline had weapons, firing shots through the air. A bullet aimed at Rylan collided into the tiled arch shielding him. The chalky dust from grout and shattering ceramic flew into his face as he dodged back. When she saw the bullet hadn't hit him, Patrice opened fire at the shooter.

* * *

Curtis approached Reverend Tucker cautiously, his hands raised in peace. Tucker only backed away as if Curtis' very presence might compromise his soul. Curtis switched his focus to the mayor, hoping he might be more rational. "We had it all wrong, Mayor Collins! So did they. We have all had it all wrong!"

Curtis' eyes widened as suddenly somewhere behind his minister's back he saw a handgun being passed sideways, hand to hand, closer and closer. "Reverend Tucker!" he shouted. "We have been wrong! Everyone has been wrong! It's not happening to the world. Only here. There are no monsters!"

Since coming to the Galleria settlement, Curtis Jackson had taken a seat every Sunday on the fifth row of the mall court and listened intently to his minister's words of comfort and guidance—explanation for a fallen world and hope for a rising one. He'd sought his counsel when the awful grief for his late wife swelled again in his heart and took strength from the preacher's wisdom. And now the preacher was staring him in the eye with the coldness of an animal about to pounce. Curtis never lifted his gaze from Reverend Tucker, even when someone passed the gun into the minister's outstretched hand. Curtis heard the shot but never saw the blast.

Doe, Allie, and Decker watched in horror as the shot into Curtis' chest blew out from his back, spewing blood and heart tissue across the floor tile. For a second all went silent, broken only by the mall guard erupting another assault of gunfire at the planters. Rylan and Patrice sprang into action, blasting their high-powered rifles into the crowd, mowing down as many of the enemy as they could, hoping it might provide Allie, Doe, and Decker enough time to run.

* * *

On the upper mezzanine, Corbin saw Colin and James watching the massacre at the rail. He tugged Genna's arm to follow, zig-zagging through their terrified neighbors making a retreat away from the battle. The Hartley's sprang up the disabled escalator treads until they reached the top. Corbin took the boys by the arms, guiding them and Genna far away from the rail. They made a run for their store at the other end of the mall, running as if their lives depended on it.

Reaching the dress shop, Corbin slammed the gate down and tucked his family near the back wall, hidden by racks of gowns and skirts. He lifted each boy's chin to face him, and said, "That is not who we are. You must understand this, boys. Every human life is precious. A Christian...a true follower of Christ our Savior, does not behave as you just saw."

Genna placed her arms across the boys and rested her hands on Corbin's shoulders. "I think we should pray for poor Mr. Jackson. And his companions."

* * *

Below, in the mall colonnade, the waving stalks of vegetation coverage grew thinner by the second with every blast from the mall assailants. Decker, Doe, and Allie saw the enemy closing in. Though most colonists lingered behind, unarmed and frightened, the front line was well-armed and winning. Then suddenly from the arcade, Patrice and Rylan opened rapid fire at the colonists, mowing enough of them down and causing the rest to run for their own cover, that Allie, Doe, and Decker made a break for it.

"Run!!!" Patrice screamed, unloading her semi-automatic into the crowd of aliens encroaching on her friends. Rylan was her wingman, firing deliberate shots at targets he knew he wouldn't miss while she sprayed the air to give their friends cover to run. Patrice saw only reptiles with every shot, while Rylan had the unfortunate clarity to know he was killing men. The blood splattering into the mob and spilling onto the floor was red, not black. Human.

Shell casings rang onto the tile like a war-twisted version of Jingle Bells as Allie and Decker sprinted towards the archway. When a gun clicked empty, they snatched a new clip from their belt and resumed the tidal wave of gunfire onto the Galleria. Both Allie and Decker fired behind themselves too as they made their way, but Doe had a different goal.

Doe wanted the Reverend. She wanted Mayor Collins. She wanted each of them to taste her blast directly, but they were no longer on the plaza. Retreating like cowards to let their underlings face the battle for them. Suddenly, Decker yelped as an enemy bullet tore into his side, but momentum and adrenaline kept him on his feet. Rylan and Patrice now stood beneath the arch's center, spraying the air around their team like an ocean spray of metal. Doe switched gears, abandoning her quest for revenge to sweep back and grab Decker under the shoulder. Allie was heading back for him too, but Doe shouted, "I've got him! Get through the arcade!"

Allie reached the arch, where Rylan grabbed his sister's wrist, slinging her inside the arcade out of direct fire. The random bullets still coming from one or two unseen shooters picked apart at the tile covering the arch as the marksman tried to hit Rylan. But Rylan's quick dodge and tuck maneuvers evaded the impact. He helped drag Decker through as Doe reached the arcade. Patrice held the enemy off but was nearly out of ammo.

"We have to get out of here!" Doe shouted, helping Allie with Decker through to the kitchen. Patrice followed but turned back to Rylan. "Come on!"

"You go!" he shouted, fumbling around the archway for something. "I have to buy us time!"

Patrice rushed back to the arch, spending the last remaining bullets left in her gun on the aliens now advancing toward the arcade. The mob had reformed and charged straight at them. They were only a few yards away when Rylan's hand found what it had been searching for. As the metal gate came rolling down fast, Patrice understood what he'd been doing. He slammed it locked and turned to go with her.

"Genius!" she shouted with a smile.

They grabbed hands, starting for the kitchen when a single shot from just outside the gate exploded through the air, slipping through the bars. Patrice felt the drag on her arm almost the moment she heard the shot. It jerked her back like someone pulling an emergency brake, then his hand slipped from hers. She felt the warm splatter of liquid and soft solids against the side of her face and neck. As Patrice turned around, believing herself to be hit, everything seemed to play out in slow motion. Rylan was toppling forward as the right side of his face exploded outward. His one remaining left eye bore a stunned look of incredulousness, as if he'd never fully believed this could be it. This was *the end*.

Patrice stood frozen over him, blood and brain matter coating her chest, neck, cheek, and hair. She grabbed his wrists, dragging him with her towards the kitchen as if he still might escape. She'd dragged him nearly there before the shock lifted enough to understand there was no saving him. Letting go, she fell to her knees beside him. In his last seconds of life, he tried to communicate something to her, but with part of his brain torn away it made little sense. He rotated his wedding ring around his finger with his other trembling hand, and the gurgling from his throat sounded as if he was saying, "raw...buried...cake." His eye closed, his mouth hung open. He was gone. Patrice twisted the ring from his finger and ducked around the corner through the swinging doors of the Dave & Buster's kitchen.

* * *

Doe was at the stove, helping Decker through the vent to exit out where Allie waited outside to pull him through. Doe's eyes saw Patrice's haunted face. There was no time for anything else. Doe hoisted Patrice into the exposed vent and followed her through.

After Decker dropped to the ground within Allie's steady hands, she quickly opened the van door, helping him inside. Once he lay back against the van wall, she pulled off his shirt, bunching it into a ball and pressing it to his wound. Blood was flowing from it, but not enough to have nicked an artery. She dashed back to the hole in the building to help the next person down.

Patrice dropped to the ground, Doe directly behind her. Allie waited for Rylan, but no one came. Doe and Patrice hadn't moved. Doe looked directly at Allie with horrified sadness. But it was Patrice, her expression empty, her eyes blank, that told Allie what had happened.

"Patrice?" Allie's voice was shaky as she uttered her name.

Patrice didn't react. She hadn't even heard her. It was like she was no longer inside her own body. Doe glanced at Allie with a solemn, tearful shake of the head. "No!" Allie said flatly. She said it again, with more certainty. "No. Rye is fine."

Decker had somehow removed himself from the van, despite the blood loss. He went to Allie, gently taking her arm.

"No," she said again, succumbing to his crestfallen eyes.

"Goddammit, Allie." Decker whimpered. "I'm so sorry, baby."

"No!!!" Allie shrieked. "Rylan is okay! He'll be through that hole in a second." As if suddenly struck with a realization, Allie exclaimed.

"Patrice!"

Allie looked once more at Patrice, seeing only now what she hadn't identified before. While Patrice stood unresponsive, looking only down at the ring in her hand, Allie slowly lifted a finger to Patrice's cheek, wiping off the matter she'd mistaken for grime from the vent. She understood now what it was.

* * *

The van was eerily silent as it ripped down the road away from the mall. Doe was driving and processing the tragic failure that had been her own plan, or if not hers completely, one she'd fully supported. Never had she imagined it could take such a sideways route. Curtis and Rylan...mostly Rylan. It gutted her heart. In the mirror, she could see the utter devastation across Allie and Patrice's faces. But the danger wasn't yet over. Decker was bleeding a lot and growing paler by the minute. If they lost him too, Allie would never recover.

Doe saw the office supply store up the road and veered the van in faster than she should have, not first issuing a warning to those in back. She didn't explain herself, only jumped from the van and bolted inside, not stopping even to consider what might be in there. But it was after all an office supply, chances of anything dangerous being there were remote. She dashed through the aisles and quickly found what she was after. Returning to the van, she ripped open a roll of packing tape with her teeth and wrapped Decker in tight layers around the midsection. The pressure would hold the wound together and stop profuse bleeding until they could get back to Vernon.

* * *

Turning onto the access road behind the school, Doe's eyes caught sight of the breach in the fence. Several Vernon friends stood huddled by the armory door. Uphill several yards, she could see a body on the ground and Dolores helping Augusta away as a ghostly figure in white swept towards them.

Patrice snapped to attention, released from her fugue as her face pressed against the van window. Her eyes tried to assess the strange sight they were returning to. "What happened? Where's Keisha?!!!"

CHAPTER 45

A STUMBLE THROUGH HELL'S GARDEN

The stench of stale automotive fluid and sanded metal saturated the air of the garage, stinging Shane's nostrils as he stood back, admiring his work. Over the low crackle of the Eric Clapton record spinning on the turntable, he caught the sharp sound of clapping from the open garage door.

"Man, I never thought you'd beat that wreck back into shape after Doe and Dasha's pinball run through the city," Penn said with an impressed grin on his lips. "But looks like you did it."

Shane turned, wiping sweat and powdered metal dust from his brow. "You and me both. But I think I got this bad boy operational again."

"How messed up was it?" Penn asked, bending down to inspect the wheel casing.

"Axel rod wasn't too bent," Shane answered. "And whatever those crazies dropped on the cab didn't make too much of a dent. That was the easy part, but that back trunk, that took some doing."

Penn gave a short, almost sorrowful laugh. "Yeah, Dasha said at the time they dodged a lot of shit falling from those windows downtown. She'd be smiling to know you beat this car back into use."

Shane opened his mouth to reply, but a horrendous crash sounded from somewhere outside. The two men bolted together through the open garage door, racing around the vocational building. Down below, just past the armory, a strange Jeep roared across the back lane behind the school—a section of twisted fencing flying off its hood! The vehicle barreled across the school property like a beast unchained. Their eyes darted to the main gate, still intact, but the fence line running downhill had been obliterated. Vernon was under attack!

Shane raced towards the armory while Penn sprinted left towards the football field. Both men moved on instinct, going where their hearts led them first. Shane hit the asphalt, spotting the Jeep abandoned near the back entrance of the school. Its inhabitants, now on foot but yet unseen, had surely infiltrated the building! Overhead, the ancient tornado siren wailed, its rotating cry slicing the afternoon air in a call to arms for Vernon's residents.

Shane quickened his pace, knowing he would need every rifle he could get his hands on to help arm his community. Rounding the corner, he saw the mangled body of one of Vernon's guards on the asphalt. He wasn't immediately recognizable, dragged no doubt under the Jeep's tires. There was no time to check his identity; Shane had to get to the guns.

* * *

Meanwhile, Penn's legs burned from the effort as he pounded downhill to the football field gardens. His heart racing as he sprinted, stumbling once on the steep decline. His ankle twisted, but he pushed through the pain, ignoring whatever damage he'd done. He had to reach the garden. This was Farrah's shift, and he had to find her!

Gunfire rattled from the garden's edge. Penn veered right to take cover behind the old concession stand, now used for garden tool storage. He twisted around to look back towards the school, where a couple of bodies now lay lifeless on the pavement. Peeking around the corner, he saw the lone gunman below, passing through the gate in the fence around the football field. From his vantage point above, Penn saw bullets ripping through the garden, shredding leaves and stalks, sending the sound of tearing paper into the sky. He couldn't see Farrah anywhere in the dense growth below, but the gunman wouldn't have ventured down there if he hadn't seen people.

Dropping low, despite the ache in his ankle, Penn eased down the concrete bleachers to the gate. He kept himself small, well below the camouflage of vegetation as his eyes desperately searched for his wife. His pregnant wife. He had to get her out of there!

He squeezed through a row of tomato plants, their fuzzy stems tickling his arms. Another bullet whizzed by as he pressed lower into the green labyrinth. Several yards away in the same row, he saw Miss Ashley curled into a ball. Penn crept, back hunched, towards her.

"I can't find Mr. Andy!" she frantically whispered.

"I'll find him," Penn whispered back. "You need to get to safety. Where is Farrah?"

Ashley pointed to the far-left end of the garden. "We were about to spread a new batch of dirt when we heard the shots. I came looking for Andy."

Repeating his earlier vow, "I will find Mr. Andy. You crawl out of here and get up the hill. Hide wherever you can."

Penn guided her into a squat, nudging her towards the garden exit, each rustle against the vegetation a risk. Ashley waddled slowly behind the heavy crops, her escape within reach. Another shot fired in the distance, but it had not been directed their way. It had hit someone, though. Penn heard the moan as the victim fell. It sounded male.

God, he hoped it was male. Penn continued crawling down the path towards where Miss Ashley had last seen Farrah. Making his way to the end of the garden was proving a gamble, as the harvest-ready plant life was bulky, almost impossible to circumnavigate as it spilled into the rows. Any bump or shake of the plants would alert the shooter to his whereabouts.

Behind him, Miss Ashley was a mere few feet from the fence. It would be only a quick sprint uphill towards the concession stand where she would be out of range of the gunman. It was quiet now, but with the only way out being the gate Ashley was nearing, she knew the gunman hadn't left the garden. The occasional snaps of twigs or vines beneath his feet echoed under the wind where only ears low to the ground could hear. Ashley sidestepped in a crunched squat slowly towards the escape route until her ears heard a terrifying sound.

"Well, hello there, young man!"

Ashley froze.

Mr. Andy, his mind clouded by his Alzheimer's, had drifted into confusion and abandoned his hiding place. As Ashley heard the cheery, affable call of her sweet father-in-law, her heart nearly stopped. He'd seen a stranger, and old Andy Sims had never met a stranger—only a yet unmade friend.

"Are you new to our little gardening club?"

The gunshot ripped the world apart. At least Andy and Ashley Sims' world. The bullet sang across the tops of leaves like a sour note in an opera house. The horror propelled Ashley upright and bolting towards the sound. She didn't see him fall—only the violent shudder of plants taking the impact of Andy's demise. A gleam of metal reached her eye as the sun hit the pistol, and the bullet meant for her exploded over the greenery.

Penn heard the second crack of gunfire followed by Miss Ashley's cry. He kept low, refusing to budge a single step so as not to betray another presence in the garden for the gunman to strike. After a few moments, he resumed his slow journey towards the end of the garden.

Farrah was crouched almost flat on her stomach behind a tipped wheelbarrow. Her eye caught Penn's, and she waved him over. As he moved to join her, he knew the rusted wheelbarrow would be no better a shield than a flap of cardboard. He had a better plan.

"What are you doing?" Farrah mouthed as he pulled her away towards the bags of soil behind her. The supply runners who'd fetched this soil for Mr. Andy's garden couldn't have known how important they might turn out to be.

The scattered bags were unopened. Without explaining, Penn pushed Farrah flat on the ground where he began dragging bags, one by one, around her. He pressed his finger to her lips each time she tried to speak. He had one mission, and that was to conceal her.

There weren't enough bags to surround her, forcing Penn to reconfigure, hoping the gunman wouldn't cross over the stack and discover her from the back. But he had enough to lay a wall of three in front of her and on the sides, then he laid the last bags on her back and legs, sealing her in. Her eyes begged him to join her, but he knew they'd surely be seen.

"There aren't enough," he whispered. She tried to rise, but his hands pressed her back into the dirt. "All I care about is you."

Her tearful eyes met his as he leaned down for a swift, and possibly final, kiss. "No, Penn," she whispered. "We both hide, or we both run. We stay together."

"We are together," he told her, reaching through the sacks to pat her stomach. "This is where you become a mother and put this kid first. I love you. Both of you."

Then, he was gone.

Farrah couldn't see where, her view too obstructed beneath the heavy bags of soil. Fighting every instinct to chase after him, she lay where he'd placed her, knowing any attempt to follow him would put him at risk too.

Penn paused under the overhead run of bean vines stretched from the goal post, waiting to hear the whereabouts of the killer's footfalls. But what he heard was something much different. It sounded like a steady, shallow tearing of something. Parting the vines of dangling beans with his fingers, he saw no gunman—only one of those terrible scaly blue aliens ripping up plants, stuffing them into its long burlap sack. Penn knew it was only a trick of the mind. He knew Portia was right, and the monsters were not real. And it hadn't been aliens driving that Jeep through Vernon's defensive wall—it was men. But despite that knowledge, his eyes saw the gunman as one of those creatures, and now that it assumed all the *demons* in the garden were dead, it was destroying—or stealing—Vernon's food supply. That would starve Vernon. Starve Farrah.

Rage exploded in Penn's chest. Before he knew what he was doing, he was sprinting directly at the monster. Time slowed in those seconds. In his periphery, he saw only a blur of green as his feet raced across the garden. Bullets tore through the tops, and Penn barely registered the hot splatters of his own blood washing across his skin against the force of his body pushing ahead. His sight stayed locked onto the hideous blue creature while his mind swirled with images of Farrah's blistered hands tending these fields to feed their people. The monster was within reach as more cracks of fire hit the air, each tearing chunks of Penn's torso away on impact. But his feet didn't stop driving him forward. And as he sprang with one final, explosive push from the ground, he propelled himself through the air at the beast. Penn's blood-soaked body, and clouding mind wondered how many yard lines he'd rushed the ball?

He landed atop the monster, grappling the fiend by the head, driving his thumbs into its slitted eye sockets. Blood spewed from Penn's open mouth as the creature—or man—screamed in agony. They crashed to the ground, momentum helping drive Penn's thumbs so far into the alien's skull that nothing could ever restore its vision. Penn's own eyes only then noticed the chunks of muscle missing from his own body ripped off by the gunfire. It made him grin that he'd still been able to take this killer out when most of his shoulder and biceps were gone. Penn rolled off into the vegetables, his back coming to a stop on top of the revolver. Above him, he saw the sightless creature staggering blindly through the rows, each plant slapping its face, startling it in a new direction. Penn slipped into death mid-laugh.

* * *

The man, Jake Voight, had been quite eager to go with Ben and Joe. Like their fourth volunteer, Dennis Witty, Jake had been inspired by Reverend Tucker's sermon and emboldened by Mayor Collin's praise as they set off to slaughter the demon nest. Only now Jake was stumbling through a maze of vegetation, his arms flailing helplessly to defend his face from the poles, wires, and scratchy foliage that kept knocking him back. His eyes were gone forever, squashed into gelatin inside empty sockets as he sobbed at God for an answer. That answer would remain just as elusive as the lone little gate that was the exit from his blind maze of hell.

CHAPTER 46

ASSAULT ON VERNON

Clinton was sprinting out of the armory when Shane reached it. He had a gun already and yelled at Shane that Terry was loading up inside too. Hearing Shane enter, Terry quickly tossed him a loaded rifle and took a pistol for himself.

Outside, the world seemed to be on mute, except for the occasional muffled crack of gunfire bleeding through the brick walls of the school on the hill. Terry pointed towards the space between the gym and the main building. "I'll take the west side and go up the switchback by the art room. I doubt whatever is attacking knows that hall is even there. You circle back and go in west."

Shane gave a nod, then split off, jumping the rail from the bus lane to the outer rooms, but his sharp eyes caught movement in the garden below. Terry hurried past the exterior-facing rooms, checking Patrice's room for Keisha, but she wasn't there. He then knocked rapidly on Mrs. Yardley's door. She gave a little whimper from inside. "It's Terry! Come with me!"

Mrs. Yardley's weathered face was etched with terror. "Get down to the armory," he advised. "You'll be okay there. The attackers are inside the school."

Shane suddenly surprised them at the rail. "Something fishy is happening on the football field. I see one of those aliens zigzagging through the crops, but I don't know why."

"I heard shots down there," Mrs. Yardley told them.

Terry and Shane exchanged a loaded glance before Shane said, "Didn't see anything but the alien, and it looks hurt. Most of our population are inside the school. I'll go back to the garden after we get the majority to safety."

"Okay," Terry nodded. "I'll go upstairs, you hit the east hall...but since you're heading that way, help Mrs. Yardley down to the armory."

"Got it," Shane said, already taking her gently by the arm.

Terry kept moving until he reached the interior door and swept up the thin switchback staircase. Darting his head into the music room and art room, he didn't spot anyone and continued to the main hall.

* * *

Lauryll almost called out to Terry when he looked into the art room, but he was gone before she could react. He hadn't noticed her at all, which meant her plan might actually work. She stepped out of the front corner, continuing her task. Her hair, tied back hastily, still had a few loose flyaways dripping paint down her forehead. She blotted it again before it reached her eyes. The old art class worktables had done a good job shielding the pool of off-white paint that covered the floor where she'd doused herself. Since Terry hadn't seen it either, her trap had potential.

She dashed back to the center of the room, propping a broom and mop against two empty chairs. Lauryll then draped them each with a black painter's smock before balancing two hats carefully on top of the handles. They were ridiculous hats. The leftover examples from a random assignment the art teacher had given her students once when Vernon had been an operating high school. But in a pinch, and to only a quick glimpsing eye, Lauryll successfully gave the illusion of two people standing in the center of the room. It hit her then—her mistake. She rushed to the art supply closet, rummaging in a dusty bin until she found what she was looking for. Lauryll went back to the figures and began dusting them with haphazard coats of red spray paint. The paint against the natural folds of the draped smocks could resemble demon skin with black blood veins—at least to a casual eye. The hats, oddly enough, when misted with red, looked more hellish than the smocks.

She picked her plan back up, now having corrected its shortsighted flaw. She sloshed more liquid from her canisters around the area behind the figures and across the floor, wall to wall, doing her best to create quite a puddle before the last vestiges of paint thinner ran out. After the trap was set, Lauryll returned to the puddle of off-white paint, swirling her fingers through it and dabbing her face in case flecks of the red had gotten on her.

* * *

Chris Pluckett had been more than a little nervous to enter the devil's den, but when Ben Noland practically ordered him to go along with him and Joe McNab, he knew he couldn't say no. Besides, his name was up next for Strike Force duty, anyway. Maybe this one mission to hit the enemy on their own turf might fulfill his obligation and spare him an entire week's deployment.

The school the hellish monsters had overtaken for a hub had been easy to get into. The heavy front frame of the Jeep tore through that fence like paper. When he, Ben, Joe, and Dennis stormed the grounds, the demons scattered like ants under a kicked mound. Dennis had raced off to take care of the ones he'd seen outside before decimating their crops. Ben, Joe, and Chris split up inside the school, opening fire on any of the devils they saw.

Chris had to admit—it was kind of fun. Watching those scorched red beasts run like sissies down the hallways or try to cower behind doors made him feel powerful. The blasts from Chris' semiautomatic ripped through wood, flesh and bone. Man, he enjoyed seeing that demon blood spurt out.

Trudging back down the school's main hall, Chris paused at a set of double doors labeled *Auditorium*. To his right, a staircase climbed to the second floor. Weighing his options, he wondered which course would provide the demons an easier way to corner him. It was then he heard a shriek down a thin, short hall followed by a loud crash. Interpreting it as the sound of one of his buddies striking down a monster, Chris abandoned his previous two options to take the one where he could have backup. He'd feel much safer exterminating this nest if Ben or Joe were by his side.

He moved down the short hall, pushing open the first door. Inside was an old art room. His eyes scanned quickly: a long wall of student artwork on the right, a cluttered teacher's desk and an easel on the left. But the room wasn't empty. Two of the demons stood in the middle of the room, their backs to him.

He stepped back into the hallway to cock his rifle, then advanced into the room. He moved fast at the devils, blasting each one rapidly. But as the demons fell, Chris saw they were nothing more than a broom, mop, and stained cloth. A sound from behind him turned his stomach into knots. He spun around only to see a single floating flame of fire. He squinted his eyes at the flame, only to see the easel swept sideways into the wall by some invisible force. But the force wasn't invisible. His eyes registered the fact far too late when the form of a woman took shape as if pushing herself out from the wall like a ghost. It was then he realized she wasn't a ghost, and she hadn't passed supernaturally through a wall. She had blended with it! Covered in the same color paint as the wall, she had gone unseen with the easel propped in front of her. But Chris realized it all too late as the grinning woman dropped her flame to the floor.

Instantly, a thin line of fire raced across the room, then exploded out on each side until a border of flames sealed him between the walls. But it wasn't over. Once the fire had blocked him from escape, another line rushed at him like a string of toppled dominoes. As it zoomed closer, Chris looked down at the puddle of shimmery liquid beneath his boots. There was no time to react as the pool ignited under him.

His agonizing cry pierced the room as crackling fire engulfed him. "Help me!!!" Searing pain wrapped his body like a sizzling blanket. He spun in circles, each movement splashing more of the fuel underfoot across his shins. Through the wall of red-yellow flames trapping him to that part of the room, he could see the satisfied sneer of the paint-encrusted woman watching him burn alive.

His mind could barely register all the agonizing sensations at once. His shirt and pants were melting like tar onto his skin as some pieces fell in singed tatters to the carpet of flames beneath him. The intensity of the pain worked quickly to overwhelm his nerves. Chris fought his brain to move, to run, to put himself out somehow, but his body did not obey. He understood now that pain, having reached its unbearable peak, could render the nervous system with no physical sensation at all—leaving only the visual horror of an incinerating body. He was naked now, clothes burned away, face bubbling up, skin sloughing off in patches across his body. His arms dangled like dripping sticks of white bone, and under the flames it looked as if his penis was melting off like a tiny stick of butter. Finally, he collapsed into the blaze, wondering if Heaven awaited him. Or was this, in fact, his righteous reward?

* * *

Clinton pressed his eye to the narrow window in the cafeteria doors, glancing out into the main hall while the others, he'd wrangled from the halls, huddled back several yards. Trisha came charging from the kitchen with a long mop. "Clinton, use this!" she cried, handing it over. Clinton slid the pole through the door handles, wedging the double doors shut against any force from outside.

Behind him, the residents sprang into action, dragging cafeteria tables across the dining hall to help barricade the door. Clinton glanced at Trisha, yanking the mop free.

"What are you doing?" she yelped.

"Ya'll got the lunchroom pretty well sealed," he answered. "I saw more people running by. Let me get out, then slide the mop back and block up this door."

Trisha tugged at his arm to stop him. "Clinton, no! Stay here where it's safe!"

"No place is safe now," he said grimly. "And I have a gun. I gotta try to help our people outside this lunchroom!"

Clinton slid through the doors, turning back to give Trisha a look through the window. He pointed at the handles, and she re-enforced the doors again with the mop. The others came pushing forward until the first long dining table slammed into the doors and wall. Then another, and another.

Clinton took bold strides into the L-shaped intersection of the two main hallways. His eyes caught sight of something moving into the office down the corridor. He broke into a run towards it.

* * *

When the alien burst through the front doors of the school, the hallway erupted into chaos. Dillon, thankfully midway in the corridor, hadn't seen the initial carnage, only the stampede of Vernon residents escaping in all directions. Some were bleeding as they hobbled past him. He gripped Keisha's small hand tightly and raced her down the hallway. His intention was to get her to the kitchen, possibly hide her in a storage closet or perhaps a cold oven, but another furious wave of residents came flowing from the connecting wing, alerting Dillon to at least one more attacker.

The only choices were the library or the stairs up to the second floor. As Keisha's terror-stricken face looked frantically in all directions, Dillon scooped her into his arms and sprang up the flight of stairs. Rounding the landing to the second flight, dread curled into his stomach. The upstairs hall was one long, exposed run flanked at either end by stairwells. If one of the monsters came up on the other side, there would be no way to go unseen. Still, the library had seemed too much of a dead end to risk when they'd been below. Reaching the second floor, Dillon didn't see any monsters yet. Doors up and down the hall were bursting open as frightened friends poured out, looking at him for answers.

"Aliens are downstairs!" he warned. "Lock yourselves in your rooms!"

Some didn't listen, choosing to take their chances below where an exit route might lie. One woman waved Dillon and Lakeisha to her room, but Dillon refused, telling her just to barricade herself inside.

He sat Lakeisha on her feet, twisting around to make sure nothing was coming the other way yet. "Shouldn't we hide in a room?" Her little voice quivered.

Dillon grasped her shoulders, falling to his knees to look into her eyes. "I can't chance you in a room. These things will search rooms."

He moved to the wall of lockers, opening one at the bottom. It had someone's things inside. He moved down, checking its neighbors until he found one empty. "Squeeze in here, sweetheart," he told her. "Tuck in your head and shoulders."

Keisha fit, but only barely. It couldn't have been comfortable, but he doubted any of the attackers would be on a locker raid. "Stay here and don't make a sound."

Her teary eyes clung to him. "But where will you hide?"

"I will be fine, baby. I just need to know you are safe. Stay put till I come get you."

Her hand reached up for his neck, silently begging for a hug he did not have time to give. "I love you. Stay here. Close your eyes. Do not look through the slits. And do not make a sound."

Dillon closed the door and eased back to the edge of the stairs, peering over to the flight below for safety before venturing back down. He was coming down the last flight when he saw Clinton whizz by. Reaching the last step, Dillon turned to look down the hall where he saw Clinton paused at the office door, then he rushed inside.

Dillon started off to help but found himself distracted by an eerie sight at the far end of the corridor. A ghostly white figure was moving towards him. He stood locked onto the strange apparition when suddenly the door beside him thrust open!

"Jesus, Doc! You scared me to death."

"Are they still here?" Corinne asked nervously from inside her office.

"I think so," Dillon muttered softly. He then pointed 20 yards down the hallway. "And whatever the hell that is."

Corinne wiped her glasses on Dillon's shirt, then put them back on. "Oh, my word! Why is Lauryll covered in paint?"

Without another thought, the two of them hurried to Lauryll, Dillon forgetting to even glance sideways into the school office where Clinton had gone.

"What happened to you?" he asked Lauryll breathlessly.

"Oh this?" she smirked proudly. "Saw it in a movie once. The important thing is I killed one of those bastards!"

At that moment, the auditorium door opened, revealing Terry. "Auditorium and bathrooms are clear," he told them. Terry then sniffed the air, his eyebrows raising. "Is something burning?"

"It'll go out on its own," Lauryll answered with no other explanation.

A sudden sound of heavy feet pounded down the topflight of stairs directly across from them. Terry acted fast, pulling Dillon, Lauryll, and Doc into the auditorium just before the creature turned on the landing and rushed down into the main hall. Terry readied his shot and told Dillon and the ladies to go down to the armory. As Terry re-entered the corridor to take down the monster, the alien was gone...but to where he did not know.

Dillon told the women he'd catch up. As Lauryll and Doc exited the auditorium's exterior door, Dillon raced back upstairs for Keisha. The monster had just come from the second floor. He prayed Keisha was still safe inside the locker.

* * *

Clinton had seen the commotion through the glass window before dashing into the office. Dolores had two file cabinet drawers clutched in her hands, the contents spilled everywhere as she swung wildly at the alien monster. Behind her, Augusta jabbed at the hissing blue beast with the tip of a flagpole, the dangling American flag swaying with each forward stab to hold it back.

Clinton saw a gun on the floor near the monster's feet, where Dolores must have knocked it free. He surged into the office, dropping to a roll and grabbing the gun! He sprang to his feet to take aim, but the alien surprised him, abandoning its attack on the women to lunge at Clinton, thrusting them both through the glass into the hall.

Dolores and Augusta rushed from the office to help, but Clinton yelled at them to run as he and the monster fought gridlocked together. Augusta dove for the fallen pistol, but Clinton and the monster rolled over it before her hand could reach. Dolores seized her arm, dragging her towards the cafeteria for shelter. Behind them, a gunshot split the air, echoing off the metal doors along the locker-lined corridor. They twisted around to look, only to see Clinton slumped lifeless against the bottom lockers, but the alien was nowhere to be seen.

"Where did it go?" Dolores stammered.

"I don't know," Augusta whispered as they slipped into the recessed alcove by the cafeteria.

* * *

Scotty and Gavin huddled together in the back of the library, hoping to go unseen behind a low rolling cart of unshelved books. They'd been in the library when the attack on the school began, the chaos of screams and crackling gunfire forcing them to stay put. And just seconds ago, they'd heard an explosion of glass in the hallway somewhere near the office. A few more seconds later, another gunshot.

"Who is it?" Gavin whispered. "Demons?" He quickly remembered, resetting his mind to its newfound knowledge. "I mean, another camp hitting Vernon for supplies?"

"I don't know, baby," Scotty muttered, his arms clutched around his boyfriend as they tried to make themselves as compact as possible behind the cart.

The carpet along the floor betrayed them by muffling the footfalls of the third person now in the library with them. And he'd heard their whispers. "Look at you!" he said mockingly as his eyes came into view over the cart. "Wrapped around each other like the two disgusting faggots you are."

"Dad?!" Scotty's voice whimpered. Though the remark was hurtful, when Scotty saw his father standing over them, he felt relieved. Surely, his dad wasn't going to kill them.

Relief quickly faded when Joe cocked the revolver he pointed at them.

"Mr. McNab!" Gavin pleaded. "It's us! I'm Gavin Tanner, and this is Scotty, your son! We aren't demons!"

"He can see us," Scotty said coldly, feeling the icy death of whatever hope he'd clung to.

"Yeah, I can see you," Joe growled. "*My son.* Letting another boy hold him like that. Comforting him like a man holds a woman."

He shifted the gun to Gavin. "Now get up! Both of you."

Slowly, Scotty rose to his feet, extending a hand to help Gavin up.

"How sweet," Joe sneered. "Helping your girlfriend up like a gentleman. You make me sick, boy! You've shamed your mama and me and gave yourself over to the devil without even a fight."

"Dad, it's not like that," Scotty pled, hands open, hoping to diffuse the tension. "We love each other. Gavin loves me like you love Mom. Or *should.*" He wasn't sure why he added the last part. It just felt appropriate.

"Love?" Joe barked. "What you do ain't love! It's an abomination is what it is! You left a holy place. A place the Lord gave us until we can go back out and repopulate His world. And you shit on His gift so you could live among the slithery underbellies of Hell."

"Dad!" Scotty cried, growing more frantic by the second. "I'm your son. Your son! How can you kill us? Kill me?"

Joe's sneer twisted into something darker. "Kill you? No, boy. I ain't gonna kill you. Your daddy is about to teach you a lesson you best remember from now on. You're gonna walk the right path and I'm getting rid of your obstacle."

* * *

Joe locked his aim onto Gavin's chest. The boys saw the twitch of his finger as he pulled the trigger! Their youthful screams pierced the air, almost overtaking the echo of the shot. Gavin fell to the ground, his eyes staring up in shock at Scotty's father. In Gavin's arms, convulsing and choking on his own blood, was Scotty. He'd jumped before Gavin in the blink of an eye, taking the death shot himself.

Joe, having meant to shoot his son's lover, stood in dizzying oblivion as his son's tortured face and brokenhearted stare held him like a prison. Gavin clutched Scotty in his arms, shrieking in gut-wrenching anguish as Scotty seized violently in his embrace.

"Don't leave me, don't leave me!" Gavin sobbed, stroking Scotty's blood splattered cheek. "Please, baby! We got this far. We got here, honey. You and me! We made it out. Don't die. Please don't die on me! I can't live without you! Stay with me, Scotty. Please!!!!"

Joe's arm fell limp, the gun still clutched in his palm. His eyes watered as Scotty's life flashed through his mind. His smiling, laughing little boy. The mischievous toddler who knew how to use a stool to reach the cookie jar on the counter. The boy who painted a picture frame with fish and hooks to give on Father's Day. Joe saw all the treasured moments, followed by the even greater lost opportunities when he might have known his son better. Like a tragic movie, the scenes played in sequence, every time Scotty tried to be close to Joe but somehow wasn't *boy enough* for him. All the attempts to win his father's love and approval, only to be dismissed, ignored, and judged.

As Gavin's head pressed into Scotty's lifeless, breathless chest, Joe suddenly observed how *he had* never cried over losing someone as deeply as Gavin did now. Not his mom, not a good friend. He didn't even think he'd be as upset if Leslie died. It was then that Gavin's shallow sobs became a different kind of bullet, plunging into Joe's tightening chest. "You...really do...love him?"

The words seemed too trivial to cover it. *Of course, Gavin loved him.* He loved him fully, and beautifully. He'd loved Scotty so unmistakably that Scotty had preferred dying for Gavin rather than living without him. It was more than Joe *had ever* tried loving him...or anyone. And now Joe had desecrated that beautiful thing and quite literally blown its heart out.

* * *

The residents barricaded in the cafeteria almost had the doors cleared to let Augusta and Dolores in, but the legs of the last two remaining tables had hung on the other, locking them together. The residents fought to pull the heavy things apart and free the doorway while Augusta and Dolores waited at the window in terror. Heavy stomping of another monster sounded nearby, coming their way. Suddenly, two hands gripped their shoulders from behind. Whirling around, they saw it was Terry!

"Come on!" he cried. "It's almost here! Let's get you out!"

He pulled them across the mouth of the main corridor just as the alien aimed his weapon from several yards away. The shot caught Terry in the arm after he'd shoved the women into the connecting hall of the east wing. Shane was already barreling towards them, firing at the alien without pause.

"Get to the armory!" Shane yelled to Augusta and Dolores.

As they sprinted away, Shane tossed his second pistol to Terry. They stood together; side-by-side, guns raised at the enemy.

"Think these assholes are human now?" Shane grunted at his friend.

Terry took Shane's flank and said, "Yes, actually I do."

The heaving beast loomed before them; its long, scaly fingers clutched around its weapon. Shane saw it for what he knew it to be—a horrifying otherworldly species set on world domination. Terry saw the same, only he knew it wasn't real. This was a man. Dangerous, but human, as he stared with bitter hatred over his pointed gun.

"I don't know what you see when you look at us," Terry called out across the short distance between them. "But my friend and I are both men. We're men. Just like you. We are all three people."

A deep, mocking laugh rumbled from the enemy's throat. The sound took Shane by surprise, but not Terry. "Do you think I don't know that?" Ben Noland said with almost sinister pleasure. "I am not as ignorant as the others I live among. I have always known what this is."

Shane staggered back against the wall. He'd heard the alien's words clearly, and now the misleading mask began peeling away layer by layer until Shane saw only the brutish man before them.

Terry was nearly as stunned, but only by Ben's admission. "You have known the whole time?"

"I've fought all over the world," Ben informed them. "There isn't a political party, a religious idolatry, or an elite liberal's song and dance that ever drew me in. This country—hell, the world—is full of people on a stupid, desperate search for anything to give them an answer. They'll buy any answer you sell them. Believe any idiot who tells them they're smart enough to believe the idiocy he's peddling."

"Then why are you here?" Terry asked, flummoxed by the man. "Why are you killing our people?"

"I am here for Stacie," Ben said. "Give me Stacie and I'll leave you to finish the morons who came with me."

"*Stacie*?" Shane asked. "Do you mean Doe?"

"Doe isn't here." Terry informed him.

"Don't play games with me, man!" Ben aimed his gun directly at Terry's head. "I know she came back here. Brought two queer kids with her. I don't give a shit about them. Keep 'em. I just want my wife."

"She isn't here, man." Shane confirmed. "She went back to the mall. Is that where you're from?"

"The mall!" Ben cried. "Why would she go back?" Suddenly, his mind raced with regret. *Had she gone back to be with him?*

"She and some others took the monster..." Shane began, stumbling over the words now. "Curtis. They said his name was Curtis."

Terry took over, his voice steady. "Curtis figured it out. He knows this was all in our minds too. Doe took him back to prove to your settlement what is really going on."

Ben seemed less imposing now somehow. The hubris, the bravado, all appeared to melt away at the chance Stacie might have wanted him back. "They'll kill her!" he exclaimed. "Nobody there will believe them, and they'll just kill her."

Shane's heart tightened. "If that's true, then you better get back there and stop them before they kill your Stacie."

Ben scratched the side of his whiskers. "Tell me, was she going back for me? Or just for Curtis?" His eyes held a hope both Terry and Shane knew was false, but they weren't telling him that.

"She wanted to show your people the truth," Terry said. "And show you too."

Ben laughed callously. "Show those dumb fuckers? Fuck them. All of them. Their simple minds can only see what they've fooled themselves into believing. None of them has ever had one profound thought in their lives. Too scared thinking too hard is a sin."

The bullet shot through the air behind him, ripping the laugh right off Ben's face, exploding his head like a squeezed watermelon. Only after they dove to the floor did Shane and Terry realize the bullet hadn't been meant for them.

Standing with a swirl of smoke drifting from the barrel of revolver, was a man neither of them had seen before. Across his face he wore an expression of utter devastation and defeat. As if his features were the living embodiment of the proverbial fool, and he had just overheard everything his friend had confessed. He looked right through Shane and Terry, possibly not even seeing them at all, and staggered out of the building.

CHAPTER 47

AFTERMATH

Augusta and Dolores stopped in their tracks just outside the school as the blue beast staggered forward. They could make a break for it and try for the armory, but their age and the monster's size weren't in their odds. Yet something else kept Augusta's feet rooted to the ground, even as Dolores tugged urgently at her arm.

The monster did not seem interested in them. In fact, it wasn't even looking at them. Its massive head hung low as it stumbled like a zombie, a seemingly forgotten gun still clutched absently at its side.

"It is a man," she whispered to Dolores.

"I don't care!" Dolores shouted. "It's still armed!"

Augusta shook away from Dolores, taking several bold steps towards the figure. Each step unveiled a little more of the illusion. The sweat in his hair and just above his lip. His trembling hand. And as he finally noticed her, he lifted his distraught eyes to meet hers.

"He was my son."

He saw the woman's eyes widen before she asked sadly, "Scotty or Gavin?"

Joe could hear her as well as he could see her. Had he not heard Ben's confession moments ago, he might still have seen her as a monster. But her eyes looked nothing like a monster's. They didn't look afraid of him either. She seemed to have pity for him.

Augusta saw the resemblance in his face and guessed. "You are Scotty's father."

"I killed him," Joe confessed. Then he repeated it, like a scratched record unable to move beyond the scarred surface.

Augusta became teary. "You killed Scotty?"

He nodded. "It isn't real," he stammered. "None of this was ever real. And Ben knew."

"We were all deceived, Mr. McNab." Augusta said gently. She reached her hand towards him, silently asking for the gun. But it was his empty hand he placed inside hers. He seemed to crave a semblance of tenderness or compassion. And though he didn't deserve it, she held his hand.

"There aren't any devils here, are there?" he asked. "There never were any devils. Except for me." Tears streamed from his eyes as the fullness of his act dawned. "He loved that boy. *Really.* Scotty died to save him."

"They loved each other," Augusta whispered.

Augusta saw the gun twitch at his side, then slowly he lifted it. "Don't do this, Mr. McNab," she pleaded. "It doesn't have to be too late for you. Just hand me the gun."

"I think it was too late for me before I even came here."

"Take my hand again, Mr. McNab," Augusta begged him. "Stay with me. We can talk more. I will talk with you for as long as you want. Let Scotty's death count for something. Your redemption."

The gun rose higher, tilting within his hand. He felt the muzzle touch his temple. "It was easier letting others do my thinking for me. Problem is...you can't know how you really think until it's over."

The ear-splitting crack of the gun sent Augusta stumbling back into Dolores. Joe McNab's head exploded across the asphalt. His legs buckled, bringing him crashing down at Augusta's feet. She stood rigid, braced by Dolores' hold, as her mind only now absorbed all that had happened in the short hour at Vernon. It was more than she could process. And yet it wasn't over.

Rambling across the green knoll, leaping through the smashed fence line, Doe plunged the van up the steep hill to the asphalt, screeching to a halt. She, Patrice, Allie, and an injured Decker jumped out, only to be met with the devastation Vernon had suffered in their absence.

* * *

The reunion was unpleasant for all involved as Rylan's absence did not go unnoticed. Augusta's questions would have to wait, as Patrice grabbed her guns from the van, readying to storm the building to find her daughter. Doe was at her side to back her up when Lakeisha's voice cried out from the armory door. Patrice ran to her, sweeping the child into her arms. Dillon was behind her, smiling at the reunion and shrugging off Patrice's gratitude for keeping her child safe. Once he saw Keisha back in her mother's arms, his focus shifted to his family. Allie was coming into the armory now, Decker under her arm as Corrine followed behind. Dillon took Decker's other side, helping guide him to the back where Corinne still had medical supplies from when she'd dissected the alien corpses weeks ago. Allie hadn't made eye contact with Dillon yet, unsure how to face her brother-in-law. But once Decker was on the exam table, Dillon took off outside to find his husband. Allie went after him, brushing past Delores, who came in to help Corinne.

Corinne went to work quickly on Decker's wound, Dolores handing over scalpels, sutures, and disinfectants when needed. Decker winced from the pain as Corinne removed the bullet and stitched him up.

Dolores squeezed his hand to distract from the discomfort, saying, "The world breaks people faster than it can mend them."

Outside the armory, Doe had just filled Augusta in, and both women stopped talking at the sight of Dillon coming out. He glanced around. His eyes scanned Patrice, still holding Keisha. Only when Keisha's tear-filled eyes met his, did Dillon grasp the silence.

"No!" he said. His eyes glassed over, shifting into an icy dissociation. He felt Allie's hands grip around his waist. Patrice reached for his hand, but the words died in her throat. She fell into sobs, trying to draw him in with her free arm, but Dillon dodged it with a steely, frozen glare.

He pulled away from Allie's hold. "Where is Rye?" he asked Doe.

Doe attempted to take Dillon's hand now too, but again he rejected it. He shifted his focus to Augusta's mournful face. "Did he go up to the school? It may not be safe yet!"

He broke towards the hill, but Allie dashed ahead of him, pushing against his chest to stop him. Her swollen red eyes did their best to contain him. "Where is he, Ale?"

She shook her head, reaching to take his face in her hands. Again, he recoiled at the touch. The only person's hands he wanted to feel right now were Rylan's. "Where is my husband?"

"It's only us now, Dillon," she whispered, wrapping her arms around his neck and pulling him against her. "We lost him."

"No. No. No." Dillon tried to pull away again, but Allie held firm. She knew him as well as she knew her own brother. Dillon would have to be forced into acceptance. It was not a place he could arrive at alone. Too accustomed to having his way, winning his arguments, and never accepting defeat, Dillon didn't accept things he didn't like. But this was something stubbornness couldn't make go away.

"Stop," Allie told him, as he continued to fight. She strengthened her hold, refusing to let him pull out. "Stay with me."

"*No!*" Dillon growled. "Rylan is not...Rylan is okay. He's just late *again.*"

"He's gone, baby," she said, removing his wedding ring from her pocket and placing in into Dillion's hand. He shivered with an escaping yelp when she closed his fingers over it. "He didn't make it."

"No." This one wasn't forceful. It came out as a whimper. His resistance was weaker too as her lock on him held firm. Allie continued holding him until finally he relented, collapsing against her in soul-wrenching grief. They held each other for a long time. Even when the crying stopped, they didn't let go. Each clung to the last vestige of family they had left. "It's us now," she finally said as they let go. "You and me."

Shane and Terry were out of the building now. Under Shane's arm was Gavin, blood-soaked and trembling, while Terry had his hand pressed around his own bleeding arm as Lauryll steadied him. Behind them, coming from the direction of the football field, a dirt-smeared Farrah stalked forward. Her face wet with tears, mixing with the brown soil she'd hidden beneath. In her hand was a shovel, bloodied from the head of the blind man she'd just killed. The man who had murdered her Penn.

Shane stopped suddenly, looking at the pavement where Joe McNab's body lay. Gavin broke into hysteria, kicking violently at it before falling to his knees, punching and beating the dead man's body. Augusta went to him, pulling him into her comforting arms as Farrah fell into Shane's. No one had to ask why. Her sorrow alone delivered the news they had also lost Penn.

* * *

Many had died, and all had died pointlessly. The battered people of Vernon leaned on each other that night in their shared mourning. Tomorrow would demand much from them. Burying their dead. Refortifying their stronghold. And rethinking how to save an enemy population that refused to be saved.

Those left heartbroken felt it the worst. Farrah had fallen into the exhausted sleep of shock, while Doe stayed with her in the room Penn would never return to. Gavin slept in Dolores' room that night. Somehow, her inexhaustible spirit and bottomless compassion anchored him when he otherwise might have opted out of life after his wrenching loss. Perhaps from this loss, Gavin would gain something akin to a mother's love—whatever that was supposed to be. It was something he'd never had and something Dolores always longed to give. Augusta sat up a while with Mrs. Yardley, the only soul wise enough to understand the burden of leading a community she considered all her own children.

But in one room, long after most of the windows in Vernon had gone dark for the night, the lights still glowed softly in the quiet. Allie sat up with Dillon in the room he'd shared with her brother. They said little to each other as they lay on the bed, but just having someone who felt the loss equally, was some comfort. Next door in the men's dorm, Decker lay awake, giving them space. Doc had removed the bullet and repaired the damage, but the leftover pain kept him up. That wasn't the only thing keeping him up. He ached for what Allie was going through. And though she'd offered to stay with him that night to look after him, Decker insisted she be with the one who needed her most. And Decker knew it was Dillon whom Allie needed most now too.

His mind wandered to the first time he'd met the three of them. He'd been outside with some of the other early residents of the school. They'd been reinforcing the fence line and welding protective bars together for the doorways when a beat-up Charger drove up to the fence. At first, Decker felt unnerved by the two men jumping out. It wouldn't have been the first time someone tried to force their way in to raid their supplies. But then a feisty, frizzy-haired blonde stepped out from the backseat. She immediately gave Decker the impression that if *Scout* from *To Kill a Mockingbird* grew up, she'd have been this lady.

In those days, Augusta required any newcomer to sequester a week before risking their coming into contact with others. Decker spent many of those days and nights sitting outside the locked door of their quarantine, chatting away for hours with them. He was so relieved to discover that it was the two guys who were the couple and the gorgeous blonde was single. Even though Decker had only seen her face for a few minutes when they first arrived, he knew he loved Allie on day three of her week in confinement just from their talks alone.

He enjoyed remembering those early days, or maybe it was the pain pill Doc had given him. Decker rarely reflected on the time behind him. Now he went even further, into territory he never let himself go. Allie wasn't much like Erika had been. Allie was feistier. More independent. Sometimes Decker didn't know how much, if any, Allie needed him. But Erika never hid her feelings. She wasn't a girl who considered relying on a man to be a shortcoming. Erika would have relied on Decker for support if she had experienced a loss like Allie. Not next door, using her strength to comfort someone else. Then again, Erika hadn't been a *Scout* kind of girl. If anything, she'd been a *Dill.* Decker wondered now if they'd have stayed together if Erika had survived the apocalypse until he'd gotten to her? It felt cruel to admit they probably wouldn't. Whatever grief he'd once carried for her had calcified into a kind of private, internal stone memorial. She'd been important to him then. But it was Allie who kept him guessing. Allie, who awakened things within him he hated so much he loved it.

Dillon and Allie were still awake on the bed, listening to each other breathe, when around 11 o'clock the door opened. Startled by the intrusion, they looked up to see the innocent, yet distraught, face.

Allie patted the mattress as Dillon opened his arms to her. Lakeisha burst into tears as she ran to the bed, falling into his embrace. "Oh, Keisha, my sweet girl," Dillon cried, wrapping her tight.

"I miss him," the child choked, sobbing against his chest as Allie stroked her back. "Why did Rye have to die?"

"He didn't have to, honey," Allie whispered angrily. "He shouldn't have died at all. We were trying to help those people."

She wanted so much to tell Dillon all of it, but she wasn't sure he could handle that just now. It was only her rage that wanted him to know, and that was a purely selfish reason to inflict more pain on him. Moments later, Patrice's head appeared in the doorway, her face apologetic. "I'm sorry, she ran away from me."

"It's okay," Dillon said, waving her in. "We should all be together tonight."

Allie reached behind her and rapped her knuckles on the adjoining wall. Within seconds, Decker joined them. The room fell quiet again while they all huddled together on the bed. Then Dillon thought of something and told the others he'd be back as he left the room. A few minutes later he returned with a cake and a handful of forks. With tears in his eyes, he placed the cake between them on the bed and handed out forks.

As she scooped out a bite, Patrice let out a sharp gasp, fully understanding now. She could barely choke out the words through her sobs. "He looked up at me, and he said, '*Strawberry chocolate cake.*'"

Rylan's last words gave Dillon an unexpected smile. They ate the cake, which was meant for Rylan's safe return, quietly together. Then slowly, exhaustion took hold, weighing their lids and drifting each of them to sleep. The four adults lay against the pillows, leaning into each other with Keisha stretching across their laps. Allie's hand now stilled in the child's hair where they'd both fallen asleep while she stroked it.

CHAPTER 48

MUHUMMED'S MOUNTAIN

Morning light streamed through the window blinds onto Dillon's face, causing his eyes to flutter groggily open. Hushed voices caught his ear as he stirred awake. Allie and Decker sat at the foot of the bed, debating something in low, heated whispers.

"I think he should know," Decker argued. "He deserves to know, Allie."

"It'll be too much for him," she insisted. "He doesn't need this right now. Not after losing Rye."

Dillon sat up abruptly. "What are you keeping from me?"

Allie's face fell as she placed her hand on his leg, nodding towards Patrice and Lakeisha still sleeping. "It isn't important."

Dillon's gaze shifted to Decker. "Tell me."

Decker ran his hand through his scruffy hair, then scratched at a beard that had needed trimming days ago. "Your parents are at the mall."

"What?!!"

His alarmed voice jolted Patrice awake. Rubbing her bleary eyes, she sat up.

"What do you mean my parents are there?" Dillon demanded. "You *saw* them?"

"Shit, you told him," Patrice sighed.

"We didn't actually *see* them," Allie clarified. "To most of us, they still look like some creature from a bad sci-fi movie. But Curtis called one of them out by name, and Rylan confirmed it. Mayor Franklin Collins."

"Did he know who Rylan was?" Dillon asked, voice sharp.

Decker nodded soberly. "Rylan yelled out who we were when the mayor was ordering his goons to attack us. Your father heard Rylan. He gave the order anyway."

Dillon sat stone-faced, his fists clenched. "My father knew you were my family, and he still sent those people to kill you?"

Allie hesitated to answer because she knew what his reaction would be. "They didn't see us as human beings, Dillon. Just like we didn't see them as human either. But yes. Your father knew your husband was there, and it didn't bother him to order our deaths."

Dillon shot off the bed, hatred ablaze in his eyes. "I'm going there."

"No!" Allie cried, jumping to her feet as she slapped Decker's shoulder. "See what telling him got us?!" She locked eyes with Dillon, hoping to convince him to forget his idea. "You can't go out there, Dillon. It won't even matter if you did. They won't see you as you are. Not anymore. This virus...or this mass delusion...or whatever it is... distorts our faces, our bodies. You won't be able to convince them it's you, and it's unlikely you'll even recognize them! I promise you."

Dillon faced her down with more fury and anguish in his eyes than she'd ever seen in him before. "I won't be going to *convince* them. I am going there to kill them."

Allie tried to calm him down, but Patrice broke into their argument.

"I agree with him," she told Allie bluntly. "And you know you feel the same way, Ale."

"This is a suicide mission, ladies!" Decker shouted, then winced from the effort.

"Not if we prepare this time," Patrice pointed out.

"Weren't we last time?" Decker guffawed. "I recall us having an excellent plan."

Shaking her head, Patrice noted, "It was a plan to reason with them. To explain our mass delusion. To expose the truth that the rest of the world is just fine while we are tearing each other apart." Her eyes shifted diabolically to Allie. "That won't be the plan this time."

Allie's eyes glanced at Dillon, then Decker, then back to Patrice. Then she looked at the sleeping face of Lakeisha, her head now resting on Rylan's pillow. "I'm in."

"For revenge, Allie?" Decker argued.

"Yes," Dillon quipped. "They love their Bible so much. Let's have a fucking eye for a fucking eye!"

Decker couldn't believe what they were saying. It was so unlike all three of them. "Our purpose was to make them understand that all the monsters we see are human. Retaliating with violence won't prove we possess any humanity. It's like you're willing to throw the goal out the window for the sake of vengeance."

Allie laid her hand on Keisha's back, staring Decker in the eye. "Not for vengeance. Preservation. This child will not have to live in a world that might kill her on any given day. The other side has proven they are not open to reason. Perhaps others out there will be, but not those people. They killed Rylan and a dozen of our people."

Decker had no better argument against her. Allie was right. "So how do we do this retaliation thing?"

Dillon's eyes turned dark, vindictive. "If the mountain won't come to Muhammad. Muhammad will blow the fucking mountain to smithereens."

* * *

"Mama, you can't go back there!" Andre pleaded. When Patrice and Doe arrived early that morning at the UAB settlement to drop Lakeisha off with her big brother, he was completely unprepared for what they had planned. "It would be equivalent to walking into a minefield blindfolded! You guys barely escaped with your lives the last time."

"We didn't escape with our lives!" Doe corrected him. "Not all of us. Not Rylan."

"I'm sorry," Andre frowned. "I didn't know him well, but I liked him." He looked back at his mother. "I don't want you to go back there, Mama."

Patrice shook her head. "If Dillon is going, he will need me with him."

Andre paced the center floor of his small quarters in the men's hospital ward. "Mama, you've got to think about your family."

"I am thinking about my family," she argued. "That is why I brought your sister here to be with you until I get back. But make no mistake, Dre, Rylan and Dillon are my family too!" She could see the bewildered look on her son's face and wished she could make him understand. "Son, when Rylan and Allie found your sister and me and took us to Vernon. They saved our lives."

"I get that. But—"

"No, Andre, you don't." She held his hand tight. "Not only did they give us a safe place to be, Rylan and Dillon...they became daddies to your sister. From day one, they made me feel like I had people behind me. Family. That I wasn't in this hell alone."

"I'm so sorry I wasn't there for you then, Mama."

"You're here for me now. Look after your sister. Mama's got a score to settle with some bigots."

Andre stood up, wringing his hands as he paced. "Then I'll go," he offered. "You stay home with Keisha, and I'll go to protect Dillon. I'd enjoy a swipe at those assholes anyway." Andre looked sorrowfully at

Doe, then revealed, "They got Rex."

"What?" Doe gasped.

Andre nodded solemnly. "There was another settlement we ran across. Nice people. They were all in an apartment building off Highway 31. We traded medicine and food for fuel. They had big gas truck."

"What happened to Rex?" Doe asked.

"They were gathering supplies to send out to the utility people, but they didn't have a reliable van. Rex stopped by to pick up their donations on his way to the power company. Those fucking blue things blew up the entire compound. Killed everyone there. Rex died with them."

Doe wrapped her arms around Andre. As he held her, he looked over her shoulder to Patrice again. "So you see, Mama, I have skin in this game too. Not just for Dasha, but Rex. You keep Keisha with you. I'll go to the mall."

Patrice smiled at her brave son, stroking his cheek. As he pulled away from Doe, she hugged him tightly herself but declined his offer. "No, Dre. You may be all grown up, but you are still my baby too. You will be here at the hospital with your sister. If anything happens to me, at least I'll know my children are safe and together."

Though Andre did his utmost to sway her, his mother was unyielding on the subject. It was Rafik who put the fight to rest, telling the two of them, "I will go with your mother, Andre. I will protect her with my own life."

"I can't let you do that, man," Andre replied.

"Those people killed Dasha. And they killed Rex. I would avenge them regardless. I shall protect your mother as you remain here and protect your sister."

* * *

Word circulated fast around the school that another mission was underway to hit the Galleria Mall. Corinne insisted Decker needed more time to heal before he could do anything with intense physical effort, but he would not allow Allie to go back to the Galleria without him.

Mrs. Yardley watched from outside her door as Decker and Allie walked down to the armory. Her mind didn't have to stray too far to wonder why. They were clearly gathering an arsenal of weapons to take with them. Mrs. Yardley attempted to call out to them, but they were too far away for her aged voice to reach.

"I'm headed their way myself," Doe said from behind, catching the old woman by surprise. "Need me to tell them something?"

Mrs. Yardley gave a snort to the air as she folded her hands together. "Frankly, Doe, we have all suffered far too much violence and loss. I regard this retaliatory move as a mistake."

"I don't disagree with you."

Mrs. Yardley seemed surprised by the admission. "Oh, from what you said, I assumed you had joined in on this escapade."

"I have," Doe replied. "I can't let them go back alone."

The senior resident lowered her head sadly. "Emotions are running high around here, after our sweet Rylan and Penn. I worry this new mission might be a misguided one."

"How so?" Doe asked.

"Tell me, Doe," Mrs. Yardley narrowed her eyes. "Is the purpose in returning to the mall to seek vengeance? Or to make another plea for them to listen to the truth?"

Doe shifted on her feet. Her reluctance to supply an immediate answer did little to ease the woman's concerns. Trying to be as transparent as possible regarding the mixed intentions, Doe replied. "Mrs. Yardley, I can't blame Dillon and Allie. But if it helps you to feel better, I volunteered to join them because I hope to make one more stab at getting those people there to listen. Maybe now that their strike force didn't come back heroes, they will finally consider what we have to say."

"That is some relief, I suppose."

"That said," Doe continued. "Not everyone going tomorrow cares anymore about healing the rift between our factions. I honestly can't tell you what will happen. Only that I will try to be a voice for peace."

Mrs. Yardley took her hands and squeezed gently. "Then I shall pray for your success."

* * *

Farrah knew enough now about how the HAM radio operated that she felt confident in what she planned to do. She found the man in the gym, shooting hoops. Though she'd never met him before, he wasn't hard to recognize. "Rafik?"

Basketball was not his sport, having made very few shots. He gladly dropped the ball and went over to the young auburn-haired woman. "Yes, I am Rafik."

"I am Farrah. I'm friends with Doe and Patrice. Can you come with me for a little while?"

It seemed very mysterious as the strange lady led him down the hill outside to the concrete outbuilding. She led him inside and to the back of the armory as if on a deliberate mission. Farrah sat down at the desk, motioning for him to take the chair beside her. She then turned to him with a fragile smile.

"It may not work," she gave as a disclaimer. "But Doe told me a little about some things you shared with Dasha. I think Dasha would want me to try."

Rafik seemed confused as Farrah clicked on the odd and antiquated machine. "I doubt we can reach them directly," she blushed. "But maybe if we can contact your home country, someone might get a message to your family in Jordan."

He understood now, and his eyes welled with gratitude. He sat silently and patiently as Farrah's nimble fingers dialed across the continents. "This is so kind of you," he whispered as she searched the airwaves.

Her face lifted, staring at him with teary eyes. "I lost the only family I had left two days ago." Her hand floated to her stomach, where only now Rafik noticed the beginnings of a baby bump. "But in a few months...maybe..." She wiped away a tear, returning to her work. "No one should be left without family. Let's find yours."

She spent nearly twenty minutes trying to reach Amman, Jordan directly. It was a far-fetched idea at best, and she was woefully unsuccessful. But just as the disappointment on Rafik's face settled in and Farrah was about to shut off the power, a voice called out, offering a glimmer of hope, albeit remote.

"YK1DA, operator Samir Haddad in Damascus. Receiving you loud and clear. Over."

"Sorry," Farrah called back over the speaker. "I was trying to reach Jordan."

"Yes, I do know this," Samir replied. "I answer to tell you of my cousin who lives in Zarqa."

Shaking her head and assuming the thick-accented man just did not understand, Farrah replied. "Thank you, sir. But again, I am hoping to reach Jordan."

Rafik nudged her. "Zarqa is in Jordan."

Farrah's face lit up as if she had won the lottery. She moved away from the radio, allowing Rafik to take over. He spoke fluently with the man in Damascus, asking if he would ask his cousin to find Rafik's parents to convey the message that he was alive and safe and loved them very much. Samir must have been willing because as Farrah excused herself to give Rafik privacy, he was weeping over the air and speaking excitedly with the generous man.

She waited outside for quite a while until Rafik emerged. Profusely grateful for her thoughtfulness, he shared with her some of his interaction. "He had a recorder," Rafik beamed. "He will play my message to his cousin, who will also record it. His cousin will find my family and play my voice for them. No matter what happens now, they will know I survived and how dear they are to me."

Farrah hugged him, nearly melting into tears herself. So often she had longed to speak to her family one last time. Now she would trade almost anything for another moment with Penn. It helped her to know that there was at least one person who was going to have the chance to reach their family again.

***

Patrice rarely ventured to the second floor of the school, but after finding the art room empty, she walked upstairs to Lauryll's room. She was sitting in an old school desk, her hands clasped together on the connected tabletop, looking expectantly at the door when Patrice came in.

"You look ready for exams!" Patrice quipped, going in. "I don't know when I last saw you outside the art room."

"I've satisfied the muse, I think," Lauryll explained. "My story has been put to canvas now, and I have my peace."

"I'm glad," Patrice grinned. "But you mustn't let your talent go dormant. I hope you paint again one day." She took a seat at the other desk across from Lauryll—the only chairs in the room. "What did you want to see me about?"

"When you go tomorrow, I want you to keep in mind what I've told you about my daughter."

Patrice raised her eyebrows a bit. "In what way?"

Pressing her hands upon the desktop as she leaned closer for emphasis, Lauryll answered with chilling clarity. "Those people cannot be brought to a place of reason. If I couldn't save my daughter, what chance do you stand with total strangers?"

"That's a rather dark outlook," Patrice noted.

As if weighing matters in her hands, Lauryl replied. "The world went dark long before we started seeing monsters. The ones who killed

Rylan are not like us, Patrice. You and me and our kind...even though we are right more times than we are not," she added with a grin. "We don't feel diminished by admitting our mistakes. Our viewpoints are strong, but still malleable. We grow and we learn."

"And you don't believe the mall colony can?"

"Some people aren't adaptable," Lauryll answered. "Some people would rather die than change."

"An extreme opinion," Patrice remarked. "I think most people are reachable with patience and respect."

"Not when they exist in an alternate reality."

Patrice leaned back on the desk with a dubious stare. She felt a little like a schoolgirl unable to digest her teacher's interpretation of Dickinson. "Don't we exist in our own altered reality? Seeing a bunch of blue reptile aliens running around instead of regular men and women is just as distorted."

With a consolatory nod, Lauryll answered, "Yes, but we have opened our eyes; they chose not to. Patrice, this is bigger than good intentions. Their reality was fed to them from a buffet of disinformation, half-truths, and prejudice. They looked to leaders who were masters of misdirection, bastardizing facts, and wrapped it all in twisted Biblical interpretation. You can't cut through that kind of muck and bravado with logic."

"Couldn't they say the same things about us?"

"*They did*," Lauryll laughed. "They thought we were just as gaslit as we believed them to be. And truth be told, who really knows which side was right—if either. But you, Patrice, belong on this side."

"What are you suggesting I do, Lauryll?"

With a gentle smile and a worried look in her eyes, Lauryll simply said, "I have few friends left in the world. I am not eager to lose another. When you go back to that place, don't lose sight of the side you fall on. If you can't open their eyes to the truth—and you won't—get out of there as quickly as you can. Get out before they kill you."

Patrice rose to leave but paused at the door as she turned back with a twisted smile for her friend. "Lauryll...I'm not going back to convince anybody of anything. That's just what we're telling Gusty. I'm going back to kill those goddamned people."

* * *

Decker and Allie hadn't expected to find Shane in the armory when they came in to gather weapons for tomorrow's mission. "I guess you are here to try and stop us?" Allie accused. "I know you don't believe that this is all mass hysteria. But even if you do think aliens have invaded the planet, you can't be against us fighting back."

Shane narrowed his eyes, stopping himself from snapping back because he knew she hadn't been there when he'd fought the aliens and found out the truth for himself. "I am not here to stop you," he said. "In fact, I am going with you tomorrow."

They were stunned by the announcement. "Really?" Decker stammered. "What caused the sudden turnaround?"

"Rylan was my friend too. Dasha was my partner. Clinton gave his life to save this place. Dillon had to shove a child into a locker to keep her safe. Even if I hadn't accepted that this is all man-made, I would still go with you to wipe out an enemy."

Allie was at a loss for words, finally muttering out, "Thank you."

Shane gave an arrogant wink to Decker and the bindings around his midsection. "Besides, you need at least one able bodied man along."

"We have to be ready this time," Allie commented. "We can't get ambushed again."

"We won't." Shane waved them to follow, leading them to the old sergeant's office. He moved to the built-in bookshelf, reaching for the hidden latch only he knew about. Behind a false panel, a small safe waited. "Found this early on when I first stocked the armory with weapons Dasha and I picked up around town." Opening the squeaky door, Shane removed two objects to show them.

"No!" Decker gasped. "How—?"

"Guess old Sergeant whatshisname kept souvenirs from his combat days." Shane slipped the two grenades into his knapsack. "I'll have these with me tomorrow. Now, if you'll excuse me, I have some preparations to make."

The sun was setting behind the trees when Shane left the armory. Most people would be in the cafeteria now for dinner. Only a couple of Patrol monitors would be outside, and the one on the roof wouldn't say anything. Clinton and Penn had been a patrol monitor too, and whatever Shane was doing to help avenge them, Patrol monitors were in full support of. He walked to the parking lane where Vernon's collected vehicles were parked. Shane cranked one of the trucks and drove it—headlights off—up the hill to the vocational building and into the open garage. He pulled the roll-down door shut behind him and went to work.

CHAPTER 49

A DAY OF HOPE OR RECKONING

As the sun lifted slowly into the morning sky the following day, all of Vernon felt wracked with tension as the yet unknown outcome of the day stretched before them like a ticking bomb. Outside, the first members of the assembling team began packing up for the mission. "You sure about going along with us?" Decker asked Rafik as they loaded the van with ammunition. "This really doesn't have anything to do with you. You can go back to your settlement, and nobody is going to judge you for it."

Rafik laid the two rifles down in the van and slid the knapsack of shells off his shoulder. "My best friend's mom is going, and he can't. And my other best friend got incinerated by those things." He paused a moment, his eyes reflecting a painful ulterior motive he wanted to share. "And they are the ones responsible for Dasha, whom I loved."

"Let's load up, boys!" Shane's voice called behind them, pulling a cart of gasoline canisters, and a pistol strapped to his shoulder.

"What's all this?" Decker exclaimed.

"I told you yesterday," Shane grinned. "I am not fucking around this time. Those assholes killed our friends. You don't fuck with Vernon."

Decker's eyes followed Shane as he rolled the cart to a pickup truck parked a few vehicles down the line. It had been far enough away that Decker hadn't noticed the change until Shane began loading it.

"Shit man! When did you do this?"

"I added some extras to it last night." Shane stood back, admiring his handiwork in the daylight. When he and Dasha found the truck abandoned on the road a few months ago, it had already been reinforced with thick protective bars over the grill. But Shane had made it into a killing machine by welding iron rods throughout the grill, forging a spiked battering ram of sorts.

From the back door of the school, Decker saw Dillon, Doe, Allie, and Patrice walking their way. "Doe and Patrice still figure on convincing the mall settlement that we are human," he confided. "Allie also thinks once Dillon sees his folks, his hate will take a backseat to his humanity, and he will try to get them to see the truth."

"I will not talk," Rafik replied with a slap onto the hood of the truck. "I'm going to finish this. And after we exterminate the mall, I'm down for hitting every nest of aliens we can find."

"Still with the aliens thing?" Shane smirked. "I hear you, brother! Hard for me to switch my brain too."

"Human. Alien. I no longer care," Rafik answered. "If Mrs. Wilson is correct, what I see as alien is a group of people who stand against everything we hold dear. If I see a man who sees me as a demon, then I know who to shoot."

The others reached the van, and Allie showed the men that she, Doe, and Patrice were armed as well. Decker glanced at Dillon. The chef turned around to show a revolver tucked into his back waistband, and a long ultra-sharp kitchen knife.

"My weapon of choice," Dillon snarled before putting it back and crawling into the van.

Decker and Allie took the front seats while Patrice climbed in after Dillon. But Doe didn't follow. Instead, she turned to Shane. "Want company?"

He held her gaze for a moment, then whatever animosity he'd recently felt toward her melted. "Dasha would want it that way."

Doe smiled respectfully and climbed into the truck. As the guards opened the gate to release the van and the souped-up pickup truck, no one noticed Augusta standing on the rooftop of the high school watching them go. Corinne was beside her, shielding her eyes from the bright morning sun.

"What will happen?" she asked Augusta. "Are they on a kill mission or are they going to take another chance of showing those people the truth?"

Augusta sighed wearily. "I honestly don't know anymore."

* * *

Not a voice stirred as Decker drove the van across the desolate lot of the Galleria Mall. Initially, he steered toward the alley where they'd made their escape last time. But Shane veered off course, waving the van to follow.

"They surely sealed it up by now," Doe shouted from the window when Decker was next to the truck. "We are going in a different way."

"There is no other way," Decker called back.

Glancing back at her driving partner, Doe laughed. "Not according to Shane."

Shane took the lead, idling the truck a safe distance from the steel-caged doors of the mall entrance. Decker held steady behind, the van engine rumbling. Shane hopped out, grenade in hand.

"Wait!" Dillon cried, leaping from the van door.

Shane looked at him with confusion until he saw for himself. Across the parking lot lay a crumpled cluster of human bodies, crows hopping atop them like ravaging vultures. Shane grabbed Dillon before he could get away, jerking him back to the van. "No, man! No, you do not want to see him like that."

Shane clutched Dillon's face and stared into Dillon's teary eyes. "You remember Rylan the way he was. And leave that graveyard over there alone. You with me?"

Dillon gave a short, reluctant nod.

"Then get back in the van and let's kill these motherfuckers who did that to him."

Shane waited for Dillon to return to the van, then he yanked the pin on the first grenade, rolling it forward into the exposed bars of the mall's reinforced gate.

"Duck!" he yelled, jumping back into the truck and pinning Doe down on the seat beneath him.

The explosion shattered the world. The mall world at least. The blast blew off the protective iron barrier, flinging debris backward in a storm of steel and flames. One gate hurdled back onto the truck, sliding through the iron spikes welded to the grill, and hitting the front with a force powerful enough to fracture the windshield into thousands of cracks and deploy the airbags.

Dusty white smoke filled the cab as Shane and Doe sat back up coughing. Doe pulled a knife from her pocket and stabbed at the two bags, deflating them out of their way while Shane pushed the shattered glass out onto the hood. Raising his hand out of the window to signal the van behind them, he slammed his foot on the accelerator, shooting the truck forward, the engine sounding like a war cry! Decker was on his heels, steering the van through the path the truck began clearing as Allie, Patrice, Rafik, and Dillon manned the open windows, guns positioned ready to fire!

Shane pummeled through the breach at top speed as the twisted metal of the second set of doors bent and moaned, giving way to Shane's joust through. The view was obscured by smoke and flaming embers, but the sound of the mounted iron bars shearing through flesh, bone, and mortar screamed through the air. There was no doubt now that those inside the mall knew what was coming for them!

The truck and van pitched violently over the rubble of concrete, steel, and possibly bodies as they infiltrated the mall. Shane didn't slow down when, through the clearing smoke, he witnessed the blue-scaled creatures scrambling like rats in a burning cellar. He felt no empathy for them, but Doe's eyes saw the terrified faces of human beings fleeing for their lives from the invaders breeching their domain.

Gunfire erupted from both sides of the van windows, its blasts appearing like fireflies dancing alongside the van. Bullets ripped into plastered walls and tore through flesh amid a chorus of frantic screams. Beneath the erupting firepower came the chorus of shattering glass from storefront windows falling to the ground like crystals on a haunted chandelier.

Shane slowed the truck enough for Doe to grab her guns and leap from the cab, taking cover behind a mall planter high with corn stalks. Once she was in place, he sped up again, tunneling through the mall's main corridor, smashing whatever lay in its path. Kiosks exploded against the rush, tables ricocheted off the sides, and screams turned to gurgles as anyone in Shane's way found themselves crushed under the tires or skewered onto the rods mounted to the grill. Their harrowing cries rang through the missing windshield into Shane's ears, but to him they were inhuman reptiles, hell-bent on consuming the earth. He watched a few of them impaled on the truck with fascination. Still alive and writhing, their long alien fingers clutched desperately at the rods trapping them. He couldn't tell if they were attempting to pull themselves free or if the poles stabbed through their midsections hurt less from the jostling if they gripped it.

In the van, things were happening a little differently for Allie and Decker than the last time they'd been there. As bullets ripped through the air, hitting the enemy like a wet slap, they no longer saw monsters.

Like Doe, now they saw people. Frightened, frantic people fled for their lives from what they perceived as demons desecrating their sanctum. While Shane continued barreling ahead, his death-truck sent mall colonists stampeding in all directions for escape. But Decker stopped his van midway through the mall.

"We are people too!" he screamed from the window as colonists scurried past. He didn't take aim at them, recognizing they were unarmed, having not foreseen this attack coming. Leaping from the van, Decker tried to grab some of them as they went by. "We didn't come to destroy you!" he shouted again. "We came to wake you up!" It was no use. Their terrified faces registered nothing but a demonic entity clawing at them.

Dillon jumped out of the van before Allie could stop him. He was already sprinting ahead; his eyes locked onto the mezzanine above. She followed, her heart thundering in her chest. Her eyes followed Dillon's stare to the upper rail where three figures stood. She couldn't be certain what Dillon thought he saw, but the way they looked down at the chaos made them seem almost aloof. Mere spectators in a battle, they kept their distance above, out of reach from the marauders below. Of course, she recognized one of them by the collar around his neck. It could be no one else but Reverend Tucker.

Dillon was heading for the stalled escalator, paying no attention to the danger coming at him now as armed forces arrived on the battlefield to protect their miniature city. Allie could see the men charging out from recessed outposts, their own guns blazing now. Others were joining the fray. The bravest of the men and women colonists poured from storefronts to join the fight, brandishing their own guns, rifles, knives, baseball bats, and hammers.

Allie shot into the crowd as it gained on Dillon. She heard more firepower coming from behind her. She turned to see Doe pressed against a center planter, shrouded by cornstalks, spraying rounds at the pursuing guards, shielding Dillon's climb and offering Allie the opportunity to go after him.

***

Patrice and Rafik flanked either side of the van moving alongside Decker, offering him cover while he waged a hopeless attempt to get someone to understand him. It seemed so futile as hysterical men and women brandishing makeshift weapons ran for cover under Patrice and Rafik's fire. Out of her periphery, she saw a man rushing forward. She turned quickly, taking aim at his chest. Hands raised, he began calling to her, "I am unarmed! I know you are all people!"

Decker waved him to the van, crouching with him behind the open door. "You can see us?"

"Yeah," the man answered. "I saw you the other day when the mayor fired on your people. I knew Curtis and Stacie. My name is Corbin Hartley."

Decker scrunched his nose. "That sounds familiar. Did you have a bunch of billboards—"

"Yes," Corbin replied, almost embarrassed. "I was an attorney. Look, my wife and our kids and another woman...we mean you no harm. We want only to leave this place."

"Get your family," Decker told him. "Head out through the hole and we will cover you."

Decker and Patrice watched as the man dashed across the plaza to a storefront where he pulled two women and two boys from behind a long counter. Checking to see if it was safe to run, Corbin guided his family behind the van towards the rubble on the mall's side where the truck had torn through. As Decker watched the man push his wife and two boys through the hole into the safety of the outside world, the second woman ran from her hiding place towards the van.

"Scotty is my nephew!" she cried, identifying herself.

Patrice and Decker exchanged grim looks.

"What?" Dorothy exclaimed. "Is he with you...at your community? His father was going after him!"

"His father killed him," Patrice shouted over the noisy fray. "I'm sorry."

"Joe killed him?" Dorothy shrieked. "He killed his own son?"

"Then himself," Decker nodded. "You need to get out of here while you can," he gesturing to the breach in the wall. "Follow your friends."

Decker and Patrice turned their attention back to the encroaching enemy. Neither saw if the woman made it out. They hoped she had. On the other side of the van, Rafik was at war with two men brandishing iron pipes. His gun was no longer in his hand. Patrice lurched across the front seat and blew a round of shots at them. She hit both men and feared she'd hit Rafik until he popped up from the ground waving his gun again. "Found it!"

* * *

At the farthest end of the mall, Shane's tirade of destruction was making its way back, veering into storefronts on either side of the plaza, shattering walls, windows and planters. As people crouched within stores, he whipped the truck closer, razing posts, structural supports, and walls, burying them back behind a blockade of debris. He could see Doe ahead. Her camouflage behind the planters hadn't held long as armed men caught the direction of her blasts and charged her way.

Their bullets came fast and without mercy, breaking sections of the planter apart under the onslaught of their blasts. A few more seconds and they'd be on top of her. But as the men spread out to surround her, Shane stepped on the gas, smashing back her way, eviscerating the food court as he steered in her direction.

The men turned their fire towards the truck, which, by now, had a shield of impaled victims taking most of the assault for him. He banked left quickly, sliding the truck sideways, toppling most of the guards to the ground like a tidal wave—many finding their legs or torsos crushed under the tires. Doe jumped back into the passenger seat and resumed her assault. Shane couldn't have come to her at a more perfect time as her gun clicked empty, spent of ammunition. She dug into the knapsack for another cartridge, reloading quickly. Shane held his gun out for her to do the same, and she popped in another round for him.

* * *

Back at the escalator, Dillon was at the top, after having to pause once or twice to duck shots coming at him. Allie was midway up behind him, but he either didn't hear, or was ignoring her shouts. At the railing several yards away, Linda Collins clung to her husband as her eyes caught sight of Dillon emerging onto the upper level. "Franklin!" Linda shrieked, cowering against her husband. "Is it...? Is that...?"

"Yes, Linda, I believe so."

They backed up several steps as the man left the escalator, turning their way. Reverend Tucker, his hands gripping the rail, was fixed on the slaughter below. Only now lifting his eyes to see the panic on the mayor's face.

"Franklin, what do you see?"

Reverend Tucker followed the mayor's trembling finger, turning around to see one of the scorched red demons stomping towards him. Tucker stood paralyzed in fear. All his talk from the pulpit about standing brave before the devil and casting him out abandoned him now. As Dillon inched closer, the minister found his voice again, screaming out from the railing to his people below. "Up here! Up here!!! The demons have opened the gates of hell and want to silence your direct line to God!"

"Shut the fuck up!" Dillon barked at him as he walked past the reverend towards his only target.

Out of breath, but finally reaching the second floor, Allie ran to the minister, pleading for him to understand her words. "We are not from Hell. We are people just like you! We have fooled ourselves into this! Into believing we are enemies. Read for yourself!"

She thrust Farrah's notebook in his face, each page detailing a new clue, fact, or radio communication she'd logged, ending with the ultimate admission from Europe of what had really happened to them all. If he still couldn't see her true face or understand the words she said, surely, he could read plain English. Tucker took the book and read the page. Allie left it with him, refocusing on Dillon. Dillon stalked closer to the man and woman. Allie knew they must be his parents. Could Dillon see them? Did he see through the alien mask? Or were they still foreign creatures in his eyes that he somehow found himself inexplicably drawn to? The mayor held his trembling wife against him as slowly their feet retreated further back with every step closer Dillon made towards them.

"It is him," Franklin stammered to his wife. "He lives among the demons. His sins claimed his soul. He is an agent of the devil now."

Dillon continued forward, saying nothing. Allie could understand their words even if Dillon couldn't, and she knew now that her guess about their identity was right. "Dillon, wait!" she cried, attempting to catch up to him. "They aren't aliens! Those are—"

With her back turned, she hadn't seen Reverend Tucker bounding forward until he had jerked her back by the arm. Shaking the notebook at her, he shouted. "What are you? You possess the ability to switch from demon form to that of a jezebel. Why should I believe any of the devil's lies you show to me?"

"They aren't lies!" Allie exclaimed. "Please listen to me, Reverend! We have all been victims of a delusion. Maybe we did it to ourselves. Our entire country got so blinded by our differences we lost our ability to see each other as we really are. Human. All of us! Our differences can't make us monsters unless we believe they do!"

"The devil is the prince of lies!!!" Reverend Tucker roared with a maniacal gleam. In one swift motion, he slung Allie against the mezzanine rail and started pushing her over.

CHAPTER 50

FOR RYLAN

Allie struggled against Tucker, but he was stronger than he looked. The rounded banister against her back acted like a roller, assisting each of his pushes by lifting her another inch off the ground. His hands drove into her chest as she fought back, attempting to claw at his face, but his arms were longer. Remembering the gun tucked into her waistband, she tried reaching for it, but removing a hand from her grapple with the reverend would have sent her right over the rail. Her feet dug behind her, searching for a space between posts to curl her foot around for leverage, but the mezzanine wall was made of thick acrylic panels with no gaps between.

Dillon, too far from her to hear Allie's cries over the chaos and gunfire below, had backed Franklin and Linda as far as the second-floor wall would allow them. Only a few feet now separated them. A shot cracked from the plaza below, whizzing past Dillon and catching his attention. He looked down to see Doe in the truck window, pointing down the mezzanine at Allie. Dillon abandoned his parents, racing to help Allie. He reached her too late as Reverend Tucker won his struggle, pitching her over the rail. She let out a blood-curdling cry, but Dillon lunged, catching her wrist. She dangled in open air, flailing, until her other hand caught his forearm. He held on tight, legs braced, heart pounding.

But Reverend Tucker, mad with fury, shoved into Dillon's back, trying to send them both over. Dillon could have easily overpowered the man, but any movement meant dropping Allie. Shots cracked overhead as Patrice and Rafik bounded up the escalator, guns blazing. Tucker fell back, shot in the shoulder, as Patrice dropped beside Dillon and helped haul Allie to safety. Rafik stood over Tucker's groaning form, raising his gun to strike again.

The alien monster writhed on the ground, squealing like a wounded pig. Only Allie could understand Reverend Tucker's words as he pleaded with the demon towering over him to have mercy. But Rafik was fresh out of mercy that day, cocking his gun back, taking another aim directly at the monster's head. Allie sprang forward, pushing Rafik's arm upward as he released the shot into the atrium. Though the upper floor recessed from any danger of falling glass, instinct took over at the splintering sounds, causing Allie, Patrice, and Rafik to curl down into a ball as a shower of deadly glass cascaded down to the plaza below.

Rafik aimed again at the monster, but Allie blocked Reverend Tucker with her own body. "He's a man!" she yelled to Rafik. "You may not see it, but he is! We can't kill him."

"Why not?" Patrice shouted. "He just tried to kill you! I thought you were on board with this Allie? They aren't like us, Allie," she said, speaking the very words Lauryll used that morning. "They can't adapt. They never could. It was their closed minds that caused all this!"

Allie turned sharply to her friend. "They are people, Patrice. Flawed, yes. But they are people!"

"People who murdered Dasha," Rafik said bitterly.

"And Rylan," added Patrice.

Allie shook her head, trying to make them understand. "I thought the same. Just two days ago, I was so angry over my brother that I was determined to wipe these people out. But haven't we have done just as much damage when we didn't know better? But when you do know better...you do better. *And* that is what makes us human."

Patrice slowly nodded, lowering her gun as Rafik did the same.

Allie looked around for Dillon. He wasn't there anymore. *When had he slipped away?* Through a glass storefront two doors down, she spotted him. Inside, with his parents cowered against a counter, staring down the barrel of his gun.

"Dillon! No!" Allie took off, Patrice right behind her.

Inside the store, Franklin and Linda Collins stared into the cold, unfeeling face of the son they had considered dead for over a decade. Allie and Patrice came in slowly, moving behind Dillon, waiting to see what he was going to do.

"I see aliens," Patrice mumbled under her breath to Allie. "What do you see?"

"A man and a woman."

"What does *he* see?" Patrice asked again.

"I don't know." Cautiously, Allie tapped his shoulder. "Dillon?"

Linda's eyes, focused on the gun in his hand, shifted her gaze to Dillon's steely, unblinking eyes. "Please, son, listen to the Lord. He has always had a plan for you."

"He doesn't hear you, Linda," Franklin scoffed. "Our son died the day he chose that life. *That man.* God washed his hands of him, and so did we."

Allie cringed at the words, then flinched at the sound of Dillon racking the slide of his gun, clicking a bullet into the chamber. She laid her hand on his arm, whispering, "They are people, Dillon."

"No, they are monsters." His words were like frostbite. "Monsters to the core."

Slowly, Allie slid her hand over his as it clutched the gun. "They only look like that because of the delusion. But Dillon, this is your mother and your father."

For the first time, Dillon turned his head away from his parents, facing Allie in the eye. "Don't you think I know that?"

Allie shot Patrice a look. Patrice stepped to Dillon's other side, staring at the blue monsters pinned against the counter. "You can see them, Dillon?" she asked. "See their human faces?"

"Of course I see them." Dillon answered coldly. He turned his icy stare back to his parents. "I know exactly who you are. Who you have always been."

Allie took her chance, gently sweeping her hand fully over Dillon's until she had taken the barrel, removing the gun from his hand, passing it to Patrice.

Dillon's father, now emboldened by safety, sneered at his son in a way Dillon remembered all too well. "Ungrateful deviant. We did our best with you, and you failed us every time."

"We loved you, Dillon," Linda said, as if expecting gratitude. "We raised you right and tried to teach you how to live like a decent Christian. But you rejected it all for that...man."

Dillon remained calm. Much too calm for Dillon, and it made the hairs on Allie's neck stand up. "His name was Rylan Daily. I am Dillon Daily. He was my husband...and this is for him."

Dillon's parents felt it before they saw it. And neither Allie nor Patrice had time to process it until they felt the warm spray of blood across their faces. Dillon had been swift, reaching behind him to pull his sharp kitchen knife from his waistband. Franklin and Linda stumbled back against the counter, eyes astonished when they looked at each other's open mouths, unable to scream as gurgling blood spurted from their slashed throats.

Patrice lifted the knife from Dillon's hand. As Franklin dropped to his knees, she wiped the blade clean on the back of his shirt, then with an approving smile, handed it back to Dillon. Linda sank to the floor beside her husband, drowning in her own blood filling her gashed throat.

"I'll be outside," Dillon said, walking out to the mezzanine and down the escalator.

Patrice and Allie moved to follow, but paused, having nearly forgotten all about Reverend Tucker. Propped against the railing where Rafik had left him before rejoining Shane and Doe downstairs, Tucker still clutched his wounded shoulder while he stared down below at the ruin of his fallen empire.

Allie made one more attempt to reason with the minister. "Sir, we must let the rest of this community know the truth. Then together we can reach other communities and in time put our entire world right again." She reached out a hand in peace for him to take. "Let's end this nightmare together."

Tucker looked at her outstretched hand with disdain. "If what you say is true, it was your people's godless, liberal aspirations that brought down the dignity of the human race. You and your people will never be a part of the new world we shall build."

A shout came from below. Patrice moved to the railing and saw everything they had missed while upstairs. The plaza was a sea of destruction and bodies—some dead, some only injured. Behind the remaining storefronts Shane's makeshift tank hadn't demolished, groups of blue figures recoiled behind lowered security gates, their last means of protection once the ammunition ran out.

Patrice could see Doe, Decker, Rafik, and Shane dousing the walls of the mall with the cans of gasoline Shane brought. She could only assume they'd faced the same resistance to peace as she and Allie had. Shane's truck was smashed against a column, which must have proven stronger than he could topple.

A shout rang out from Decker: "Come on and let's get out of here!"

Patrice waved down, then motioned for Allie to go ahead of her, citing she wanted a last word with the good reverend. Allie made her way down the broken escalator, as Patrice looked down at the misguided minister, who peered below at his lost Eden. She wanted to pity him, but it wasn't within her.

"You were wrong, you know?" she said, towering over him. "Arrogance usually is."

"You call loving God arrogance?"

"No," Patrice shook her head. "I love God too. And I love how He moves us forward, little by little, as our minds can understand it. Fire. Clean water. Electricity. Airplanes. Spacecraft. The Internet. Modern medicine. He leads us slowly, so we can adjust." Patrice squatted next to Reverend Tucker. "But your kind doesn't adjust. Fear of change holds you back. And it is your arrogance that deceives you into believing you have nothing left to learn."

"I know what I know."

"And that is precisely the problem," Patrice replied. "Because everything you know is all you will ever know. And you miss so much that way."

Tucker looked down at the gasoline-drenched mall. "You are killers. That I do know."

Patrice let out a sigh as she stood back up, starting for the escalator. As her hand gripped the black rubber rail of the broken lift, she looked back at Reverend Tucker for the last time. "You are right," she admitted, garnering a glint of surprise from him. "Sadly, you've forced us to be executioners. Those of us who understand the value in our differences must weed out the ones who can't. The unadaptable animals always die out. Darwin, Reverend. Darwin. Perhaps you should have also studied him in your day."

* * *

Dillon slipped out of the mall without being seen by his friends. His parents' blood now drying on his sweat-stained face felt like war paint, and he a medieval warrior having slain the dragon. The birds of prey scattered at his approach as he climbed the mound of dead behind the mall. Somewhere among these putrid corpses dragged from the mall after the prior battle was Rylan. Dillon would find him.

Shane had been right; Dillon shouldn't have had to see his husband that way—mutilated from his mortal wound and half decomposed under the summer elements. Flies, maggots, and all the unspeakable accouterments of death awaited him. But love was stronger than a churning stomach. Dillon pulled Rylan's remains free of the others and kneeled at his side. His tears were a blessing, helping to blur the unsightly leftovers of his husband's body.

He had worn Rylan's wedding band along with his own since Allie had given it to him. Dillon now placed it back on Rylan's rotting finger. "Cuff up with me, my beautiful love. And this time, I promise eternity."

* * *

Patrice and Allie reached the van where the others waited. "Dillon said he'll meet us outside," Allie told them. Decker guided the battered van over the broken kiosks, shattered glass, fallen bodies, and dust-laden rubble as the watching eyes of the surviving mall colonists stared from behind the safety of their gated storefronts. Decker could squeeze through the original hole Shane had opened in the wall when they had first arrived, and within seconds the turbulent van bounced into the bright sunlight of the fresh outdoors.

He stopped the van just outside the ruined entrance to the mall. Allie searched through the windows for Dillon but did not see him. Then...she did. Allie tore out of the back of the van, running to the pile of dead. Decker went after her, reaching her only seconds before her eyes could fully capture the scene. He spun her towards him, saving Allie from the retching sight. She fought against him, but Decker refused to let go. He would not let her spend her life haunted by the image. Instead, he painted a picture for her as he clutched her face to his chest.

"It's the way he wanted it, Allie," Decker said, choking back tears. "It's rather quite beautiful. Dillon is lying across Rylan. Rylan's hand is clutched in Dillon's. Their two wedding rings are touching. Dillon's cheek is against Rye's chest. He used his kitchen knife to pierce his heart...just like in Romeo and Juliet. Dillon's eyes are closed, and he is smiling. The guys are together now. They always will be."

* * *

When Decker got Allie back to the van, Shane and Doe stood before the wall's breach. Each had a flare gun in hand. With a nod to each other, they fired. The flares shrieked through the hole, erupting the plaza into flames. Heat surged from the shattered entrance. Glass cracked, metal screamed. Smoke billowed skyward from the broken atrium. Rising with the cloud of black rose the first screams from the blistering lungs of the fools who had sealed themselves behind cages.

No one spoke as the van pulled away.

When the van hit the open road, no one looked back. Inside was only silence. They didn't speak of justice. Or revenge. Or God. Not yet. Only after the mall vanished behind them did the irony settle in. A society that had twisted faith into a weapon had met the hellfire of which they preached. And maybe from that smoke, a better world could begin. One that might welcome anyone willing to learn from the mistakes of those who came before them.

ABOUT THE AUTHOR

Micah House is the author of *The Blanchard Witches* series which has won several awards since its debut, including the NYC Big Book Award, The Indie Excellence Award, and The BookFest Award. His southern style of storytelling weaves drama, humor, emotional connection to characters, and plenty of page-turning suspense. He currently resides in Birmingham, Alabama with his husband and son and their five dogs.

www.ingramcontent.com/pod-product-compliance
Lightning Source LLC
Chambersburg PA
CBHW030330120726
47901CB00007B/1741